Boomer

Star Watch Series
Book 3

Mark Wayne McGinnis

Edited by:

Kim McGinnis

Lura Lee Genz

Mia Manns

Avenstar Productions

Boomer Ebook:

ISBN: **978-0-9974514-0-5**

Boomer Paperback:

ISBNB-10: **0997451416**

ISBN-13: **978-0997451412**

To join Mark's mailing list, jump to:

http://eepurl.com/iCGBXk

Visit Mark Wayne McGinnis at:

http://www.markwaynemcginnis.com

❀ Formatted with Vellum

Prologue

Legs outstretched, Boomer sat on a layer of accumulated black ash. The ground was still warm beneath her. She just needed to quickly catch her breath—a moment, or two. Nighttime's darkness had turned to dawn—a narrow band of scarlet was breaching the far-off horizon. She waved away a fluttering, glowing ember. Looking at her soot-blackened hand, she noted she was missing the tip of one finger—her pinkie. She examined the cauterized stub as if it were an inanimate thing ... something apart from herself. She looked up, now that the fallen forms around her were taking on shape in the early light, and silently acknowledged those dead. They were all dead. She surveyed the surrounding battlefield and the recently fallen. The impact of what she was seeing, she knew, was being internally compartmentalized. She wasn't ready to acknowledge the loss of those she cared about. Not yet, anyway. Looking around her, she saw the bloodied—more often blackened—smoldering bodies. Death lay everywhere. And now the stink of death was filling the morning air in this ancient place—recently so beautiful, with its endless amber desert dunes and meticulously preserved ruins. Built by a people who'd warned this day would come. Apparently ... no one had listened.

Boomer rested her open hand on the cool, triangular-shaped metal strapped to her forearm. She fingered the lines on its engraved surface and let them speak to her: *Deek mog Mirrah— lor eej Pol* ... Strength of Spirit will vanquish all enemies. She almost laughed out loud but a tear inexplicably fell onto the surface of her enhancement shield. With the heel of her palm she ground its moisture into the black soot.

She felt subtle vibrations beneath her. *They're coming for me.* Without looking down, she reached for the small metallic device on her belt and depressed the two inset tabs. Three times she repeated the same action and three times nothing happened. The SuitPac device was dead anyway—her battle suit's auxiliary power completely exhausted. "Screw it ... the thing just gets in my way."

She stood, keeping her eyes fixed on the sky's ever-growing color band—now pink and amber and more beautiful than anything she'd ever witnessed. *It's a good day to die.* She turned to face the approaching column of Sahhrain warriors, who moved ahead with steady, unhurried purpose. Harpaign's morning sun washed over the backs and sides of the warriors, shimmering off their metallic breastplates and flowing capes. The sight was both beautiful and horrible. Her eyes easily settled on Lord Zintar Shakrim. Bigger than expected, he was a hell of a lot bigger than his brother, Vikor.

Shit.

Chapter 1

"Why am I even here?"

"Oh, come on ... how can you ask that?"

"It's not like we were close. I haven't seen her in ... what? Three years?"

Jason tightened his jaw. It was two years since he'd last seen Boomer. He'd been the one to encourage her to go. If only he could do things differently—do things all over again.

Mollie said, "I'm missing finals this week. You know that ... right?"

"I don't care; you can make them up."

Mollie continued to stare straight ahead, out the forward observation window. "It's not like high school. In college certain expectations have to be met. Grades matter."

"So does attending your sister's funeral ... or whatever they call it on Harpaign."

Jason knew Mollie well enough to know she was dealing with Boomer's death in her own way, by acting indifferent—deflecting. The truth was, Boomer wasn't actually her sister. She wasn't, in fact, even a different person. They shared the same

DNA. Their bond was profound and Mollie, he knew, was as devastated by Boomer's loss as he was.

He glanced over to her, noting the physical resemblance between both daughters, but he had to look for it. Mollie, now sixteen, was as near a polar opposite to Boomer as one could imagine. Mollie's brown hair, streaked with wheat-colored highlights, was worn long and straight, reaching down past the middle of her back. Fashion-conscious, she was dressed in a crisp, white button-down shirt tucked into a short gray skirt. Refined and proper, she intended to be a lawyer, like her mother. Boomer, on the other hand—at least the last time he'd seen her—had her hair dyed black and cut short and was wearing oversized camo-pants and a black, torn, AC/DC T-shirt.

"You're sure Mom's going to be there?"

"She's probably already there by now. Why don't you NanoText her and see for yourself?" Jason said as he entered the necessary code to call up an interchange wormhole.

Mollie raised her chin and took in her surroundings. "This is new."

"Perk of the job," Jason said. Actually, *Stellar*, a fifty-five-foot-long space yacht, was built to his own specifications. It was a luxury transport vessel that made extended space travel more comfortable. With the galaxy enjoying relative peace for the last year, Jason was spending more and more time on diplomatic missions. At forty-five, he was still in his prime as a commander ... as fleet Omni ... but he did enjoy, occasionally, the softer bed and plush-cushioned seating the *Stellar* afforded.

"It's nice ... I guess. A little swanky." Mollie let out a long breath, using manicured fingernails to pull non-existent lint from her skirt. "I thought I'd see Dira here. She still on Jhardon?"

He nodded. About to ask her about school, Jason noticed

she'd just plugged ear buds into her ears and was scrolling through what seemed to be an endless list of songs or playlists on her iPhone. Adding to that, she'd slightly turned away—an indication further conversation was over.

Soon, Jason became lost in his own thoughts. *Has it really been two years?* He unconsciously nodded. It was hard to believe that nearly five years had passed since he'd taken on the role of Omni, the U.S. space fleet's supreme commander position. Boomer had been at his side through what must have been a hundred Star Watch missions. She'd been a warrior in every sense of the word. He overheard more than once that she was a badass and even far worse things than that. It was common knowledge: Not only was she the Omni's daughter, she was the daughter of the former President of the United States. Make a pass at her and risk a slow torturous death—from Traveler, a seven-foot-tall rhino-warrior, or from Jason's best friend and fellow Navy SEAL, Billy Hernandez, or from a slew of others, who protected Boomer as if she were part of their own family. So any ill-advised romantic advances, or overtures, had not been a problem. But even at fourteen, the last time he'd seen his daughter, she was not interested in boys. Kahill Callan pretty much occupied the entirety of her personal universe. Boomer was a Tahli warrior—a master of that Blues ancient martial arts since she was eleven years old. She was tough—had a no-nonsense, no bullshit attitude, and her departure left a void on board the *Parcical* when she went off to complete her training elsewhere. But there had been vulnerability there too. As accomplished and fearsome a killer as Boomer had become, still his daughter was vulnerable in other ways, perhaps even more so than Mollie. Inside, she possessed a childlike innocence that was in stark opposition to the badass demeanor she tried to exude outwardly.

And now she was dead. Jason closed his eyes and willed

himself to hold back the tears—search for something ... anything ... else to think about. They were entering the interchange wormhole. He made a few unnecessary adjustments to the controls and chewed at the inside of his cheek. From the corner of his eye, he could see Mollie looking at him over her shoulder. Just as quickly, they were already emerging from the wormhole, where no less than twenty imposing Blues' warships were within visual range.

A small Craing man entered the bridge. "Captain, shall I request permission—"

Jason cut him off with a slight wave of his hand: "No ... that's okay, Ricket, the AI's already taken care of that."

For the first time in more than an hour Mollie smiled, then concern filled her eyes. "Hi, Ricket. It's good to see you. You look ..."

Ricket's face brightened seeing Mollie and he hurried to her side. He placed a hand on her arm and said, "I've made some adjustments to my physiology. I didn't anticipate how dramatic the repercussions from doing so might be physically. Is it disturbing?"

"Disturbing? To me?" she laughed, and before he could react, she flung her arms around him and pulled him in for a hug. "I love you, Ricket ... there's absolutely nothing you could ever do that would ever disturb me."

It was good to see Mollie smile. Apparently, only her parents were on the receiving end of her perpetual cold treatment. Once released from her embrace, Ricket, blushing and obviously flustered, smiled and looked awkward.

"Ricket, can you let the others know we've entered the Dacci system and we'll be saddling up to the StarDome within the next ten minutes?"

"Yes, Captain." Ricket left the small bridge and Jason turned his attention to the distant space structure. The Blues had completed construction on the StarDome less than a year earlier. With Lord Vikor Shakrim long dead, and the subsequent defeat of the Sahhrain, the Blues had flourished. The StarDome—a vast space station in the Dacci system—was both a military stronghold and a legislative capital. Hundreds of thousands of beings lived and worked there.

But now the nearby, sand-colored planet, lying just beyond it, consumed all Jason's attention. *Harpaign.*

"Is that where it happened?" asked Mollie. "Where she ... where her body is?"

Jason turned toward Mollie and nodded. "That's Harpaign, and yes—that's where your sister's body is being held."

Mollie's eyes were fixed on the bright planet. "I hate this place. Why did she ever have to come here?"

"She had a connection with this planet that went far beyond my, or anyone else's, understanding. In some ways she was more a Blues than a human. Besides, except for the *Parcical*, this planet was her home."

Mollie's face darkened and there was a coldness in her voice Jason had never heard before. "Let's just get this over with. I don't want to be here."

Chapter 2

Positioned snuggly in the *Stellar's* StarDome berth, Jason put the yacht's systems to sleep. He rose to his feet, and saw Mollie waited for him at the bridge hatchway. Her backpack was slung over one shoulder, and he saw what looked to be the top edge of a photograph, peeking out from one of the bag's numerous front pockets. Jason gestured toward it with his chin. "May I?"

Mollie shrugged indifference, and he plucked it free from the pocket. It was a photograph of Mollie and Boomer together. He instantly recognized the background—their home back on Earth—the family scrapyard. His father's latest project, an old Skylark, was still in the midst of repair work at that time.

"This photo has to be four years old," Jason said.

"Closer to five," she corrected.

Laughing, both girls—about twelve years old—were wearing shorts and T-shirts and had their arms casually slung over each other's shoulders. They were covered from head to toe in brightly colored splotches of paint. Their grandfather thought it a good idea to buy them paint guns and use the scrapyard as a battlefield. Jason remembered the day the picture was taken—

how much fun they had and how both girls received a myriad of cuts and bruises on their legs and arms. Scolding his father for letting the girls use the scrapyard as a playground, his father sloughed it off saying, "You grew up playing in the damn scrapyard ... didn't you turn out okay?"

"We better go, Dad," Mollie said, pulling the picture from his fingers and tucking it back inside its pocket on her backpack. They entered the main cabin, appointed more like a lavish living room than a spacecraft, which held sectional leather, couch-like, seating; indirect lighting; and wraparound observation windows on both its port and starboard sides. Ten or more passengers were making this solemn journey on board the *Stellar*. It had been quite some time since all of them had been together in one location. Traveler loomed over everyone and looked uncomfortable amongst, with the exception of Ricket, the humanoids. He spent most of his time these days, when back on Earth, in an area allocated to other rhino-warriors in North Korea. He'd avoided taking any direct leadership position up to this point, but Jason suspected that could be changing.

Jason watched Mollie approach Traveler, taking hold of his hand. Together, they headed out of the vessel.

"Swanky."

Jason turned—it was Billy Hernandez, referring to the plush accommodations inside the main cabin. He ran several fingers over the top of a leather seat, then over an embossed Mercedes Benz symbol. "Guess it was only a matter of time," he said with a wry grin—the laugh lines on his face briefly coming to light. Like Jason, he was wearing his dress reds. Red was the official color of all U.S. fleet officer uniforms these days and Billy wore his well.

An unlit cigar hung from Billy's lips and his expression turned serious. "You're not alone here, Cap ... we're all hurting. Not like you ... I know that ... but just know, her loss ..."

Jason nodded and put a hand on Billy's shoulder. "I know, my friend. Thank you.

"Countless times a day I find myself thinking about it. Shit, it's the worst kind of gut punch," Jason said, not wanting to talk any more about it. He saw Orion talking to Captain Perkins on the other side of the cabin and subtly nodded to her. Her eyes flicked toward Billy and she shook her head. She and Billy had been inseparable for years, but now, even getting them to stay in the same room together took something like this to happen. Jason knew Orion would wait for him to finish conversing with Billy before she'd approach.

He shook Billy's hand. "I'll catch you later, Billy. Let me make the rounds ... I'm not sure how much time I'll have to catch up with everyone at the service."

"What's that going to be ... um ... like? Do you know?" Billy asked.

"Not sure. The Blues have their own deep-rooted spiritual beliefs. We'll just have to go along for the ride." Jason gave Billy a pat on the back and moved off.

Orion, like Billy and Ricket, was among the crew he saw on a daily basis. Stationed on the *Parcical*, they each could have moved on to higher officer positions anywhere in the fleet, but apparently they were content right where they were. Secretly, Jason suspected that Billy and Orion didn't want to venture too far away from one another—somehow hoping things could be reconciled between them—though neither would ever admit to that.

Orion opened her arms and pulled Jason in for a hug. He felt the strength in her arms—felt the flexing of her biceps beneath her uniform. Although she looked African-American, she wasn't actually from Earth. Gunny Orion was once a sports star on her home planet of Tarkin.

They separated and she continued to gaze at Jason with

compassion. Her face was intricately tattooed, covered with minute geometric symbols. From what Billy had attested to him in a pub on a return visit to Trom—when they both were inebriated—there wasn't an inch on her body that was not similarly marked. And Billy had checked and rechecked that fact.

"We'll get through this. You'll get through this," she said.

Jason didn't answer right away. "Thanks, Gunny. The problem is ... I'm not sure I even want to." He turned his attention toward Perkins, who was hovering nearby.

"Captain Perkins ... how's life on the *Minian*?"

"Life is fine, sir. The *Minian*'s been out of service for the last two weeks—maintenance overhaul."

"That's right. I remember signing off on that. She's a fine vessel. I hope you appreciate her."

"I do, sir, every day I serve on her. And the *Parcical*, sir?"

Jason stopped and thought about the question for a moment. "As soon as I think I've got that little ship figured out she offers up something new to surprise me. An amazing vessel. I too am honored to serve on such a fine craft."

As fleet Omni, it was expected Jason would eventually settle behind a desk. He tried it and quickly found he wasn't well suited for that kind of physical inactivity. The truth was, he didn't see any need to do so. With their modern, advanced, communication systems he could be anywhere in the galaxy, virtually speaking, in moments. But he knew the time was coming for change. Increasing pressure was coming from fleet headquarters—the Alliance's new Liberty Station back in the Sol System. With Nan Reynolds no longer president, her influence was far less prominent these days, and he was quickly losing command favor. His past *carry a big stick* methodologies no longer fit with the kinder, gentler philosophy that Alliance politicians wanted exemplified. Perhaps they were right, and he was a leftover relic from another time. *Whatever.*

Jason was being hailed. "Go for Captain."

"Where are you?"

Jason heard the impatience in his ex-wife's voice. "Star-Dome ... we're just leaving the *Stellar* now. And you?"

"On the surface. We got in last night. They have shuttles, commuting down to the surface on the hour. If you hurry, you can make the 1:00."

"We'll make it," Jason answered flatly. A palpable heaviness underlay the tone of Nan's voice and the ensuing silence went a beat too long. "Anything else?" Jason asked. They'd fought each time they spoke, since hearing the heartbreaking news. Nan hadn't come right out and said it, but it was clear she blamed him. Blamed him for the life, and the inevitable death, Boomer had chosen.

"Well ... we'll see you soon."

She didn't reply for a moment, then asked, "How's Mollie doing with all this?"

"She's acting like she doesn't care. Playing it cool."

"I know it's killing her," Nan said. "She's hurt and angry."

"At me?" Jason asked, already knowing the answer.

"Yes ... she's furious with you. We both are."

With that, she cut the connection.

Chapter 3

two weeks earlier...

Boomer had mixed feelings about the day's quickly approaching ceremony and butterflies continued to flutter in her belly. She had tried eating something earlier but soon realized that was a really bad idea. Everything would finally conclude today. Looking back, there were far too many hardships to recount—all those extended years away from her family.

Bands of light—dancing dust particles glittering in the morning sun—filtered down from two open apertures above her. She looked at herself in the mirror, then shifted in her chair to study MarGiline, whose coarse-braided dreadlocks, the color of snow, were worn long—hanging down to her waist. No less than one hundred and fifty Earth years of age, she was meticulously threading gold and silver beads into Boomer's dark, shoulder-length, hair. Tall, but bowed with age, she hummed to herself as she worked.

"Stop fidgeting, young Master Tahhrim Dol," she scolded.

Boomer closed her eyes and used the meditation technique

called *baskile* to bring peace and tranquility to her agitated mind. She gently blocked errant thoughts from pushing their way into her consciousness. Realistically, there was a chance she would not survive the day. Some did not. Those that did would become a *Goldwon* Warrior—what the last two years of her training had led up to. Certainly, being a human did not help her in the least. The ceremonial edicts, rules of the trials, set forth several millennia past, did not allow any compensation for one's inadequacies. She was genetically ill-suited to become a Tahli warrior in the first place, let alone the victor—the *Goldwon*—akin to a Blues' lord—of which there were so very few remaining.

"What is the count?" Boomer asked.

"It should not matter. A *Goldwon* would not be concerned ..."

Boomer's expression halted her lecturing. "I am a mere servant, my dear. What I have learned is but second- and third-hand knowledge."

"And?"

"And, at last count, there are an even ten."

Boomer nodded, adjusting to the information. More than she'd hoped, but it could be worse, too. She'd heard of graduation combat trials having as many as twenty, and some as few as five, contestants. Others would be graduating today—but there could be only one victor—only one *Goldwon*. Thinking about it, she wasn't in fear for her own mortality as much as coming to terms with injuring—perhaps even killing—nine other Tahli warriors. She was certain of only two others, also vying for the revered title, competing today—Dromit Sagent and Carmotta Piaget. Carmotta was as dear a friend as she had ever had and Boomer dreaded going up against her. Could she even do it? End her life, if necessary? Boomer let that question stay unanswered, turning her thoughts over to Dromit ... *Drom.* She blushed, just thinking about him. He was the most beautiful being she'd ever laid eyes on: Tall and muscular, with a strong inner sense of wellbeing ... no, not wellbeing—patience. Boomer was well aware that her infatuation with the Blues male was one-sided. If anything, she was an aberration ... a curiosity to the young Tahli warrior. Although he had taken her under his wing, stood up for her presence there ... as a *Calhoom* ... a freak human, she suspected she'd become more like a sister to him than anything else.

Part of her Tahli warrior training, now occupying more than five years of her life, was dedicated to furthering her Kahill Callan mastery. Two of those years were spent right here, on Harpaign, in pursuit of becoming a Goldwon Warrior—perhaps even *the* Goldwon. Part of her felt unworthy of even contemplating such a feat ... such an honor. She'd embraced every aspect of the Blues' way of life—even their strange cultural and spiritual predispositions. Kahill Callan was a package deal. Boomer had known that from the start, when she first entered the underground cavern five years ago, and sipped *Jahhlorine*—the transformative potion that initiated her journey toward mastership. What she didn't know then was that becoming a Kahill Callan Tahli warrior, albeit a great achievement in itself, was but one step toward the ultimate goal—to become elevated to what was akin to a *lord* status—the *Goldwon*—something even her dear friend and mentor, Prince Aahil Aqeel, had not aspired to.

Boomer looked at herself in the mirror and nearly laughed out loud. *Who the hell is that looking back at me?* After three hours of primping and painting and beading, Boomer hardly recognized herself.

"You are beautiful, no?" MarGiline asked, seeing her stunned expression.

"I don't know. It's embarrassing." Boomer, a tomboy as far

back as she could remember, had never before worn makeup. Perhaps she should have been born a male. She quickly shooed away errant thoughts of Drom again. *Well, maybe not.* But viewing herself in the mirror—her outlined, accented eyes looked twice their normal size and appeared captivating, even to her. Her lips, now painted bright yellow, looked full and ... she searched for the word ... *kissable?*

She let her eyes fall to her exposed neck and bare shoulders and the violet band of leather covering her small breasts. Using the fingers on both hands, she attempted to tug the fabric higher up.

MarGiline slapped at her hands. "Do not hide your femininity, Master Tahhrim Dol ... or do you not think they too are a weapon?"

Boomer looked at her cleavage ... *When the hell did that happen?* Then again, she was sixteen now—no longer a young girl. She shook her head—no way! She'd never played that card—never even thought she could, realistically. She'd no more use her body like that than allow herself to cheat or steal —if she couldn't prevail on an even playing field, she'd rather lose.

"How long do I have to wear this silly outfit?"

MarGiline stopped with her beading and tilted her head.

"When do I change into my Shadick?"

MarGiline snickered. "No, no ... you will not be dressed like a common peasant on this important day, my dear."

"Oh no, there's no way I'm going into combat dressed like this!" Boomer stood and gestured toward the mirror. The leather-like material barely concealed anything. The narrow band, covering up her chest and leaving a bare midriff, was bad enough, but the skintight leather leggings, conforming to her body like nothing she'd ever worn before, left zero to the imagination—hugging every inch of her long legs and derriere. She brought a hand up to her mouth and scowled toward the mirror. *Oh my God ... Drom will see me like this.*

"You should be thankful you were born when you were. A mere two hundred cycles past, contestants were unclothed during the trials."

Boomer tried to imagine past combatants running around all butt naked with their long pratta-shafts and enhancement shields. She let out a breath, still looking at her body. MarGiline had used a perfectly matched skin-color makeup to conceal the scores of small scars and lacerations normally visible on her exposed upper arms and torso—accumulated over the years. A part of her felt angry they were hidden: She'd earned those scars ... each and every one.

MarGiline tied the last of the tiny knots into her hair and stood back. Together, they appraised Master Tahhrim Dol's reflection. "You are ready, my dear. May the Gods of *Arkain* protect you and lead you to victory today." She moved behind Boomer and wrapped her in her own long, slender arms. "My heart and best wishes go with you, Boomer."

It had been years now since anyone had used her Earth name. Boomer patted the old Blues woman's arm and with a bemused smile said, "Guess it's time I go kick some ass."

At some point, two ceremonial guards had entered into the chamber, and now stood both erect and stone-faced on either side of the arched stone entrance. Boomer enviously took in their silver metallic breastplates and their draping, scarf-like, wraps of azure blue. What she would give for even one of those body-concealing wraps.

She glanced back at MarGiline, then, with her head held high, walked into the adjacent, larger Master's chamber, located within the ancient Acropolis, where Prince Aahil Aqeel stood waiting for her. Master Sahhselies, standing several paces behind him, looked frail, as ancient as the Acropolis itself. He bowed in concert with Aqeel. Both had been instrumental in her training over the years. Prince Aahil Aqeel, much like an older brother, was more than a mentor—he'd become her friend and confidant.

"You look beautiful, young Tahhrim Dol."

"I'd rather look scary and frightening ... but I'd settle for formidable."

Approaching her, the prince said nothing as he affixed her enhancement shield to her left forearm. He tested it, ensuring it was secure, then stood aside for Master Sahhselies, who, extending his arm, held out a long pratta-shaft. "This spear was my father's and his father's before him, Master Tahhrim Dol. May past generations of Sahhselies warriors help bring you victory today."

Boomer took the long staff from him and held it vertically before her. More than a foot taller than the top of her head, the staff's razor-sharp point held steady, now caught in a band of sunlight. The three stared at the reflective pinnacle.

"A good omen ... it seems supernatural elements are definitely at work here," Master Sahhselies told her.

A chorus of Tasmillian trumpets began playing somewhere within the stadium, outside the chamber's walls. Both Aqeel and Sahhselies, bowing in deference toward Boomer, looked toward the entrance. "It is time," Prince Aqeel said.

For the first time Boomer saw *something* in the prince's eyes. *The look of foreboding?*

"What is it?" Boomer asked.

"You need to concentrate on the Trials that lie before you, Master Tahhrim Dol."

"Will you not be escorting me to the arena?" she asked, aware something was amiss.

"My presence at your side will not serve you today, young Tahhrim Dol. You must own this moment by yourself." His face became tight—his gaze even more intense. "You must win and take possession of the Goldwon effigy. Boomer, you must not relinquish it to anyone ... do you understand me?"

She held his eyes and nodded. "I will do as you say, Prince Aqeel." She then turned away, heading toward the heightened cheering outside.

The solemn-looking guards left the chamber, waiting for her just outside the archway. Now, an audible rise of cheering voices could be heard coming from the stadium. The other combatants were emerging from their own respective chambers too: Each of these nine Tahli warriors—who likewise spent years in disciplined training—was among the very few selected from those hundreds and hundreds of others, within the Dacci system, who had not made it this far. Those competing today, in reality, had already graduated and would be honored with a *Goldwon Warrior* title—that is, if he or she survived the day. They were the best of the best and today they would race and fight until either too incapacitated to fight any longer, giving the sign of Drench—*surrender*—or were killed in battle. Only one would become the *Goldwon*.

Chapter 4

If the Dacci system's Tahli ministry had their way, Boomer would not be standing among them today. A mixture of politics, favoritism, and out-and-out prejudice had constantly been at play. Along with that came two years of extended, nearly impossible, roadblocks. Always an extra physical challenge the others were not required to meet—like a new match against older, and far more experienced, opponents she had to prevail against. But, in the end, the Council of One, the true elders of the Blues, put their collective foot down—*Enough! She's more than earned her rightful place to compete.*

Now, as Boomer stood upon her four-foot-square crystal pedestal, she took in the spectacle around her. Apparently, the ancient stadium held close to fifty thousand souls. No open seats could be found here on this most important day. The crowd, all Blues, had been cheering non-stop for the past ten minutes. Boomer let her gaze move from contestant to contestant, standing upon their own crystal pedestals, around the oval-shaped, ancient—eroded by time and wear—stadium. Each contender stood tall, with legs apart, a vertical pratta-shaft clenched in one fist. Hanging in front of each raised pedestal was the contestant's banner, which bore the warrior's home symbol, suspended in a field of bright colors. Twice Boomer's height, the banners were well over ten feet tall and were dramatically whipping and flapping now in the mid-morning Harpaign sunlight. She'd been allowed to choose her own home symbol and, perhaps as a secret measure of defiance, she'd selected the bright red lips and extended tongue of the Rolling Stones on a field of white. Truthfully, she didn't particularly like the Stones' music—but that was beside the point. She liked knowing the symbol was offensive—vulgar, in fact—to virtually any Blues individual upon seeing it.

Directly across from her, and looking right at her, was Carmotta. Dressed nearly identical to Boomer, her exposed, well-toned, light-blue skin practically glowed. While most Blues inherited thickly matted black hair—like dark steel wool—hers was black but straight ... a clear sign of interbreeding, somewhere back in her lineage. Carmotta had joked more than once that Boomer, being a human *Calhoom*—had taken the spotlight off Carmotta's racial impurity. They'd been like sisters for two years—while ferociously competing against each other. Honing their individual skill levels ever higher and higher.

Purposely, Boomer avoided looking over in Drom's direction, at the narrowest end of the stadium. She felt his eyes on her. Felt the heat of his stare on her exposed body. There were seven males competing, wearing the same skin-tight leggings, but they were bare-chested. Drom's physique was crazy—his chest pectoral muscles round and prominent—his abdominals ridiculously chiseled. She was embarrassed, seeing him compete without his loose-fitting Shadick on.

Why am I thinking about Drom? Think about the match ... the obstacles.

The floor of the stadium had been transformed into multiple zones—each contained its own death-defying obstacle.

Boomer studied each sectioned-off area: One had multiple pools of flesh-eating Gamby fish; another had a tower of jutting, knife-like rocks that seemed to leave only a few places to make a stand. Below, directly in front of her were large sand dunes, mimicking much of the terrain of Harpaign itself. She already knew the dunes were nearly impossible to stand erect upon. Off to her right, directly below Drom, sat a Shintuco Cat. Easily twice the size of a Bengal tiger, the greenish-furred feline was all claws and teeth. Secured to a post by a long chain, attached to a thick collar around its neck, the creature had free rein of its zone. The obstacle was not to kill, or even harm, the deadly dangerous beast. An endangered species, protected by law, the zone was all about avoiding the big cat while going up against your opponent. It just so happened that the zone was directly below Drom's position. Easily, the two most dangerous aspects to the competition were initially paired. It was never a secret that Drom was expected to win today—becoming the next *Goldwon*.

There were other zones—other obstacles. Boomer took it all in and formulated a battle strategy for each zone one by one. Eventually, her eyes moved to the center of the stadium. Elevated, even higher than the combatants' respective pedestals, stood a towering tower, black as obsidian. One hundred and thirty feet in height, just climbing to its top, with its near-vertical sides, presented a formidable challenge. Atop the tower awaited the Goldwon effigy—a seventeen-inch-tall diamond-like statue of a half-bird creature, half-warrior. It was said to be the creation of the Gods of *Arkain*—older than the Acropolis—even older than the Capital City. Boomer could almost see it up there ... or perhaps she only imagined she could.

But before attempting that feat, one first had to defeat all of the other nine contestants. In a perfect situation, no one would die today. There was no dishonor in leaving due to injury, or even by Drench, for that matter. But surrender, at some point, would be forced onto most contestants in order for only one combatant to prevail. Either that or fight to the death, which was rarely the case. *But are these warriors different? Would they carry things too far?* Boomer briefly wondered. How would she personally react in that kind of situation? Was she willing to stake her life on winning at all costs? How important was victory to her? At the end of the course—if indeed one even survived it—the sole victor would stand tall on that center pedestal. Then, no longer a mere Tahli warrior, he or she would be proclaimed *the* Goldwon. Boomer, perhaps for the first time, realized then how much she wanted ... needed ... to become the Goldwon.

The trumpets sounded again. Boomer found the blaring irritating and narrowed her eyes in the direction of the horn-blowers below her. They were all waiting for the last of the official observers to take their seats—first came the ten Tahli ministry members, filing in now, wearing long, hooded, black robes. One by one they took their seats near the top row of the stadium.

Eventually, the Council of One—dressed similarly in hooded robes, but in spectacularly gleaming white ones—entered and waved to the heightened, cheering crowd. Boomer was well aware those Blues elders were capable of looking virtually any age—young or old—like shape-shifters. She found it interesting that currently they each appeared very old. Were they revealing their true state of being today?

One of the elders remained standing, and the crowd's enthusiasm hushed down to a low murmur. Although she spoke to the full stadium in a normal tone of voice, Boomer, and everyone there, could still hear her every word. She spoke in their native Dacci—relating the history of the impending tournament. She spoke of the honor of becoming a Goldwon, and then of the two previous ceremonies where virtually every contestant suffered harm of some sort—some seriously, and several were even killed—either by another opponent or via one of the treacherous stadium obstacles. The elder, whom Boomer recognized as Lord Manna, raised both her hands, palms outstretched, and commenced saying holy words Boomer did not understand, in an ancient dialect foreign to her.

Boomer's thoughts wandered unchecked for several seconds, which nearly cost her her life. Once the elder took her seat, the graduation completion ceremonies immediately commenced—no final blast from the horns, no drum beating, no hitting of a gong.

Carmotta was the first to fire off violet distortion waves from her outstretched enhancement shield. The spectacular bright waves crossed the stadium at close to the speed of light and hit Boomer directly in the chest. Nearly catapulted off from her perch atop the pedestal, Boomer landed on her back, and was propelled to its very edge. Her clawed fingertips grabbed for something—anything—to gain purchase. She knew that falling from the far side of a pedestal instantly disqualified a warrior from further competing in the challenge.

Boomer's head and upper shoulders slid over the far side of the pedestal before she was able to maneuver her own shield. Pointing it backward, she fired a wide swath of distortion waves over her head to slow further forward momentum. She came to a precarious halt, nearly at the tipping point of going head-over-heels backward. Heart pounding in her chest, she had to smile at Carmotta's clever strategy to take her out so early in the competition. Boomer next used strategically pointed waves to elevate herself up onto her feet and spied her friend crouched several hundred feet across from her. Both smiled.

Carmotta jumped down from her crystal perch to the floor of the stadium and was immediately engaged in battle with another young Tahli warrior. As much as Boomer wanted to watch her friend fight for her life, she had a dire engagement of her own to attend to. A small tornado of spinning sand particles began to take shape directly below her, atop the sand dunes. Just as suddenly, its movement began to slow. In its dissipating wake, Boomer recognized warrior Clive Sha, from the farthest planet away within the Dacci system. He now stood upon the highest dune, his feet submerged beneath several inches of sand. Beginning to sink into the sand, he cleverly used his shield to hover in place, instead of attempting to run across the shifting sand.

"Get down here!" His words were snarled in hatred as he beckoned her using a curt gesture to come down. She'd heard about him from Carmotta. Clive Sha, apparently one of her most adamant denouncers, had argued Boomer did not belong there—was unworthy of the honor of becoming a Goldwon Warrior.

An advantage Boomer did have over the other contestants was her years of battle experience. From the age of eight on she'd faced multiple adversaries—often forced to kill to stay alive. She doubted any of the others were as battle-hardened as she.

He stared up at her with contempt—waiting for her to meet him in battle down on the sand. Instead, with lightning speed, she thrust her pratta-shaft downward in his direction and watched as its point disappeared into the sand between his feet. Eyes open wide, he jumped back—then stumbled and fell backward onto the sand. He flailed desperately but, in an instant, his body started to disappear beneath the sea of sand. In moments, his screams were drowned out beneath its surface. Lighter than Clive—and sinking at a slower rate—Master Sahhselies' pratta-shaft was still visible.

Boomer jumped down from the pedestal, directly onto where she guessed Clive Sha's now-submerged, hidden legs were buried. Landing directly atop them, she had just enough support to avoid getting sucked under. She used her enhancement shield to keep her body elevated. Then, in one fluid motion, she thrust a hand into the sand, reaching down for Clive Sha. Her fingers touched his matted thick hair and, in a single move, she both grabbed and hauled him upward.

As the top half of his body rose out of the sand Clive Sha desperately coughed and gasped. Boomer, still standing on his legs and holding his head up by his dreadlocks, waited for him to stop coughing. His eyes met hers in a stare filled with hatred.

"Say it! Say the word, Sha," Boomer ordered, just loud enough for him to hear her.

His voice, barely a croak, said, "I'll say it, but you'll see, nobody here today ... nobody will accept surrender when your turn comes. Your death is a forgone conclusion."

She waited.

"Drench! Drench," he yelled, loud enough for those in the nearby stands to hear.

Boomer, increasing power to her shield, pulled Sha up and out of the deadly quicksand. She dropped his body, unceremoniously, onto nearby solid ground then turned her back on him, the first contestant to formally give up. She wondered if it was true. Had the others made some kind of secret agreement? Would any surrender from her be ignored? Surely Carmotta and Drom would never go along with such a thing. *Or would they?*

The first defeated Tahli warrior was dragged from the stadium floor by Sahhrain guards to a flurry of boos and hisses. She suspected the catcalls were aimed more toward her than Clive Sha. Boomer knew she was not popular. *Well, screw them ... screw them all!*

New cheers emanated from the seats. Boomer realized they were in response to what just occurred across the stadium floor, where Carmotta had vanquished her own combatant. Apparently, she'd been watching Boomer while her left foot held steady upon her prone opponent's throat. One quick thrust and a crushed larynx would be the result. Apparently, her opponent chose to shout Drench, instead. The crowd cheered and soon more guards were dispatched to escort another Tahli Warrior from the trials.

Carmotta and Boomer quickly saluted each other before each turned to face her next battle challenge.

Boomer stopped and appraised what lay ahead. She did not know her name—had never seen the stocky female before today. Somehow she'd managed to navigate upward to a flat section within the rock tower—the tower of sword-like blades. Startled, Boomer heard a distant scream. Though out of view, she knew it came from Carmotta.

Chapter 5

present day...

J ason first wanted to visit where it all had come down—where his daughter, and so many others, had been killed. *No ... slaughtered.* Checking his internal nano-devices he noted it was 12:40, Earth Pacific Time. He had over an hour before Boomer's memorial services would commence. Initially, the Blues' security official, Magistrate Peele, was not receptive to non-nationals visiting the still-under-investigation battle scene. "You do realize that the Blues are suddenly at a state of war. I'm sure you understand, Omni Reynolds. We cannot have the area tainted by outsiders tromping around down there."

Jason had abruptly disconnected linkup with that intergalactic communication channel. It took less than two minutes, speaking directly to the brother of the injured Prince Aqeel, a Blues dignitary in his own right with substantial influence, for all such restrictions to be waived. The unspoken reality, and one not lost on the prince, was that Jason and the U.S. fleet had literally saved the Blues from an assured mass extinction, at the hands of the Sahhrain, a mere five years ago. The prince and his brother owed him—hell, every living Blues citizen owed him.

The wide, bus-like, shuttle dropped down from Harpaign's higher atmosphere at a seemingly lackadaisical pace. Quelling his impatience, Jason steadily watched the nearing planet's surface come into view below them. Everywhere were the same, mile-after-mile, orange-colored sand dunes—all the way across to the far horizon.

He felt a tap on his shoulder. "There!" Mollie said, an outstretched finger pointing off to the right. "Is that it? Those are the Capital Ruins ... right?"

He squinted against the harsh bright sunlight and nodded, then shrugged. Harpaign had hundreds—thousands even—of ruins since new excavation programs were enacted over the past few years.

Ricket, now standing at the same observation window, said, "Those are indeed the Capital Ruins, Captain."

Jason kept his eyes on the approaching devastation. The ancient city, small in terms of most sprawling, modern-day metropolises, would normally be scarcely distinguishable from the area's surrounding sandy landscape. But now, with so many of its stone structures both pitted and scorched black, the terrain seemed almost moon-like, with countless craters of varying sizes scattered about. It obviously was the site of an epic-level attack.

Jason heard Mollie's rapid intake of air and turned to see her staring wide-eyed, her hands covering her mouth, and an expression of disbelief on her face as she scanned the rapidly approaching carnage below them. "No one could survive that," she said with chilling finality.

The truth was, apparently some had: Those sitting at the north end of the stadium, including the dark-robed Tahli ministry members. They were protected by powerful, albeit localized, shield projectors. Although initially designed to shield against attacks instigated inside the stadium itself, the shields did offer sufficient early protection from incoming enemy plasma blasts for some. They escaped to a hidden subterranean vault beneath the stadium, hiding there in safety, while the world above them became decimated—first aerially, by a formidable Sahhrain warship; then by two ground garrisons of Sahhrain warriors.

It took substantial willpower for Jason to unclench his white-knuckled fists. He looked forward to meeting the cowards, those hiding beneath the city while tens of thousands, including his daughter, were being butchered above.

Vibrations from the shuttle's large downward-pointing thrusters rumbled through the craft as everyone prepared to disembark. Jason stayed at the window, watching the group of Blues emissaries standing beneath a poled tarp. One by one, they left the comfort of their shady confine to welcome their arrival.

"I've seen that face before," Mollie said, glancing up. She'd stayed next to her father, waiting for him. "You want to kill them."

Jason pulled his heated glare toward those outside the shuttle away. He nodded. "Every fucking last one of them."

Everyone moved out of the sun, now standing sheltered beneath the tarp's cover. There were six Blues officials, sporting sidearms on their belts. The one who seemed to be in charge wore a uniform that reminded Jason of a janitor's ill-fitting overalls. He mumbled something, then bowed his head at the assemblage of ten foreigners standing before him. Pacing back and forth, the long-faced Blues official had elongated ears and two puckering, wrinkled lips. He briefly hesitated as he approached Traveler, who towered, like a perfectly sculpted statue, over him. Regaining his composure, he said, "I am Storvan. I am chief of security for all the Blues antiquities within the Dacci system." He looked back and forth at their unimpressed blank faces. "Please listen carefully. You must stay within the cordoned-off areas at all times. You must not touch anything. You must not take anything from the battle site. Anyone who deviates from those guidelines will be arrested and taken back to the Star-Dome, where you will be prosecuted. If these conditions are understood—"

This is bullshit! Jason took a quick step forward, his hands already clenched into two vise-like fists. Then, abruptly, a voice came from the back of the group.

"I have a question."

Everyone, including Jason, turned. Leon Pike moved up to the front—his eyes on Jason as he spoke to Storvan. "Um ... would it be possible to interview some of the survivors?"

Storvan, who'd recoiled at Jason's approach, turned his eyes toward Leon. "No. That will not be possible. They are very busy now, dealing with far more important ..."

Jason appreciated Leon's attempt to mollify the situation, but he'd had enough. Again, he stepped forward, this time taking the Blues official by surprise, and grabbed a fistful of fabric beneath his pointy chin. He pulled him closer—their faces inches apart. "Listen to me carefully. My name is Jason Reynolds ... perhaps you've heard of me? You can address me as Omni or Captain—either will suffice. Just recently, the Blues ... those exclusive of the Dacci System ... renewed their inclusion with the Alliance, of which I am the military commander—in charge over millions of planetary bodies. I am taking command of this site and you, Mr. Storvan, will do exactly what I tell you to do. You will instruct your people to bend over backwards to appease our every request." Ending on that note, Jason's brows rose questioningly.

Storvan's eyes shifted left, then right. No one was coming to his defense. He nodded twice. Jason released his grip and smoothed down the wrinkles. "Very good. I'm sure we'll get along splendidly from here on out. Now stop wasting our time. Take us into the city's battlegrounds."

Jason broke them up into four smaller teams: Traveler, Leon and Hanna were in group one; Billy and Rizzo in group two; and Orion and Perkins in group three. Mollie, along with her ever-present hovering droid, Teardrop, and Ricket, were with him in group four.

"What are we looking for, Cap?" Billy asked, as they headed off toward the ancient city.

Jason shrugged. "Answers. Over the next hour I want to piece together what really happened here. Our own evaluation, not what the Blues are spoon-feeding us."

Each team had commandeered one of Storvan's security men. Storvan, surprisingly, stayed with Jason and his group. As they entered through the city's high walls, sooty smoke still hung in the air, plus the putrid stench of rotting, charred, flesh. The four groups split up, heading off in different directions. Jason glanced over to Mollie, the least dressed for such rough surroundings. She didn't seem to mind. In fact, she was more engaged now than when she first arrived to board the *Stellar* earlier.

Mollie, addressing Storvan, asked, "Can you take us to the battlefield ... the one where ..." She let her words trail off.

The security man looked to Jason for approval before

detouring them to the right, away from the nearly-leveled stadium, a quarter of a mile away to their left.

It took them less than ten minutes to reach the battlefield. They didn't need Storvan to say anything. What looked like bright-red twine was stretched between makeshift wooden poles, intended to keep one from entering any further onto the actual battlefield. Jason held up, looking across acres upon acres of what must have been a long, and horrific, encounter. Though their dead bodies had been carted away still remnants of their fight remained: broken and splintered pratta-shafts, dented and bloodied breastplates, scorched blast marks on the sand. Blood—now turned the color of dark rust—was everywhere.

Ricket began to fiddle with the droid. He opened a small panel on its triangular torso and made some kind of intricate adjustment within it. A moment later, he closed the panel and, after exchanging subtle nods with Jason, turned back to Teardrop. The droid quickly rose higher in the air before crossing over and into the battlefield. Jason flashed the security guard a stern glance that said *don't say a word*.

Immediately, Teardrop dropped to within inches of the ground and moved back and forth, in what seemed a pre-programmed pattern. It soon began traversing the cordoned-off area at incredible speeds.

"What's Teardrop doing, Dad?" Mollie asked.

"Full spectrum scans."

"He's looking for her DNA ... isn't he?"

Jason held her eyes a moment, but didn't answer.

Teardrop suddenly halted, one hundred yards away from their position—moving in a spherical range of ten or so feet.

Ricket, two fingers up to his ear, said in a soft voice full of compassion, "It has been confirmed. Her DNA—significant amounts of it—is present there."

Jason had been informed of the very same thing some days

earlier. What they suspected was that Boomer's charred body had been collected and moved to a nearby, temporary morgue setup. The body was beyond recognition—beyond retrieving DNA samples from, though the dried pool of blood was another matter, where part of a finger was also found.

Jason felt his chest begin to restrict, finding it hard to breathe. It was time to come to terms with the harsh reality that his daughter was dead. Accept it, as Nan and Mollie had. He looked over to Mollie, ready to be there for her; provide her all the loving support she needed. What he didn't expect to see in that moment was what showed on her face: A broad, confident, smile.

"She's not dead ... Dad."

Chapter 6

two weeks earlier...

Carmotta's scream threw her off balance. Boomer's natural instinct was to rescue her friend. *What then? Rescue her, only to fight her again later on?*

The stocky female before her hadn't moved from her perch amongst the rocky shards. Smiling, she beckoned Boomer forward with an inward waving gesture. "I am Latchki ... the opponent who ends your quest for the Goldwon," she chided.

Boomer returned her own gesture—one far less friendly, which instigated a ferocious round of distortion waves in her direction. She blocked the first round but misjudged where the second round would hit, and took the full breadth of Latchki's energy punch to her solar plexus. Boomer stumbled and nearly passed out. *Crap that hurts.*

Shaking it off, Boomer kept moving around the lower perimeter of the rocks—her eyes constantly scanning for each potential safe haven landing spot. She'd counted four so far and committed them to memory. She was well aware that one mistake ... one misjudgment ... would mean a certain, painful, death.

"Come on, little Calhoom, don't be afraid. I will kill you fast. No need for the alternative pain you'll face if you make this difficult for me."

There's that word again ... *Calhoom*. She didn't know *precisely* what it meant but she'd let the obviously derogatory term get under her skin. A handful of young Blues Tahli warriors spent time in the infirmary recently—all regretting they'd called her that same stupid word. She threw her pratta-shaft and saw Latchki casually block it with her shield.

Boomer had now spied five isolated safe regions, some no wider than a few inches, located throughout the rock tower. She came around from the back of the tower and made eye contact with the stocky girl, who then fired off three quick distortion wave bursts. Boomer used her shield to fire off her own deflecting salvos, then abruptly went airborne, using her shield to propel herself thirty feet up onto the tower—ten feet behind, and to the right, of her opponent. She precariously landed on one foot—all there was room for—between a series of razor-sharp spikes. Again, she used distortion waves, to help her maintain balance, while staying consciously aware of her opponent, now turning in her direction.

Boomer, slow to make a move, took a glancing blow to her upper shoulder. It was enough to throw her off balance and she fell backward, toward five, or more, upward-pointed rocky spikes. Spinning around, the highest of the skewer-like rock spikes impaled her upper thigh. By sheer good fortune, she was able to grasp ahold of the next spike an inch before it entered her left eye socket. She couldn't adequately use her shield since she was holding on to the spike with the same hand. Cheers from fifty thousand Blues erupted—clearly anticipating her imminent demise.

Laughter, then a light-hearted song came up from below: "Calhoom ... Calhoom ... the Calhoom's going to diiiiiiee ..."

Boomer was stuck. The white-hot blinding pain in her leg made it nearly impossible to think, or to move, and she was losing blood. The first of Latchki's distortion waves began to pound against Boomer's unprotected back, and she felt the skin there start to blister. *A truckload of MarGiline's makeup's not going to hide that scarring.* Tears filled her eyes and she clenched her teeth—not wanting to give her opponent the pleasure of hearing her scream. In an all-or-nothing effort, Boomer wrenched her skewered leg sideways and felt the spike snap in half. She was free—but her fleeting strength had nearly dissipated.

"Hey—Thunder thighs! Sing that song again ... will you?" Boomer yelled from the tower.

She heard her laugh again and then there it was ... that same stupid song.

It did the trick. Infuriated, Boomer, her fist still tightly wrapped around the spike a mere inch from her face, thrust her arm downward, then propelled herself backward, away from the spike, and into a sideways spin. At last, she was now able to use her shield. In less than a second she managed to stand vertically again, even on the leg still impaled with a broken-off rock spike. Boomer did her best to recall each one of the other safe havens she'd noted, then made her next move. Using intense violet distortion waves, she propelled herself upward, over the head of her opponent, and landed on a slanted plateau of rock just wide enough for both feet. She'd caught Latchki off guard. With anger unbridled, Boomer let go with a battery of violet—now fringed with red—distortion waves, directing them toward Latchki's head.

Boomer quickly took to the air again, heading for her next safe haven. Solely from memory, she landed with her legs apart

—coming down on two separate, narrow, flat outcroppings. Shield up and ready for her next attack, Boomer hesitated. Latchki's face looked decimated—her nose was virtually non-existent—her lips an oozing pulp mess. One eye was seared shut while the other held Boomer's stare. Latchki tried to say something ... wobbled ... and Boomer knew, beyond any doubt, she purposely let herself fall forward. A four-foot-tall shard of rock entered her chest, killing her instantly. The yelling crowd went quiet.

Before Boomer could fully digest what just happened, she heard Carmotta's voice off in the distance, taunting her opponent. Words that surprisingly comforted Boomer, in light of what had just occurred.

Something flashed above her and she turned toward the middle of the stadium. There, high above on the center pedestal, sun rays struck the small statue in just the right way. Its glittering reflection reminded Boomer of why she was there. *I haven't forgotten about you, little Goldwon. Don't worry—I'll be up there with you ... soon.*

Boomer heard the distant Shintuco Cat's roar—loud enough to drown out the erupting cheers of the audience. Boomer dreaded going near that end of the stadium—because of the big cat, for sure; but even more so—Drom was there.

First things first: Boomer inspected the damage to her thigh. The tip of the rock spike was still imbedded, at least several inches deep. It hurt, but hadn't incapacitated her so far. Best to leave it be for now. For all she knew, she'd completely bleed out if she pulled it free.

Maneuvering toward the south end of the stadium, she noticed several contestants' banners had been pulled down from their pedestals: Clive Sha's, Latchki's, and three others. They were all dead. Both Drom's and Carmotta's, plus two others, and her own, still remained up. *Five down ... four to go.*

Farther down from the quicksand-like dunes, on the same side of the stadium, was another death-defying zone—*The Pendulums.* Looking between the tall, swinging back and forth, half-circular, honed blades—no opponents could be seen nearby. The closer she came to them the more she heard their *swooping* sounds and felt the rushing of air on her skin. Some of the swinging blades nearly touched the ground, while others were closer to head-level; all of them, probably close to fifteen total, moved independently of one another. Boomer came to an abrupt stop, catching sight of something she'd not anticipated to find there—a twenty-foot-tall, un-climbable, glass-like panel. The whole area to the right of the wall obstacle was considered out of bounds. To get to the next zone, Drom's zone, she'd need to move through the myriad of swinging pendulums. Boomer contemplated turning completely back around—retracing her steps, going counter-clockwise, around the stadium. But in doing that she knew she'd only have to face other obstacles. And, not to forget, her friend, Carmotta, too ... eventually. No. She'd face this obstacle head on, and persevere.

But she couldn't see how to do it. *Come on ... come on! There has to be a way through the blades by timing my advances,* she thought. *Right?* Boomer's eyes followed the rhythm of the long swinging blades, watching for openings—where and when she'd need to hold up. The roars coming from the Shintuco Cat tugged at her concentration: Twice she lost focus and needed to start over. *What the hell is that?* She thought she could see movement, on the far side of the zone. Boomer twice visualized her progression through the maze of blades, and realized there wasn't any way to move forward without being split in half. Frustrated, she stomped her foot. "Damn!"

Then she heard his voice—barely audible above the yowl of the big cat and the cheering crowd. "Come on, figure it out ... you can move sideways too ... not only forward."

She recognized Drom's voice. It was Drom she'd seen moving around on the obstacle's other side. Of course, why hadn't she thought of that? She went back over her mental steps-counting, only this time, when there was no clear way to proceed forward, she looked instead for ways to move sideways. *Yes! That's it!*

Boomer by now knew the rhythm of each blade. Knew the beats to count—whether to hold up or go on. She waited for the first two outer opposing blades to cross then jumped. She was in! She counted four beats and jumped forward again, now crouching low, for the next swinging pendulum hung a foot and a half lower than the last. Hold five beats, then rolling, head-over-heels, forward, she stood up straight, in the middle of the obstacle. It seemed darker and cooler there, where all forward movement was impossible. She counted eight beats then sidestepped three times and halted. Again, ducking low, Boomer froze. Here, the blades in front of her were all smeared with blood ... dripping with blood. She became aware of other objects ... grizzly things ... spread over the ground. Body parts. She knew that losing her concentration and focus now, missing a count, would be the end of her. Three beats ... four beats ... she jumped forward, immediately sidestepping to the right. She saw the head-height pendulum blade swinging toward her head and leaned back an inch, holding her breath. *Shingggg*—several strands of her hair flew into the air and drifted around her. *That was way too close.* She jumped forward and ... *oh my God, I've lost count ... I've completely, fucking, lost count!* Her breaths expelled fast and short. The pendulums seemed to have increased speed and were zipping around her on all sides. *Oh God, I'm trapped here. Think!* Then she thought of something ... something divergent. Two of the swinging pendulums, the ones forward and to her right, were significantly smaller. Certainly just as sharp and lethal, but they weighed far less than the other blades. There didn't seem to be another course of action—could she do it?

Boomer closed her eyes and, using *baskile*, relaxed and let the world around her fade away into the ether. The sounds of the big cat, the crowd, and the rhythmic swooping of the blades became muted, then drummed into silence. Now, only the two, small, swinging pendulums remained in her consciousness. She saw them clearly and let all fear ... all dread ... dissipate away. When she was ready, she raised her enhancement shield—pointing its face toward where the pendulum blades would cross in front of her—and fired off a massive, bright-scarlet-colored stream of distortion waves.

The abrupt, very loud clanging of metal hitting metal startled her from her deep meditation. The swinging pendulums continued to move in their deathly trajectories—except for the two smaller blades, both destroyed. As easily as walking through a doorway, Boomer stepped forward and to the side into the next zone, to a stunned, silent, arena.

Apparently waiting for her, Drom casually stood there, using his upright pratta-shaft to support his weight. Blood covered much of his body. Boomer was unsure how much was his, or if the blood belonged to his recent opponents. What was left of a shredded one ... or maybe two, dismembered Tahli warriors, lay behind at the feeding big cat's feet. She saw Drom's crooked smile ... a smile that conveyed both relief and awe she'd managed to survive her own fearsome obstacle.

"I wouldn't be turning my back on that beast if I were you," Boomer said, gesturing toward the snarling Shintuco Cat behind him.

Drom gave a quick glance over his shoulder. "He and I have come to an agreement."

"Yeah? And what's that?"

"If he keeps his distance I won't keep aiming distortion waves at his testicles."

Boomer nodded and slowly turned in a circle. One by one, she noted the home banners missing from some pedestals. Her gaze stopped, spotting the symbol of a bright-blue palm on a field of black. He said, "I guess it's down to just the three of us, kid."

Boomer was about to respond *that's the way I'd hoped it would be*—but she never had the chance. It started as a vibration —then a rumble. The ground beneath them began shaking. Someone in the crowd screamed—something about a warship. But Boomer had already seen it: Massive and ominous, it slowly moved into view as it crested over the top of the stadium. Only then did it fire off its big plasma cannons. The nearby south section of the stands went up in a fireball, and with it—thousands of Blues' lives.

Chapter 7

Jason continued to stare at his daughter. He knew this was an emotional time for her—in spite of her obvious *put on* nonchalance. "Look, Mollie, I know this is a difficult time for you ... it is for all of us."

"You know, Dad, I was afraid to come here," Mollie said.

Jason slowly nodded, not sure where she was going with that comment. "Of course you were."

"I knew I'd be able to feel her last moments ... maybe even see her death," Mollie said. "The thought of it scared me ... terrified me. It's happened before—too many times to count—those constant life and death situations. It's why I hate her. Hate her for the connection I have with her and what I've had to ..." Mollie's voice trailed off.

Jason was aware the girls were bonded, possibly like no other two people in history, but he hadn't been aware that their bond was on such a deep, inner, level. He looked at Mollie with new compassion. Her strange tie, connection, to Boomer, of all people—one who repeatedly threw herself into dangerous, death-defying situations. Having to experience such perils, even though secondhand, would be miserable.

"You never told me," he said.

"Yes, I did. You and Mom just never listened. But it's gotten stronger over the last few years. I'd be sitting in class, taking a test or something, and all of a sudden I'm seeing what Boomer's seeing—a huge Jonga-beast chasing after her, or she's caught in a maze of swinging pendulums. Each time she's about to die, it's almost as if she's telling me goodbye! God, I hate her!"

Jason watched as tears streamed down his daughter's cheeks. She wiped them away with a swipe of one hand. Mollie looked out to the battlefield, pointing to an area Teardrop had hovered over just moments before. "She was there. I saw her look at her hand ... noticing the missing stub of a finger. It was her pinkie. Go ahead—check it out and see for yourself."

Mollie and Jason turned toward Ricket, who told them, "I would first have to covertly access the Blues' StarDome network ... locate the database and find Boomer's—"

Mollie cut him off, "Hack in, Ricket. Just do it!"

Ricket hesitated and looked up at Jason. It was tantamount to an act of war to breach another sovereign's network system. With that said, Ricket was no ordinary systems engineer. It would be a walk in the park for him to hack in and not leave a traceable trail. Jason lowered his voice to a mere whisper. "Do it."

"It is done," Ricket said a moment later. He brought up his virtual notepad, expanding a virtual form image before them.

Mollie let out a groan as she took in the projected image of a blackened, completely charred body, lying upon a metallic-surfaced table.

"This is one of three database morgue images allocated to the female Boomer Reynolds. It matches the height and esti-mated weight of Boomer before she was struck by a powerful plasma blast. There were no viable DNA, or other viable organic substances, to confirm that this is truly her body, with the exception of ..." Ricket switched to the next image, providing them a close up of a severed finger tip, "this fingertip, found beneath the charred body. DNA and other identifiers confirm this was indeed a section of Boomer's finger." He changed to the last image, showing a large, nearly black, pool of congealed blood. "Nearby the body was this excessive amount of blood ... also confirmed to be of Boomer's DNA. So an assumption was made—the body's identity was solely linked to the fingertip and the blood." Ricket brought up the 3D image of the charred body again then manipulated the image—flipping the body onto its side. He next zoomed in on the body's charred left-hand fingers. Ricket shrugged and smiled, letting the hovering image speak for itself. Although obviously charred, the pinkie's fingertip was still present. Ricket then flipped the image the opposite way, zooming in on the body's charred right-hand fingers. There, too, the pinkie's fingertip could be seen still attached.

Both Mollie and Ricket looked to Jason. The implications were enormous. His daughter quite possibly was still alive.

"Mollie, have you had any ... other visions or impressions since then?" Jason watched as she mentally searched through recent memories.

"I'm not sure ... maybe. More often, it's her strong emotions —like fear or excitement or anger—whatever she's feeling at the time. For anything visual ... well, something epic has to be going on. Still, with all that said, I think she's alive."

Jason was being hailed.

"Go for ..."

"Where are you? Damn it, Jason, it's your daughter's funeral service. I can't believe this ... that you'd miss—"

He interrupted Nan's tirade. "Boomer's not dead."

Nan continued, "I don't know if this is some kind of denial ... or maybe guilt you're feeling, but this is unconscionable! Wait ... what did you just say?"

"Nan ... there's a good chance she's not dead."

There was a long silence over their NanoCom connection. "Don't you dare tell me that, Jason."

"The body ... it's not Boomer. I don't know whose it is, but it's not our daughter."

Jason heard Nan break down. She was hundreds of miles away probably surrounded by other mourners—a solemn funeral service of sorts—and she was sobbing, unable to speak. It took several moments before she spoke again. "Okay ... I need to get away from here. You're really sure?"

Jason let his eyes fall on Ricket, questioning him. As if reading his thoughts, Ricket not only nodded, he appeared hopeful. "Yes, Nan, I'm sure."

Immediately after leaving the surface of Harpaign, aboard the same meandering shuttle, they made their way back to the Star-Dome—everyone reconvening there within the deluxe privacy of the *Stellar*. Nan, along with her ever-present, five-man presidential-protection detail, showed up less than a half-hour later. Now, a total of sixteen mingled aboard the Omni's personal yacht. Mollie rushed into her mother's embrace. Jason waited several moments before approaching his ex-wife. She looked tired and, eyes puffy, had obviously been crying her eyes out for days now. Just now forty-five, her long dark hair pulled back into a ponytail, she had only become more beautiful. Seeing Jason over Mollie's shoulder, Nan patted her daughter's back twice before stepping aside.

"Jason!" With no hesitation, Nan stepped forward and hugged him, too. "I can't believe it ... she's alive ... possibly?" Her words were muffled against his chest. She pulled away enough to look up at him—hope in her eyes. "I'm sorry I've been such a bitch. I know you've been suffering as much as me ... maybe more so, since she's always been close to your side. I've been horrible to you."

"Let's just find her," he said, stepping free of her embrace feeling somewhat self-conscious. With a disappointed expression, he said, "I thought Michael would be ..."

"Come on, Jason ... our son's a little too young to be involved in all this ..."

"No, you're right. I just miss him."

Nan and Jason's son was now going on six. Jason saw far too little of him. Something he planned on rectifying, soon.

"You know ... you could come visit more ... he misses you. Talks about you incessantly."

Pangs of guilt clutched at Jason's constricted throat. He nodded. This was not the time for this. His mind turned back to matters at hand.

Jason at this point knew they needed to get a clearer indication of exactly what transpired on the surface of Harpaign. The official Blues' accounting of the Sahhrain attack on their planet was sketchy at best. Although clearly an act of war, there was only the one attack. The Sahhrain had left Blues' space then and didn't return. Military support from the Alliance, specifically from Star Watch, was scheduled to arrive in force there within days. Since no further attacks had been instigated, Jason —as Omni of all U.S. fleet assets—although tempted, didn't order immediate retaliatory action. Although the Blues unequivocally declared war immediately on their neighbors, the Sahhrain, that didn't necessarily mean the Alliance would do so, as well. The underlying fact of the matter was the Sahhrain, too, had been an Alliance member for the past five years. It was complicated.

Jason moved to the middle of the cabin. "Look, we have a limited amount of time before Star Watch arrives in force. At that point, my priorities mandate that I take command of the arriving fleet. For now, I'm simply Boomer's father, and the rest of you are here on a non-official basis. We need to be careful. This is how wars start, and the last thing we need now is to inadvertently trigger something between the Blues and the Sahhrain ... and the Alliance ... that could be best settled through negotiations."

Jason looked at those around him. "This is what we know so far: According to the official logs, Boomer and nine other Tahli warriors were competing in something called the *Goldwon Trials*. Boomer, not allowed to speak directly with anyone on the outside, and far out of reach of NanoCom communications, sent word two weeks ago through Prince Aqeel. I received a personal communiqué from him that Boomer was on the verge of completing her years-long training period, and that there was only one more important, and dangerous, testing regime she had to undergo—more like a contest."

"Why weren't we invited to the contest?" Nan asked with brows furrowed.

"Apparently non-nationals ... non-Blues ... weren't allowed there."

"Boomer's not one of the Blues," Billy said.

"I know. But they conceded special allowances for her a long time ago. Anyway, from what the Blues' logs tell us, it was during the contest the attack occurred. Tens of thousands of Blues were killed. Useful details have not been entered into their logs up to this point. Why? I'm not sure. Something fishy is definitely going on."

"Can we talk to Prince Aqeel directly?" Nan asked. "I can use my former position of president to—"

"Aqeel's here ... and near death. Apparently he has suffered burns over most of his body. He's in the hospital, under heavy guard."

"Why the hell don't they put him in a MediPod and be done with it?" Billy asked, bewildered. "And what's with guarding him? From whom?"

"I don't know. We've given them ten pods over the last few months. And they're right there, on the StarDome. Something strange is going on. The Blues are being increasingly tightlipped. The more I press them to get answers the more resistance I'm getting."

"So what should we do?" Mollie queried.

"The next step—I pay a personal visit to Aqeel's bedside. If necessary, I'll bring him back with me."

Chapter 8

"Here? Like ... onto the *Stellar*?" Leon asked.

"Sure. We need answers now. There's a fully functional MediPod below. Granted, it's a cramped medical department, but everything necessary is available there to help Prince Aqeel recover," Jason said, showing pride in his new space-voyaging luxury yacht.

"Everything but an actual doctor ... like Dira," Mollie said, immediately regretting her words. "Sorry, Dad ... that was mean of me."

Jason couldn't blame her for saying what everyone else was probably thinking. He and Dira, married four and a half years, had seen little of each other since their vows. Although the world of Jhardon had transformed from a monarch-ruled government to one successfully democratic, its populace was disinclined to forsake their royal heritage family, and their favorite royal daughter. In some respects, Princess Dira was the beating pulse of that nearly destroyed world. Beautiful and passionate, she'd become an advocate for the masses, against a less compassionate political machine, ruled with detached authoritarianism. Jason's stolen getaways with her were often filled with arguments. Adding to that unrest, invariably each was frequently hailed to put out fires—Jason with Star Watch and the U.S. fleet, and Dira with matters of state on Jhardon. It was never a matter of waning love for either. In fact, the opposite was true—their long, many separations had been heartbreaking for both.

Jason offered up a one-sided smile and said, "Ricket certainly doesn't have Dira's great legs, nor her warm bedside manner, but remember—he is an accomplished doctor in his own right." He looked around the cabin—other than Dira and his father and Michael back on Earth—these were the most important people in his life. "I want to say something here: Over the next few days, I'm planning to do something other than act as the fleet's Omni. I'm going to be breaking rules. I'm going to break a shitload of laws. I'm going to be selfish—attend to the needs of my family—my missing daughter. So I cannot ask any of you to join me on my ... whatever this is ... crusade. You have careers to think of; loved ones of your own to consider."

A grunt came from the back of the semicircle. A steamy snotty sprout shot into the air as Traveler, obviously agitated, pushed his way to the front of the group. "No, Boomer is also my family, Captain. Did she not risk her life for me ... more than once? She is a brave warrior. Yes. I will gladly die to protect the one we call Boomer." Traveler assumed a new position, standing tall behind Jason.

Billy, his hands on hips, nodded empathically. "I agree. As annoying as Boomer could be, she was, is, as close a daughter to me as I'll probably ever have." Billy's eyes flashed over to Orion before continuing: "I'm with you, Cap ... let's break some fucking laws."

Jason put both palms up, in mock surrender. "Hold on ...

hold on, everyone. Let's let those who wish to return to the Sol System do so now. What you don't know, can't be used against you later."

Everyone looked around—as though daring anyone to break up the group's solidarity.

"I'm sorry, Captain," Perkins said, looking nervous. "I can't be a part of this. I've worked too hard to get my own commission. Besides, I'm needed back on the *Minian*. My crew counts on me."

"Uh huh, of course they do," Hanna said sarcastically, her head cocked and her arms crossed over her chest, an expression of disgust on her face. Jason knew Hanna was not a huge fan of Perkins—his words only substantiated her feelings.

"That's fine," Jason said, giving Hanna a disapproving glance. "There's a U.S. fleet light cruiser moored just on the other side of the StarDome. They'll be leaving within the hour, so go ... make haste, Captain Perkins."

"Again ... I'm sorry, Captain ... Omni." Perkins purposely avoided eye contact with any of the others. Looking as if he wanted to say something else, he abruptly rushed toward the hatch. It opened as he approached, then closed just as quickly after his departure.

"Anyone else? Now's the time," Billy asked, sounding annoyed.

Nan bit her lip. Looking reluctant, she said, "As much as I want to be a part of this ... need to be a part of this, I don't know how I'm able to help you. I'm not a warrior, like the rest of you. Perhaps I can better serve your efforts by remaining in Sol space in the background. Deflect attention off of what you're doing, while still keeping you apprised of what's happening."

Jason saw her protection detail of five visibly release long collective sighs of relief. It was unrealistic for a recently departed POTUS to gallivant around the galaxy, and it could bring undue attention to what must stay a highly secretive mission. Nan pulled Jason into a hug, her words lowered for his ears only: "Find her, Jason ... if anyone can, it's you."

"I won't come back without her, Nan," he vowed.

Nan stepped away, keeping eye contact for several more beats. She turned, nodding to her detail, and headed for the hatch. Halfway across the cabin she suddenly halted and turned toward Mollie. "Are you coming?"

Mollie shook her head. "I'm staying."

Nan's smile was nearly imperceptible as she looked back at Jason. "Watch her." With that, they were gone.

Jason let out a breath, ready to move things along.

"What?" Mollie asked, glaring at Hanna.

Hanna, her arms still crossed beneath her breast, shook her head in Mollie's direction. "I'm sorry, Captain, but I don't think any of us should be babysitting your daughter when things might get ... you know, dicey."

All eyes went to Mollie, including Jason's. He was about to say something when Mollie took three quick strides forward to plant herself in front of Hanna. Standing straight—not a hair out of place—her white button-down shirt and short mini-skirt looked as fresh as they had when she put them on that morning. Under his breath, Billy murmured, "Oh boy ..."

Mollie said, "I don't know who the hell you are, lady, and frankly I don't give a shit. What I can tell you is that I have as much battle experience as you. Maybe more. I died from a plasma bolt to the heart when I was eight. I escaped the fangs of Serapin-Terplins, and I personally fought and killed more Craing than I care to remember. I fought at my mother's side, against hundreds of zombie peovils, and lived to talk about it. Before there was a Boomer, there was me. Just me. So if you really want to know if I'm tough enough, just keep giving me that pretentious, superior, look!" Mollie's index finger came up, pointing toward Hanna's chest.

You could hear a pin drop, no one uttering a word. Ricket was the first to move. As the two females glared at each other, he went to Mollie's side and took her hand. "Mollie, I am sorry I shot you in the heart."

Rizzo, who'd quietly stayed in the background, was the first to let out a chuckle. Then one by one, the others followed suit. Soon, Hanna too let a smile cross her lips as the cabin erupted in laughter. Mollie was the only one not seeing humor in the situation after her heated rebuff.

Dramatically, with her hands up, Hanna bowed in reverence toward Mollie several times. "I stand corrected. You are officially one badass chick and I've been properly chastised." Hanna offered her hand and Mollie finally smiled and reluctantly shook it.

"Okay, that's enough drama for one day." Jason turned to Leon. "You and Hanna can man the helm and get us clearance to leave StarDome. Traveler, Billy and Rizzo, I'll need your help. Everyone else, hang tight. Oh ... and Orion, there's a small tactical station on the bridge. We may need your expertise there."

Orion nodded.

"What do you want me to do?" Mollie asked.

"Go down to Medical with Ricket. We're about to acquire a new patient. Hopefully one who'll be able to answer some questions—help us find Boomer."

"Captain, I've forwarded the phase-shift coordinates, showing Prince Aqeel's estimated location in StarDome's hospital," Ricket said.

"Thank you, Ricket." Jason was first to initialize his battle suit, as Billy, Rizzo, and Traveler followed suit.

"You have any weapons on this little luxury liner, Cap?" Billy asked.

"I set up the *Stellar*'s armory, so what do you think?" Orion asked, leaving the cabin without looking in Billy's direction.

"Wait ... the Benz has an armory?" Billy said.

Chapter 9

Jason waited for the *Stellar* to disengage from the StarDome and move some distance away. Even at thirty miles out, the immense space station was still visible—an impressive display of modern design and ingenuity.

A dazzling gateway into the Dacci System, the StarDome was primarily designed and constructed by several commercial, mega-conglomerates on Earth, cropping up over the past five years. Big money was being made—via commerce between Space and Earth—and the U.S. and China and the re-configured USSR were taking full advantage of it. As part of the deal, the Blues demanded that they provide the bulk of laborers, which meant prolonged delays—expanding the training and education tools now required of their workforce. In the end, the StarDome did materialize and the Blues gained invaluable knowledge and experience from the joint endeavor, propelling them to develop even further their own recent manufacturing businesses—building and outfitting new space stations and ship-building platforms. Eventually, advanced space freighters and other spacecraft were built. All occupied space within the Allied territory. With a workforce that charged sums only a fraction of those levied within the Sol System—Liberty Station, the Alliance's, and also the U.S. fleet's, replacement for the destroyed, but now nearly operational, old Jefferson Station— the Blues also contracted work out to their three newly formed construction companies. Advanced electronics and weaponry implementation were provided entirely by U.S. military contractors.

Again, Jason and his team reviewed the virtual schematic of the StarDome's hospital and its surrounding compartments.

"It's a simple nab and grab, Cap. Rizzo and I alone can get in and out of there within two minutes," Billy said.

Looking at the virtual diagram, Jason had to agree. Perhaps it was overkill for Traveler and him to go along. The last thing they needed was a team tripping over itself. Jason hailed Ricket: "Can you come up here?"

Thirty seconds later Ricket appeared, now standing at his side.

"How recent are these plans? I want to scan this area here—"

"I'm sorry, Captain, but the *Stellar* does not have military-grade, short-range sensors to breach StarDome. Those schematics are at least three years old. Only from inside will you be able to scan the facility."

"Seriously?"

"Most U.S. warships' sensors are unable to see inside the StarDome. Only the *Parcical*, with her more recent Caldurian technology, would be up to the task."

"Yeah, well ... bringing her here would add an even higher level of attention to what we're planning to do. Best we keep this on the downlow." Jason looked over to Billy. "No. It will be the four of us." Pointing to a color-coded section on Level 83, he added, "This looks like some kind of supply room. We'll phase-shift there first, and should we need to, we'll back right out."

They unslung their multi-guns, then lowered their visors. "Do us the honor, Ricket?"

"Yes, Captain."

In a brilliant white flash, they phase-shifted from the *Stellar*'s main passenger cabin into total blackness.

Jason quickly reviewed his HUD readings and found no other life forms in the near vicinity. With their helmet beams coming on, they took in the tight, close-quarters surroundings. It was definitely a storeroom of sorts. *So far so good.*

Billy approached the hatch, and it automatically opened. He peered out then turned back. "Cap ... um ... you're going to want to take a look at this."

Jason looked past Billy into the dimly lit passageway. Taking two strides, he slid past Billy and peered out. Yes, indeed, it was the hospital, but it was completely deserted. He walked over to a circular hub—a station for attending doctors and nurses—and ran a finger over the countertop, leaving a streak in the thin layer of dust.

"What the hell?" Jason, pointing fingers in different directions, said, "Let's split up and take a look around. Stay on the open channel." Jason then headed down, from what he remembered seeing on the schematics, the hospital's primary hallway. A doublewide hatchway appeared off to his right, and once through it, he entered into what he knew was the largest compartment within the hospital itself. Jason stepped closer to the nearest object and pulled a plastic tarp away, letting it fall to the deck. A brand new MediPod sat there, its shipping straps still intact. Peering inside, he noticed a container, filled with unused mounting hardware. Moving to the next covered object, he pulled its tarp away and let it too slide to the deck. Again, another uninstalled MediPod. One by one, he pulled the tarps away—a total of ten pods—none installed.

"There's nothing going on here, Cap," Billy said, over the open channel.

"Copy that," Jason replied. He wondered what the hell was going on in here? Had the Blues forgotten about this level, or were they interrupted in some manner before it could be brought completely online? Leaving the compartment, he shelved his questions—for now.

The foursome converged back at the central hub station.

"Anything?" Jason asked the other three.

"This hospital is not being utilized," Traveler said, expressing the obvious.

"There's close to two hundred levels in total on this space station. Maybe they're using an area somewhere else for their hospital," Rizzo suggested, shrugging.

Jason, communicating with Ricket via comms, didn't bother acknowledging Rizzo's remark. He studied his HUD, running a scan for Prince Aqeel's life signature. "There he is ... he's there ... down on Level 4."

Billy tilted his head and Jason nodded an unspoken confirmation. After years in space, boarding too many space stations to count, Jason found it typical for their lower levels to be used mainly for maintenance and other rudimentary functions. He called up the StarDome's schematics and zoomed in on the lower levels. Sure enough, the maintenance and supply sections of the station were there. He found the area where the prince was located. "This shows he's in the ship's brig," Jason said.

"I don't get it. He's like Blues royalty, isn't he? The last place you'd expect to find him would be the brig. Maybe we go spring him out of there?"

Jason continued to stare at the diagram. As much as he liked Prince Aqeel, he was still somewhat reluctant to jeopardize interstellar relations by taking covert action against the Blues. That's what diplomats were for. But Boomer was missing, and he had a strong feeling the prince was tied into that ... somehow. He selected their next phase-shift location and inputted its settings. "In for a penny ... in for a pound. Here we go ... be ready—I'm detecting quite a few life forms milling around down there."

They found themselves standing at one end of a long, curved corridor. At this lower-level section within StarDome, the space station was at its most narrow. The setup here was different— not like a typical station brig arrangement. The phase-shift had brought them into the middle of what was obviously a large-scale prison system, where scores of active energy fields glowed a bright aqua-blue. Jason had configured their combat suits for stealth mode, which would conceal them no more than two minutes. After that, they would be fully visible.

There were hundreds of prisoner cells there, each one occupied. *Who were all these prisoners?* But what got Jason to stand with his mouth agape were the ten or more guards visible from their present position. Several were uniformed Blues, but most were the far larger Sahhrain, also wearing uniforms. The Blues hated the Sahhrain—this didn't make sense.

"We're down to a minute-thirty before we go visible, Cap," Billy said.

"Copy that," Jason said, hurrying down the corridor and as quietly as possible sidestepping an approaching Sahhrain guard as he moved past him. Keeping an eye on the flashing life icon on his HUD, he kept going until he found the right cell—where the prince was being held. Behind the fluctuating energy field within the small eight-by-eight compartment was what remained of Prince Aahil Aqeel. Jason, uncertain, knew he would have to rely on the science behind his suit's sensors to be fully positive of the man's identity. The individual lying prone on the shelf-like bed was unrecognizable—nearly as blackened, with charcoal-crusted skin, as the dead body they'd earlier assumed to be Boomer's.

"Holy Christ ... the guy must be in agony," Rizzo said.

Jason saw the body move and heard a muffled groan coming from the cell.

"I will carry this dying prince," Traveler said, in his commanding, deep baritone voice.

"Thirty more seconds, Cap," Billy said.

"Thanks, Big Ben. You do know I have the same HUD mission-counter as you, right?"

Knowing he would be faster inputting the shift settings than the rhino-warrior, Jason went ahead and phase-shifted Traveler to the other side of the energy field.

All at once, Billy, Rizzo, and Jason stood visible, midway down the long corridor. It would take time for their suits to recharge sufficiently to have that limited cloaking function available. All three stayed still, hoping not to be noticed.

Traveler was working on his second attempt to slip his hands gently beneath Prince Aqeel's prone body when agonizing screams erupted again, even louder this time. Traveler, with puffs of snotty mist forming above his head, looked unsure how to proceed. Nervously, he turned back toward the other three.

"Just pick him up!" Billy and Rizzo yelled over comms in unison.

Jason's attention was quickly drawn toward the guards—four Sahhrain and two Blues—who'd just registered their presence. Hands moved to the guards' side arms and a klaxon began wailing from above. Jason was the first hit with a plasma bolt, mid-torso, and Rizzo and Billy were both struck too, a second later. Jason figured, with the advanced capabilities of their battle suits, it would take a lot more than what these six prison guards could dish out for them to be in serious trouble; unless, of course, additional guards appeared.

A glance to his right confirmed to Jason that more prison guards were now approaching them from the opposite end of the corridor. He cursed inwardly. Two were carrying substantially larger plasma rifles. Almost at once, they too began firing.

Immediately, Jason's HUD warned him of possible suit failure. Rizzo turned and raised his own multi-gun, but Jason pushed its muzzle down. "We're not starting a galactic war here, Rizzo. Damn it, Traveler ... grab ahold of him. Now!"

The prince's unending writhing and screaming, the howling klaxon above them, and the barrage of incoming plasma fire caused Jason to reach the end of his patience. He no longer cared if Traveler had a hold on the prince, or not. They needed to go ... to leave now. In a flash, he phase-shifted the lot of them back to the *Stellar*.

Chapter 10

two weeks earlier...

Screams continued to echo from those trapped in the stands high above them. The Blues had nowhere to run to, nowhere to escape. The gargantuan spacecraft hovered ominously overhead—firing off one thunderous plasma bolt after another. And with each strike, another thousand souls became enveloped in a fiery ball of hell. In a matter of seconds, any semblance of sanity in the stadium vanished—all that was left was total, complete, mayhem.

Nearby on the arena floor, Drom and Carmotta were staring at her—both screaming something. Their voices were drowned out by the horrific cries, the noisy explosions, and the ever-present, low rumbling noise from the ship's propulsion system.

Carmotta reached Boomer first—taking her by the arms and spinning her around—forcing Boomer to look into her eyes. Only then did Boomer notice Carmotta's injuries. Sections of flesh on both legs and arms were missing, from the massive bites she'd received earlier, when ravaged by Gamby fish. Like large piranha on steroids, the aquatic beasts had horribly disfigured her once beautiful body.

Carmotta slapped Boomer across the face, bringing her attention back in focus. "Listen! Listen to me, Boomer! You must get the Goldwon. They've come for it. It's everything to them. We can't let that happen. Hey ... are you listening to me?"

Boomer shook her head. "Why? I don't understand."

Now Drom was there too, standing next to Carmotta. Only then did she notice his torn flesh, like shredded ground-beef— claw marks running along one side of his back. Boomer's eyes went wide—bile burned at the back of her throat. Feeling dizzy, she wanted to throw up: Too much was happening, all at once.

Carmotta and Drom lowered themselves down to one knee and bowed their heads. Boomer stared down at them in confusion and screamed, "Get up! What are you doing? We need to go ... to get out of here!"

Then she heard their words—first from Carmotta, "*Drench*," then Drom, "*Drench*." They had both surrendered to her. *Why now? And why did that even matter?*

Drom staggered to his feet and pulled Boomer close into him, his lips by her ear: "Our injuries ... too severe. It is up to you ... only you. Get to the center tower and claim the Goldwon. Go! Are you listening to me?"

Boomer nodded, still trying to comprehend what was happening around her.

"We need to get off this planet! Get away from the Sahhrain!" He pushed Boomer toward the center of the arena, and mumbled, "Go!" then turned to help Carmotta to her feet.

Another explosion brought down the remainder of the south end of the stadium. Over the rubble, and through the black smoke, Boomer could just make out incoming Sahhrain warriors. Seeming more like ancient Roman soldiers to her, with their metallic breastplates and bright colored capes, they were an army, preparing to conquer, and they were fast approaching.

Boomer ran, then quickly staggered and fell. She looked up in time to see the charging Shintuco Cat—its huge mouth was open wide enough to envelop half her body. It leapt toward her, with bared, outstretched, claws. Boomer's thoughts flashed to the sight of Drom's back. It was all too much. *I'm going to die.*

Three bright-violet distortion waves struck the cat simultaneously. It burst into a fireball, and what little remained of its smoldering corpse dropped lifelessly two feet from her. Boomer turned to see Carmotta and Drom, both pointing their enhancement shields toward the fallen cat.

"Get up! Hurry now!" New excited yells reached her from the opposite direction. Boomer rose to her feet and saw Prince Aqeel, now running toward her from the far side of the arena. She noticed the shield on his forearm and realized he sent the third wave out to help bring down the big Shintuco Cat. She ran toward him, meeting him midway.

Out of breath, he said, "Take this! Your suit device is inside. Everything is explained within this satchel." He removed the strap from his shoulder and thrust the leather bag at her, pointing then to the center of the arena.

Boomer took the bag and held up a palm. "I already know ... get the Goldwon. But what about you?"

"Go now!" He was already running toward the gaping opening at the south section of the stadium. Running also, Carmotta and Drom were soon by his side. They were going to fight the approaching Sahhrain warriors together. *Three mortals against a hundred? For sure, theirs was a suicide-act in the making.*

Another two violent explosions erupted in the stands and their concussive blasts nearly toppled Boomer off her feet. She opened the flap of the satchel, rooting around in it until she caught the reflection of a small metallic device. She hadn't seen it for two years, since she'd last handed it over to Prince Aqeel, when she first came to Harpaign to complete her training.

With shaking fingers, and taking a deep, steadying breath, she slid the clip of the SuitPac up to the top waistband of her leggings, then depressed the two inset tabs. Within three seconds, the segmented combat suit enveloped her entire body. As if it were yesterday, she took in the readings on her helmet's heads-up display. She heard Drom's words repeat inside her head: *Get to the center tower and claim the Goldwon. Go!*

Now sprinting, Boomer threw the satchel's strap over her head and reaffixed the enhancement shield to her forearm. *Why am I running?* And again, it all came back to her. She spotted the top of the glossy black tower ahead and glints of light reflecting off the Goldwon. Mid-step—in a flash of white light—Boomer phase-shifted.

One hundred and thirty feet up, Boomer instantly reappeared—her forward running momentum nearly carrying her over the side of the tower. She had to use her enhancement shield to halt herself mid-stride, before coming to an abrupt standstill. From her high-up vantage point she could see the true measure of devastation from the attack. With the exception of the north area of the stadium, which was relatively left undisturbed, all else was in total ruins.

Boomer looked up toward the ship—one so tall even craning her neck up she could barely make out its top. She searched the outer perimeter of the stadium grounds. *Where are you?* There! She saw Drom and Carmotta—both wielding their enhancement shields and battling multiple Sahhrain warriors. A handful of Sahhrain lay dead, their bodies scattered around the field.

Boomer scanned the nearby grounds for Prince Aqeel, and soon found him battling three, much larger, combatants. Also nearby the flowing white robes of the elders—the Council of One—could be seen. Several had fallen already, while others fought valiantly on against seemingly impossible odds.

Looking down at her feet, Boomer saw the foot-and-a-half-tall Goldwon statue—unbelievably beautiful in the midst of such surrounding horror. She snatched it up with one hand and opened the flap of the satchel with the other, then tucked it safely inside. Drawing the strap tight, she repositioned the satchel over her back. With another glance out toward the ensuing battle, Boomer said to herself, "I'm coming ... this is what I do best."

Chapter 11

Boomer, on the verge of phase-shifting off the tower and directly into the battle below, had already entered the necessary phase-shift coordinates into her HUD when she felt a familiar sensation—a cross between a chill and *something else*—perhaps more akin to a magnetic pull. Whatever it was, over the years she'd learned to trust it. Not heeding it in the past had nearly cost her her life. What she knew in that present moment was that dark emotions were at work out there. Someone's attention ... *somewhere* ... was on her—was consumed with her.

She looked back over her shoulder and scanned the upper north stands—pretty much the only area of the stadium still intact. Standing alone in the stands, and wearing a long black robe, was one of the Tahli ministry members. His hood was up and dark shadows obscured much of his face. It occurred to Boomer that not even one of the Tahli ministry was seen fighting down below, engaging the Sahhrain warriors. As with the Council of One, all Tahli ministry members were highly trained in the ancient martial arts of Kahill Callan. *Why are they not fighting alongside their brethren on the battlefield?*

Boomer

Even as the robed Tahli ministry member turned away, she felt his lingering hatred—his unabashed ill-will toward her.

Suddenly, in a flash of white light, Boomer appeared next to Drom, who was managing to hold his own against four Sahhrain warriors. A concerned flash in his eyes told Boomer that he didn't immediately recognize that it was indeed her—hidden as she was in some kind of advanced combat suit.

She had made one quick detour before joining the battle. With Prince Aqeel's near frantic concern for the Goldwon effigy, Boomer had found an appropriate hiding place to stow the satchel. A hiding place that, for the most part, guaranteed its safety until she, herself, could retrieve it later.

With four rapid blasts from Boomer's integrated wrist-mounted plasma guns, Drom's four opponents fell lifelessly to the ground. "You can thank me later," she said, without looking back. Her face immediately flushed, and she cursed herself for saying something that sounded more like a sexual proposition than a casual remark.

Thirty yards forward, Carmotta was not faring nearly as well as Drom. Driven down onto one knee, she was obviously struggling, now gasping for breath—no longer able to adequately fend off her opponent. Dissimilarly to the other warriors, this Sahhrain wore no cape and his breastplate was matte black. She then noticed a small but visible family crest embossed over his heart. Boomer recognized it as the royal Shakrim family moniker. She'd heard of it—he was next in line to rule. Zintar's son, it seemed, was not much older than Boomer herself.

The young Sahhrain's advanced attack movements—his *Jarta* moves—were well practiced and he moved with a level of grace she'd observed in few others.

To fight against the skill-level of this opponent, she'd need to retract her combat suit. Boomer knew from past experience it would only hinder her movements. Without a second thought, she entered the necessary HUD command and felt her suit retract back into the SuitPac device clipped to her waistband. Never taking her eyes off the Sahhrain, she watched as he thrust his shield forward, firing off a burst of distortion waves at Carmotta, who deflected them—but barely. He swung one of his legs behind him, turning his body ninety degrees counterclockwise, and used his shield's edge, in a tilted, swiping motion, to propel his body upward, six feet into the air. Once there, he used the opposite edge on his shield to halt forward progression.

Boomer fired—just barely missing her friend while distracting the Sahhrain from making a lethal strike. He elegantly dodged and deflected, moving sideways to safety, as if he'd known ahead of time precisely what she was going to do.

"Get down, Carmotta!" Boomer yelled as she cartwheeled up and sideways.

When the Sahhrain warrior flew into the air again, Boomer was already on the move and anticipating his next position.

Boomer propelled herself forward in his direction while firing off distortion waves. She misjudged his movements and found him no longer before her. She'd made a catastrophic mistake. *His speed was remarkable.* Attempting to abruptly turn and face him, she saw him momentarily suspended in her peripheral vision. He quickly flipped his feet up and backwards —all the way over Carmotta's head—landing gently behind her now totally exposed flank.

Boomer, falling fast and trying to bring her own shield to bear—caught sight of Carmotta's astonished expression—one, in that instant, already acknowledging her defeat by a higher-skilled opponent. It was evident that Carmotta knew only one thing remained: Her opponent's killing strike.

It was something Boomer would never forget: A momentary second when the Sahhrain combatant hesitated, then smiled. A smile that said volumes—perhaps mutual respect for another Kahill Callan master whose training might be superior to his own.

In a move of desperation, Boomer dove toward Carmotta—either to knock her out of the way or to shield her friend from harm, whichever came first—but her action was in vain.

He fired. His shield's distortion waves were bright scarlet in color—a torrent of thunderous, glowing energy. Horrified, Boomer watched as Carmotta suddenly burst into a white-hot fireball. Still high in mid-air, there was nothing Boomer could do but propel herself away from the blazing heat. In a blur—the Sahhrain warrior was gone from where he'd last stood.

Boomer landed, readying for another attack, but an attack never came. He was already gone. Reluctantly, she brought her eyes back to her friend. Carmotta had died instantly, even before a scream reached the young Blues warrior's lips. Tears filled Boomer's eyes and she was finding it hard to breathe. *I'm so sorry, Carmotta!*

She sensed movement—an incoming spear. Only partially blocking its trajectory, pain erupted first in Boomer's hand and then in her lower back—a glancing blow from a pratta-shaft. It was enough to jar her from the horror of what had just occurred —the loss of her best friend. She glanced down at her bleeding hand. A finger was missing.

In the distance, the Sahhrain warrior moved with purpose toward an awaiting *dune-skipper* ... a speedy one-man craft—popular transportation these days across Harpaign's vast deserts. As he gained elevation he banked and headed for the center of the arena. *He was on a quest to find the Goldwon.* Boomer tracked him with her eyes for several seconds and vowed, one day, she'd have her revenge.

She reached back and felt the gaping, open wound; copious amounts of blood began to flow freely down her legs. Instinctively, she reached for her SuitPac device to reinitialize her battle suit. Thanks to her suit's tech, and her own internal nanites, she knew she'd recover fine.

The raging battle around her continued on. In the distance, Boomer could see Drom, still holding his own. Prince Aqeel was there, too, fighting valiantly alongside three, white-robed, elders. But there were still easily ten Sahhrain warriors to every Blues.

She kept seeing Carmotta's horrified face in those last seconds of her life. *Stop!* She pushed her emotions down— buried the sorrow—the loss that was on the verge of overwhelming her. As she reassessed the battlefield before her, she felt a detached—almost robot-like—calm come over her. She headed toward a group of approaching enemy combatants coming toward her and, one-by-one, committed to destroy them ... destroy them all.

Simultaneously firing off integrated plasma guns, she dispatched lethal bolts, sequencing them with a myriad of Kahill Callan Jarta moves. She spent as much time in the air as she did on the ground. Always moving—spinning—cartwheeling —while being nearly impossible to be targeted by the enemy.

Day had turned to night—how many hours had passed while fighting in near total darkness? Time had lost all meaning —primal action and reaction held the entirety of her focus, until the repetitive alarms and verbal warnings from her HUD ceased, and her combat suit, utilizing the last of its completely drained power reserves, retracted back into its SuitPac.

At some level, Boomer was aware she'd killed scores and scores of Sahhrain. It was getting lighter again. The lifeless bodies, some stacked two or three deep, had become a grotesque, and obscene, reflection of her inner turmoil.

Chest heaving, Boomer gasped for breath and lowered

herself to her knees, utterly exhausted and totally spent. Suddenly, she jerked her head to the left, but could see no one there. Her adrenalin—artificially still amped-up via her internal nanites—had yet to normalize. Jittery, she was still in battle mode.

Dawn eased into the harsh Harpaign landscape. The silence was startling. Slowly, she took in the carnage, turning 360-degrees around. There was no one—not a single Blues or Sahhrain warrior still on his feet. No movement—even the air was perfectly still. With that knowledge came the realization that Drom, Prince Aqeel, and even the elders, were probably dead.

Feeling light-headed and nauseous, Boomer eased herself down to the ash-colored ground. A deep sadness crept over her, such as she'd never experienced before. Emotions she'd repressed about Carmotta were back tenfold. She freely wept until the tears no longer came. *What now?*

Bringing her hand up, she contemplated the loss of her pinkie, at least a good portion of it gone during her battle with the Sahhrain in black. She wondered if a MediPod might fix that. Would she even get the chance to find out?

Glancing up, she wasn't aware the huge vessel had returned. *Had it ever left?* Through teary, blurred, vision she contemplated her fate. *Maybe I too should have died here, along with my friends.*

A column of fresh Sahhrain warriors began making their way slowly through the distant sands ...

Chapter 12

Having tried to re-initialize her battle suit without success, Boomer wearily stood up, mentally preparing herself for what was to come. She was prepared to die. She'd already sent many of the enemy to an early grave, and she knew, eventually, her time too would come. That was a warrior's life—the life she had chosen.

Her eyes moved toward the hulking, unmistakable figure at the head of the approaching column. He towered over all the other Sahhrain warriors, who marched in step behind him.

"So you're Zintar," Boomer said out loud. At one time, she'd come up against Zintar's smaller brother—the infamous Lord Vikor Shakrim. A horrific battle flashed into Boomer's mind, back to five years earlier, when she and her father fought together, side by side, within a virtual habitat nearly identical to Harpaign. Lord Vikor Shakrim not only outsmarted them then, he'd come close to defeating them both, utilizing his mastery of *Sahhrain* Kahill Callan. In the end, Lord Vikor had been killed —but at a high cost. Many Blues warriors and U.S. fleet Sharks perished that day also.

A chill ran through Boomer as she observed the dark and

foreboding Lord Zintar Shakrim. He radiated something primal —almost beastly. Methodically moving closer, she noted he was easily eight feet tall.

Although she'd never actually laid eyes on Zintar before, she had seen a statue of him on the planet Dacci, years earlier, before her training began. She didn't know much about this Sahhrain leader other than he'd become the immediate successor to his brother, Vikor. The truth was, she didn't know too much about such things, as interaction with events outside her small, protective world was strictly forbidden. Fleetingly, she allowed herself to revel now, knowing those days were behind her. Her training was complete—she'd survived the trials. *Is it really true? Am I now the Goldwon victor?* Her heart rate jumped, thinking of her father and mother, then of Mollie. For the first time in many months, she let herself remember them—along with a life she once cherished. A way of life she'd said goodbye to five years ago. Watching the ever-growing procession of warriors now approaching, all hope of seeing them again vanished. More than likely she would die today. She forced herself to stay focused on the here and now.

Boomer walked toward her steadily advancing adversaries, coming to a halt atop the highest sand dune of the battlefield. She wanted Lord Zintar Shakrim to see her—to fully comprehend all that happened today: That Master Tahhrim Dol, a Tahli warrior—perhaps known to him as Boomer—was the same girl who, at eleven years old, had sent his wretched brother straight to hell. And she was there now, standing right before him.

She felt his eyes on her. Felt him sizing her up. He held up a hand and those behind him came to a halt. What came next was unexpected: Lowering his other hand he fiddled with something on his belt. Boomer watched as segment by segment his bulk became completely enshrouded within a combat suit.

Outside of the U.S. fleet, she was fairly certain such technology was highly uncommon—certainly not available within the Dacci system, and definitely not with the Sahhrain, who were put on a tight technological leash after their defeat.

Boomer reached for her SuitPac device. She pinched the two inset tabs and, again, her own combat suit would not initialize.

"Fine ... then I will die like a true Tahli warrior. You better have brought your A-game on, big guy, because I'm not going down without taking a shitload of you with me."

Something was happening: What began as a low hum, like the sound of an approaching insect, grew louder—sounding less and less bug-like. Boomer turned to see three rapidly approaching dune-skippers. Two were single-man crafts, and one was larger—a three-man model.

Boomer froze, wide-eyed, as realization set in: It was Drom! Standing at the controls of the leading, low-flying dune-skipper, the wind in his hair and a smile on his face, he looked as happy to see her as she was to see him. Speeding along on a dune-skipper right behind him was another Tahli warrior. Off to his left were three white-robed elders, each hanging on for dear life, riding in an open dune-truck—bigger and wider—but similar to the other two dune-skipper crafts.

Boomer looked back, seeing a billowing, kicked up, dust cloud forming. The column of Sahhrain was now at full advance and she recognized someone—Carmotta's killer. *So he survived the night's battle.* Quickly pulling away from the Sahhrain behind him, and straddling his own dune-skipper, the black-clad Sahhrain Tahli warrior was accelerating fast.

"Hurry! Get on!"

Boomer turned in time to see Drom almost upon her, barely slowing. At the last moment he leaned out and extended his arm. She ran toward him, took his hand, and jumped on behind him. She noticed he was wearing his Shaddick—bloodstains from his back's wounds had seeped through the thin material. As he kicked the throttle forward, the engine whirled into a higher pitch and gained speed. With a quick look over her shoulder, Boomer noted their accompanying dune-skipper and dune-truck were right behind them. The one piloted by the Blues male she didn't know, while three Council Elders, on the larger dune-truck, she recognized—but even more important, she saw Elder Pauli, who had been her most influential mentor over the past two years. She gave Boomer a reassuring nod before looking away.

"Where is the Goldwon?" Drom asked, craning his neck to look back at her, his face full of concern. "Tell me! Where's the satchel Prince Aqeel gave you?"

"I ... I hid it. So they couldn't get to it," Boomer said, gesturing back toward the distant Sahhrain ship.

Drom turned the dune-skipper sharply left and Boomer, arms gripped around his waist, pulled herself in closer. She pointed over his shoulder. "Go that way." She'd kept an eye on the trailing Sahhrain, riding on the dune-skipper behind them. "We're being followed!"

Drom glanced back at her with an annoyed expression, implying that she was saying the ridiculously obvious.

Boomer stood up on tiptoes to get closer to his ear. "Look, only I can get to it. This dune-skipper won't be—" The wind in their faces made it hard to hear.

"What are you talking about?" Drom asked, irritably.

Once again, Boomer tried her SuitPac. Instantly relieved, she felt the suit expanding over the contours of her body. She yelled, "Just keep going straight. Don't worry, I'll find you." With that, she used her enhancement shield to propel herself upward—back-flipping over the small convoy. She scooted down behind a rise in the dunes and hugged the sand.

In less than a minute, their pursuing dune-skipper was upon her. Again, Boomer propelled herself into the air, simultaneously firing off both integrated plasma guns. The Sahhrain's dune-skipper exploded in a ball of fire and the black-clad Sahhrain rider was thrown off. It wasn't the right time to reconvene their earlier battle; she phase-shifted away.

In a bright white flash Boomer returned to her favorite underground hiding place. For months she'd been coming there alone—always by foot, since she didn't have access to her combat suit. Getting there entailed taking a treacherous, five-mile-long trek. There were few places she could find solitude on Harpaign—where she could be alone with her own thoughts. Carmotta brought her there a year ago, to the shore of the underground salted lake. There was even a beach, of sorts. Crystal stalactites hung from the cavern ceiling above—composed of some strange mineral, they glowed continuously, somewhat like the silent flickering of a thousand candles. Below, the sea reflected shades of yellow and amber. The magical surroundings never ceased to take her breath away. Once, Boomer had fantasized about bringing Drom there. She pushed the thought away ... *he doesn't think of me that way.*

The satchel was where she'd left it, nestled deep into a crook between two rocks. She lifted it out and felt the heft of the Goldwon within. With the strap secured over her shoulder, she phase-shifted to the one place she hoped to find Drom.

A moment later, she stood atop the tall, center tower, back inside the mostly destroyed stadium. The wind had come up, and even through her combat suit she felt it buffeting her back and legs. The Sahhrain warship still dominated the distant skyline and too many warriors to count moved about the arena directly below her. Undoubtedly, they were searching for the very item she possessed, hidden within her satchel. *Why?*

Turning around twice, Boomer's eyes finally locked on to three, fast-moving, dune-skipper vehicles. They were about two miles away. She knew she could have more easily used her HUD sensors to find them but she was out of practice relying on technology. Smiling inwardly, she phase-shifted.

Boomer appeared behind Drom without him noticing. She retracted her battle suit then put her arms around his waist. He didn't react to her sudden presence, other than saying, "You know, that's a bit creepy ... popping up like that, so unexpectedly."

"Sorry if I frightened you," Boomer said, bemused.

"Hey ... come on! You didn't frighten me."

She didn't reply. Instead, she concentrated on the distant horizon. She was well aware her lack of a response would only annoy him more. She liked that she could tease him in this way, but a part of her wondered if there couldn't be something more. She was like a child in his eyes, she knew, but suddenly that was not nearly enough.

Chapter 13

I t was a prearranged understanding that the center area of the *Stellar's* passenger cabin was its phase-shift zone. Hang around that part of the ship overly long and you might find yourself inadvertently, and violently, thrown aside when crewmembers phase-shifting in showed up there unexpectedly.

The small assault team arrived all at once, accompanied by Prince Aqeel's constant, agonized screams. As the prince writhed in Traveler's arms, the flustered rhino-warrior looked to Jason for direction.

"Follow me," Jason said, heading for the *Stellar's* closest DeckPort, one of the many modifications Ricket had made to the ship's standard factory-design configurations. Of Caldurian technology, DeckPorts allowed one to walk into an elevator-sized energy field and walk out another, like going through a doorway.

Mollie came running from her cabin, located on the forward

section of Deck Two. Wide-eyed, she took in the horrific sight—
the unrecognizable form in Traveler's arms.

"Where's Ricket?" Jason asked, running aft. Traveller
followed, holding Prince Aqeel, in close pursuit.

Mollie said, "He's in ..."

"I am here, Captain," Ricket said, peeking his head out,
cutting Mollie off mid-sentence. Jason held back at the hatchway, pointing into the small medical compartment, as Traveler
hurried inside. Noticing that the MediPod's clamshell lid was
already open, he laid the prince within it and stood back.

Ricket made several last-minute setting adjustments to the
pod's control panel before the clamshell began to close. They all
watched as the lid sealed, making a sucking *thump*. Immediately, a slow-spinning, bright blue 3D representation of the
prince's anatomy was viewable, hovering above the MediPod.

Jason watched Aqeel's virtual image—his red, color-coded,
rapidly beating heart—and wondered if they'd gotten him there in
time. Through the pod's window, the mostly blackened and charred
figure looked more like a piece of burnt firewood than a living being.

"We must let him be. This will be a longer process than
typical, Captain," Ricket said.

Jason nodded back. "Okay ... let's all give the prince some
privacy." He then brought two fingers up to his ear; he was
being hailed.

"Go ahead, Gunny."

"Cap ... not sure what you guys did back on StarDome, but
we're being ordered to hold our position. Blues' command
dispatched a handful of Arrow fighters."

"Yeah well ... it's more like Sahhrain command than Blues ...
I'm guessing. Where are we positioned right now?"

"As instructed, we've pulled back from the station. We're
about four hundred and fifty miles out."

"I'm on my way up."

"Are we to engage the fighters?"

"Hold on ... I'm on my way."

As Jason entered the *Stellar*'s small bridge, Hanna got up from the co-pilot seat to move to a seat behind and across from Orion at her tactical station. Jason filled her vacated seat and nodded toward Leon, seated at the helm's controls.

Orion said, "They're almost upon us, Cap ... they're locked on, weapons hot."

"We need you on comms now, Hanna."

"I'm already on it, Captain." A moment later, she reported, "We have an incoming, high-priority hail from the lead fighter. It's for the captain of this vessel."

Jason spun around to look at Hanna and hesitated, contemplating his next decision.

"Another hail's coming in," Hanna said. "It's a long-range communiqué from Liberty Station."

Jason, expecting blowback from his decision to grab the prince, knew it was either go ahead and reply to the communiqué, or kiss goodbye a chance of finding out what actually happened to Boomer. Even with that urgency in mind, instigating interstellar friction with the Blues was not a good idea. "Who is it?"

"Admiral Stark," Hanna told him, providing a sympathetic shrug.

Stark wanted Jason's job—there were no two ways about it. He wanted to become the fleet's Omni. Demands on the Star Watch fleet to attend to conflicts spanning to the farthest reaches of the galaxy led Stark, for some time now, to vocally state that a centralized command structure was needed within the Sol System. More times than Jason cared to remember, the two had butted heads. But mostly they differed on command methodologies. As far as Stark was concerned, there was no place for Captain Reynolds's often reactionary, often violent, tactics, when faced with alien disagreements. These were modern times and Jason's antiquated, even rogue, gunslinger-style mindset was a thing of the past. Disputes today should be handled through properly conducted negotiations.

Jason tried explaining to Stark that his diplomacy-first methodology was simply unrealistic—that the Craing Emperor Quorp, and the evil Ot-Mul, had nearly destroyed Earth. And that the pirate, Captain Stalls, and even more recently, Lord Vikor Shakrim, if initially left unchecked, easily would have invaded Sol System. None of those leaders had had the proclivity for, or interest in, civil negotiation. Jason said there was only one way to deal with their type of aggression—defeat them fast or die trying—but his words fell on deaf ears.

Admiral Stark had many friends within the U.S. fleet and was a growing political influence within the Alliance of planets. For five years, with the exception of smaller flare-ups, recent times had been good. Commercialization of space was going full throttle and money was being made hand over fist. As far as Stark was concerned, it was long past time for the Reynolds' father and son leadership legacy in space to end.

How soon they forget, Jason thought. He let out a breath and closed his eyes for a moment. "Put him through," Jason said flatly.

"Captain Reynolds, good to see you looking so well," Admiral Stark said. He, like Jason, was wearing his dress reds. Jason took in Stark's round face, his round rosy cheeks, atop his roundish, squatty, body. The man's demeanor was all about big smiles and hearty pats on the back—his slow Southern drawl exuding friendliness and likability. And it was all bullshit.

"Captain Reynolds."

"It's Omni Reynolds, Admiral."

The admiral wobbled his head back and forth as if he'd forgotten something trivial. "Yes, yes, of course, Omni Reynolds. Um ... we've received several urgent, and quite disturbing communiqués from the Dacci system. Actually, from the Blues high command there. That is where you currently are positioned ... am I correct?"

Stark knew perfectly well where the *Stellar* was situated. Beyond a doubt, he was personally tracking their exact coordinates within Dacci space.

"Apparently someone ... an assault team, of sorts ... has broken into a secure area of the StarDome and ..." the admiral looked away momentarily, as though reading the report verbatim, "and absconded with an important prisoner." He looked back with a perplexed expression. "It mentions specifically that one of the intruders was definitely a rhino-warrior."

Jason kept his expression impassive. "Admiral Stark, I do not report to you. Are you aware of that?"

"Yes, but ..."

"And I am sure you understand that there are high-level decisions being made that do not always involve you."

"I suppose. But as the ranking officer on Liberty Station—"

"Look, I'm here to attend the memorial service of my deceased daughter. Were you aware of that?"

"Yes."

"Do I need to return there and do your job for you, Admiral?"

"No ... of course not, sir."

"Even now, in this most upsetting time, can't you manage up a little diplomatic wrangling? Hell, I thought you were all about diplomacy. You acknowledged you're not privy to all my decision making, so I'm sure you wouldn't deliberately throw a fellow officer—your commanding officer—under the proverbial bus now, would you? Especially in light of the fact that you don't exactly know what's transpiring in the Dacci system."

"What is it you would like me to do, Omni Reynolds?"

"Do what you're best at, Admiral. Pile on the bullshit and keep the Blues placated while I conduct important U.S. fleet business. You'll be brought up to speed ... in good time."

"Yes, Omni."

Jason nodded in Hanna's direction and she cut the connection.

"Not bad, Captain," Leon said, looking impressed.

"Well, Admiral Stark's not the only one who can pile on the bullshit."

"There are five Blues *drawback* fighters now positioned around the *Stellar*, Cap," Orion said.

"They're still hailing us, too," Hanna added. "Threatening to fire on us if we don't accompany them back to StarDome."

Jason was tempted to simply phase shift three thousand miles away and be done with it. The issue was, the *Stellar* was not supposed to possess such capability. There were only a few vessels known to have that advanced Caldurian technology— most notably, the vessels that comprised Star Watch, twelve including the *Parcical*, plus the *SpaceRunner*. He'd protected knowledge of this technology from outsiders, along with other Caldurian tech, because of its far-reaching level of advancement.

The ability to move about in space in the blink of an eye, or anywhere, within several thousands of miles, was an immensely powerful tool, but also provided a powerful weapon. A weapon he would far rather control today than be pitted against later on. Numerous clandestine attempts to replicate the onboard Caldurian phase-shift synthesizers had failed. There were only two, possibly three, individuals capable of understanding the principles at work with this Caldurian technology—Ricket, Bristol, and perhaps Granger, who was, in fact, an actual Caldurian. All were loyal to Jason. But showing his hand right now, his own hypocrisy, wasn't really desirable.

"What do you want to do, Cap?" Orion asked.

"*Phase-shift* us as far away from here as possible."

Chapter 14

Rizzo and Billy played cards on the starboard side of the cabin while Traveler, sprawled out on one of the couches, lay sleeping.

Jason and Mollie, sitting off by themselves, watched Prince Aqeel enter the main cabin through the DeckPort, with Ricket by his side. He was wearing a plain white Shadick that Ricket manufactured for him via their onboard replicator. He looked confused and hesitant as he took in the ship's environment and those seated around the cabin. His eyes suddenly locked on to Jason, spurring relieved recognition.

"Is that you, Captain Reynolds?"

Jason stood and approached the prince. "Prince Aqeel, let me help you to a seat."

"I'm fine ... just a little unsteady on my legs."

Jason guided the Blues prince over to the same group of seats and helped him sit down. Again, Aqeel took in the surroundings. "I'm sorry ... I'm at a loss. Where exactly am I? Why am I here?"

Before Jason could answer, the prince took in an excited

breath—his eyes went wide as they settled on Mollie. "Young Master Tahhrim Dol!"

Mollie's reaction was a quick furrowing of her brow.

"This is Mollie," said Jason. "My other daughter. They are ... nearly identical in appearance."

"So not a Tahli warrior then?"

"No," Jason said. "She's enrolled in a university on Earth."

"She must begin her training. Already old to begin doing so."

Jason and Mollie exchanged a look. "She is not—"

"I'm not Boomer," Mollie interjected, indignantly. "I don't do everything she does ... we're actually two separate people ... in case you haven't noticed."

The prince nodded, although clearly not accepting her response.

"Prince Aqeel, are you up to a few questions? It's imperative we learn what happened on Harpaign. What happened to Boomer ... to Master Tahhrim Dol." The prince suddenly jerked upright, concern filling his eyes. "The Goldwon!"

"Please ... easy now, Prince Aqeel. Your body has undergone much trauma," Ricket interjected.

"Don't you understand? Everything, and I mean everything, depends on the whereabouts of the Goldwon effigy!"

Jason watched the prince as recollection of recent events came back to him.

"The trials ... I should never have allowed the actual Goldwon effigy to be used."

"Can you start at the beginning? Just take us through everything that happened."

The prince, still lost in thought, his eyes unfocussed and moving about, seemed to be searching his memories. Eventually, he nodded, then said, "It was the Goldwon Trials—a competition, a race to the finish, as well as a graduation ceremony, for those Tahli warriors who had completed years of training. The victor is *the* Goldwon."

"What exactly does that mean?" Jason asked.

"To have completed the years of training ... for one to be inducted into the Goldwon Trials, is quite rare. So rare, that there are only a few participants still alive within the Dacci system. Less than one hundred, and many of those graduated Goldwon Warriors are elderly now. Actual winners? ... *the* Goldwons ... a mere handful.

"They are considered Lords and are given ultimate admiration and respect."

"Talk to me about the competition ... the trials as you call them."

"As a Tahli warrior, Boomer had to defeat nine other Tahli warriors, also young—the very best competitors within the Dacci system, while traversing through extremely hazardous obstacle zones. Only then could she claim the Goldwon effigy ... the ancient sacred statue, situated high up on an obsidian tower."

"Boomer competed to be a Lord?" Mollie asked skeptically.

Aqeel stared back at Mollie. "Competed and prevailed."

"She won? Like ... the whole shebang?" she said.

"Boomer is the Goldwon."

"So what happened, what went wrong?" Jason asked, urging to stay on track.

"The trials were concluding. Out of ten competitors, only three Tahli warriors remained active."

"What happened to the other seven?" Mollie asked.

Aqeel shrugged. "Severe enough injuries to take them out of competition, and Drench, of course: those that surrendered," he said.

"What happened?" Jason prompted.

"It was then that the Sahhrain warship—a Vastma-class ship ... a massive vessel—approached Capital City. It hovered by the arena." Moisture filled the prince's eyes. "It began firing its powerful weapons. The destruction, the loss of life, was terrible."

"What were they after? Why attack a stadium ... an innocent crowd? Why not a military installation ... or hell, why not StarDome?"

Aqeel leaned back, looking defeated. He also seemed ashamed. "For five years, the constant presence of the Allied command ... the U.S. fleet ... within the Dacci system, imposing its strict new laws and regulations, has been tremendously burdensome. Although the Alliance's impetus was to limit the Sahhrain's ability to wage war again, side effects affected the Blues too, perhaps as much as they did the Sahhrain. It wasn't long before resentment grew. Resentment turned to hatred. Soon, the Blues realized there were far more similarities between their culture and the Sahhrain's, than with that of the oppressive Alliance. Memories are short, Captain Reynolds." He looked at Jason and shook his head. "I suspected the Sahhrain were inveigling themselves into Blues politics, and even into the military. And why wouldn't they? With the Blues' newfound wealth—new construction contracts awarded on a daily basis—the Sahhrain became the Blues' new best friends."

"And you stood by and said nothing?"

"The Council of One—the elders—were the only ones to vehemently oppose the Sahhrain's presence. Personally, I stayed clear of politics, but I regret that now."

"So how does that tie in with the Goldwon, with them wanting that statue-thing?" Mollie asked the prince.

He looked at her, then over to Jason. "You are familiar with Glist?"

"Sure, it's what enhancement shields are comprised of."

"Among other things, yes. It has incredible ... magical, if you will, properties. It is what the Goldwon is comprised of."

Jason nodded, prompting the prince to move things along.

"Over the last few years, much attention ... a resurgence ... has been placed on antiquities—on both the Blues' and Sahhrain's heritage. On Harpaign, excavation of ancient ruins turned up the lost Dacci scriptures—an amazing, and profound, find. From those writings we discovered there were actually four effigies: The Palwon, the Nordwon, the Lortwon, and the Goldwon.

"When fitted together, the wons produce distortion waves of magnificent power: Powerful enough to breach the very fabric of reality. A virtual bridge to other dimensions."

Jason was suddenly feeling uncomfortable. He didn't like the direction their conversation was going.

Aqeel continued, "By your expression, you know what I'm going to say next."

"Rom Dasticon."

"There was a time, thousands of years ago, when he strad-dled this realm, as well as others, Captain Reynolds. It is now the dream of the Sahhrain, and of many Blues today, to again bring forth Dasticon's dark power. A power believed to be a birthright among Dacci brethren ... a power that will elevate their place within the universe. With darkness, *Rom Dasticon* will take ahold of this realm. This is no fable deity or religious imagining, as so many—even among the Sahhrain and the Blues—believe. *Rom Dasticon* is real—the true Sachem—and the surviving brother of Lord Vikor Shakrim, Lord Zintar Shakrim, will stop at nothing to find, and bring together, the four wons."

"Why not simply destroy the one you already had, the Goldwon, and be done with it?" Mollie asked.

Prince Aqeel replied, "The Glist castings ... the *won* effigies ... are impervious. They cannot be destroyed."

Jason looked toward Ricket and raised his brow, questioning.

"It is possible, Captain. I would need to examine an actual statue to be certain. There are ancient fables, or tales, concerning Glist, once mined on the planet, Dacci. It speaks of an alchemy process ... the transference of one type of mineral, Glist, into another."

Aqeel continued, "The statues are indestructible, take my word for that, Captain. With that in mind, they were separated from each other—here within the Dacci system—then each hidden and placed where no individual can get near them."

"How was that accomplished?" Jason asked.

"It is what the Goldwon trials were originally based on: insurmountable obstacles. Obstacles that make even the current zones of the Goldwon trials look childish ... simple."

"How would anyone know where to look for them? The other wons?"

"Three weeks ago, within the grounds of Capital City, another tablet was uncovered. It was a map ... of sorts. It showed the location of the hidden wons—all were hidden here, within the Dacci system. The tablet was held, or secreted, by the Council of One."

"Let me guess, it was stolen."

Aqeel nodded. "We suspect by the Tahli ministry. They have far-reaching ties to Rom Dasticon that are not acknowledged openly. Using their Tahli powers, only they have the capability to breach our formidable security system."

"Sounds like you need to find the other wons, fast ... before Lord Zintar Shakrim does," Mollie said.

The prince gave Mollie a long, intense stare. "That is what I intended Boomer, our young *Goldwon* Tahhrim Dol, to do.

Unfortunately, she met her demise at the hands of the Sahhrain ... on the battlefields of Capital City."

Jason and Ricket looked at one another.

Mollie said, "You're wrong. She's alive. That I'm sure of. If you ask me ... she's looking for them right now ... those other statues."

Chapter 15

Tossing and turning, Lord Zintar Shakrim was having another sleepless night. He belched and passed gas in unison, evoking an appreciative smile. Within moments, a sleepy, irritated groan spewed forth from one of his wives—he wasn't sure which one.

He patted his ample belly and debated if he should just get up. His mind wandered. After years of planning and preparation, he could see events—once no more than distant hopes or dreams—now coming to fruition. His anticipation of what lay ahead had grown these last few weeks. So much had transpired. It wasn't all about revenge; he hoped he was better than that. It was about righting a wrong—about setting in motion a new chain of events that would alter the destiny of a strong, proud, people ... his people: the Sahhrain. And to think that all had nearly been lost, only five years earlier. Vikor had been an idiot. An idiot, but still his brother, and after his humiliating defeat there needed to be an accounting.

Zintar's mind flashed to the battlefield of Harpaign's Capital City. Of the figure standing upon the dune crest. From small girl to young Kahill Callan warrior, she had blossomed.

Even at a distance he saw ... felt her haughtiness. She was the fly in the ointment. Had her presence here been foreseen—chiseled into uncovered ancient tablets? Tablets that had been immediately destroyed—turned to dust.

Zintar stared up at the ceiling, listening to the almost imperceptible hum of the ship's six powerful Nauticus drives. Drives that allowed his Vastma-class command ship to travel at unheard of speeds. Maybe his ship didn't possess the capability to phase-shift, or call up an interchange wormhole—crossing vast distances of space in the blink of an eye—something Star Watch vessels were easily capable of doing, thanks to their Caldurian technology. Just the same, this latest technology, *Nauticus*, was far and above anything the Sahhrain had been capable of producing on their own. He supposed he'd have to acknowledge that the Blues were instrumental in that regard. They were a means to an end. Their emerging technical prowess was more than a little impressive. But did they really think all would be forgotten? That siding with the Alliance over their fellow Dacci brethren would ever be forgiven? Very soon, that inequity would be remedied—the Alliance would fall, and the Blues right along with them.

Zintar's mind turned to the Sol System—thirty-eight light-years away—and he pictured it in his mind. Even with the Alliance's combined assets, including the U.S. fleet, they were destined to fall. Again, Zintar savored the thought of possessing that small fleet of advanced ships: possessing Star Watch. Anyone in command of those twelve vessels would surely rule the galaxy. Soon now, he'd have the means to snatch them.

And now he had the means to an end. A wonderful fluke of good fortune—after excavation of another monotonous, ancient Harpaign buried ruin, more rock tablets were uncovered. But this time, nothing less than a miracle had come about. Zintar had heard the fables since early childhood—stories passed down from past generations—of the four *wons* that would open a gateway to Rom Dasticon. Dasticon would simply be a means to an end ... useful to a higher purpose—his and the Sahhrain's.

This next phase—the final phase—would be the most crucial. It required possession of all four *won* effigies, which would open the gateway into that distant realm—Dasticon's realm. Zintar possessed one already. He suspected the young human girl possessed another—the Goldwon, most likely. Zintar's fists clenched. The very same child female who'd defeated his brother, Vikor, in battle, humiliating a whole race of people in the process. He pushed the thought of her from his mind. He would deal with her himself—make an example of her. Killing her was an option but making her a slave—perhaps a barracks whore—would be far more fitting.

He shifted his thirteen-hundred-pound bulk onto his side and heard the bedding beneath him strain under its colossal weight. Two of his three wives were asleep, lying in the huge bed beside him.

One wife, Glorra, sleeping on her back, her mouth slightly agape, was gently snoring. Tormaline, on the other side of Glorra, lay on her side, facing away from Zintar. Beneath the dim cabin lights, Zintar's eyes took in and followed her gentle naked curves, where her waist broadened at the hips, then let his gaze travel on further, down her long muscular legs. *What amazingly strong legs this wife has!* His eyes returned to her buttocks—small and round—and noticed the still visible impression of a handprint—his handprint—on one cheek. He'd given her a good whack there, during their recent lovemaking. The memory of it brought a brief smile to his lips.

He abruptly sat up, then stood. Stretching, he made his way to the quarters' head. As he relieved himself, he contemplated bathing. It had been several days, a point Tormaline brought up just hours earlier. Perhaps tomorrow ... He dressed in yesterday's black uniform of leggings, heavy boots, and a near floor-length uniform jacket. He avoided looking at his reflection in the large mirror. He knew he was unattractive. His lips were full, on a wide-set mouth. His furry brow protruded out ridiculously—like those of his ancient Sahhrain ancestors, a million years back. He was a fucking beast—thick and hairy, even a glance at his own reflection was enough to depress him for the rest of the day. He quickly left his ornate and spacious quarters and his two sleeping wives.

Lord Zintar entered the Vastma-class warship's bridge. The fleet command ship, she was a hive of constant, bustling activity. In this compartment alone there were sixty-three bridge officers, always busy at work. The vessel was immense—as large as a city —spanning miles in circumference. On board, the crew consisted of close to a thousand Sahhrain, and just as many warriors were hoarded in the ship's barracks.

Heads turned in Zintar's direction as he approached the throne-like command chair toward the front of the bridge. From a chorus of deep male voices came the usual welcoming chant, "Lead us, Zintar!"

He smiled and they smiled back. Unlike his late brother, Vikor, Lord Zintar Shakrim was not only respected among his crew—he was also liked—even loved. He was fair and often used humor to relieve onboard tension. Even with that said, he dealt with disobediences swiftly—usually by his own hand. But that was a rare occurrence among a crew more than willing to please. They knew what was expected of them—what their commander most desired. All anyone had to do was look high up, where the bridge compartment's forward bulkhead narrowed and curved. A virtual series of five three-dimensional warriors hovered in various poses of battle. At the center was Captain Jason Reynolds, his daughter Boomer at his side. She was wielding an enhancement shield, he a plasma rifle. There was also a horned beast, known as a rhino-warrior, holding a large hammer in one fist. There were two others—another human, Billy Hernandez, and a small, odd-looking creature, known as Ricket, who had an intellect like no other. Those five were the architects of the Sahhrain's defeat, five years past. Each one, in their own way, still yielded a powerful influence over thousands, if not millions, of people and the U.S. fleet. One by one, he contemplated them actually hovering up there. Soon, those virtual images would be erased—just as their lives would be.

Lord Zintar settled his girth into the command chair and was soon joined by his second-in-command. Zintar said, "Don't keep me in suspense, Brakken. Tell me what's been happening in my absence?"

Brakken, at seven feet tall, was handsome, and had refined Sahhrain sensibilities. Slender, though chiseled, muscles hid beneath his uniform, and he was a cunning warrior that few would ever contemplate going up against. The only one known to have beaten him, while sparring within a combat rink, was Lord Zintar. That was not a surprise, for none had defeated Zintar in battle before—or since.

"It has been a mere three hours, my Lord. Why not return to your colossal bed and your three needy wives?"

"Two. One has run off ... somewhere." Zintar looked over at Brakken with a sideways glance. "If I find out that Danamie is now warming your bed sheets—waiting for your shift to end— I'll be most upset."

"No, my Lord, I'd be far more inclined to entice Tormaline into my bed."

Zintar laughed at his second's candor. "Talk to me about our mole."

Commander Brakken shrugged. "It is just as you expected. He has, albeit reluctantly, agreed to our latest terms."

Lord Zintar stared blankly at his friend. Humans never ceased to amaze him. While some were among the most courageous of beings—others were solely motivated by power and greed, and that disgusted him. Eventually it came down to weeding out and tempting the right highly placed officer—one having little, if any, scruples. But finding someone as high up in the chain as a general—well, that seemed almost too perfect. The fleet officer offered to do small favors at first, in exchange for monetary compensation. Over time, though, he approved hundreds of construction jobs for Blues contractors. A strong advocate for the Blues, he became secretly wealthy in the process. It was only a matter of time before the Blues became the primary builder of most U.S. fleet space stations; then later, of all new warships. The high-up fleet officer had even gone so far as to encourage the Blues as they opened their arms wide to the Sahhrain sharing their vast technological advances and had even worked in tandem with them—building a secret fleet of Blues/Sahhrain warships, on a par with those of the U.S. fleet. Zintar marveled at the general's treachery toward his own people and reminded himself to never trust the arrogant Calhoom.

"There is a problem, my Lord," Brakken volunteered.

Zintar already knew what he was going to say: "Let me guess ... the mole is becoming worried about working with us ... the Sahhrain?"

"He is terrified that the knowledge of his subversive actions over the years will become known to the high fleet command—namely the Omni—his brother."

Lord Zintar and Brakken exchanged another smile and looked up at the hovering image of Captain Reynolds. "What I would give to be there, when the Omni of the U.S. fleet is told of his brother's ongoing transgressions: that Brian, now the rank of general, is a traitor to his own kind. Ahh, to be a bug on that wall," Brakken said.

Zintar sat back in his chair, keeping his gaze on the lifelike images. For all the malice he felt toward Captain Reynolds, it paled in comparison to the venomous hatred he felt toward the young girl warrior. But she too, unknowingly, was now being played.

"Go ahead and strut, little Goldwon master—in the end all the *wons* will be mine. Then you will have to face me, and pay for your actions."

"Lord Shakrim ... there's an Alliance vessel quickly approaching. A personal craft," the Sahhrain officer said, looking up from his board with a startled expression. "The Blues' database has it registered to the U.S. fleet's Omni."

Chapter 16

"No! It's not, Gunny, look again. Have you ever seen that kind of symmetry ... or organization ... in open space?" Leon asked, glancing up as Jason entered the bridge.

"What's all the hubbub?" Jason asked.

"I hate to admit it, but I think Leon may have a point," Orion said. She stood aside as Jason leaned in to take a look at the small, hovering, tactical display.

Jason asked, "Can't you expand this a bit more?"

"On the *Parcical* I could, Cap," she shot back, sounding a bit frustrated.

Jason stood and turned toward the forward observation window. "I agree ... if it were a belt, individual meteors would be positioned randomly. And it's not moving ... there's no drift. No, we're not looking at some deep space natural occurrence." Saying that, Jason was well aware of the implications—quite possibly there were thousands upon thousands of foreign objects adrift in the far reaches of the Dacci system. Perhaps some were spacecraft, but that didn't really make sense.

"There are high levels of radiation in that part of the system.

It's an area of space seldom traversed ... no commercial traffic to speak of," Orion said.

"What do the charts say?" Jason asked.

Orion scanned her board readings. "There is a meteor belt, but the readings indicate it's two light-years away from these coordinates."

Hanna, sitting quietly at the comms station, continued to adjust her settings. "Well, hello there!" All eyes turned in her direction.

"What have you got?"

"I didn't pick up on it at first. It's not on any of the standard communications channels. In fact, it's only showing up on an obscure channel—one dedicated to drone telemetry."

"What are you hearing?" Jason asked.

"Dacci ... they're speaking Dacci. Because they've over-loaded the channel, it's scratchy as hell—everything's distorted." Hanna looked up, then said, "Captain, there are hundreds ... thousands ... of open, live ship-to-ship channels."

Jason took a seat at the helm. "Take a seat, everyone."

Orion sat down at her station as Leon moved over to the co-pilot's seat.

"Cap, we'd need five separate phase-shifts to get in close enough to see what's really there," Orion said. "Unless you want to call up a wormhole."

"An interchange wormhole would be far too noticeable, so five phase-shifts will be fine. Go ahead and input the coordinates, Gunny."

"Done, Cap," she reported a moment later.

Jason saw their proposed jump pattern highlighted on the small forward display. He tapped at a touch-sensitive virtual key. In less than a second, five distinct white flashes later, they'd traveled hundreds of thousands of miles.

The extended silence in the cabin was broken when Billy

suddenly entered the bridge. "Sweet Jesus, tell me I'm not seeing what I'm seeing." No one answered.

Jason didn't expect them to be positioned this close to the enemy. As he visually scanned space before him, he did a quick mental tally and stopped counting at ten thousand warships.

"Somebody's been busy," Billy said, now standing at Jason's side.

"Cap, we're looking at three separate fleets here. Most vessels are on a par with our own Craing light and heavy cruisers: Advanced shielding, high-yield plasma cannons, FTL capability. It's an incredible assemblage of assets," Orion said.

"Would have been nice if you'd picked up on them before," Billy said, without looking back at Orion.

"Yeah ... and it'd be nice if you'd get sucked out of an airlock," she snapped back.

Jason gave them both a stern expression. "Gunny, zoom in on their closest ship." She did as told. Jason leaned forward, then asked, "What's that?" Orion zoomed in again.

Billy said, "Well, I guess that removes any doubt."

Jason nodded. They were looking at the starboard hull of the closest warship. An emblem or crest depicted the Sahhrain flag on its background and a symbol of an enhancement shield in the foreground. The *Stellar*'s AI translated the Dacci lettering above the emblem, *Honor and Sacrifice*, and below it, spelled out, was *Rom Dasticon*.

"What are they waiting for?" Orion asked. "This is a serious threat ... a threat the U.S. fleet would have a hard time holding off, let alone defeating."

Jason's irritation was growing. Irritation that this buildup had gone without notice by the Alliance—and more so, by himself.

"I think I can answer that," Hanna said. "Much of the jabbering I'm picking up concerns someone named Zintar."

"That's probably Lord Zintar Shakrim."

Hanna shrugged. "Could be. Anyway, he's apparently on a quest of sorts, looking for something—something that would allow this Zintar fellow to open up some kind of gateway. I'm not sure if that's the right word for it."

"Close enough," Jason said. "That pretty much confirms what Prince Aqeel told me earlier. He's looking for four effigies ... small statues. They're hidden all around the Dacci system. Whoever brings them together ... *apparently* ... can open a bridge to the realm where Rom Dasticon resides."

"Him again? I thought we sent that shit-bag packing five years ago," Billy said.

Jason didn't answer, continuing to study the enemy's mass of military might, stretching out as far as the eye could see.

Billy said, "I lost a hell of a lot of men the last time we went up against those guys, Cap. Truth is ... I'd rather nail my balls to my knee than have to go through all that again."

For some reason, his comment made Orion giggle. Billy glanced back, seeing her trying not to laugh, but failing miserably. He too laughed out loud.

Jason shook his head. "You two sure picked a hell of a time to start playing nice again. Let's back away from here, before someone sees us."

"Too late," Leon said, pointing out the forward observation window.

"Shit!"

"Thirty Arrow fighters ... Sahhrain versions of what we saw before, but bigger and meaner. We're way outclassed here, Cap," Orion reported.

"Phase-shift us out of—"

"Can't, Captain," Leon said, "we're still regenerating the synthesizer power after our last five phase-shifts."

"Someone get Ricket in here," Jason ordered.

"We're taking fire—but shields are holding," Orion said.

"Time to deploy Big Baby, Gunny."

Billy almost lost his balance as Jason kicked-in the *Stellar*'s two antimatter drives, whipping their small ship up and over, then banking tightly left, as a flurry of yellow plasma bolts streaked past both side windows.

"Yes, Captain, how may I be of assistance?" Ricket asked, suddenly standing at Jason's side.

"What do you need to finish getting Big Baby operational?"

Ricket turned back, sending a glance toward Orion. "We need to junction the gun to the auxiliary power plant—the feeder to the anti—"

Jason cut him off mid-sentence. "Just tell me, how long will it take you?"

"I could do a temporary coupling. Maybe five minutes?"

"Make it two! Where do you need to work?" Jason asked.

"Aft ... between the drives, in the Engineering hold space."

"Go! Get it done!"

Jason continued to maneuver the *Stellar* through radical lefts and rights. "Hold on!" He jerked the nose of the ship down and into a forward dive.

"G-force compensators red-lining, Cap," Leon said, as the *Stellar* violently shook.

"Three direct strikes. Shields down to forty percent."

Leon said, "The good news ... we're a hell of a lot quicker than those little Arrows."

Jason opened up a NanoCom channel to Ricket: "Talk to me!"

"Well, Captain, it won't be quite as simple a ... fix ... as ... I first thought," Ricket said, his voice strained, like he was using physical exertion, doing whatever he was doing.

Two more violent shakes and the bridge momentarily went dark, then became illuminated again.

"Um ... uh oh," Orion said under her breath.

"I don't like the sound of that, Gunny."

"I've heard of these vessels ..." Orion continued. "Vastma-class warship. Makes our Craing Meganaughts look like little play toys."

Jason noticed the Goliath-sized vessel was slowly pulling away from the cluster of parked warships. Something moved past them in a blur. It was pure instinct that prompted Jason to jam the controls in toward his own body, bringing the *Stellar* into a tight, ass-over-teakettle, barrel roll. Before them, a solid wall—a Vastma-class warship—blocked their way. Billy staggered, losing his balance, falling backward onto the deck.

Completing the barrel roll and leveling out, Jason spotted a different kind of wall approaching—one made of Arrow fighters. "Shit shit shit!" A series of green plasma bolts streamed by their starboard windows—each one the size of a full-sized school bus.

"Those plasma bolts were fired from the Vastma ship. We won't survive even a single hit from that ship, Cap."

Jason heard Ricket's voice in his ear.

"I believe Big Baby is operational, Captain," Ricket said.

"Copy that. Gunny?"

"I heard. I'm on it."

Another virtual display suddenly appeared above the forward console. It was a duplicate display of what Orion was viewing on the tactical station. Jason watched as the *Stellar's* upgraded AI targeted no less than ten Arrow fighters.

"Fire at will, Gunny!"

Big Baby—deploying aft—was mounted to an underbelly turret and was unlike any other weapon in existence, at least according to Ricket, who'd invented the weapon over the past several years. It was untested in battle—still in prototype-phase —and was supposedly propelled by a spinning matrix of plasma and gallium-energy waves. Ricket said it was a good fit for the Omni's personal craft.

"Shields down to five percent," Leon said.

The *Stellar* began to vibrate, as Big Baby spewed off a torrent of bright red energy spheres toward each locked on target—*thump thump thump thump thump*—and the Arrow fighters disintegrated on contact. Their shields seemed to provide little resistance against the *Stellar*'s powerful barrage. Within twenty seconds, the wall of Arrow fighters had been destroyed.

A massive external punch, coinciding with a thunderous *crack*, and the *Stellar* went twirling uncontrollably through space. Those on the bridge were violently wrenched out of their seats and thrown to the deck.

The AI's voice filled the small space: "Warning, hull breach ... Warning, hull breach ... Warning, hull breach ..."

Jason half crawled, half slid, toward the forward console. His stomach protested; he needed to get the *Stellar*'s spinning under control fast.

Leon, regaining his seat first, held out an arm to help Jason back onto his own seat. "Everything's offline—G-force compensators ... propulsion ... even weapons systems," Leon yelled above the blaring klaxon and the AI's continuous alerts.

At least they had auxiliary power, Jason thought. He addressed the AI directly: "*Stellar*, deactivate audible warning alerts."

The bridge suddenly went quiet.

"*Stellar* ... status of all major systems. We need to get the propulsion system back online. And reengage compensators!" He turned back to see that Hanna and Orion were basically holding on for dear life. Billy was lying on the deck, unconscious. Right then, Jason noticed the bridge hatch was secured and closed. His mind flashed to Mollie ... *where did the hull breach occur?*

"*Stellar* ... where, specifically, is the location of that hull breach?"

"Hull breach is on Deck Two, forward portside cabin. That section of the ship has been sealed off, Captain."

That was Mollie's cabin. "Status of onboard personnel!"

"All crew and passengers accounted for, Captain. Billy Hernandez is unconscious but his injuries are not life threatening. Traveler has lacerations to his face, which are not life threatening. Rizzo has a dislocated shoulder, which is not life threatening."

Jason let out a breath through puffed cheeks. "Propulsion and compensator systems cannot initialize while vessel is operating in auxiliary power mode," the AI continued.

Glancing out the forward observation window, Jason saw a blur of white streaks. He closed his eyes and held back an almost uncontrollable urge to throw up. He heard Ricket's voice in his head.

"Captain, we took a direct strike from that Vastma-class warship."

"I gathered that. What's fixable?"

"I am within the Engineering hold space. Whatever repairs I make will be temporary. I am attempting to initialize the starboard drive now. Ship power levels should be coming back online. But it could take me several hours before we have the compensators operational."

"And no nav-control?"

"No, I am sorry, Captain."

Jason noticed that the phase-shift synthesizer status indicator had just gone green. "Ricket, do we have phase-shifting capability?"

There was a long pause. Hanna announced she was going to vomit any moment just as Billy began to stir on the deck.

"The phase-shift synthesizer is back online, Captain," Ricket affirmed.

"I'm on it, Cap," Orion said. "Looks like the closest planet to our current coordinates—one with breathable air—is Dule. But this is a hostile ..."

Leon spoke over her, "It'll be another five phase-shifts. Once we're there, know we're going to be stuck there for a while."

Jason had made up his mind. "We need to be gone from here before that Vastma warship shows up again."

Suddenly, Hanna threw up, and Billy, in the process of sitting up, threw up, too. Leon covered his own mouth and closed his eyes.

Jason, seeing that Orion had provided the phase-shift telemetry now showing up on his display, tapped the flashing key. The *Stellar* flashed away.

Chapter 17

"Hold on!" Drom said, as he brought the dune-skipper higher up and banked around a tall rock spire. They'd crossed out of the dunes and onto the barren rocks ten minutes earlier and had followed along a ridge-line for several miles. On one side, the ragged red cliffs fell away to a thousand-foot-deep chasm. Boomer avoided looking down. One mistake—one miscalculation on Drom's part—and they would be shredded on the rocks below. Either that, or they'd fall all the way to the chasm's bottom and certain death.

The small dune-skipper dropped suddenly, and they began speeding along a narrow winding passage within the chasm walls. Boomer guessed she could touch the parallel walls by simply reaching out with both hands. Their speed hadn't changed, yet up ahead the chasm appeared to be coming to an abrupt end. There was a solid rock wall thirty yards before them. She hugged Drom's waist and prayed he knew what the hell he was doing. At ten yards out, and ready to scream, the dune-skipper suddenly dropped another twenty feet. In a blur, they plunged into total darkness. Boomer buried her face into Drom's back.

"Aaaa!" Drom yelled. "Easy on my back!"

Boomer had forgotten all about his injuries, courtesy of the Shintuco Cat. "Sorry!"

The temperature had easily dropped twenty degrees, and the blackness was turning to varying shades of gray. Rock outcroppings flashed by as they periodically turned one way then another. It became evident to her—Drom had traversed this passageway many times before.

Boomer felt them slow, now dropping in altitude at a far quicker rate. She peered around his shoulder and caught the distant glow of firelight. She looked behind her and saw no sign of the pursuing Sahhrain.

Drom looked back at her and smiled. "I think you're going to like this."

She nodded, doubting that anything could compare to this—having her arms wrapped around his muscular torso. But she was wrong.

Like others, she'd heard the term *oasis* spoken of countless times. But until that instant, she'd never actually seen one. Not like this. They were at the bottom of the chasm, one thousand feet, or more, down. What she'd earlier thought to be firelight was actually sunlight, filtering down through lush, tall trees. The chasm gradually widened, becoming hundreds of feet wide. High green grasses swayed in the shifting breeze. A winding creek, with crystal-clear waters, meandered down the middle of the expanse, where a female, dressed in a Shadick, squatted, filling a container. She looked up and waved. Three sheep-like animals quickly skittered out of the way as the dune-skipper approached. As beams of bright sunlight fell across Boomer's face, she raised her chin and closed her eyes to absorb its warming rays—letting the peacefulness in the *oasis* engulf her.

The dune-skipper throttled down and they came to a stop. Her eyes opening up, Boomer realized Drom was watching her.

"What do you think?" he asked.

Startled, she took in a breath and held it. Before her was a city built into the cliffs—a city of glowing blue—as blue as the enhancement shield on her forearm. "Glist!"

Boomer was led upward, to an area of the cliff-side city called Conclave Hall ... or simply Conclave. To Boomer, it felt like a holy place, a sanctuary, where speaking in low tones would be expected. Earlier, Drom reminded her that when entering here one left both anger and ego behind. They had climbed a series of stairways, traversing across several narrow bridges, to get there. The Conclave was about halfway up, nestled within the cliff city. There were no windows—only open balconies. She was told temperatures were kept at a constant 72 degrees, even with the occasional warm breeze drifting in from the distant desert dunes.

"They have been alerted to our arrival. It won't be long now," Drom said.

Boomer stood before a Glist balustrade next to him. They were standing upon the largest balcony in the city, where before them lay a panoramic view of the *oasis* chasm. Treetops swayed rhythmically—back and forth—and Boomer could hear the tinkling sounds of a waterfall somewhere below them. If there were such a thing as paradise, this, most certainly, could be it.

"What is this place called?"

"It has had many names throughout the ages. Those living here now call it Loma City," Drom said. "You know, I was born here ... this is my home."

Boomer stared up at him. "Nice place to grow up. You must have had a charmed childhood."

"Phsssst," he snickered at her comment. "You would think so, but no ... I did not."

She waited for him to elaborate, but he didn't speak further.

A young Blues female, who looked to be about twelve or thirteen, approached them, carrying a folded tan Shadick. She stopped and held it out with both arms as she bowed her head.

Boomer glanced over to Drom, who nodded. She took the garment, saying, "Thank you."

The female smiled and bowed again without speaking. Then she left the way she'd come.

Suddenly self-conscious of what she was wearing—the same skintight leggings and just as revealing top—her midriff wide open at the waist, Boomer said, "I'm sorry ... what I'm wearing must seem pretty inappropriate for this place, huh?"

Drom shrugged. "I wouldn't worry too much about it."

Boomer slipped the Shadick over her head and ran her fingers through her hair, which she knew looked a mess. "Better?"

Giving her a nonchalant shrug, he said, "Sure ... I guess." He looked over his shoulder. "Ah ... they're arriving. We must take our seats."

They stepped back inside the Conclave, which to Boomer looked like a temple, or perhaps a cathedral, not really sure about such things. It was circular in shape and light streamed in from the balcony, as well as from multiple high-up, outer-facing apertures. No less than twenty massive, fluted pillars followed the contours of the cathedral walls—each reaching hundreds of feet up—supporting a vaulted ceiling high above them. Virtually everything was made of Glist. A bluish glow emanated all around, only adding to the hall's heaven-like ambiance.

Drom led Boomer to the archway that separated the balcony from the Conclave.

"Can we go in?"

"Best we stay here where we can talk quietly," Drom said. They were about fifty feet back from a raised area that looked like a stage, or dais. She surmised that was where the elders would be seated.

Boomer nodded and watched as the Conclave began to fill up behind them. Blues, Loma city residents, were wearing Shadicks of muted tans and pale greens. By the size of the still-growing crowd, as one after another plopped down onto cushions, she suspected the whole city—thousands—would be attending.

The first of the elders to arrive was Elder Pauli. She wore a pristine white robe, which fell and gathered below her bare feet. She moved to the center of the dais and stood quietly as more elders filed in behind her, to sit on a row of cushions that spanned the width of the dais. There were eight elders in all. Seven cushions remained untaken.

Elder Pauli held out both palms in a gesture of welcoming and smiled at the congregation. Respectful silence replaced the crowd's low murmuring, and again the distant soothing sounds of rustling branches, and the tinkling waterfall, could be heard.

She spoke and her words echoed around the large chamber: "It is good to be among you; we shine together, as we shine alone —we shine into eternity—offering up our spirit into the Light."

The congregation repeated the words after her. Boomer had heard the same phrase a thousand times before—had said the same words herself too many times to count. Her training to become a Tahli warrior—and then a Tahli Master—had been as much a spiritual journey as it was a physical one. The beliefs of the Blues were indeed unique, but at the same time Boomer had found them to be surprisingly similar to other religions, or spiritual paths, such as some back on Earth. The truth was, she didn't feel she was a particularly spiritual or religious-leaning person. As far as she was concerned, her beliefs were her own affair, and until she figured things out—was given some kind of proof of an afterlife or experienced some deity's lofty presence —she'd keep her mouth shut and go with the flow.

"As you can see, the Council of One has been decimated," Elder Pauli said. She glanced for a moment at the open cushions near her. "My heart is heavy in my chest. With those seven elders gone ... I'm at a loss for how to continue. But continue on we must. Those we do not see today are the thousands upon thousands killed within that ancient arena of Capital City. Those Tahli warriors who gave their lives in defense of Harpaign." She paused and glanced toward another section of the dais that Boomer hadn't noticed before—where ten cushions, all black, sat unoccupied.

"As you can see, none of the Tahli ministry have joined us here today. Just as absent as they were on the battlefields, when a Sahhrain warship decimated the city ... decimated our people. Our reunification with the Sahhrain—our hope a thousand years of war between us had finally come to an end—well, that hope is gone now. We have been led down a path of trickery and deceit. Was it not our brethren, the Tahli ministry members, who opened the channels of communication with the Sahhrain high command? Was it not the Tahli ministry members who ensured us that Blues and Sahhrain, working together, would establish a new dynasty within the galaxy? Was it not the Tahli ministry members who had rallied, over much hesitancy from the Council of One, for independence from the Alliance? Why did we not see what was coming? Are the Blues so gullible?"

Boomer leaned in close to Drom, whispering, "What do the Tahli ministry members have to do with the Sahhrain?"

"The Talhi ministry always remained close with the

Sahhrain. Although they are Blues, they follow the path of the dark power—that of Rom Dasticon—just as the Sahhrain do."

Elder Pauli's voice was full of emotion—frustration. "Since the Sahhrain-Blues war ended, five years past, the Blues have had five years of wonderful prosperity. Our hardworking people are sought out now throughout the sector—by the U.S. fleet, in particular, as evident by their own new Liberty Station and now, by our own magnificent StarDome."

"The Blues are constructing space stations now?" Boomer asked.

"Yeah ... cheap labor. Think about it ... a Blues worker is typically twice as strong as a human ... can work more hours. The Blues workforce is in high demand. We can do the manual labor that droids aren't well suited for."

Elder Pauli continued over their whispers, "But in recent years, in secret and under the prompting of Talhi ministry members, we have joined with the Sahhrain high command in constructing tens of thousands of warships." She paused to let her words sink in.

Boomer leaned in. "Why would the Blues help the Sahhrain build warships?"

"Shhhh, keep your voice down. Let me listen."

"Now these warships will, undoubtedly, be turned against us and the Alliance—the U.S. fleet. Those same allies who came to our rescue a mere five years ago. I am ashamed ... we have forsaken the very ones, the very saviors, who aided us in our time of need. I would like to put the blame on the Talhi ministry members, which I do, but we ... the Blues ... are just as responsible. We made it possible."

Boomer listened to Elder Pauli with rapt attention. So much had happened while she was sequestered in her two years of training. She had no idea the Blues and the Sahhrain were even communicating, let alone had reestablished such close ties. And the Blues had become some kind of manufacturing power-house? Building warships? Warships intended—at least by the Sahhrain, to go up against the U.S. fleet?

She felt her face flush; was she a part of something that could harm the Alliance ... Earth? Could the lives of her own family be at risk now? She would not be a part of that. When she looked back toward Elder Pauli, she saw the old Blues master looking directly back at her, as if she were reading her mind.

Boomer returned her stare—her own expression of mistrust evident. In an avalanche of emotions, Boomer realized something fairly profound: *These are not my people. These are not my fucking people!*

Chapter 18

Feeling more and more impatient, Boomer waited outside on the balcony. She thought about using *baskile*, but the truth was, the last thing she wanted to do was meditate ... she wanted to be on edge—had every right to be angry. Where the hell was Drom? She turned away from the views of the chasm and peered back inside Conclave Hall. Most everyone had left. Only a few stragglers stood around, talking in small groups.

She heard footsteps and saw Drom, along with Elder Pauli, walking toward her. They must have entered onto the balcony from somewhere else. Boomer crossed her arms beneath her breasts and leaned back against the balustrade.

The old elder bowed, offering Boomer a smile that carried with it pain, and perhaps foreboding. "Congratulations, my young warrior. You are now a Goldwon master. One of very few."

Boomer stood up straighter, fighting to keep her emotions in check. "I didn't know the Blues and the Sahhrain had become so chummy while I was hidden away, in training on Harpaign."

"Those in training need to stay focused. I'm sure you understand that."

"No. The Sahhrain have killed thousands of my people. I watched my father nearly beaten to death by Lord Vikor Shakrim. The Sahhrain are a bunch of ruthless killers!"

Protectively, Drom took a step forward, pushing his chest out, his fists clenched. "How dare you speak to—"

"Step back, Drom," Elder Pauli said, resting a placating palm on Drom's arm. "She has every right to be upset."

"My people are in jeopardy; have been for months ... or years. I've spent time here when I should have been protecting my own people. You've made me into a traitor."

The elder maintained a bemused smile. "Listen to me, Boomer. You are not a traitor. That, I know, is something you could never be. Listen to me ... not all Blues have forsaken their commitment to peace. Not all Blues are 'chummy,' as you put it, with the Sahhrain. The massacre today at Capital City will be proof enough that the Sahhrain, as well as our own Tahli ministry members, are rooted in the ways of darkness ... of ruthlessness and deceit."

"Well, I want to leave. Now ... this minute," Boomer said.

Elder Pauli considered that for a moment, then said, "Do you want to leave, or do you want to help those you love?"

"What do you mean?"

Elder Pauli let out a breath. She walked over to the balustrade and gazed out at the darkening landscape beyond. "You have been one of ... if not *the* most proficient warrior we have ever trained here. You have mastered the skills of Kahill Callan to the point you have improved the very martial art itself ... injecting new and innovative methodologies. But while that aspect is true, you have failed to grasp the equally important non-physical side of true mastership."

Boomer didn't like being called a failure. If she was a failure, then why was she standing here—the new Goldwon—and not Drom or Carmotta?

Elder Pauli continued, "Sometimes things happen for a reason ... for a reason that is not always apparent. I want you to let go of your anger for a minute and consider something else ... something, perhaps, even *supernatural*. I want you to consider that others foresaw what happened today. That the convergence of destiny and fate and much patience were at work."

"The elders ... you foresaw this?"

She didn't answer.

"Why didn't you say something! So many died—"

Again, Drom's body became rigid.

"What happened today was horrible. Horrible, but necessary, too. It was our gift of far-sightedness, our clairvoyance, which kept us from doing what you have suggested. Stopping the massacre today, as wonderful as that would have been, would lead to millions, perhaps billions, of Blues, and many humans, massacred later on."

Boomer thought about that, wanting badly to protest against everything she was hearing. Her mind flashed back to that morning, when explosion after explosion blasted within the ancient arena; scorched and dismembered bodies lay everywhere.

"You were brought here for a reason, Boomer. And it wasn't to become a great Tahli Master or even become the Goldwon. You were brought here to save us ... and to save your own people."

Boomer made a face and shook her head. "I'm sorry, but that's simply crazy. I'm only sixteen. I don't even know things most other sixteen-year-olds know. My sister is already in college; she's so much smarter than me. My mother was the interim President of the United States. My father is Omni of the U.S. fleet. They are true leaders. And my sister, too, will become a great leader someday. But me? I don't know anything ... I'm not educated. I'm not smart like they are. Sure, I know how to fight, but that's not enough. So, Elder Pauli, you can't place the entire responsibility onto my shoulders."

Elder Pauli pulled Boomer's hands out from beneath her chest and held them in her own. She looked into Boomer's eyes for a long moment. "Boomer, we all have a purpose. Your purpose was clear since you were a little girl. You have always been the defender of what is right. You have always been willing to sacrifice everything, even yourself, for the ones you love. You came here for training for that same reason, although you may not have realized it at the time. You did not know what you actually *do* know on a much deeper level ... what the elders had foreseen, you did so as well."

Boomer did her best to blink away the tears in her eyes. Was what the elder said really true? Had she come here for reasons other than mastering Kahill Callan? Deep in her heart, she suspected that was so.

"We have little time, Boomer," Elder Pauli said quietly.

Noting the tension in the elder's face, Boomer refocused her attention. "Time for what?"

"The Sahhrain ... Lord Zintar Shakrim won't make a move until he has opened a gateway to Rom Dasticon. He will not repeat the mistakes of his brother. Only with Rom Dasticon by his side will Shakrim make his big move to defeat the Alliance, along with Earth's powerful U.S. fleet. The gateway into Rom Dasticon's dark realm must never be opened. Never."

"So how do you stop him?"

"Zintar is currently searching for all four won effigies. One of them you possess, hidden in your satchel. We suspect that he, too, may possess one of them already."

Boomer's mind flashed back to the hundreds of Sahhrain

warriors searching the arena—she understood now that they were searching for the Goldwon.

"There are three others: the Palwon, the Nordwon, and the Lortwon. All are similar effigies, made of Glist and other compounds, and all are said to be indestructible. Listen carefully, Boomer ... the being who possesses all four wons, and connects them together properly, will have the capability to open the gateway into Rom Dasticon's realm. A bridge that can be traversed either way, like a portal. That can not be allowed to happen."

"I understand."

"No, you don't. Not really. But you will, young Master Tahhrim Dol. You will come to understand why you were brought here; why you've learned what you have learned; why you perfected the unique skills that only you possess. The Goldwon Trials were created to be insurmountable. And that is why, year after year, most fail and so many die. The trials prepared you for what is to come."

"What is it I must do?"

"She just told you," Drom said.

Boomer scowled up at Drom. *Why is he being such an ass?* "I know, Drom ... find the other effigies. But how? Where do I go?"

"This is for you. It must never leave your possession, is that understood? You will die before you let another being take it from you." Elder Pauli pulled a small scroll from her sleeve, untied its attached leather thong, and unrolled it. "This was copied from a two-thousand-year-old stone tablet. Only two such maps were ever created. The original tablet no longer exists. Lord Zintar Shakrim possesses the other map. They are nearly identical ... but not quite identical. Ultimately, owning both would be best. The hidden locations of all four won effigies are depicted on this map; specifically, where each may be found.

You need to venture to the other three locations and retrieve those effigies."

"But you said so yourself: Lord Zintar Shakrim probably has possession of one of them."

Elder Pauli and Drom exchanged a quick glance. "That may indeed be a fact. If that's the case, you will have to take it from him."

"It may be on his command ship," Drom added.

"That huge thing that fired on the arena?"

Drom shrugged. "Could be."

"We'd need an army to do that, and time to train."

Elder Pauli said, "We've trusted only a few with this information. There will be six of you, of course all Tahli warriors. Drom will be one of them."

"And a ship?"

"Your travels must go unnoticed. You will move about the Dacci system aboard a trader barge."

Boomer continued to stare at Elder Pauli, then at Drom, with utter disbelief.

"Others are looking for the effigies ... both foes and friends alike. They may think they have accurate maps, although they do not."

"What friends?"

"That does not matter. Complete the task, then hide them in a place only you know about."

"No, you should have them. And this one too," Boomer said, releasing the satchel strap from around her shoulder.

"No! Listen to me, Boomer ... trust no one. Find the won effigies and hide them where no one can find them. Either that or die trying to do so."

Chapter 19

A t least the ship's unrelenting spinning had finally come to an end. Nothing else mattered but that. Jason willed his mind to ignore the stench from their heavy retching, and the fouled air from Hanna and Billy's vomit. The planet's gravity forced all floating-in-the-air chunks to fall to the deck. He looked down at his legs, also splattered with the muck, and thought, *terrific!* He then glanced over at Billy, still sprawled on the deck, but attempting to sit up.

Billy looked green. "I thought I had a sailor's cast iron constitution ..."

Orion looked down at Billy with an expression of disgust, then back at Jason. "We're still in one piece, Cap. I'm not picking up any structural damage to the *Stellar*."

Jason hailed Ricket.

"Yes, Captain."

"Good, you obviously survived the battle ... the spinning. How soon can you get started on repairs, Ricket?" Jason leaned forward to peer out the forward observation window. "I'm not so sure that we've phase-shifted into the friendliest of places," he added.

"It is too early to provide you with an accurate time estimate, Captain. Would it be possible to provide me with some assistance?"

Frustrated, Jason thought about Boomer. Another obstacle in the way of finding his daughter. "Let me check on how the others are doing. Maybe Rizzo can join you back there." Jason cut the connection and stood, scanning the outside landscape. They were situated within a lush green jungle. Startled, he saw something black fly past the window in a blur.

"What the hell was that?" Leon asked, craning his neck to peer up into the trees outside.

"Ask me that after Ricket makes the repairs," Orion said, shrugging. "Sensors are down."

"Okay ... let's all exit the bridge. I'll send Mollie's droid in here to clean things up." Jason was the first to leave the bridge.

Mollie was just stepping out from the DeckPort when Jason entered the passenger compartment.

"Dad! Where are we? You know, there's something out there!"

"What happened to your head?" he asked, moving her hair back from her face, after spotting a bloody scrape on her temple. "Mollie, you need to get yourself into the MediPod."

"I'll live, and the pod's going to be occupied for a while—with the prince first, then with Traveler—if I can find a way to squeeze him into it. They each broke a limb due to all that spinning in space."

Jason thought about poor Aqeel, who'd just gotten out of the pod. "Hey, can you fetch Teardrop? Bridge needs some ... maintenance."

Mollie made a face. "Teardrop's in my cabin. I'll go get her."

Jason nodded and watched her re-enter the DeckPort. *Her?* He tried to remember if Mollie had always referred to the droid that way.

He saw Rizzo and gestured him over. "You, OK?"

"I'm good, Cap."

"Can you help Ricket? He's in the Engineering hold space, making repairs."

"I'm on it, Captain. Um ... no offense, sir, but you really reek," Rizzo said apologetically, hurrying off toward the rear of the compartment.

Traveler sat alone on one of the couches, cradling one broken arm in the other.

The *Stellar* shook and those on board reached for something to grab on to. Jason staggered over to the wraparound window and peered out. The cabin went quiet as he leaned forward, trying to make sense of what he was seeing: *Big black tree trunks. Furry tree trunks?*

"Are those ... legs?" Orion asked, her words barely audible.

Her question immediately became moot when the black legs moved and the *Stellar* was jolted again. Then the craft was tossed high into the air and Jason felt stomach bile rise to his throat as the ship pitched back and forth as though on a turbulent sea.

Instinctively, Jason reached for his SuitPac and initialized his combat suit, as the others around him did the same. Jason scanned his HUD readings, simultaneously hearing Billy's voice come over his comms.

"Look at all those life readings!"

Jason had already done that. In addition to the ginormous beast that had grabbed the *Stellar*, there were countless other equally large life forms in the all too close vicinity. This was obviously a planet where the scale of organic life was massive.

Movement.

Taking his attention off his HUD, he refocused on whatever existed outside the *Stellar*. Two enormous green eyes stared back at him.

Suddenly, multiple screams blared over his comms, coming from Mollie and Hanna.

"Everyone, if you haven't done so already, initialize your combat suits," Jason ordered, primarily thinking of Mollie, still below deck.

"He drops us and we're screwed," Billy said, over the open channel.

"Ricket ... can we phase-shift again?"

"Only combat suits, Captain. The *Stellar* won't have that capability for at least another thirty minutes."

"Okay, then you and Rizzo keep on doing what you're doing."

The face of the beast was now in clear view and Jason gasped. It was like nothing he had ever seen—more swine- or wild boar-like than either ape or bear. It had a flattened, panting snout, with four moist quivering nostrils; a row of six yellowed, curved, tusks protruded just above its thin black lips. Suddenly, yellowed fangs appeared, and Jason heard a rumbling snarl penetrate in through the *Stellar*'s outer hull.

A flash came off to his right and Orion appeared, holding four multi-guns. "Hope you don't mind that I raided your armory." She handed them out to Jason, Leon, and Billy, keeping one for herself.

"Hanna, I want you on the bridge. Stay on the open channel," Jason said, then noticed Traveler was up, wearing his combat suit.

"With that busted arm you best stay here, Traveler."

"I am fine ... I have fought with far more serious injuries." Jason had earlier spotted the fracture, halfway along Traveler's left forearm. At least it wasn't his hammer-holding arm.

"Fine. Then let's go see if we can get that *thing* to put the *Stellar* down gently ... somewhere."

Mollie, with Teardrop close behind, nodded once toward Jason, then headed into the bridge.

He used the group setting on his suit's HUD to phase-shift the five of them to the surface.

In a flash, the group appeared thirty yards away from the two hoofed feet. Looking all the way up, Jason got a full, head-to-toe, view of the beast. Easily fifty to sixty feet tall, the two-legged, two-armed, swine beast, was holding the *Stellar* in both hands—which were more like three-fingered claws. The *Stellar* was as large as the tall beast, which spoke to the strength of the awesome creature. It was hefting up many tons of dead weight that appeared to take minimal effort.

"What's your plan here, Cap?" Billy asked.

"Maybe it's intelligent," Orion said. "Perhaps we can simply ask it to put the ship down."

"Yeah ... now there's a great idea for you," Billy muttered sarcastically.

Fully aware that his daughter, and several others, were still on board the craft, he was willing to try anything. He adjusted the external audio volume settings on his combat suit, then phase-shifted to the top of the *Stellar*'s fuselage. The bright white flash must have startled the beast, and Jason felt the ship waver beneath his feet. He was positioned midway between the bow and stern atop the gentle curve of the hull. He was finding it more and more difficult to keep his balance. Staring up at the massive face, he looked for some semblance of intelligence behind those forest-green eyes. He too was being appraised, and Jason considered the thought that he, possibly, was being considered for his next meal.

A sudden flash and Ricket appeared, standing to his right.

"Captain, I apologize for showing up unannounced, but you do not have the translation capability necessary to speak to this species."

"And you do, Ricket?"

"Yes and no, Captain. Beatrice has a vast language database," he said, referring to his own internal AI, named Beatrice.

"Well, don't just stand there—hurry up, ask the beast to put the ship down!"

Ricket, his attention on the looming face above them, rattled off a mixture of squeals and whines that Jason didn't understand. The swine's eyes widened, and its large head tilted both left and right. What emanated from its mouth next was deafeningly loud and Jason and Ricket protectively turned their heads off to the side. Jason raised his multi-gun—readying himself, if necessary, to fire.

"Captain," Ricket said.

Jason looked down at the small Craing and saw fear in Ricket's face. "What did it say?" Jason asked.

"Two words: intruder. And kill."

Both Jason and Ricket lost their balance as the beast frantically began to stomp around. Jason hoped the team below had enough good sense to get the hell out of the way.

"You ready to drop that big pig, Cap?" came Billy's voice.

Before he could answer, an influx of even louder noises surrounded them. More nearly identical creatures had joined the fray. He turned, noting Ricket was now gone. He'd either slid off the fuselage or phase-shifted away. The gyrating motion of the ship had made it impossible to stay here. Jason phase-shifted down to the surface and saw Ricket was there and getting back up to his feet. Around them were a dozen or more swine-like beasts. Open mouthed, he watched as the *Stellar* was tossed around among them. Flipping end over end, the vessel was nearly dropped. Sounds of screeching filled the jungle air as their game of *catch* continued.

Using his HUD's phase-shift menu, Jason located and locked on to those still on board the ship and in a flash, Mollie, Rizzo, and Hanna appeared beside them.

"Where's Teardrop?!" Mollie yelled, looking among those around them.

"And Prince Aqeel?!" Hanna added.

"Damn!" Jason watched in horror as his personal, multi-billion-dollar yacht continued to be flung, from one set of hairy arms to the next. "Ricket ... I need some help here," he shouted. He wasn't getting a lock on Prince Aqeel's location.

"The prince is within the MediPod. We are not able to phase-shift him here while it's in mid-operation." Ricket sounded desperate.

"Can you get Teardrop?" Mollie yelled, when suddenly the droid appeared in a flash by her side. She looked instantly relieved.

Jason watched in shock as the *Stellar* dropped toward the ground—only to be snatched up at the last moment by a huge female swine.

Orion caught Jason's eye. "I'll go. I can get the prince out of the MediPod, then phase-shift us both out."

"No ... I'll go," Jason said, already adjusting his HUD settings.

Mollie yelled, "Oh my God!"

Jason looked up, seeing the *Stellar* fly through the air in a high, wide arc. The beasts were done playing catch. The vessel was about to crash to the ground, some fifty feet away, and there was not a thing he, or anyone else, could do about it. Not only would the prince be killed—their only ticket off this planet would be gone—destroyed.

Ten feet above the ground, the *Stellar* disintegrated.

No one said anything—even the swine-like beasts went quiet—all eyes focused on the spot where the ship had last been.

"I thought the *Stellar* couldn't phase-shift, Cap," Billy said.

Jason looked around and found Ricket.

"That was not a phase-shift, Captain."

The beasts began angrily clamoring again. A shadow passed overhead—the original swine was back with one of its legs held high in the air. Jason phase-shifted away just as a stomping hoof impacted the ground where he'd been standing.

"They're angry about their lost toy!" Hanna said, running for cover. The others scurried into the thick foliage too, as stomping hooves crashed down all around them.

"Time to go," Jason said, readying to phase-shift the lot of them away—to anywhere but where they were standing. Before he could do that, two of the giant swine-like beasts erupted into magnificent hot fireballs.

Multiple plasma bolts rained down from above. One by one, the rest of the huge beasts scurried off in a frantic chorus of squeals.

Jason had to smile when he heard the familiar, squeaky voice over his comms: "What the fuck were those things?" He watched as the one-of-a-kind Rogue Class warship appeared in the sky above. It was the *Parcical*.

"Bristol! You have impeccable timing ... and I think you've just earned yourself a promotion."

Chapter 20

"I'm not wearing this ... this god-awful thing," Boomer said, staring down at the garment Drom had tossed over to her.

"It's called a Tammy Wrap. What's wrong with it?" he asked.

With an incredulous expression, she answered back. "Have you looked at your own reflection? Don't they have mirrors on this old barge?"

He shrugged. "I have no idea. Who cares? Look around you, it's what all the Bassilion traders are wearing."

"Fine." Boomer stooped over, picking up what looked like a pile of rags off the deck, and disappeared behind a nearby bulkhead. She slipped out of her tournament clothes and let them fall to the deck. Suddenly conscious of her total nakedness, she hurried—holding up the fabric and spinning it around until she found both armhole openings. She next realized there were thin ventilation slats in what she'd thought was a solid bulkhead. In the dim light, she saw Drom's form, standing where she'd left him only seconds before. He caught her staring back at him and looked away, self-conscious.

Embarrassed also, Boomer hurried, throwing the garment over her body and letting it fall in place. She wrapped it tightly around her, then tied the belt snug. The truth was, it was similar to her Shadick, while Drom's garment, it just so happened, looked ridiculously short, and dress-like, on his oversized frame. She grabbed up her tournament clothes and retrieved her SuitPac device. Stashing the clothes into her rucksack, she came back around to where Drom waited.

"I guess it's not so bad," Boomer said, hoping to avoid discussing what had just transpired. "You, on the other hand, still look ridiculous."

Drom shrugged, not bothering to reply. Standing in the bow of the little ship, he gazed out toward open space. Boomer joined him there, but instead rested her backside against the railing behind her to take in the odd little craft. At first impression, the ancient, dilapidated-appearing trader vessel reminded her of something back on Earth. *Where did I see it?* She'd visited the place with her father years earlier. *Was it Bangkok?* Yes, that was it! This vessel reminded her of an old Bangkok canal barge. It even had sails. She looked up and took in the immense, dark orange, solar sails that spanned thousands of feet out; like a giant fan, they encircled the entirety of the craft. She noticed the craft's dim running lights reflecting, shimmering, off the sails above. Someone back toward the stern was plucking strings on a small ukulele-type instrument. *Why didn't I notice it before?* It was all breathtakingly beautiful—a different world. *Is this what others consider a romantic atmosphere?* she wondered. Several distant sparkles of light flashed and just as quickly dissipated. The open-decked vessel was completely encased in an invisible atmospheric field. She knew that what she'd observed above were simply several tiny meteors, igniting when they hit the energy field, but beautiful just the same. She glanced over to Drom, and breathed in his pleasant, musky scent. He looked unsettled, creases bunched together on his brow.

"Hey. Can I see that map again?" she asked. Her question pulled him back to the moment. "Um ... sure." He withdrew the rolled scroll from inside his Tammy Wrap, untied the leather thong, and spread the scroll wide before them.

"Explain what it is I'm looking at. It looks more like gibberish than a real map ... to me."

"This scroll was copied from a tablet which was made when ancient Dacci had little resemblance to today's modern language. As you can see, it's mostly symbols. But first ..." He flipped the whole thing the opposite way around and laughed: "I had it upside down. See how the map is actually broken down into four quadrants?"

Boomer now saw them too. Wavy lines separated the four areas from each other. "And a *won* is hidden within each—"

He cut her off. "Remember, we already have one—the Gold-won. And Elder Pauli said there's a good chance Lord Zintar Shakrim possesses one, too."

"And we don't know which one is hidden where, or on what planet?" Boomer asked, staring at the scroll.

Drom shook his head. "We'll start here." He tapped the top right quadrant. "That's the symbol for the Dacci system constellation—called Pratta's Mate." As if anticipating her next question, he continued, "In that group of heavenly bodies, there's only one planet with a friendly enough atmosphere. We've had to make some assumptions along the way; one was that the *won* effigies were each hidden where there was enough oxygen to breathe."

"How old did you say those *wons* are?"

"Two thousand years ... plus change," he said.

"So how did a bunch of ancient Daccis, or whatever they called themselves back then, travel to distant constellations? I know as a fact that space travel only became commonplace here within the last few hundred years."

"I have no idea."

"This ... expedition of ours doesn't seem very scientific. A lot of guesswork."

"Maybe, but guesswork that's been going on for thousands of years. It's the best we've got. The potential cost to my people ... and yours, if we do nothing, is not an option."

Boomer let it go and brought her attention back to the scroll. "What's that symbol there?" she asked, pointing to a geometric shape that resembled a box, with two angled lines right above it.

"That's one of the easier ones," he said. "It represents a dwelling. See ... those are its walls and that's the roofline."

"Oh ... okay. I kinda see it. And this one here?"

Startled, both Boomer and Drom looked up as a slightly hunched, elderly Bassilion trader scurried past them. Similar to humanoids, Boomer was initially taken aback by their appearance, as they all had long, snake like tails. What's more, their tails were exposed, hanging out the back of their Tammy Wraps. That explained the small hole she'd noticed on the lower back of her own garment when first getting dressed. The Bassilion smiled warmly—his tail wagging back and forth as he moved past them—descending down a flight of stairs and out of sight. She briefly wondered what that would be like—having one's emotional response so readily apparent to others by possessing an uncontrollable wagging tail.

"That's the sign of death. Or, in this case, a life-threatening element," Drom said, gesturing to the scroll.

"Like one of the trials or hazards back in the arena?"

"Yeah ... exactly. This first one ... I believe is where the Nordwon effigy is hidden. The course itself has to do with patience ... or maybe it's balance," he said, nodding.

"Balance? That doesn't seem all that perilous."

"I don't know ... we'll just have to see."

He pursed his lips. "How about I redraw this, using symbols you'll better understand? It shouldn't take me long."

"You'd do that for me?"

"It's for the expedition. Don't make too much out of it ... it's not that big of a deal. There are four other Tahli warriors on this expedition ... they'll make good use of it."

I've irritated him again, Boomer thought, just when things were going so well.

"I'm tired. I'll return to my cabin now and get started." He rolled the scroll back into its long tube, tucking it under his Tammy Wrap, and left her standing at the bow of the barge without another word. She wanted to be mad at him, return his sudden hostility, but—seeing him walk away in the way-too-short garment that looked more like a dress—she smiled instead.

Boomer turned around and faced forward, looking out at the vast space beyond. "How long will we be traveling?" she wondered aloud. Part of her was fully content to stay right there; avoid what she knew would be coming. A high-up grouping of three bright stars looked similar to the Orion's Belt system she was familiar with seeing from the Sol System. She then noticed that they, ever so slightly, were not stationary, and that anomaly had probably drawn her attention to noticing them in the first place.

Boomer glanced back over her shoulder to see if there was anyone around her, and there didn't appear to be. She slid one hand inside the folds of her Tammy Wrap and touched the cool metallic device she'd clipped there. Depressing its two spring-tabs, she immediately felt the combat suit expand over her Tammy Wrap-clothed body. Through her helmet's visor, she again found the same three moving lights above in space. Using her HUD, she increased magnification to its maximum parameters, then took in a quick breath. Definitely spacecrafts. They were also the same type of vessel that attacked Capital City's arena.

"I see you up there, Shakrim. Soon ... very soon, I'll be coming for you."

Chapter 21

Boomer suddenly awoke from what had been a restless sleep. Startled, she sat straight up and tried to make sense of where she was. She looked about the small, dimly lit, compartment, and remembered she was in her cabin, aboard a small trading vessel, on a mission to retrieve the three hidden wons.

There was angry shouting coming from the outside deck. Boomer's eyes searched the dark recesses around her until she found her rucksack. Among other things, her enhancement shield was tucked inside it. More shouting emanated above her, followed by a loud crash. A hatchway, more like a flimsy doorway, had been kicked in. Obviously, someone was searching for the ship. Beyond any doubt, she knew they were searching for both Drom and her. She leapt out of bed, needing to look out the single porthole in her cabin—positioned nearly even with the deck itself. A military gunship, equally small to their own ship, was stationed alongside the barge—small, yet lethal looking. Several sets of legs hurried by her porthole window—once past her, she needed to crane her neck to follow them: three

Sahhrain warriors—all wearing, characteristically, metallic breastplates and capes.

A whimper came from the opposite direction and Boomer turned her head, looking toward the stern. A Sahhrain warrior had a Bassilion trader down on the deck, his head held firmly under the boot of his captor. *Oh my God!* It was the same sweet Bassilion who'd shuffled by her and Drom last night on deck. Their eyes even met. No! She couldn't allow something to happen to him.

Boomer spun toward her rucksack and was immediately encircled in two strong arms. A hand came over her mouth, holding her tight. She strained to see who had grabbed her and found Drom's eyes glaring back at her. He moved his lips next to her ear: "Don't ... say ... a ... word," he whispered, and released her mouth.

Boomer felt his grip on her relax and she shoved him away, furious. They stared at each other for several beats before she mouthed the words, *"We can't let this happen!"*

He shook his head, looking equally upset, and whispered back, *"The mission ... it's too important!"*

She turned and looked out the porthole again. The Bassilion trader and the Sahhrain warrior were no longer in sight. She let out a breath and relaxed a little. Her eyes moved back to Drom and, showing some defiance, she stepped quietly over to her rucksack. Opening it, she withdrew her enhancement shield. As she attached it to her forearm, Drom glared back at her.

She barely whispered, "We don't look like Bassilions ... we don't have fucking tails!"

His eyes shifted and then he nodded, withdrawing his own small shield from inside his Tammy Wrap, and securing it above his wrist.

Boomer listened to a cacophony of new sounds. The soldiers were moving below onto their deck now, searching the cabins one-by-one. Drom gestured toward the bed and took a position to the left of the hatchway. Understanding his meaning, she jumped back into the bed and brought the bed covers up around her, leaving only her head exposed.

"Try to look more vulnerable ... like you're scared or something," he whispered. She glowered at him, then did as he asked. The truth was, she *was* scared.

Boomer's eyes went wide as saucers when her hatch door was kicked open. She shrieked—only partially acting. A gigantic Sahhrain warrior filled the open hatchway, nearly obscuring the two warriors standing close behind him.

"Get out of bed, you Bassilion whore! Show me your transport papers."

Boomer furtively glanced toward Drom, hidden behind what was left of the swung open hatch door.

One of the two Sahhrain in the back said, "Ah ... she's young and pretty. We'll take her back with us ... let her make the rounds in the barracks for a while."

Boomer had heard stories about *barracks whores*—sexual slaves, passed from one assaulter to another for months—even years, if they survived that long.

"Not much in the way of tits ... but she'll be nice and firm ... and the bitch will scream." All three laughed in unison.

Boomer glanced to the left. *Uh oh* ... she thought. The fury she now saw in Drom's eyes was nothing short of epic. *So much for keeping quiet to save the mission.*

Drom, moving swiftly from his hiding place, brought up his enhancement shield. Violet distortion waves pounded the forward Sahhrain in the face—driving him abruptly up and backward—right into the other two Sahhrain. The three crashed backwards, with Drom following after them, continuing his relentless violet barrage until they all lay still upon the deck.

Boomer moved through the hatch to join Drom's side.

Together, they looked down at the fallen warriors. She knew instantly they were dead. Their faces looked misshapen. Drom had shattered their facial bones and turned their brains to mush.

She glanced up at him. "Maybe a little excessive. You think?"

He ignored her comment. Then said, "Crap's about to hit the fan."

She rushed down the passageway toward the stairs. If they were going to take on more Sahhrain, best to be in a place where they had more freedom of movement.

By the time Boomer reached the top deck, she was wondering where the other four Tahli warriors were. That thought no sooner entered her mind than she sighted Gain and Tam, rounding the corner on the opposite side of the top deck. Both Blues were shorter than Drom, and close friends of his. In fact, they had grown up together, back in Loma City. The other two Blues she hadn't seen yet. They'd gone below and into their respective cabins before she'd come on board, and they hadn't reappeared since.

"We're here ..."

Boomer turned to see two Blues females ascending the same stairwell she and Drom had just climbed and froze: The one in the lead looked remarkably like Carmotta.

"I'm her sister. You met me before, Boomer ... a year ago," she said, reading Boomer's expression.

Boomer nodded, now remembering Carmotta's pretty younger sibling. She'd actually met her several times. Rogna idolized Carmotta—had followed in her footsteps—even starting her Kahill Callan training when only a toddler. Whereas Carmotta was a natural warrior, Rogna was not. Technically, she knew the moves, the positions—but she was overly empathetic. That translated into hesitancy when she'd come up against an opponent—a characteristic that didn't bode well for a

Tahli warrior. Although they were probably the same age, Boomer considered her to be younger, for some reason.

"I'm very sorry about your sister," she said, noting Rogna looked as if she was barely keeping her emotions in check. "But Rogna, what are you doing here?"

"She's here because she was selected to be here," a low voice muttered, coming from the second Blues beside her.

Boomer took in the plain-looking female Tahli warrior now standing next to Rogna. She exuded an aggressive, masculine energy and seemed to have an apparent chip on her shoulder.

"And who are you?" Boomer asked.

"I'm Bren," she answered, with an incredulous expression, like Boomer should already know who she was.

The five Tahli warriors stared at Boomer. Self-conscious, she asked, "What?"

"What do you mean *what*?" Drom questioned, perplexed.

"Why is everyone standing around looking at me? There's more Sahhrain—"

Cutting her off and impatient, Bren said, "Either lead us, or someone else needs to take over!"

Boomer turned to Drom. "You are the Goldwon, Boomer. Not to mention, you have years of real-life battle experience. We do not," Drom said. "Didn't you know that this was your expedition? You are our leader ... so you better start leading."

"Um ... we have company," Gain said, pointing.

Ten Sahhrain warriors were quickly funneling out from the alongside gunship and crossing onto the barge's top deck. Each one was equipped with an enhancement shield. Several held pratta-shafts.

As if an internal switch had turned on, Boomer took in their situation and immediately said, "Tam and Gain ... move to the starboard side and come back around from the stern. You'll be the rear flank. Drom and Bren—head to mid-ship; you'll also come at them from the starboard side. Rogna, you're with me. We'll go welcome our guests, head on. Go!"

One thing Boomer knew for sure—Carmotta would want her to watch over her sister, although she would not have wanted her to be here in the first place. Rogna wasn't nearly ready to engage in battle yet.

The Sahhrain warriors, now on board, were fanning out. Boomer and Rogna were the first to reach them. Over her shoulder, Boomer asked, "You know how to use that enhancement shield?"

"Of course, I do!"

"Then start using it!"

Both dove to the deck as white-hot distortion waves filled the air. Boomer scooted in behind a three-foot-tall air vent, while Rogna continued to roll left as distortion waves tore up the decking around her. Four of the ten warriors had remained with them and all four were going after Rogna.

Boomer leapt high in the air spun around—and, with a sideways swiping motion, let loose with her own barrage of energy waves. Three of the combatants were hit low, their legs knocked out from under them, and they fell to the deck like bowling pins. The lone standing Sahhrain fired back in Boomer's direction. She easily parried the distortion waves when she landed, and, just as quickly, cartwheeled in behind him. She next spun one hundred and eighty degrees, hitting him broadside in the face with her enhancement shield. He fell to the deck like a sack of bricks.

Suddenly, Drom was at her side and punching off quick consecutive waves at the three downed warriors who were attempting to rise to their feet. They all went down and this time they stayed down.

Battle sounds could be heard toward the barge's stern and Drom headed away. Boomer rushed over to where Rogna was sitting, her back placed against a low, inside wall of the hull. There were black scorch patches on one of her shoulders.

"How were you hit?" she asked, crouching down next to her.

Rogna, wide-eyed, smiled, shaking her head. "You moved like ... like you knew where they were going to shoot ... even before they knew!"

Boomer pulled open the top of Rogna's Tammy Wrap and saw that the flesh on her upper shoulder was red. A few heat blisters had already formed there. Relieved she was okay, Boomer said, "Fix your clothes ... we're not done yet."

Chapter 22

Boomer and Rogna reached mid-ship where two Sahhrain warriors lay dead on the deck, the work of Drom and Bren. Boomer caught sight of Bren up ahead, running toward the stern of the barge.

"Come on, Rogna," Boomer urged, also heading aft.

They arrived at the stern—the widest section of the barge—to find Drom and Gain finishing off the last two Sahhrain warriors. Boomer already knew Drom was exceptional in the combatant arts of Kahill Callan, but it was clearly evident, by his swiftness and sheer creativity, that Gain was no slouch either. Drom and Gain worked well together and seemed to play off each other's strengths—completely overwhelming their inferiorly trained opponents. The second Sahhrain also fell.

Then Boomer noticed Tam, lying on the deck off to the right. Gain rushed to his side and placed an open palm on the young Blues' chest. He lowered his head as tears flowed freely down his cheeks. It was a sobering reminder that they were all quite young—only big kids.

"And six becomes five," Drom whispered, standing now at her side—loud enough for only Boomer to hear his words.

Gain looked up and found Boomer's eyes. "We can't leave him ... not like this. I should take him home."

Two Bassilion traders, heads bowed—their tails low and immobile—joined Gain's side. Empathetic hands reached out to him and one of the traders pulled him into an embrace. The other Bassilion attended to Tam, folding the young Blues' arms across his chest. He carefully slid his arms beneath the still body and lifted him up.

Boomer said, "Let them attend to him, Gain. They'll take good care of him."

Gain stared after them looking lost and devastated. "They were closer than brothers ... we all were," Drom said.

Boomer nodded, then turned around.

"Where are you going?" Drom asked her.

"I suspect there are more Sahhrain on board the gunship." Now heading forward, she continued, "So we should keep moving."

Boomer, along with Drom, Bren, Rogna, and a reluctant Gain, moved swiftly. At mid-ship, Boomer approached the Sahhrain gunship, still moored alongside their barge. Its hatch, now closed, made access inside impossible.

Bren said, "Closed up tighter than a glatcha's sna—"

"Hey!" Drom cut her off. "Can we watch our language here?" He glared at Bren.

Boomer smiled. "If you're trying to protect my innocent little ears, don't bother, Drom. I've grown up around foul-mouthed sailors my entire life." She looked over to Bren, and said, "And it's not sealed up tighter than a glatcha's snatch. Whatever a glatcha is ... I've got ways of getting inside. Hold tight, everyone. I'll be right back."

They watched as Boomer initiated her combat suit, and then, in a white flash, phase-shifted away.

Boomer had a fairly clear indication of the gunship's layout from her HUD's sensor readings already. Now, standing within a circular compartment, not more than ten feet from her fellow Tahli warriors outside, she figured she was inside a dual-purpose airlock and armory. Five vertically mounted pratta-shafts lined the bulkhead on one side, and five enhancement shields were also mounted, across the compartment, on the opposite bulkhead. There were about fifteen or so empty spaces—weapons obviously removed by the now-dead warriors, their bodies still on board the barge. Directly behind her was the secured outer hull hatch, and to its right, a light was glowing green, with a series of touch pads affixed beside it. Her HUD translated the symbols for her. She depressed the appropriate pad and the light changed over to red—the hatchway slid up and opened.

Boomer signaled for the team of Tahli warriors to come aboard.

"So how do we get a suit like that?" Bren asked, looking more than a little impressed.

"You get accepted into the U.S. fleet," Drom said.

"Actually, only Star Watch offers this level of technology. And getting accepted into Star Watch is no easy feat," Boomer added.

"How many more are there aboard?" Drom asked.

"I'm picking up another ..." An overhead klaxon alarm interrupted her mid-sentence. She raised her voice, "Another eight crewmembers."

"What do we do with them?" Rogna asked, as Boomer and Drom exchanged glances.

"I'm sure there is a small hold somewhere on this ship. By the looks of things, they're not armed. If they don't put up too much of a fight, we'll secure them right here." Boomer turned, closing the outer hatch.

"I think we should let them take a walk into deep outer space," Gain said.

Boomer approached the inside hatch—located on the opposite bulkhead—and depressed the appropriate pad, watching as the hatch slid open.

"Rogna ... you're with me. We need to secure the bridge. The rest of you, clear the ship. Put any remaining crew you find into a locked hold."

Boomer headed forward, with Rogna close behind.

"You're babysitting me, aren't you?"

Boomer glanced back at Rogna, but didn't answer.

"I'm not completely incompetent, you know. The others are going to think less of me."

Boomer slowed as she approached what looked to be the ship's mess. Several tables were strewn with trays, holding plates of half-eaten meals, that gave the impression that discipline among the ranks was quite lax. Boomer gestured for Rogna to stay close.

A Sahhrain, wearing an apron of sorts, came out from an adjoining kitchen, his hands held high.

"Who else is here with you?" Boomer asked, her enhancement shield held up, facing him.

"Just me. Look ... I'm only the ship's cook."

Boomer, scanning her HUD readings, confirmed he was telling the truth. She looked back to Rogna. "Find something to tie his hands behind his back, then take him to Drom and the others. Can you handle that?"

Rogna gave Boomer an impatient scowl and moved off toward the kitchen. Boomer looked at the cook. "Give her a hard time and I'll come back and flambé your ass."

He looked momentarily confused, and then, comprehending, nodded.

Boomer hurried from the mess and down a passageway lined with secured hatchways. Since no life-form readings showed in this part of the ship she kept moving on, eventually locating a wide, mechanical system—a cross between an escalator and an open elevator or lift. It took her a moment to figure out the controls and when it started moving, she hopped on the rising platform. Knowing there were four decks on the ship, she stepped off at the next level. According to her HUD readings the bridge, such as it was, was on this level, not more than twenty feet forward. There were no access controls at this hatch. Again, checking her HUD, she saw there were three crewmembers behind the closed hatch. She phase-shifted into the bridge, taking the three Sahhrain crew by complete surprise.

They were standing close together... seemed she'd caught them in the middle of a raging argument. Yelling continued between them until her presence was noticed, and they became silent, more than a little shocked.

Boomer quickly took in her surroundings. The bridge was compact, holding five stations and seven open seats. "Who is the captain or commander of this vessel?" she asked, already knowing the answer as she took in their uniforms. None wore the typical Sahhrain warrior garb—metallic breastplate and colorful cape. The three were very practically dressed, in overall-type apparel; the one in the middle had several silver-angled stripes running across the upper part of his shoulder. *A fancy touch*, she thought.

"You there—what is your name?" she asked.

"I am the captain of this vessel."

"I know that; what's your name?"

"Brith. Captain Brith."

"I'm taking over your ship, Captain Brith. Please open the hatch."

"No."

"You do understand that I could just as easily have killed you," Boomer said.

Captain Brith shrugged, keeping his gaze steadily on her. But another's eyes—the one on his right—flicked to something behind her. By the time she checked her HUD it was too late.

Chapter 23

The droid was already moving toward her before she had a chance to react. Three consecutive plasma bolts aimed at her head drove her backward, in between the officers standing on the bridge, and into the opposite bulkhead. Her combat suit saved her life. It was the second time she'd witnessed a type of advanced technology the Sahhrain should not have had access to. First, it was Lord Zintar Shakrim, wearing a retractable combat suit, back on Harpaign, and now a hover-droid—looking remarkably similar to her own droid Dewdrop. Were the Sahhrain being supplied with Caldurian tech?

Boomer thrust her arms out straight and, using her integrated wrist guns, fired back toward the droid. One of the bridge officers was caught in the crossfire and immediately dropped where he stood. The other two dove away, finding no place to hide within the cramped confines of the bridge. Unable to get to her feet, Boomer took four more direct hits to her abdomen. Her HUD lit up and she saw:

WARNING – EXTERNAL SHIELDS DOWN TO 8%

Beyond doubt, she knew another blast like the last ones and she'd literally be toast. Boomer used her enhancement shield to propel herself up and away from the attacking droid. By pure chance, she landed behind the now-crouching Captain Brith, and the droid ceased firing. A fleeting smile reached Boomer's lips. *Of course ... thing's been coded not to fire on the crew.* She attempted to haul the captain onto his feet, while staying hidden behind him.

"Get up!" She pushed her arm out from beneath the captain's armpit and fired continuously. The droid dodged left then right—moving remarkably fast. It was attempting to get a better angle on her, but her combat suit's firepower soon became too much for it and it went silent.

Black blast marks now covered most of the droid's exterior. It continued to drift about—aimlessly hovering and bumping off whatever it came into contact with. Boomer, on guard and ready to fire should it become necessary, moved in behind the droid's rear side where she found the tiny access panel, located in the exact same position as the one on Dewdrop. She lowered the panel door and peered inside. The good news—it didn't possess the latest technology. The bad news—Caldurian tech was definitely used, but significantly older than what she was accustomed to seeing. She turned the droid's power source completely off and stood back as it crashed down hard onto the deck.

"Captain Brith, where did you get that droid?" she asked, just as a loud pounding came from the other side of the hatch. Boomer stared at the other officer: "Well, open it!"

The Sahhrain officer looked over to the captain for some sign of capitulation.

"Don't look at him ... he's no longer in charge. Open it. I won't ask you again."

The officer moved across to one of the stations and tapped a touch pad and the hatch slid up. Both Drom and Bren stood there—Bren looking apprehensive and Drom looking relieved to find Boomer unhurt. The front of his Tammy Wrap was badly ripped, exposing his chest. Boomer temporarily froze at the sight of his heaving, muscular body.

Behind her visor, Boomer's face flushed pink with embarrassment; she only hoped Drom hadn't noticed. Fighting Sahhrain warriors or crazed droids was fully within her wheelhouse—but dealing with her feelings—strange new urges—well, that was another matter entirely.

She spun about and scowled toward the captain, repeating her question. "Where did you get that damn droid?"

"It's new. Delivered right before we left ... left our system. One was delivered to each Sahhrain gunship. It was supposed to be virtually invincible."

"Who's supplying the droids? Should you lie to me, I'll know."

"The Blues. They come from the Blues. The Sahhrain have received thousands of them."

"That's impossible! How would they—"

Captain Brith raised his hands in mock surrender. "The Blues. They get them from someone in the Sol System ... one of your own kind."

"A human?"

"Yes. I think he's been trading with the Blues for several years now, but that's all I know."

Boomer turned her attention back to Drom. "The ship?"

"Cleared. Five crewmembers are secured within a hold. We should go; get underway on the barge before another gunship arrives," Drom said.

"We're not returning to the barge," Boomer responded. "As

it is, we've already brought undue attention to our Bassilion trader friends."

Drom appeared confused as he looked around the small bridge. "How ...?"

"If necessary, I can pilot this vessel ... I think. But Captain Brith here, along with his first mate, will be seated at the helm." Boomer looked directly at Brith. "Unless he'd prefer I end his life right here and now."

Brith glanced down at the disabled droid on the deck. "I'll do as you say. All I ask is that you spare my crew ... and us."

"One more thing, Captain. You need to make this vessel invisible to your fleet. Cut off contact—shut down all connections you have with the Sahhrain."

He nodded his agreement.

"You still have that map handy?" Boomer asked Drom.

"Yes, but showing it to him ... that's a bad idea."

"We're out of time, Drom. Without this ship's speed, and help from the captain here, we're running blind."

"You trust him?"

"God no, not at all. But my suit has highly advanced sensors —I can tell when he's lying. He's already indicated he's in favor of keeping both himself and his crew alive." She turned toward the captain. "Lie to me ... even once, and you're finished. You do understand that?"

The captain nodded. "Show me your map."

Drom pulled the scroll from the folds of his Tammy Wrap, then spread it out on the forward panel. "It's written in ancient Dacci—"

"I can read it. Sahhrain are taught Old Dacci in grade school." He studied the confusing array of intricate symbols. Nodding, he took in a deep breath and looked at Boomer.

"Well?" she asked.

"As your Blues friend over there stated, it shows four

different locations. Separated here, here, here, and here. I recognize them—they are all located within the Dacci system."

Boomer looked at him with a strange expression, before asking, "What is it? Captain ..."

"Brith."

"Captain Brith, what were your orders?" Drom asked.

Captain Brith raised his chin ever so slightly. "To find her ... the child warrior."

"I'm hardly a child," Boomer spat back defensively.

This time the other officer spoke. "It was foreseen ... on the ancient tablets. You are the child warrior. You are the one who must be defeated."

"Enough with this child crap," Boomer said. "Exactly what do these tablets say I'm supposed to do?"

"Bow before Rom Dasticon."

Boomer snickered. "You know, I once had a glimpse of him ... years ago. I'll die before I bow before him, or that tub of lard, Shakrim."

The offensiveness of that remark was clearly apparent on the two Sahhrain faces. Even Drom and Bren looked taken aback. Boomer didn't care—Dasticon wasn't her god and Lord Zintar Shakrim didn't frighten her in the least.

"Show me the nearest of the locations," she commanded.

Captain Brith hesitated, then tapped at the second section on the map.

"How far? How many days to reach that planet?"

"Not days ... hours. We are quite close."

Boomer resisted the urge to high-five Drom, keeping her expression flat instead. "What else does it say?"

"There are four different locations: four different hardships to endure. One must overcome, best, each hardship in order to uncover the four wons' positions. I'm sure you already know that, or you wouldn't be here."

"Are any specifics given regarding the closest hardship?"

The captain reassessed the map and shrugged. "Only the one *in perfect balance* will prevail."

"What is that supposed to mean?" Bren asked, still standing at the hatchway.

The captain shrugged again.

They arrived, orbiting Clorvious Noles three hours and ten minutes later. Boomer debated how to best handle the crew on board the Sahhrain gunship. She obviously couldn't trust the captain, or his first officer—named Commander Brolin. In the end, she decided to lock them in the hold with the other crew prisoners.

Boomer brought their small team of Tahli warriors together in the mess compartment. For the last hour, they'd filled their canteens and rummaged around for food in the galley. There was no telling when they'd again get the opportunity to find something to eat. Although a food replicator was in the kitchen, none could make heads or tails on how to configure it to Blues' tastes. Sahhrain liked their food hot and spicy—to the extent most non-Sahhrain couldn't tolerate.

Rogna sat on a tabletop next to Boomer, eating something brown and rice-like from a bowl. Her mouth full of food, she asked, "And you're sure the coordinates are correct? That little map is like ... impossible ... to read."

The others nodded their heads in unison.

"Again, how can we trust anything Captain Brith said?" Bren asked.

"We'll know within the hour. We're closing in on the drop location now." Boomer wasn't sure why so much apprehension was coming from those around her.

"Drop location? We're flying down to the surface?" Drom asked.

"No, it's safer if the ship remains in orbit. We don't really know what's down there, and we can flee back here to safety, if it becomes necessary."

"So how are we getting down there?" Rogna asked, swallowing.

"Phase-shift. I should be able to get all five of us down there at once."

"You're talking about that *flash* thing you do ..." Gain said.

"Uh huh."

Boomer watched as the others got wide-eyed. Drom looked as if he was about to be sick. "There has to be another way. We're ... I'm ... not comfortable doing that."

Boomer found their pre-phase-shift jitters amusing and made no attempt to hide it. She initialized her combat suit and waited for it to expand over her body. Drom began to protest, still shaking his head. She held up a single finger and placed it over his lips. "Shhhhh ... it's all right. I promise."

She took his hand in hers, then phase-shifted them 2,800 miles down to the drop location on the planet's surface.

Drom staggered, holding out both palms to steady himself. He nervously looked around, taking in the alien environment, as Boomer scanned her HUD readings—finding no other life forms in close proximity. She then assessed the atmosphere and radiation levels and noted they were well within safe, comfortable levels.

The landscape seemed like an extinct volcano site. Although some trees and sandy areas could be seen, for the most part the terrain was flat and rocky. Visible in the far distance were snow-capped mountain peaks.

"You okay?" Boomer asked, smiling at Drom. He seemed to be calming down some.

He nodded and then smiled back. "Actually, that was rather enjoyable."

"Told you. I'm going back to get the others. So hold tight here."

"Grab my satchel and a pratta-shaft, okay?"

Chapter 24

Boomer phase-shifted back onto the gunship. She was somewhat apprehensive about leaving Drom below alone—almost tempted to phase-shift right back to the surface. She let the thought go, needing to bring the rest of them down too. Rogna was going to be a problem. Boomer knew from experience that sometimes one needed to *show*—rather than *explain*; especially to those uncomfortable with the prospect of having their molecular particles phase-shifted across far distances in space. The most expedient way, to her, was to provide them with an example—in this case Drom—illustrating the procedure was safe. Unfortunately, her reasoning may have backfired.

"I can't believe you did that!" Rogna said, obviously upset.

"Where's Drom?" Gain and Bren asked at the same time.

"He's down on the planet ... waiting for the rest of you," Boomer said, looking around for Drom's satchel. She found it on the deck, near where he'd been sitting earlier. She threw it over her shoulder, next to her own rucksack, and hurried out of the mess. Behind her, she heard someone call after her, *"Now where are you going?"*

Boomer returned, carrying four pratta-shafts, along with two Sahhrain enhancement shields. She handed shafts to both Bren and Gain, then two to Rogna. "One is for Drom.

"Okay ... everyone ready?" Boomer asked. She saw the anxiety on their faces and fought back a laugh. They were among the most highly trained Tahli warriors in the system and they were afraid of something as easy as phase-shifting.

"Maybe we should reconsider taking the gunship down to the planet," Gain said.

The others nodded, appreciating his suggestion.

"I think you may be right," Boomer said. She looked from one face to the next, then the next. "Maybe we need a group *baskile*. It's a big decision ... right?"

"As a group?" Rogna asked, making a face.

"Of course. It's easy. Truth is, I'm a little surprised none of you have heard of it. Maybe your Kahill Callan training hasn't progressed to that level yet ..."

"Oh ... I've heard of it; I just forgot," Gain replied with confidence.

Again, Boomer had to stifle a giggle. "All right then—gather around and have hand or arm contact with another person." Boomer was fairly certain none of them knew she'd transported Drom to the surface simply by holding his hand.

With pratta-shafts grasped vertically in one hand, their free hand held on to the person's arm next to them—making a circular link.

"Close your eyes and center yourselves," Boomer said. Then, observing they'd complied, she double-checked—noting they were each in proper contact. She instantly phase-shifted all four of them down to the surface.

The intense flash was enough to startle them into instant hyper-awareness of their new surroundings. But Boomer was more concerned with Drom. He was gone. She checked, then rechecked, her HUD and then her phase-shift coordinates.

"I knew you were going to do that," Gain said. "You didn't fool me, not for a second."

"You think you're real smart ... don't you?" Bren asked, annoyed. "I don't like being deceived like that."

Boomer, still preoccupied with her HUD readings, thought, *Where is Drom? Where is his life form?* Suddenly, feeling guilt, she looked at those around her. Only then did she realize none of them were showing up as life forms on her HUD either. *Must have something to do with the landscape here,* she thought. Studying the composition readings of the volcanic rock they were standing on, she realized the site was actually highly magnetized. She used her settings to compensate—increase sensitivity—for the organic composition of the rocky surface. Immediately, the bottom of her HUD lit up. *Oh my ...*

"There he is!"

Boomer spun around, watching Drom emerge from a cleft in the surface rocks. She strode over to him, and the assembling group around him. "You shouldn't have gone down there," Boomer told him, in a more accusatory voice than she'd intended.

"Why ... what was I supposed to do? Stay in one spot till you returned? You said it was safe here—"

"Well, I was wrong ... or possibly wrong. I'm picking up life forms here now."

They waited for her to continue, with expressions of guarded anticipation.

"What kind of life forms?" Rogna asked.

"There are a few different species here, in different sizes. The most prevalent, according to my suit's database, are called Pogoes."

"I've heard of them," Gain said.

Boomer gave him a wary look, getting fed up with his know-it-all bullshit.

"Seriously—they're on several worlds within the Dacci system. Freaky one-legged things."

Boomer checked her HUD to find he was actually right.

"They bite. Some of them are poisonous," he added.

Drom said, "I haven't seen anything alive around here, including below ground. Although it was so dark down there ..."

"We need to stay together until we locate the first *won* site," Boomer said.

"Well, there's nothing here. Just look around—it's totally barren," Rogna said, again making a face; Rogna's immaturity was becoming more and more apparent to Boomer the longer she was in her company.

"According to Captain Brith, this must be the location. The symbols provided a mathematical equation that are based on nearby planetary landmarks—in conjunction with the location of this world's two polar caps."

"Why would we trust that Sahhrain ass in the first place? Now we're stuck down here without transportation," Bren added. Her pessimism was starting to wear on Boomer almost as much as Rogna's naivety.

"Fan out ... but keep close enough to still hear each other," Boomer said. She headed off in her own direction. Her HUD readings weren't accurate, and she felt frustration building up. She thought of her father. *How does he do it ... lead a crew of hundreds, a fleet of thousands? I can't even lead a team of four without wanting to scream.* She felt a pull on her heartstrings—she made the conscious decision two years ago not to think of her father, or any of her family, as she missed them so much it could almost be crippling at times. Especially Mollie, which was strange, since she'd actually been with her the least over the past five years. Their mental connection had inexplicably grown, though. She'd heard of such things happening with twins, but they weren't actually twins. *What are we then?* They were close —they were the *same* person—at least they were, at one time. Time ... *time* performed a miraculous phenomenon in their case. Her thoughts returned to Mollie. How different they were—she was so much smarter. Who enters college at sixteen? And she knew about boys. *Somehow,* Boomer had been there too—her consciousness pulled into that dimly-lit college dorm room— when Mollie received her first kiss. Her face flushed, re-experiencing the memory—the passion. More and more, it was like that in recent years whenever a highly charged or emotional situation occurred. She suspected Mollie was with her during her own super-charged experiences. She was certainly there during the Goldwon trials. And knowing that comforted her still.

Boomer stopped in her tracks. Wait! *Do they think I'm dead?* Her mind flashed back to the devastation left behind by the Sahhrain warship. The demolished arena—a battlefield strewn with bodies. *How could I have been so selfish?* Her thoughts turned to her mother—she'd be devastated! Dad—*oh God, please know I'm not dead!*

Startled, she felt a tug on her shoulder.

"What's wrong with you?" It was Rogna. "I've been yelling to get your attention."

"What is it?" Boomer asked.

"We found it. We found a ... I don't know what it's called— like a village in a valley."

Boomer looked past Rogna to where the others were standing, at least a hundred yards away. *Did I lose track of time? Of where I was?* She placed a hand on Rogna's arm and phase-shifted them both across the rocky landscape.

"I hate it when you do that!" Rogna said, pulling her arm

away from Boomer. "Would it kill you to warn somebody first, when you're going to do that?"

But Boomer's attention was focused on what lay before her. Elder Pauli had not exaggerated. Her training—the Goldwon trials—was designed to prepare them—*her*—for this event. What they were seeing was an immense obstacle course.

"Look! Is that one of those Pogoes things you were talking about?" Rogna asked, pointing to a one-legged creature ten feet away. Before Boomer could answer her, seven more hopped into view.

Chapter 25

Mollie poked her head in the room from around the corner. "Dad, I think everyone is here."

Jason, with Orion at his side, was sitting at his ready room desk. He replied, "Thanks, Mollie. Tell everyone to hold tight for a few minutes while we finish up here."

She disappeared from view, back into the conference room.

Jason and Orion had spent the last hour conducting their own investigation. They both agreed in advance that their inquiries needed to be done in secret. At least, until they figured out who the primary players were—who was responsible for supplying the Blues with their fleet's highly-classified technical specifications.

"It had to come from Executive level; no one else had the authority to approve such a thing," Orion said.

"Since there's not an actual paper trail ... or comms trail, it's evident our traitor has done a good job covering his tracks." Jason stood. "Let's join the others."

Jason and Orion entered the conference room and took their seats. He scanned the faces around him. Noticeably absent was

Traveler, dealing with a personal issue back on HAB 170. Present were Billy, Rizzo, Ricket, Bristol, Sergeant Major Gail Stone, Hanna, Leon and Mollie. Mollie looked confused, probably unsure why she'd been asked to attend.

"Feels good to be back on the *Parcical*. We have a lot to discuss. Let's start with the *Stellar*," Jason said.

All eyes moved to Bristol.

"Easy! I can give it to you in three words—beat to shit."

Jason stared at Bristol blank-faced, waiting for him to continue.

"Substantial hull damage, drive, antimatter initiator, alignment issues, and the bridge smells like shit."

"Vomit," Mollie corrected.

"I stand corrected," Bristol acquiesced. "Vomit."

"Status of the repairs?" Jason asked, surprised by his own concern for the vessel.

"To put it in Earth terms, she'll be up on blocks for an indeterminate amount of time. Since there's no Mercedes supply-parts depot here in the Dacci system, I'll have to manufacture what we need."

"Where are we with your assignment, Ricket?"

"With Beatrice's help, I've been able to make some headway. The technology transfer that was required to build a fleet, such as the one we observed with the Sahhrain, would need to be massive. Their conduit, obviously, was the Blues. As suspected, the Blues and the Sahhrain reestablished trade several years back. That much was verified by Prince Aqeel."

Jason nodded. "Let's get him in here."

Mollie got up, preparing to notify him.

"It's OK, Mollie," Jason said, gesturing for her to sit back down. "*Parcical* ... please notify Prince Aqeel to join us in the captain's conference room as soon as possible."

"Yes, Captain," came a pleasant voice, from nowhere in particular.

Ricket continued, "I did find something of interest, Captain."

Jason raised his brow.

"As we all are aware, much of the *Minian*, plus the other Caldurian Master Class Caldurian vessels, remains virtually unexplored. There are compartments that have remained undisturbed since we acquired the vessels."

Jason knew that to be true, more so than most others. As the *Minian*'s former captain, he'd explored a portion of the mile-long vessel, her twenty-three decks—many of them closed off. There were vast amounts of unexplored space—not only on the *Minian*, but on the other ten similar Master Class ships in the Star Watch Fleet. Jason shifted in his seat, uneasy with where the discussion was leading.

"While exact missing contents are indeterminate, not logged, what I have found are fluctuations in the ship's overall bulk tonnage."

"Does that normally change?" Leon asked.

"Oh yes. Every time a vessel lands in the flight bay—or deliveries are made of parts or food stores. Also, crew levels change. The overall tonnage of a vessel is constantly being monitored. Everything is tied into the ship's AI—a vessel's weight affects multiple systems in various ways. In our case, subversive actions, if any had occurred, may be tracked."

"Good work, Ricket. What have you determined?" Jason asked.

"That corresponding log entries were made for every fluctuating weight change, with the exception of these." Ricket tapped on his virtual notebook, prompting a 3D display to jump forward onto the middle of the table.

"What are we looking at here, Ricket?"

"The *Minian's* fluctuating weight log is on the left. I've filtered the output of the report—only showing alterations of high tonnage. On the right is the corresponding log of flight bay ingresses and egresses, and all deliveries. Again, it's filtered down to show only high tonnage amounts." Ricket scrolled through the list—thousands and thousands of entries. Then several color-coded red lines came into view.

"What are those?" Jason asked.

"This is when the discrepancies started ... about three and a half years ago."

Jason watched as more and more red lines of text appeared. "Stop on that one there." He read the text, then said, "Those four lines, alone, amount to over two thousand tons removed from the *Minian.*"

"That is correct, Captain. And as you can see, there are no corresponding log entries to explain what or why."

Jason pursed his lips and rubbed the scruff on his chin. "Can you determine, specifically, where the weight was removed from?"

Ricket smiled. "Good question, Captain. The answer is yes." Ricket brought up an image. "From a mid-ship compartment on Deck 17."

Jason searched his memory. "That part of the *Minian* was off-limits ... closed off." He continued to study the image, studying what looked like any other medium-sized hold area on the ship. It was empty. "So we have no idea what was in there ... stolen from there?"

Ricket zoomed in on a small object in the corner of the compartment.

"I know what that is," Mollie said. "It's part of a droid. An arm segment. Teardrop has something similar."

Ricket smiled toward Mollie. "She is correct, Captain. The object is a Caldurian combat droid's upper arm segment."

"Why is it black?" Orion asked. "I thought Teardrop was all white?"

"The technology on this droid would have been years—many years—older than Teardrop and Dewdrop. With that said, I suspect droids in the hold were still highly advanced, combat ready, and approximately the same size and weight as the newer versions. That fact is important."

"Why's that?" Jason asked.

Ricket smiled, obviously pleased with himself. "Knowing that, we can make the assumption the hold was used as a storage location for many of those out-of-date droids. And we can estimate how many droids were stolen. From this hold alone ... approximately two thousand."

Everyone stared at Ricket in silence.

"There are five more holds on this level, with miscellaneous broken droid parts strewn around inside them. At a minimum, we are looking at ten thousand droids that have been pilfered."

Jason felt a cool chill running down his back. Ricket's findings were not good. He saw Sergeant Major Gail Stone shaking her head, causing several strands of her long platinum hair to fall free from behind her ear and hang over her eyes.

"What is it, Master Sergeant?"

Gail Stone directed her question toward Ricket. "Do the missing droids account for all the weight discrepancies?"

"No, Master Sergeant, not by any close measure. I took it upon myself to dispatch security droids to all unexplored ship compartments, and provide me with a detailed accounting of what, and how many, items were found within them, including partial or broken items, such as droid arm segments."

"I don't think we want to hear this," Billy said.

"Shush," Orion said. "Go on, Ricket."

"There are various plasma weapons—some similar, but not as advanced as our multi-guns; there are spacecraft parts—for example, for our shuttle, drone, and manned fighters; even parts used to construct DeckPorts."

"How about phase synthesizers?" Bristol asked with alarm.

"No ... I do not suspect phase synthesizers, or any parts associated with the manufacture of synthesizers, were compromised."

"That's good—we hand over that technology and it's game over, lights out," Bristol said.

"Why is that?" Hanna asked.

"Onboard phase synthesizers are what make DeckPorts work, and JIT munitions, and weaponry. But, most important, the ability of a vessel to phase-shift thousands of miles across space."

"It's what separates the technical supremacy of the vessels of Star Watch from the rest of the U.S. fleet," Jason said. "I've always kept a tight grip on that technology. As fleet Omni, I've imposed rigid guidelines on who has access to that technology. A growing sore point with the rest of fleet command, to be sure, who ardently believe all fleet vessels should be equipped with the same Caldurian tech."

"Why don't they simply copy what's on the *Minian*, and the other Caldurian ships?" Hanna asked.

"There are only two, maybe three of us who have that capability—or smarts—to do such a thing. Even with a phase synthesizer sitting right in front of them," Bristol added. "Me, Ricket, and maybe Captain Granger ... though he's doubtful."

"So those weapons and droids, and God knows what else, are now in the hands of who?" Leon asked.

"The Blues and, unfortunately now, the Sahhrain." The answer came from Prince Aqeel. He entered the conference room, wearing a Shadick and looking, for the first time, perfectly healthy. He gestured toward an open seat next to Ricket.

Jason nodded.

The prince sat and said, "I am Blues. My loyalty is to my people first. I've known of the reestablishment of relations between Blues and the Sahhrain for some time. Although wary at first, my people believed our Dacci brethren were sincere in their efforts to bring our warring people together again. We had defeated them and, with the help of the U.S. fleet, maintained a military hold on the entire system. What did we have to lose by thawing relations?"

More than a few at the table audibly scoffed.

"Did you know about the buildup—that huge Sahhrain fleet we witnessed?" Orion asked.

He hesitated. "Not exactly. I knew the Blues were building their own assets. Obviously, space stations, and, more recently, our own warships. That aspect was kept secret. I did not know we assisted the Sahhrain in building a power fleet. I do not have access to all high-level decision-making."

"So, thanks to the Blues ... the Sahhrain have taken the ball and run with it," Jason said. "The price paid for that was the Capital City massacre. That, and the Sahhrain are now poised to not only conquer the Blues, but probably attempt a war with the Alliance and the U.S. fleet."

The prince looked down at the table and slowly nodded.

"And because of some asshole traitor among our own ranks, incredible technology—droids, weapons, and who knows what else, has flowed into the hands of the Sahhrain. All thanks to the Blues," Leon said.

Jason broke the silence. "Where is my daughter? Where is Boomer?"

The prince looked up and held Jason's stare. "My last memories on Harpaign were of the Sahhrain attacking. The warship bombarding the arena ... the battlefield. I saw Boomer and instructed her to retrieve the Goldwon effigy, located within the nearly destroyed arena. It wasn't long after that when I was struck down. Young Master Tahhrim Dol, Boomer, would have been up against ... insurmountable odds. I am sorry," he said, looking at Mollie with eyes full of sympathy, "but I do not see how she could have survived."

"Well, she did," Mollie said.

"Let's assume she's alive. Where would she go?" Jason asked.

"Her rucksack had instructions, but she would need help. If there were others left alive—perhaps Drom, or even an elder—they would head to Loma City."

"Why is that?"

"It would be a safe refuge—hidden and nearly impossible to find. Even tracking sensors are useless in that area. If she is still alive, she has already been dispatched on a quest. That was discussed by us in recent days. The winner of the Goldwon was to gather a small team and find the three remaining wons. The elders, the Council of One, were opposed to reunification with the Sahhrain. They would rapidly push for locating the other wons—thereby disrupting any chance for the return of Rom Dasticon."

Jason was being hailed. He'd left explicit instructions on the bridge that he did not want to be disturbed.

"What is it, Seaman Gordon?"

"You have two holding inbound communiqués, sir. One's Admiral Stark, Captain. He insists you take his communiqué. And Captain, there's something else ... I don't know if I was supposed to see it, but there is a high-command warrant out for your arrest."

"Terrific ... and what's the other one?"

"From Jhardon, Princess Caparri, sir."

Jason's mind was filled with an image of Dira's face. *Oh no ... Was she going to finally do it ... do what he feared more than anything?* Would this be the day she told him she wanted a divorce? That she's going to put an end to their marriage?

"Tell the princess I'll have to get back to her ... patch in the Admiral, Seaman."

Chapter 26

He cut his NanoCom connection to Seaman Gordon. The conference room went quiet and all eyes held fast on Jason.

"What's wrong?" Orion asked.

"Seems there's a warrant out for my arrest, courtesy of Admiral Stark."

"On what charge?"

"I don't know yet."

"You think Stark's behind the selling-off of our weapons to the Blues?" Billy asked.

"I won't know until I talk to him."

"You think that's wise ... to talk to him before we have any proof?" Leon asked, prompting several heads to nod assent around the table.

Jason thought about his predicament. He was in trouble, but that didn't mean his crew was too. "Look ... I'm not surrendering to the admiral at this time. Not until I've found Boomer. With that said, all of you need to return to the Sol System, in the *Parcical*. I'll take the *Stellar*—she's not a fleet vessel."

"I'm staying with you, Dad."

Jason nodded.

Billy was smiling, which must have been contagious, because the same smile spread across the other faces.

Jason shook his head, already knowing what was coming. "Look, what I'm doing is tantamount to going AWOL; guilty or not, running off against fleet orders is a court-martial offense. You need to think of your careers."

Leon and Hanna looked first toward each other, then Leon said, "Um ... we're private contractors. I've been on the run before. We're with you, Captain."

"I may not be as wealthy as you are, but I still could have retired ten years ago. I was there at the start ... back on *The Lilly*. I might as well see where things end up," Billy said.

"Goes the same for me," Orion added.

"Me too," Rizzo said.

Jason wasn't surprised. But some there hadn't been around from the start. "Master Sergeant ... Gail ..."

She cut him off. "I've been on your bridge for five years. You really want to insult me at this point?" she asked, looking offended.

Jason shook his head. "Gunny, have several shuttles prepped for departure. There's close to two hundred crew, including Sharks, on board the *Parcical*. Find a friendly world nearby, where we can start unloading our people. We'll instruct the fleet later where they are located."

"Will you make the unloading voluntary?"

Jason didn't answer for several moments. The truth was, something very wrong was going on—having some semblance of a crew on board could be the difference between future success or failure. He nodded assent. "Voluntary."

Jason sat in the command chair, mentally preparing himself for his conversation with the admiral.

"I've given the order for the shuttles to be powered down," Orion said.

"Still no volunteers?" Jason asked.

"Not a one."

"Seaman Gordon, do you have an open channel to Liberty Station yet?"

"Yes, Captain. And Admiral Stark is waiting."

"Put him up on the display."

The *Parcical*'s overhead three-hundred-and-sixty-degree 3D display, currently showing the open space around the ship, suddenly segmented and a new forward video feed, showing Admiral Stark, appeared. Gone now was his typical, painted-on, over-sized smile. His expression—an attempt to appear stern—came across instead as one being more righteous, or pompous, than anything else.

"Admiral Stark," Jason said, devoid of all friendliness.

"Omni Reynolds. Were you not notified, more than three hours ago, of my need to speak with you?"

"I was busy. But since you have my full attention now, I suggest you make the best of it."

Stark, clearly not accustomed to being spoken to in such an abrupt manner, made no attempt to hide his irritation. "Your immediate return to Sol System and Liberty Station is demanded ..."

"Uh huh. Last I checked, Admiral, I don't report to you."

"I'm sure you understand that no one is above the law. Even someone who's appointed himself the fleet Omni."

"What offense do you think I've committed?"

"This is a conversation that should be carried out on private comms."

"You mean private comms, *sir*," Jason corrected the admiral.

"Sir."

"Speak freely, Stark. I want my bridge crew to hear this too."

The admiral shifted in his chair before speaking again. "Evidence has been presented—irrefutable evidence I might add—that connects you personally to a number of illegal acts; the least of which is the sale of contraband. Fleet technology—advanced weaponry—the list goes on and on. I can see by the expression on your face you already know what I'm referring to."

Jason did know and was only surprised to hear the admiral was aware of it too, since he had just learned of the ransacking of the *Minian*'s holds, and possibly other ships' holds too.

"Your name is literally all over this, Omni Reynolds," Stark said, not even attempting to rein in his condescending smile.

"What does that mean ... my name?"

The admiral let out a long breath, blinked, and slowly opened his eyes wide, as if the mere act of explaining was burdensome. "Much can be done to doctor AI logs. Even security video feeds in this day and age are easily manipulated. But items impossible to change are command-level, log instruction entries. From what I've been told, any modifications to the AI logs require a verifiable, corresponding, signature. The AI verifies its authenticity—to a degree, I'm told, that simply cannot be circumvented. The thefts on board fleet assets took place at specific times and locations. The AI system and security logs were manipulated to hide that fact. Guess what? The manipulated logs match identically with the theft timeframes and ship compartment locations. Again, your name is all over these. It took a crack technical team to find the log entries, which were expertly hidden I might add, but they were found just the same."

Jason felt perspiration forming on his brow. He wasn't guilty but at this point he probably looked it. He needed Ricket's help to dig through the data. As if on cue, Ricket appeared at his side.

"What the admiral is saying is true, Captain."

The all-knowing admiral nodded in response.

"What exactly does the log signature say?" Jason asked.

"This is getting embarrassing, Omni Reynolds. Embarrassing for you. Let's dispense with the—"

Jason cut him off. "Humor me."

Someone handed the admiral a virtual notebook and he read, verbatim, what it said: "U.S. fleet—Executive Command Level Personnel. Crew: Reynolds." He looked back up. "There is no Omni classification, as far as the AI is concerned. And, as you know, Executive Command Level ... well, that is Admiralty. Added to that, you are indeed crew: Reynolds, yes?" The admiral looked up, his brows arched high, questioning.

Jason sat back and stared at Admiral Stark in silence.

"If I may ... that is not entirely true, Admiral," Ricket interjected.

Jason had already made the other connection when Ricket continued with, "The military command position of General also holds the Executive Command Level Personnel designation."

Oh shit. What the hell has Brian been up to?

Sudden comprehension registered on the admiral's stunned face as well. Jason guessed it was due to his dashed hopes of an immediate rise in rank to the level of fleet Omni.

"There is no clear evidence that General Reynolds had anything to do with those thefts. Personally, I believe you are grasping; and, quite frankly, I am disappointed you would stoop to the level of throwing your own brother under the proverbial bus ..."

"Watch yourself, Admiral! I may be a lot of things ... but a thief is not one of them. Why would I pilfer from fleet assets? Money? I have more than I could spend in three lifetimes."

"You—the *Parcical* and her crew—need to return to Liberty

Station at once. If what you are telling me is true, well ... we'll conduct a thorough investigation."

"I'm glad to hear that. And I'll make sure that you do exactly that. But as for me and the *Parcical* returning to Liberty Station now—that's not going to happen just yet."

"There is an active warrant out for your immediate arrest, Omni Reynolds—"

"Be quiet and listen to me! This is far bigger than the pilfering of droids and weapons. The Blues and the Sahhrain have been covertly working together for several years now. Did you know that? All those construction contracts offered to the Blues for over five years now—the incredible technology that's been transferred, handed over to them, to build advanced space stations, and, more recently, warships. Guess what? That same technology also went directly to the Sahhrain. Listen carefully, Stark, they have amassed a fleet of warships—"

"Who? Who has amassed a fleet? You mean the Blues?"

"It may have started out that way, but then turned to a covert, joint Blues and Sahhrain endeavor. What we personally witnessed were many thousands of advanced warships, at the ready, in the Dacci system. Those warships were all Sahhrain built."

The admiral stared back at Jason, clearly astonished at what he was hearing.

"You've already received the reports on the attack of Capital City. The possible death of my daughter in a brutal massacre. That was the Sahhrain. It's started ... they've double-crossed the Blues, ready to go to war."

"Why am I just hearing about it now? This is ... preposterous!"

"The *Stellar* was attacked by the Sahhrain when we stumbled upon their fleet. The *Parcical* responded to our distress call, so now you are hearing about it. Damn it! What you need to know is that, with the possible exception of our Caldurian Star Watch assets, the level of technology possessed by the Sahhrain fleet is far superior to our own. Put ten Craing Heavy Cruisers—hell, a Meganaught—up against one of those immense Sahhrain warships and you'll be picking through space dust to find our crewmembers' DNA. Here's something else, Admiral—all that I've told you is still not the worst of it. Go back and read the logs on someone called Rom Dasticon. The Sahhrain are doing everything they can to bring him into our realm of existence. An entity ... a force ... so powerful—"

The admiral interrupted, "I know perfectly well who Dasticon is." He held up a palm and shook his head. "All this is —well, to be honest—incredible, if not unbelievable. Again, you must return to Liberty Station. A full investigation will—"

"Have you not listened to a damn word I've said? We are on the verge of full-out war! I'm ordering you to ready the fleet. I'm bringing Star Watch here, to the Dacci system, to see if we can nip the upcoming war in the bud ... early on."

The admiral shook his head.

"What are you doing? Stop shaking your fat head."

"You are no longer fleet Omni. Star Watch is under my command until, as I said, a full investigation has been conducted. As for the allegations about your brother, those too will be investigated. Come home and we'll take it from there."

"I always suspected you were an idiot, Stark. Now I'm certain of it. My first priorities will be finding my daughter and stopping Dasticon. You need to ready the fleet. Do it now! Send Star Watch to the Dacci System." Jason gestured for Seaman Gordon to cut the connection.

Chapter 27

"**D**isgusting. They look like slugs," Bren said.

"Yeah, slugs that can stand and bounce around," Gain added.

"They look harmless to me. They're kinda cute ... don't you think?" Rogna asked, taking several steps in the direction of the clustered, knee-high creatures.

"Stay away from those things," Boomer said, standing at Drom's side, and taking in the strangely constructed obstacle course, cloistered in the valley below them.

"She's right," Drom said. "Get back, Rogna!"

Boomer pointed to the left. "So I'm guessing the starting point of the course is at that end of the valley."

"That's my assumption too, as well," Drom said.

"Why even bother going through all those obstacles? Why not just climb down the far side over there, toward that end, and complete the last obstacle? You'd then be done with the whole thing," Gain said.

Boomer shook her head. "No, I thought of that myself. The constructors of this course—whatever it's called—would have designed the obstacles to be done cumulatively and consecutively. Different from the Goldwon trials, where we could change the order of the challenges and still complete the course. Here, I'm betting that once started, only by completing the previous obstacle would you be allowed to progress on to the next one. Not worth the potential risk of deviating from the intended."

"What are those?" Drom asked, pointing.

"Bones. Using my HUD, I zoomed down on the ground. There must be several hundred bones scattered around down there," Boomer said. "Obviously, we weren't the first ones attempting to defeat this course."

"And there's no way for us to know if it was successfully completed? If the won effigy has already been found ... taken?" Gain asked.

"Get back, Rogna!" Bren yelled.

Boomer turned in time to see Rogna twenty paces away, along the lip of the valley. She was crouching down, holding something out before her—probably food from her rucksack— and offering it to the little group of Pogoes. Excited, high-pitched yipping sounds erupted as the hopping slugs moved closer—slowly, at first, then hopping forward frantically. Rogna looked back over her shoulder. "They're so cute!"

Bren, who was closest to Rogna, was the first one to jump into action. Using her enhancement shield, she jumped up and over Rogna, placing herself between the girl and the approaching Pogoes. Then the slugs attacked—coming straight at Bren.

The speed in which the Pogoes moved took Boomer completely by surprise. Before she could even react, three of the Pogoes leapt onto Bren—two onto both thighs and one onto her exposed neck. The white, translucent-colored Pogoes immediately changed color, from pinkish to dark red. They were filling up on Bren's blood.

Bren screamed and flailed. Using both hands she tried to pull off the Pogoe clamped on to her neck. Drom raised his enhancement shield.

"No! Not accurate enough. Let me," Boomer said, rushing closer in and raising her arm. "Take your hands away, Bren!"

Bren's legs turned wobbly, her blue skin now a sickly white color. She lowered her hands and fell to her knees. Boomer fired one quick plasma bolt from her suit's integrated wrist cannon. The Pogoe flared into bright flames, before shriveling—becoming charred and black—and dropping away. Two more plasma bolts left the two other Pogoes dead.

In a swiping motion, Drom used his enhancement shield—turning the remaining Pogoes into a gooey paste.

Boomer and Rogna rushed to Bren's side.

"I need to take her back to the ship," Boomer said.

"It's too late," Drom said, looking down at Bren.

Boomer knew he was right. Bren's eyes were open and fixed—her life form icon, showing on Boomer's HUD, had blinked off. Boomer felt sick to her stomach, saddened, and suddenly overwhelmed with doubts. They hadn't started the course yet and they had already lost another team member. Why had Elder Pauli placed her trust in them? After all, they were nothing more than a group of kids, for God's sake!

"This is all your fault!" Gain said, looking at Rogna. "How many more times are you going to do stupid things that get another of us killed?"

"It was an accident," Boomer said. "I'm sure those things would have attacked at some point anyway." She looked over to Rogna, and said, "Bren just saved your life. I hope you appreciate her sacrifice."

Tears filled the young Blues' eyes. "I didn't mean it. I just wanted to ..." Rogna buried her face in her hands and wept.

Boomer said, "I'll be back in two minutes. Nobody let your

guard down. The Pogoes aren't the only predators on this planet." She took Bren's lifeless arm in one hand and phase-shifted away.

Boomer returned to the surface, finding the others pretty much where she'd left them several minutes earlier. In the distance came the sound of the Pogoes' chatter, getting increasingly louder.

"Bren?" Drom asked.

"I found an out of the way place on the ship to put her body where it won't be disturbed. Here's her rucksack ... no use letting her food go to waste."

Drom took the bag and swung it over his shoulder, next to his own. "I figured you could do that phase-shift thing you do, and take us down to the entrance."

Boomer nodded and gestured for the three remaining Tahli warriors to huddle in close and make physical contact. Taking another look down into the valley, she set new phase-shift coordinates and they flashed away.

Once down on the valley floor, the four spread out to get a better look at what was before them—an ancient-looking stone block, with crudely-formed metal fittings, designed to weather the ages. Five chiseled stone steps led under an archway that actually began the start of the course. Boomer estimated the small valley to be approximately fifty feet wide by two hundred feet long. The obstacle course, built on the site, took up almost the entire valley. The ground was gravel-like and, as she'd noticed when looking down from above, bones were strewn about all over the place.

"Look at the size of this one!" Rogna said, picking it up and standing the long white bone virtually on its end. It was nearly as long as the pratta-shaft she held in her other hand.

Boomer and Drom exchanged a look. That bone was neither a Blues nor Sahhrain bone. Boomer pictured something more on the scale of a small dinosaur.

"So who's going to do this?" Drom asked, standing with his hands on his hips as he looked up into the archway. "The scroll mentions something about balance ... or having good balance."

"I have good balance, and I think I should be the one attempting to do this anyway," Boomer said. "Why don't you follow along on that parallel path running off to the side? The three of you can give me suggestions along the way."

"You going to wear that suit?" Gain asked.

"No. From what I'm getting, completing this course needs to be accomplished fair and square. I'm not even sure I should wear my enhancement shield ... probably not." She climbed up the steps, holding still on a flat, pedestal-like, rock surface that must have weighed five tons. The stone-carved arch above her head spanned twenty feet into the air. But the course lying before her had fully captured her attention: complicated looking, with various heights of stone platforms and open vaults which, from her present perspective, seemed black and bottomless. She followed the course with her eyes—one section at a time. Each looked more impossible to conquer than the one that preceded it.

Drom hurried around to the side, climbing on the path paralleling Boomer's. He pointed in front of her: "There are wheels, which will need resetting, at the beginning of each obstacle. The first thing you do, once you succeed through an obstacle, is reset the wheel behind you. It's the only way you can move forward, too, I'm betting."

Boomer watched as Gain and Rogna joined Drom on the pathway. They all looked apprehensive.

Boomer removed the enhancement shield from her arm and reluctantly shoved it into her rucksack. She retracted her combat suit and unclipped the small SuitPac device from her Tammy Wrap. She hesitated but then placed that too inside the bag. If she was going to do this—it would be as a Tahli warrior— no tricks, no special technological advantage. She closed and tossed the rucksack over to Drom, then. The first obstacle before her spanned twenty feet. She stepped to the edge and looked down, not seeing a bottom. Looking over to the opposite side, she saw the metal wheel that Drom spoke of, the one she would need to reset.

"You need to jump from one spire to the next," Rogna said.

"I know that," Boomer said, looking ahead at the three skinny rock spires—each no more than four inches square. She'd need to jump more than six feet, landing one-footed on the first spire, then holding her balance there. Could she even jump that far?

"Maybe I should do this one," Drom said. "I have a much longer stride than you."

"Shush! I'm trying to concentrate."

Boomer took in a deep breath and let it out. She took several steps backward—held steady there for a moment—then ran and leapt. She landed one footed on the small four-inch-square spire. She waved her arms up and down to balance herself and realized the skinny stone tower was swaying back and forth.

"How are you going to jump to the next one? It's not like you can get another running start," Rogna asked.

Boomer briefly wondered how Carmotta had endured her younger sister for so many years. She took a quick glance downward and instantly regretted doing so. The blackness was absolute. Considering the sun was almost directly overhead, she should be able to see something down there.

She brought her attention back to the next spire. About to

agree that the leap was impossible—she smiled. *The swaying!* She couldn't get a running start, but she could let the swaying tower, beneath her right foot, propel her over to the next tall pillar. That is, if she timed things just perfectly and could maintain her one-footed balance.

"You can do this, Boomer," Drom said.

"Don't fall," Rogna added.

First, leaning her upper body somewhat back, and then a little forward, Boomer began to sway the rock spire several feet in both directions and the momentum began to build. Obviously, the time was coming when the spire's motion would be too fast—making it impossible to keep her footing. She needed to jump before that happened. Back and forth, the tall pillar swayed, closer and closer to the next one. Their distance apart—down to about four feet—seemed doable, so she leapt. Halfway over to the four-inch rock square, Boomer realized she was going to miss it. She'd over-shot a left-foot landing. She felt her heart restrict in her chest and clenched her teeth, certain she was about to die.

Chapter 28

Boomer's eyes locked on the rock spire, as she felt herself begin to fall. She reached out with both arms, realizing her fingers were mere inches from touching it. But it may as well be a thousand miles away. No, she was going to die —that was for certain. In a matter of moments, she'd be swallowed into the darkness beneath her. She contemplated the eventual impact. Would she even feel her death when it came? In a split second her mind raced, flashing to her family and those she loved. She thought of Mollie and hoped she wasn't experiencing her last few seconds too—but with their connection, she knew she was. *I'm sorry, Mollie.* Resigned now to her inevitable fate, she turned her head toward Drom and the others. Rogna and Gain were there, looking back at her, horrified. *Wait.* Where was Drom? Suddenly frantic, Boomer needed to connect with him one last time—even something as simple as eye contact. It was important. The top of her head was below the spire, as crisp, cool air rushed up from the dark depths below. She was falling faster.

And then she felt a *Thump!* As though someone had kicked her squarely in the back. It hurt a lot—and propelled her up—

face first into the rock spire. The unforgiving ragged surface struck her right cheekbone—splitting open her cheek. Her arms and legs instinctively wrapped around the pole-like spire and her descent slowed, then stopped. As warm blood flowed down her cheek, she closed her eyes, leaning her forehead against the cold, hard surface. She continued to gasp for breath until her heart rate slowed, realizing that she might not die today, after all. Based on the all-too-familiar sting she'd felt on her back, she knew Drom used his enhancement shield—had fired off distortion waves at her as her body descended. It had done the trick.

"Boomer?"

The voice was distant, unmistakably Drom's—the most perfect voice in all creation. The voice of a saving angel.

"I'm all right," she called back.

The next voice she heard was female and anything but angelic: "Are you going to finish it or just stay down there all day?"

"Bite me, Rogna," Boomer yelled back through smiling lips. She stared up at the ten feet she'd need to climb. *I'm never, ever, going anywhere without my SuitPac on again.* It took several minutes before she reached the top, and then another few minutes to get her foot securely positioned on the small square stone and stand atop it.

Drom moved back to where the others were and smiled at her. She mouthed the words *thank you.* He shrugged. Once again he'd been there for her—had saved her from certain death.

Using the same method as before, Boomer got the rock spire swaying back and forth. She had a much better idea now about the effort she'd need to propel her to the next small pedestal. Back and forth, she continued the spire's lateral movement until the time was right—and she leapt. Her left foot landed perfectly on the small square of rock, but her fast momentum caused her to fall off again. This time, though, she clung to the spire and held on for dear life. She waited for the spire to cease movement, then climbed up.

Boomer repeated the process again, but this time she nailed her landing. Excited clapping came from her onlookers. The worst was over—all she needed to do now was jump over to the next ledge. She swayed back and forth on the spire several times and leapt, landing on solid rock. Letting out a long breath of relief, she looked across to the others and noticed Drom studying the scroll. He looked over to her and made a face.

"What ... what's wrong?"

He gestured with his chin. "All that ... back there ... um ... it was okay for you to have on an enhancement shield after all. I understand the symbols better now and it clearly speaks of Tahli warriors and enhancement shields." Again, he shrugged. "Hey, at least now you know you're—"

"Just throw it over to me," she said, more relieved than she wanted to show.

She caught her shield one-handed and secured it onto her left forearm.

"Don't forget to reset the wheel," Drom said.

Boomer turned and found the dark metal wheel, located on the far-left side of the small plateau she was standing on. It reminded her of a ship's old fashioned steering wheel. She turned it in one direction without success, then the other way, and felt the wheel slowly turn. It took five full revolutions before it locked into place, and she heard an audible scraping of stone against stone. The spires behind slowly changed orientation—as one moved to the left another one moved to the right. They'd completely repositioned. Boomer turned, recognizing the next obstacle had reconfigured as well.

"Look, they're moving," Rogna said, pointing out the obvious.

The new obstacle had a thirty- to forty-foot span. Five metal rings, each six feet in diameter, were supported by poles of varying heights that continuously spun around at different rates of speed. Standing upright between the five rings were more rock spires.

"Crap! Are you kidding me? Again?!" Boomer mumbled, as she wiped blood from her split cheek.

"I think you're supposed to time it—jump through the rings and land on the little rock squares."

"Uh huh ... thank you, Rogna."

Now that her enhancement shield was again on her arm, Boomer's confidence had restored. In fact, she thought, this challenge could be fun. She watched the spinning rings, got the timing down pat on when they were all aligned—the exact time to clear the rings and land on the rock squares. From what she'd seen, it was a two-minute cycle. Catch it just right and she should be able to cruise through this obstacle course all the way to its end. A new cycle was coming up and she poised herself to leap.

The black-clad Tahli warrior, Commander Jarial Shakrim, watched from his hidden position within a rocky cleft at the top ridge of the valley. The young Sahhrain had enjoyed watching the girl traverse the first obstacle. *And she'd accomplished it without the aid of an enhancement shield!* She was very talented —but then again, he already knew that.

The girl dove through the first ring—tucked into a forward spin—and used distortion waves from her enhancement shield to halt forward progression. She landed on one foot, without so much as a waver. *Now she is just showing off!* The same obstacle had taken him hours, nearly killing him. The girl, *Boomer*, was again on the move. She dove—this time not stopping on the next spire's square but using it as a steppingstone to cartwheel right through the next ring, and ... *oh my* ... she landed —a one-handed handstand—holding perfectly still a moment, then back-flipping into the next open ring. She'd made it safely to the other side, as if she'd practiced the feat a thousand times before. The others clapped their hands and cheered; Boomer smiled back and bowed. *Go ahead ... enjoy your brief moment of accomplishment. In the end, you'll find the reward you seek, the Nordwon, was already claimed—by me—two weeks ago.*

Jarial peered out from his hidden perch to the pathway below, where the two Blues males, and the pixyish-looking female, were standing. Their days were numbered. The taller of the two males—he'd noticed him before, back on the battlefield of Capital City—was well-trained, but no match for his own, far-superior, Kahill Callan training. He debated killing the three of them right then, while Boomer progressed through the obstacles. He smiled at the thought of her finding them, all missing their respective heads. Father ... Lord Zintar Shakrim, certainly would approve. But no, they were helping her out, which meant they were helping him too. Jarial had journeyed to the other won sites and attempted to retrieve the Lortwon on the planet where it was hidden. He had failed to complete the obstacle course miserably. It had almost cost him his life, so now he would wait for this Kahill Callan master to retrieve the effigy from that course — and then he would take it from her.

He watched Boomer, now balancing on a long, razor-sharp section of the final obstacle, and shook his head—feeling a mixture of admiration and jealousy ... and hatred. Was she really *the one* ... the one described in the ancient tablets? Of course, she was. Letting her live was a dangerous proposition. Every moment she lived, their opportunity to get close to the gateway into Dasticon's realm was jeopardized. Their Sahhrain legacy ... very existence ... could be eradicated. He should kill the human now. He could blame it on the obstacle course. But Jarial never lied to his father. And the truth was, he couldn't deprive his father of doing the one thing he desired most—avenging his brother's death.

Renewed cheering from below brought him back to the here and now. He needed to return to his small ship—parked nearby —before it was spotted by these young Tahli warriors. Jarial took another glance at Boomer.

Chapter 29

Rushing to get things done, aware that his team was waiting on him, Jason promised them he'd only be a quick second. He took the incoming communiqué in his ready room.

"Hey ... I'm just on my way out, Nan. Can this wait—" but his words were cut short. As he lowered himself into his seat he saw his son's five-year-old face staring back at him—his little forehead furrowed with concern. "Well, well, little man. I didn't expect to see you up and about this time of day." Jason figured it was early there, about six o'clock in the morning in Colorado.

"I smelled pancakes cooking," the little boy said.

"That'll do it."

"Daddy ... Mommy says soon I'm gonna be big enough to visit you in space."

Jason's son, Michael, now five, was perched on his mother's lap. Squirming around, like most other five-year-olds who'd just consumed copious amounts of syrupy sugar.

"Well, kiddo, we'll have to see about that. Going into space is really a big boy thing to do. Why don't you go play and let Mommy and me talk about it?"

"Okay, Daddy ... bye." He jumped down off Nan's knee, and three seconds later Jason heard the back porch door squeak open then slam shut. A dog barked in the distance, and suddenly Jason yearned for those simpler times.

"That's all he's been talking about lately. He wants to be like you. He wants to be a fleet captain someday."

"And I'd like to be more like him—a kid running around the back yard. I miss him. I need to make more time ..."

"Don't start making promises, Jason. Talk to me about Boomer. I'm worried sick and I haven't heard from you. She is alive, isn't she?"

"I'll know more after we speak with survivors of the massacre. Prince Aqeel is taking us to a hidden city—Loma City —on Harpaign."

"So we still don't know for sure?" Nan asked, frustration showing on her face.

"How can I? But I'm going to get answers sometime today ... I promise."

His words didn't seem to mollify her anxiety. "Change of subject," she said. "You're in trouble, Jason. I don't know whom you pissed off over the years, but you've got the U.S. admiralty seeking to bring you to justice. Something about stealing technology."

"Well, they do have part of it right. It was carried out by an executive officer with the same name—Reynolds. Only they have the wrong Reynolds. It was Brian. At least, it looks that way. Not sure what he's up to. And I don't have time to dig into any of that right now. Of far more importance, we have first-hand sightings the Sahhrain have amassed a massive fleet of warships that would give the U.S. fleet more than a run for their money. The Alliance is in jeopardy, and for some inconceivable reason, I can't get anyone on Liberty Station to take the matter seriously."

"I heard about it. Admiral Stark brought that up to a joint committee but it's evident he doesn't believe you. I've been getting information secondhand. I'm not in those circles anymore, but I have had discussions with several close contacts that are still involved there. Watch your back, Jason. There's politics going on and certain people want your head on a platter. There were even rumblings about sending Star Watch assets to apprehend you."

"Let them. My priority right now is to find Boomer and bring her home. From what the prince tells us, Boomer may be on some kind of quest ... to find a bunch of little statues."

"That sounds crazy, in light of everything that's going on," Nan said, befuddled.

"Apparently, whoever acquires all four statues has the means to bring Rom Dasticon into our realm."

"Not him again! Didn't we deal with all that nonsense years ago?"

"I thought so, too. Look, I need to go. I promise I'll give you an update just as soon as I learn more. Okay?"

"One more question?"

"Honestly, I have to go ..."

"Have you heard from Dira?"

"Not for a few days ... she's busy. I'm busy ..."

Nan nodded. "Get back to me about Boomer ... okay?"

Jason nodded and cut the connection. He sat there for a moment, suddenly unable to move. Why'd she have to bring Dira up? *Why now?* It had taken all his willpower to keep her from his thoughts lately. Now she was all he could think about—her pretty face—her violet skin and those amazing eyes. He forced himself not to think of her body, her ...

"Hey, we going to do this or not?" Billy asked from the open hatch.

Jason got to his feet. "Let's go."

"Dad?"

Jason turned to see Mollie coming out of the kitchenette.

"Where are you going?"

"I'm late, Mollie ... we're still tracking down leads to find Boomer."

"Then I'm going with you."

"Not this time ... it's too—"

She cut him off, "Dangerous?"

Jason just stared at her.

"I need to tell you something. I was there, wherever she is ... was. She was falling. Falling to her death. It was real. Not a dream."

"What are you saying? That she ... died?"

"No. Somehow she was saved, or she saved herself."

"Where was this?" Jason asked.

"At first, I thought it was back at the arena—at Capital City. I thought maybe I was somehow reliving her past experience, during an obstacle course, or something. But I knew what I was seeing, or experiencing, was happening right now, in that very instant. She was traversing a dangerous obstacle course, and she almost died."

"How fast can you get dressed?"

Leaving the *Parcical* in orbit around Harpaign, Jason, Billy, Rizzo, Ricket, Mollie, and Prince Aqeel phase-shifted down to the surface of the planet. Since Aqeel did not know the specific coordinates, and even the *Parcical*'s advanced sensors couldn't locate the hidden city, they decided to get in as close as possible, based on Aqeel's input, then hoof it in the rest of the way from there.

In a white flash, the team of six suddenly appeared on the

rocky surface. Rizzo released his hold on Prince Aqeel, the only one not wearing a combat suit. Jason took in the beautiful, albeit harsh, landscape. As far as the eye could see, a jagged, orangey-red, rocky terrain spanned off to the horizon. Deep crevices—some more like valleys—would make traversing the large area nearly impossible.

"I don't know. We may need to bring down a shuttle," Jason said, turning three hundred and sixty degrees around, shaking his head. "It all looks the same ... be hard not to get lost here."

"And this heat. The prince will cook without a suit on," Billy added.

"No need," Aqeel said. "First of all, I'm used to the climate here, and second, I know exactly where we are. I recognize the rock formations over in that direction," he said, pointing. "If you could phase-shift us—is that the right terminology?—over to that plateau in the distance, we'll be closer."

Rizzo put a hand on Aqeel's arm. Jason gave Ricket a nod—prompting him to set the distant drop location—then went ahead and phase-shifted the group. They flashed again.

Aqeel staggered. "I don't know if I'll ever get used to that."

Ricket said, "Captain, although rather faint, my internal sensors are picking up readings of nearby life forms." He pointed to the nearest deep crevice.

"He is correct, Captain," Prince Aqeel said. "But as mentioned before, you cannot approach the city wearing a combat suit or carrying weapons other than enhancement shields."

"How long a walk is it?" Rizzo asked.

"From here ... about two hours."

Jason removed his day pack and deactivated his battle suit. He was already properly attired in a Shadick. The others, following his example, also wore Shadicks beneath their battle suits. Pulling enhancement shields from their packs, they affixed them to their forearms, except for Ricket and Mollie, still untrained in their use.

"Lead the way, Prince. It's only getting hotter, the longer we stand around on this rock," Jason said.

The six descended into a nearby cleft where the temperature immediately dipped down to an almost tolerable level. They climbed down a steep section of rock facing, using what weren't exactly steps, but more like chiseled out, worn, foot holds. Strategically cut into the rock, they were useful but also imperceptible, unless specifically looked for. As they progressed along a narrow pathway, Jason studied Prince Aahil Aqeel ahead. There was no way he could have gotten them this close without first knowing the coordinates. He just didn't want to share them with the crew. A secret city remains secret only so long as others don't know how to find it.

"Captain."

Jason turned and waited for Ricket to catch up.

"I thought you would want to know; we are being watched ... more like shadowed."

Without making any sudden movement, Jason scanned the narrow canyon they were walking through. "How many?"

"Not definitive, Captain. The readings are faint, almost imperceptible. I don't have specifics."

"I guess that makes sense," Jason said.

"They know me, of course. So I don't expect there to be any trouble," Prince Aqeel said.

Jason had a feeling that they were being watched for the last few miles. Ricket's words only confirmed it. But there was something else not right. The problem was, he couldn't quite put his finger on what. He glanced over to Mollie, whose eyes were locked on to something ahead, off to the left, on the other side of the gorge.

Chapter 30

"What is it?" Jason asked.

"I thought I saw something ... up there in the rocks. Like a reflection," Mollie said. "I may only have imagined it, though."

Jason looked to Ricket, who seemed to be lost in thought. Jason knew he was checking his internal sensors.

"We are approaching Loma City. The abundance of Glist there will affect your ability to scan the area—"

They were the last words Prince Aahil Aqeel would ever speak. His head was vaporized in a flash as multiple streams of violet distortion waves caught him mid-step. His headless body remained standing for several moments before folding to the ground, like a lifeless rag doll.

"Get down!" Jason yelled, his hand instinctively moving to his SuitPac device, concealed within the folds of his Shadick. His fingers found the two inset tabs and he squeezed. Nothing happened.

The entire team dove to the ground, with the exception of Rizzo and Mollie. Together, they crouched low and scurried in behind a large, nearby rock.

Jason discovered his NanoCom was also down. Attempting to hail Billy, at the rear of the group, was futile. *Shit!* Realization of their dire predicament dawned on him with stark clarity. Not only were their internal comms down, but they were also virtually defenseless without functioning combat suits. He couldn't even remember the last time he felt this vulnerable. *Why on earth did I let Mollie join the team?*

"Ricket!"

"I am right here, Captain," Ricket replied.

Jason found him huddled nearby, cowering on the ground close to Aqeel's headless body. "How many?" he asked.

"Between five and ten ... I cannot be more accur—"

"Where are they?" Jason interrupted.

"There and there," Ricket said, pointing in the same location Mollie had pointed to earlier, as well as toward another position, directly in front of them.

"Remove the enhancement shield from the prince's arm. Throw it over to Mollie ..."

Ricket looked back at him quizzically. Jason wasn't sure why —perhaps because he hadn't suggested Ricket put it on his arm. Tentatively, Ricket crawled closer to the body, unstrapped the shield, and back-crawled a bit. Turning, he found Mollie peering around from a large rock twenty paces back and tossed her the enhancement shield. It landed ten feet short of the target, in the middle of the path.

Startled, Jason saw Mollie dart out from her hiding place, snatch up the enhancement shield, and dive back for cover.

A new blaze of violet distortion waves filled the air above their heads. Plumes of rock and dust erupted from the nearby cliffs down onto the path.

Furious, Jason yelled, "That was incredibly stupid! No more of that shit, you hear me, Mollie?"

She didn't answer.

"Jesus ... we're sitting ducks here, Cap!" Billy yelled out behind him.

For several years Jason had religiously practiced Kahill Callan. He attended Boomer's classes and, under her tutelage, had become fairly adept using an enhancement shield. The same went for Billy and Rizzo. But later demands on his time made Jason's visits to the gym less and less frequent. *Perhaps, though, it's like riding a bike.* Truth was, they had little choice. Either take the offensive and make a charge, or just sit there, waiting to get picked off—one by one.

"Rizzo. Keep her safe. We're making a run for it!"

"Where the hell to?" Billy yelled back.

"Forward—that way—anywhere but here. Now! Go! Go! Go!"

Three strides forward, Jason took a glancing blow to his right shoulder of white-hot energy. Immediately, he felt his skin blistering, could smell his own scorched flesh. Raising his enhancement shield, he fired off a continuous burst of distortion waves—relieved the use of the weapon had come back so easily.

After fifty yards' advancement, the enemy group—those ahead on their same path—came into view. The gorge was wider there, allowing them to assume positions higher up on the cliffs. Perfect for an ambush. The Sahhrain were situated at various points, taking cover behind rock outcroppings. *What I would give for a multi-gun right now*, Jason thought. He gestured for those behind him to keep to the right—hug the cliff walls. A series of bright bursts came from behind, and a Sahhrain warrior in the cliffs tumbled forward, his metallic breastplate briefly catching the light. His red cape tangled around him as he descended down the steep rough terrain to disappear into the gorge below.

"Stupid fucking costumes ... can you imagine having to wear that shit?" Billy asked, suddenly appearing at Jason's side.

"That your shot?" Jason asked.

"Rizzo's."

"Impressive. How many more do you count?" Jason asked.

"Four more up ahead, just around the path. And at least three on the other side of the gorge. Although I've no idea how they got over there."

"I believe their method of transportation is called a dune-skipper," Ricket said, joining them and clearly out of breath. "There is one parked up ahead," he said, pointing.

Jason squinted his eyes, thinking he saw something in the distance, but unsure. He recalled Ricket's latest MediPod enhancement procedure—a zoom feature for his eyes.

"Why don't you use those new eagle eyes of yours to help pinpoint enemy positions? We're far too exposed here."

Ricket scanned the distant cliffs on the opposite side of the open gorge. "There, Captain. Between those two cone-shaped pinnacles."

Both Billy and Jason repositioned their footing for a wider stance, then fired off multiple bursts of distortion waves. Neither let up until all the rock in that localized area burst and shattered. Subsequent to that, a scream emanated from the immense plume of dust.

"He's toast," Billy said. "Where else, Ricket?"

"There ... thirty-three feet to the left. Almost directly across from us."

Before Jason and Billy could get him in their line of sight, the Sahhrain let loose with his own barrage of energy waves. Billy was hit and all three dove to the ground.

"You okay?" Jason asked, keeping his eyes on the distant cliffs.

"I'll live."

Jason came up on one knee and fired off a series of distortion waves. Two other streams of energy joined his, coming from behind. Glancing back, he saw they'd come from Rizzo and Mollie. Mollie, it seemed, was getting a quick introduction on the basics of enhancement shield usage. Between them, another Sahhrain warrior was killed.

"Any better idea on how many we are up against now, Ricket?"

"There is still one across the gorge. At least six more are up ahead, on this side. They are on the move, Captain."

He heard the distant hum from multiple vehicles. Across the gorge, moving fast, was a Sahhrain warrior, standing at the controls of what looked like a flattened jet ski. A dune-skipper, Jason surmised.

"They are leaving," Ricket said. "Moving in the same direction we are heading."

"Most likely repositioning themselves further up—within Loma City," Billy said, his voice stifled from pain.

Jason did a double take. The right side of Billy's head was scorched black. It appeared his right ear was missing too, no longer attached.

"That looks like it hurts bad," Jason said.

"You think?"

"Your head trauma will be repairable within a MediPod," Ricket unnecessarily added.

"Let's move," Jason said. He gestured for Billy and Ricket to head off, then checked to see if Mollie was still doing all right. She and Rizzo were in a deep discussion. He was moving his enhancement shield around—holding it in different positions before his body—and she was following his example, mimicking his actions.

Their pace as a group had slowed. The enemy could easily be hiding around every bend, or in the rocks on either side of the gorge. Ricket's sensors were becoming completely useless as they approached the city. Again, Jason was struck by his limited capabilities. For years he'd communicated with his team using nothing more strenuous than mere thought. Not being able to initialize his combat suit now was humbling—what it felt like to be an ordinary human again—before he discovered *The Lilly*, eight years ago. Before he reconnected with his father ... before he met Dira. He pushed the thought of her away.

Billy and Ricket had slowed down their pace ahead, Billy's shield held out in front of him. Ricket fell back to walk behind Jason. They were entering Loma City. Jason hadn't paid any notice to it as they made their descent to the bottom of the gorge, now seeing the gorge had opened up into a wide valley, with a crystal-blue stream flowing off to their left. But the sudden awe-inspiring sight before him brought Jason to a standstill. A spectacular oasis: green lush trees—an abrupt contrast to the red rocks of the surrounding cliffsides. In the distance lay a massive cliff city—a city glowing as blue as the enhancement shield on his arm. A city made of Glist.

By the time Jason and the others fully registered the sound of approaching dune-skippers they barely had time to scurry into the trees for cover. Billy and Ricket, close behind Jason, ducked down by the base of some adjacent trees. Looking back, Jason saw Mollie, still standing on the path, out in the open. Rizzo was pulling on her arm. *What's wrong with her?*

Jason ran back to her side. "Take cover, Rizzo!" He shook Mollie then grabbed her by the chin—forcing her to look at him. "They're coming ... we need to take cover. Mollie!"

Her eyes finally focused on Jason's. "A beast ... it's after Boomer ... she's running for her life right now!"

"What are you talking about?"

"Boomer ... she's in danger ... oh God!"

Chapter 31

Completing the obstacle course, Boomer heard the others cheering and applauding her success from the nearby path. The obstacles—so similar to the kind of trials she'd endured back on Harpaign—certainly were difficult. But to be really honest with herself, she had expected something more—expected them to have a higher degree of difficulty. If she was able to best this course, wouldn't others have done so also? But, then again, who would ever want to come here in the first place? The planet, Clorvious Noles, was selected for one reason. No one would visit here by choice. It was off the beaten path of most space routes and an inhospitable planet, to boot. The ancient Daccis knew that, deciding it was the perfect location to hide a *won* effigy.

Now, standing atop the final raised platform of the course, Boomer stared downward. A section of rock slowly descended below, revealing a chiseled stone stairway. She stepped closer and peered into the black void below. Cool air rose up from its depths. She glanced up and caught Drom's eye.

"You want me to go with you?" Drom asked.

"Yes. But it's probably best I go alone. Who knows if something's rigged—if more than one person progresses from here on in. Let's just hope this doesn't close up on me while I'm down there."

Both Gain and Rogna nodded their heads.

Drom said, "Be careful."

Boomer stepped onto the first step, then waited a moment to see if anything new happened, triggered by her added weight. Satisfied, she progressed down slowly, quickly realizing she wouldn't be able to see much of anything soon in the growing darkness. An idea came to her. Holding her shield out, she directed a low-level distortion wave into the shadows. Emanating bright energy cast a violet glow ahead, illuminating the space around her. She continued down the stone steps for what seemed an eternity. She guessed she'd descended several hundred feet when she finally reached the bottom. Three things immediately became evident: One, beyond this point the Dacci hadn't changed the stark natural surroundings. She was standing in a natural, below ground vault—an underground world that looked pretty much untouched by civilization. Two, the only non-natural item in view was off to her right. Barely able to make out what she was seeing, the object appeared to be four or five feet tall—perhaps rectangular in shape. *Like a pedestal?* As she slowly moved forward in its direction, a third thing occurred to her. The little life they had encountered above ground didn't seem to reflect a similar reality below ground.

Boomer was keenly aware of the movement of many small critters down here—well hidden in the dark recesses around her. She stopped as a question occurred to her—what caused the hundreds, no thousands, of bones scattered throughout the obstacle course above ground? Boomer shivered. Seeing a mist rising from her outgoing breath, the temperature below, she realized, had to be near freezing. She took several steps forward, still pondering on the bones, when her thoughts flashed back to

Rogna—standing next to a bone that looked as long as her pratta-shaft. *What kind of an animal did that once belong to?*

Reaching her destination, she confirmed that it was, indeed, a pedestal of sorts. She increased the amount of emanating distortion waves to better see in their light the circular base pattern of what had once sat atop the cut piece of rock. The outline matched perfectly the size of her own Goldwon. She obviously, then, wasn't the first to successfully complete the obstacle course above. Someone else had plucked the effigy from this pedestal. Was the missing *won* in the hands of Lord Zintar Shakrim now?

She gave the top of the smooth rock surface a few pats, coming to terms with this new setback. Time for them to move on to the next won.

About to turn away and return to the surface, a different kind of roar echoed forth from the darkness beyond her—a noise carrying both substance and weight. Boomer glanced over her shoulder, back toward the stairway. Thirty yards. At a dead run —with the aid of her enhancement shield—she could make it there in seconds. She should run—*now*! But curiosity got the best of her and she peered ahead, toward the escalating snarling sounds. Again, she increased the power of her shield, moving it in a slow arc—like moving the beam of a flashlight. Nothing there. Wait ... she brought the violet swath of light back a quarter turn, this time swinging it around much slower. Then she saw it. It would be easy to miss. Its coloring was the same as the rocky walls, a brownish gray. But walls don't have glowing, bright green eyes.

The beast was easily twenty feet tall. Dread washed over Boomer as she stared into its two unblinking orbs. The face was wide and horrible, as if it were inside out. Massive, yellowed teeth reflected off the light, along with an exposed musculature —pinkish tendons and gooey flesh. Gobs of thick moisture—

drool—dripped down the sides of enormous jaws on a cheekless face.

Boomer ran the light up and down the creature's powerful-looking body. The rest of it was thick and hairy. *Of course it is!* As expected, she also saw long claws on more than two sets of arms—claws like those on a grizzly bear—only much, much larger.

Transfixed, Boomer didn't immediately react when the beast charged. She simply watched it move, as if her feet were somehow affixed deep into the ground. Only its terrible roar snapped her from her trance-like state. *Fight or flight?* She turned and ran—using her enhancement shield to propel her both upwards and farther forward. Soon, she was practically flying. She reached into the folds of her Tammy Wrap. *Where is it? Where is my damn SuitPac device!* She then remembered; she'd given it to Drom ... *Crap!*

Thunderous stomping filled her ears—somehow—the beast was already upon her. Boomer knew she couldn't make it all the way to the stairs. Her mind flashed to Mollie, and she knew, without a doubt, that Mollie was experiencing this same terrifying moment right along with her. *Welcome to my world, Sis.* A smile spread across Boomer's face—even in light of her dire present circumstances. Knowing she wasn't alone beneath the surface of this dreadful planet gave her the psychological boost she needed.

Fight ... not flight.

Boomer repositioned the face of her enhancement shield downward, concentrating with all her willpower to slow her forward momentum. She sensed, rather than felt, the swiping motion of the beast's claws several feet below her body. A blow, if it had reached her, would have undoubtedly killed her.

With another swipe of her shield, she back-flipped even higher. Briefly upside-down, she gazed upon a face she'd not soon forget. Its breath—a mix of rotting meat and the sour stench of something putrid—perhaps death itself—caused her to gag reflexively. Mere inches from its gaping open jaws, Boomer brought her shield up, putting everything she had into that next burst of distortion waves. No longer violet—the bright-red waves coursed into the beast's garage-sized mouth. For a split second, the inside of the beast's throat was illuminated. Then it was gone—blown apart, along with the whole back section of the creature's head.

It fell backward, as Boomer continued her own flip rotation. Landing softly on the ground and facing in the opposite direction, she didn't look back—knowing it was dead. She walked somewhat unsteadily toward the softly illuminated staircase before her and turned her thoughts back to the latest connection she'd experienced with Mollie. She recognized her surroundings —they were unmistakable—*Why is she at Loma City? Who was shooting at her?*

Boomer emerged into bright sunlight and saw Gain, Rogna, and Drom still standing about where they were earlier.

"Where is it?" Rogna asked, looking disappointed. "Couldn't find it?"

"I found where it *used* to be—before someone else grabbed it," Boomer said, jumping across onto the pathway where she joined the others.

"So that was the one—the won effigy Lord Zintar Shakrim has," Drom said.

"Could be."

"Hey ... we heard a ship taking off ... above ... beyond this valley. I tried to get up there, but I must have just missed it. I think someone was observing you," Drom said.

"Observing me? You mean when I was traversing the obstacles?"

Drom shrugged.

Boomer flushed. She'd looked like a spaz. She remembered falling and needing to be saved by Drom. She idly wondered who had come to watch. Pursing her lips, she nodded, suspecting who it might be.

Chapter 32

Back on the Sahhrain gunship, along with their few remaining teammates, Boomer and Drom released the Sahhrain crew from the hold and soon everyone converged into the small, onboard mess. Boomer ate little—the mental image of Mollie in danger weighing heavily on her mind. *She's here in the Dacci system. So close, which means Dad must be nearby too!*

"Where ya goin'?" Rogna asked, over a mouthful of something green.

"Don't worry about it," Boomer said, getting up abruptly from the table and rushing from the mess. She needed to get away from the others; her heart was racing and her palms suddenly felt moist and clammy. It had been years since she'd spoken to anyone in her family. Long ago, she'd disallowed her thoughts to even ponder them ... miss them. The heartache she first endured no longer having them as part of her life. So why was this moment so difficult? Boomer hadn't used her NanoCom for over two years—she had told her father she was deactivating it until she was finished training. "Don't even try to contact me," she had said to him. But her training was now complete, and they were apparently within range of one another. Truthfully, there was nothing she wanted more than to reconnect now with her family. She regretted the years apart, feeling remorse that she'd somehow lost perspective of what was truly important. After all, what was more important than family or kinship? *Nothing.*

Boomer stood in the empty gunship passageway, her back flat against a bulkhead. She inwardly stared at the floating menu option, hovering right before her eyes:

Reinitialize Nano-Devices?

She realized she was trembling. *Oh, for God's sake ... get a grip, girl!* Sure—she could go up against the worst villains and monsters imaginable, but simply calling home made her want to pee her pants.

She affirmed the virtual selection.

Nano-Devices Reinitialized

Within a split second, her internal nano-devices began springing to life within her consciousness. With the reconnection to advanced technology now activated, an influx of sights and sounds she'd taken a sabbatical leave away from came alive. A flurry of virtual menus flashed into view—some she dismissed, mentally waving them away, others she pondered over, and eventually either affirmed or declined activation. She was over two years behind in implementing new updates to her nano-devices.

She'd forgotten how tedious being *connected* could sometimes get. Apparently, her internal nanites had been faltering for months now too, unbeknownst to her. She affirmed the virtual updates and instantly, like a jolt of caffeine, felt a surge in energy. Eventually, NanoCom menus began to pop up. Older audio messages she had never listened to streamed in—a growing list—heightening her anxiety. Some messages were stored from two years ago. When time permitted, she'd have to listen to each and every one of them. Suddenly, they were all extremely important to her.

Boomer scanned the most recent messages, hoping to see one from Mollie or her father. But the most recent one was from her mother—and only two minutes ago. She selected it and gasped, not realizing it included a hi-def video. Hovering before her eyes was her mother, holding a flailing child on her lap. Tears filled Boomer's eyes. Her baby brother seemed immense—chubby and unrestrainedly happy. Her mother wrapped her arms around Michael and laughed at his antics.

"Boomer ... I so hope you are receiving this message. I miss you and I love you. You must be tired of hearing me say that in all my stored past messages, but it's true. I ... we ... all of us thought you died on Harpaign ..." Tears welled in her mother's eyes. "I have to keep this short since I'm scheduled to shuttle up to Liberty Station later today." Finally, she released Michael from her grasp, and he ran from view. Nan's face turned serious. "Boomer, your father and Mollie are looking for you—out there, in the Dacci system. On Harpaign. The problem is, we can no longer contact him. Some localized interference down on the surface, apparently. I cannot reach any of the team, including Mollie—"

Boomer cut the playback message off in mid-sentence. She hailed her father—old functions coming back to her as if no time at all had passed. He wasn't acknowledging her hail. She tried Mollie and got the same result. Frustrated, she stamped her foot down on the decking. She thought quietly for another moment, then, with no other option apparent, hailed Orion.

"Go for Gunny. Boomer? Is that you, girl?"

"Orion!" The tears began to flow down her cheeks in streams. *What the hell is wrong with me?* she thought, swallowing and trying to speak.

"I'm so happy you're alive ... so happy to hear your voice—"

Boomer cut her off, "Me too, Orion ... you have no idea ... but where is my father?"

"He's looking for you, Boomer. Your sister Mollie, Billy, Ricket, Rizzo, and the prince are too."

"Prince Aqeel?"

"Yes. They're on Harpaign ... headed for Loma City."

"I knew it!"

"What?"

"I ... I saw a vision ... through Mollie's eyes. She ... they ... were being attacked. By the Sahhrain."

"Are you sure?"

"Yeah, I'm sure."

"I'll send another team. What about you? Your father will want you on the *Parcical.*"

"It's here? In the Dacci system?"

"Yes, you need to come—"

"I can't do that, Orion. It's a long story, but I need to track down two more won effigies. It's all about keeping Rom Dasticon ..."

Orion finished her sentence, "from entering our realm. We're aware of that. Your father knows, or at least had a pretty strong hunch that you were doing just that. Okay ... keep on mission, but don't turn off your nano-devices ever again!" Orion scolded.

"I won't, I promise. But let me know the second you hear from Dad. Let me know if I should return to Harpaign."

"We'll find them. And if the Sahhrain are there ... they're going to have to deal with the *Parcical.* So go! We've got this, Boomer." Orion cut the connection.

Boomer closed her eyes and let out a long breath.

"What are you doing?"

Boomer blinked away the virtual menu option, seeing Rogna approaching. "Drom wants you." She smiled at her own statement. "Well, we all already know that, but he wants you on the bridge. Something about where we're going next."

Does Drom really want me? Like in a romantic way? Boomer wondered.

"Why are you still standing there? You look ... sad. I'm sad too. I miss Carmotta," Rogna said, going over and joining Boomer, resting her back against the bulkhead next to her.

Boomer felt the girl's need to connect. With the loss of her sister, Rogna had transferred her dependence on Carmotta over to Boomer. As annoying as Rogna could be, she was Boomer's responsibility now. She owed that much to Carmotta.

"Come on. Let's get back to the others. We still have two more stupid statues to find."

Drom was seated next to Gain at the back of the bridge. Both, hunched over, were studying the now-open scroll and looked up as Boomer and Rogna entered. Boomer noticed Captain Brith and Commander Brolin were back, now seated at their respective panels. Looking no worse for wear, neither looked particularly enthusiastic to be back, having to again pilot the vessel for the enemy.

"You left the mess ... in a hurry," Drom said.

Boomer shrugged his comment off. "I had to take care of something. Did you figure out our next stop?" she asked.

"According to the captain here, who has a far better grasp of ancient Dacci, the next closest planet would be Draggim."

"Let me guess: It's barren, inhospitable, and situated in a remote part of the Dacci system."

Captain Brith said, "That's a good guess, with one exception. It's not barren. In fact, that small world teems with life."

"What kind of life?" Gain asked before Boomer could.

"I'm guessing ... insectile. There are bugs on that world the size of this ship and I'm not exaggerating about that. The planets in this system have been deemed off-limits to non-scientists for over a hundred years. Too many visitors—thinking they could build strong enough structures to keep the native inhabitants out—found that out the hard way. Nothing will or can stop them when creatures attack or insects swarm. So you won't find shipping lanes going anywhere near these places today."

"I hate bugs," Rogna said, making a face. "Maybe I'll stay on board the ship while you go looking for your statue-thingy."

Gain said, "No way! Just because you don't like bugs won't excuse you. Not a one of us like fucking bugs."

"How far away is this Draggim world?" Boomer asked.

"Few hours ... we're en route there now," Brith said, turning his chair forward.

"You want to go over the symbols ... what we've figured out about the next set of obstacles?" Drom asked Boomer. He then looked at Gain, his brows raised.

"Oh ... I guess that's my cue to leave." Gain stood and made an elaborate gesture toward his open seat. "Come on, Rogna, I'll show you how to replicate Sahhrain ice cream in the kitchen."

Boomer took his vacated seat and felt the warmth of Drom's body close to her, their shoulders touching. She tried not to overthink how the simple contact of their arms could fluster her so much.

"First of all, I don't want any argument from you."

"What are you talking about?"

"I'm running the next obstacle course."

"Why?"

"Because I want to and because I'm not afraid of insects. I collected them as a boy. I think they are ... interesting. Even kept a small colony of shank beetles till the age of twelve." He said this as if it was supposed to mean something to her.

Boomer hated bugs. If Drom expected an argument from her, he'd be disappointed. "No problem, Drom ... go for it!"

Chapter 33

Jason, not waiting for Mollie to snap out of her trance, picked her up and flung her over his shoulder, then dashed back to find cover within the trees. The incoming distortion waves had increased, up to the point that it was obvious now they were definitively outnumbered. Only five against an untold number—and Ricket was unarmed.

"I'm fine ... put me down, Dad!"

He set Mollie down—she'd begun to squirm in his arms and was loudly protesting.

Once behind cover, Jason immediately joined Billy and Rizzo in returning enemy fire with his enhancement shield. Mollie was soon by his side, too. He noticed she was increasingly more proficient using the Dacci technology, firing off her own volleys of violet distortion waves in the general direction of the Sahhrain.

"Any guess how many we're up against?" Jason yelled into the group of trees, twenty yards off to his left, where both Billy and Rizzo had taken cover.

"Maybe fifty," Rizzo said.

Billy said, "They're making steady progress moving up on

our position. It's just a matter of time before they wage a full-on attack."

Jason found Ricket, cowering behind a lone tree several paces behind him. "How about your comms? Can you send a message, Ricket? Or a NanoText?"

"I am sorry, Captain. The quantity of Glist here is very high. My nano-devices are not responding."

Jason took another quick glance back at Ricket, noting that the small Craing looked disoriented. He definitely was being impacted physically by all the Glist, which made sense. Over the years, Ricket had steadily increased ever more nano-tech into his physiology, which reminded Jason of someone addicted to plastic surgery. One more nip and tuck—here or there—always justifying their need to have another procedure to correct this or that.

"I don't know what I'm even shooting at!" Mollie said, frustration in her voice.

"Let's hope they don't either," Jason replied, then ceased firing. "Hear that?"

In the distance, he heard the low droning sound of multiple vehicles approaching.

"Shit!" Billy said. "Dune-skippers. Over there! They're moving along that far side of the valley. They get in behind us, flank us, and we're ..."

"Screwed," Rizzo interjected.

Billy crouched low, making his way over to the next crop of trees. He began to fire at four now-visible dune-skippers. Each held two Sahhrain warriors, making steady progress one hundred yards away.

"Dad!"

Jason spun around to see ten warriors moving through the trees, off to his left. *Of course! They want to flank us on that side too*, he thought. Together with Mollie, having actual live targets to concentrate on, he initiated a steady flurry of distortion waves toward their enemy combatants.

"I got one!" Mollie yelled with enthusiasm. "I love this thing!"

In that moment Jason had to smile. Knowing the odds of their surviving were looking less and less promising, he realized how much he'd missed Mollie's presence. Missed his daughter's unique, quirky enthusiasm—for different things, situations, and life in general.

Jason also picked off two Sahhrain. First one and then the other were propelled backward, off their feet, and into some trees, falling lifeless at their trunks. He too was getting more and more familiar with using the Dacci weapon.

"You know what's coming, don't you, Cap?" Rizzo asked.

"Full frontal," Jason said.

"Full frontal?" Mollie repeated quizzically.

"Their dual flanking moves have two purposes—to secure both sides and eventually limit our retreat. They also act as a diversion for when they implement their bigger attack, which will come from the front—full frontal," Rizzo said, giving Mollie a crooked grin.

"Whatever," she said, smiling back at him.

Jason only half-listened to their back-and-forth chatter. He knew it was a good way to relieve some of the tension around them right then—no comms to call in reinforcements; they were highly out-numbered; and their present position was all but invisible to the *Parcical.*

Suddenly he spotted the enemy approaching, an oncoming full-frontal attack. No less than thirty Sahhrain red capes could be seen moving in the distance—periodically becoming visible between the trees. His mind flashed to the Revolutionary War and the British, red-coated soldiers. Red uniforms were stupid back then, and equally stupid for the Sahhrain combatants now.

Although the way things were going, the Sahhrain would probably have the last laugh still.

Once more, Jason fingered the small SuitPac within the folds of his Shadick and again nothing happened.

"Here they come!" Rizzo yelled, moving out from the cover of his tree while steadily firing toward the quickly approaching Sahhrain onslaught.

"Hit the deck! Down, everyone!" Jason yelled, as the small forest lit up all around them. Instinctively, he dove in the direction of Mollie, wanting to protect her from what seemed as close to Armageddon as he'd yet experienced. The trees—all of them —instantly erupted into billowing balls of flame as hundreds of crisscrossing distortion waves passed inches over their heads. The Sahhrain were now moving in from all sides. Mollie curled her body into a ball, her hands covering her head. Jason slithered like a snake across the ground, reaching her and trying to cover her body with his own. He felt the first of the distortion waves hit him squarely in the back, another in the thigh, then another in the arm. The pain was incredible. Mollie too was hit —her screams filled his ears—and he hoped, for her sake, that their end would come fast.

Only partially aware of the muted sounds of more dune-skippers arriving, Jason continued to shield Mollie—attempting to protect her from distortion waves and the burning branches, now raining down from nearby trees. Hot embers ignited the sleeve of his Shadick, and he hastily patted out the flame. This was it ... the end ... the end of everything had come.

The sound was wrong ... not dune-skippers.

Several sets of legs approached, and Jason moved the face of his enhancement shield toward them. He hesitated, recognizing the unique camo patterns worn by the *Parcical*'s Sharks. The blast from powerful multi-guns, simultaneously firing off countless plasma bolts, was one of the most beautiful sounds he'd ever heard. Distant screams from an army in retreat foretold they would survive the day, after all.

Strong arms pulled Jason off Mollie, and he looked into Gunny Orion's smiling face. He didn't know how in hell she could possibly be there—but he was never happier to see anyone in his life. A thought quickly crossed his mind. "Don't kill them all ... we'll need to question some of them."

"Already a step ahead of you. We've got six prisoners, now being held within the city," she said. "You've both been hit. You need an evac to the *Parcical*."

"Later for me."

He looked over at Mollie, slowly getting to her feet. "Later for me too," she said, "although that hurt like—"

"A bitch," Rizzo said, approaching and smiling.

"Cap ... where's Billy?"

Jason saw the concern in Orion's eyes. He looked over to the right, toward the cliffs. "He moved off, to cover our right flank."

Both Jason and Orion hurried off in that direction. "Billy?" Jason called out.

"Dammit, Billy ... where are you?" Orion yelled, her voice tight with concern.

Eventually they emerged from the trees where a crystal-clear stream babbled. Three abandoned dune-skippers, one half-submerged in water, and six dead Sahhrain warriors, implied a recent battle had taken place. Orion walked among the dead, then stopped and looked at Jason. There was pleading in her eyes. Pleading that Billy wouldn't be found there, also dead.

Jason said, "You know as well as I that we don't give up on Billy's ability to survive a battle, even when the odds are stacked against him."

"If he's alive he would have answered us ... our presence is pretty obvious!"

"Just calm down ... we'll find him," Jason said, moving

further downstream, looking for anything—any clue—to where his friend might be. The truth was Gunny was right. If he were alive—conscious—he'd have called out for help.

Up ahead, a toppled tree trunk made a natural bridge over the water. As he approached, he saw two legs—extending from the far side—unmoving.

Orion sprinted past Jason, obviously spotting them as well. Right on her heels, he joined her on the other side. Orion stopped in her tracks and peered down at the man sitting in the water—his back propped up against the tree. His eyes were closed, and his face was blackened to the point he was barely recognizable. Billy's ears were both gone now—instead of just the one.

Orion's hands were covering her mouth, as tears filled her eyes. She turned toward Jason—all hope gone from her face. But upon noting Jason's expression, she looked down again at Billy; his eyes were open, and he was smiling up at her.

"You asshole! What are you doing just sitting there in the water like an idiot? Why didn't you answer us?"

Clearly, Billy had survived a whole lot of distortion wave fire. As awful as Jason felt, enduring his own painful set of injuries, Billy looked to be in far worse shape.

Orion continued to yell down at him when he pointed to an ear—where an ear used to be.

Billy shook his head—confused. "I can't hear a thing ... my ears," he yelled.

"He's totally deaf, Gunny," Jason said, kneeling down in the water next to his friend, and giving him a couple of pats on the shoulder. "See ... both ears are gone."

Orion continued to stare down at Billy, her expression a mixture of anger and relief. Billy, on the other hand, was all smiles, seeing that she was worried about him.

Jason stood. "How did you get down here, Orion?"

"Three shuttles, full of Sharks; Leon and Hanna came down in the *SpaceRunner*." She helped Billy to his feet. His legs went wobbly beneath him, and she placed her shoulder under his arm to support the bulk of his weight.

"But how ... how did you know we needed your help?" he asked, looking at her, confused.

Orion suddenly brightened. "Oh yeah, I got a NanoCom hail from someone you know."

Jason took in a breath and waited. "No! Not Boomer?"

"Uh huh ... she's alive and she's okay, Cap."

Jason felt a tremendous weight suddenly release from his shoulders. He suspected she was still alive, but until then he didn't know for sure. He gave a silent *thank you* to the stars above.

Orion supported Billy, heading back toward the burnt-out trees, where, Jason suspected, one of the shuttles was parked. "Wait, how did Boomer know we were here?" he yelled after her, hurrying to catch up.

Orion and Billy kept walking forward. She said, "You'll have to get the full story from her. Apparently, she saw Mollie *somehow* and that she was in danger. How that happened I have no idea. Boomer said she recognized Mollie's location. That is, here, in Loma City, and that she was under attack."

Jason took that in. Mollie had spoken to him about her and Boomer's growing connection—their shared visions. "That still doesn't explain how you found us."

"It took us a while to track you. Since your comms were out, we had to track you from your last phase-shift location. Actually, it was Leon and Hanna who found this gorge and followed it. Eventually spotting Prince Aqeel's dead body. After that, finding the rest of you was pretty easy. I need to get Billy evaced out of here, Cap. He's unconscious and not looking so good."

Chapter 34

Lord Zintar Shakrim entered the sanctum, immediately feeling the familiar chill. As if the cold itself were a conscious being, it slithered and wrapped around his body, beneath his garments, as though hungrily seeking out what it was not—a thing alive. Zintar waited for his eyes to adjust to the darkness and eventually the soft glow of an amber light above him became visible. The compartment, built to exact specifications, was immense. Miles and miles of open space, right there on his command ship. If it still bothered him that much of the space had been appropriated—he also knew it was far too late. He'd already made a deal with the proverbial devil.

He let his eyes wander, unable to focus on anything in particular. There was nothing around but a heavy, all-pervading, mist—dreadful wet air—as close as possible to approximate the native environment of the god-like being. He detested Rom Dasticon, whose virtual visits had been increasing of late. Zintar had zero illusions—allowing the aberration, that harbinger of evil, into their realm in actual physical form would hardly prove to be inconsequential. Everything would change. Once done, it could not be undone. But the Sahhrain people had come extremely far in only a few years. Zintar could not deny them—their reemergence from seeming near obliteration to where they were now—on the verge of becoming an intergalactic superpower.

As Zintar contemplated the enormity of it all—the mounting influence of the dark being, from a completely separate multiverse realm—he couldn't help but ask the same question one more time: *Am I making a huge mistake?* And the same inevitable answer came back to him: *Am I willing to risk the Sahhrain suffering defeat, again, at the hands of the humans?*

Rom Dasticon's sudden presence crept up on Zintar. He felt foolish, caught off guard, by the disembodied voice, coming from so close behind him. Zintar did not turn, or even make a move. For several moments, he simply stared off into the mist. He would not tremble, or cower down, like he'd seen so many others do in the past—even his own brother.

Rom Dasticon moved—more like floated—into Zintar's line of sight. There—in the moist silence—his hooded form wore a different kind of darkness. He was like an anomaly—a black hole—stealing what little light there was in the huge space; greedily sucking it all into himself.

"And again ... you do not lower down to a knee. Your pride will be your undoing, Lord Zintar Shakrim."

Zintar waited for Dasticon's hooded features to become more visible in the haze. For the virtual eyes to be revealed. Ah ... there they were. Cold, calculating, and utterly ruthless.

"I am at your mercy, My Lord Rom Dasticon."

"I know you are. We have accomplished great things together, you and I. For that reason, I have forgiven your minor transgressions."

Zintar watched the form turn away, as if surveying the surroundings. "And what is the progress of the terraforming, those preparations underway for my home here, within the Dacci System?"

Zintar knew that would be his first question. Dasticon's physical presence required a planet environment similar to this hellish improvised sanctum: dark, cold and wet. The planet, a world dwarfing all others within the planetary system, was located at the farthest reaches of Dacci space. As far as anyone was concerned, it was a dead planet. No one decided to go there purposely, but it was perfect for Dasticon's needs. It only required a few terraforming alterations to match his native environment.

"Moisture levels are nearly sufficient. Temperatures are still too low—very little sunlight reaches all the way down to Caspian."

"Better too cold than too warm," he said. "Now talk to me of the four won effigies. Everything we've done comes back to acquiring all four."

"I have one and the human ... the girl ... holds another. As we speak, the last two are being recovered."

"By the human," Dasticon spat back with contempt.

Zintar was uneasy with the present line of questioning. "Whether it is she or my own agent who recovers the final two effigies matters not. Either way, they are as good as in my possession already." For the first time Zintar saw the outline of a smile form beneath the hood's dark shadow.

"And you savor the moment she no longer serves a purpose —the moment when you can avenge your brother's humiliating defeat. Tell me, how old was the human then? Ten, or eleven, years of life?" Dasticon asked.

Zintar was well aware he was being taunted. "Yes. She will not be underestimated this time."

"Let's hope not, for your sake. Isn't it true your own ancient writings speak of an alien child who joins with the

God-force? That does not bode well for you, Lord Zintar Shakrim."

Zintar did not answer.

"Assure me that it will be done. That the four won effigies are brought together, just as I have instructed, and placed upon a Glist pedestal at the planet's polar axis, on my new world Caspian. And this will happen within five cycles of your sun."

"Five days?" Zintar scoffed. "That was never our agreement. I have no control over when—"

Dasticon interrupted—moving in closer: "Five cycles, or I will make this endeavor of ours far more personal than simply about revenge for your murdered brother. You have a son ... Jarial. Yes?"

"Do not go there, Dasticon. You threaten my son, you threaten me."

"Yes—that is exactly my intent."

In that moment, Zintar's hatred for the dark demi-god elevated to a new level. His fingers balled into tight fists, his teeth were clenched, and his eyes narrowed down to slits. He willed himself not to do something the Sahhrain people would have to pay for—for an eternity. And what could Dasticon do now—this virtual representation, anyway? Albeit even his image seemed powerful—standing there before him—taunting him.

"My new fleet of warships ... I trust they stand at the ready?"

Zintar had been waiting for this question, as well. He inwardly bristled at Dasticon's possessive reference to what was, in reality, the fruits of his own labor—not Dasticon's.

"It is a fleet like none other. More warships than the Allied and the Earth's U.S. fleets combined. Over one million souls— Sahhrain, Blues, and slaves from neighboring systems, not to mention countless numbers of drones—all have contributed to the construction of the many thousands of warships."

Like a deathly reaper, Rom Dasticon pointed a sleeved hand into Zintar's face: "What you do not know is that the fleet has already been detected. That element of surprise you so counted on is gone."

Zintar, of course, did know that, already having gone up against the small, private, vessel from the Sol System. But he'd hoped the ship had since been destroyed or, at the very least, had crashed onto a nearby planet.

"You should attack now, before the Alliance fleets have time to coordinate an attack. It is not, as you must know, a forgone conclusion that even thousands of warships will be able to best the Caldurian technology."

"Caldurian ships are just a fraction of their assets. Most are older Craing vessels, far inferior to what we have constructed. When we attack, it will be a massacre of epic proportions, Rom Dasticon."

"Then you should make your move now."

"We agree that ... your presence here, your influence, will all but guarantee success. Three cycles ... that is all I require to reunite the remaining won effigies; to invoke the bridge between our distant realms." Zintar surprised even himself to be making this argument. He watched as Dasticon's chin rose; a condescending smile appeared on his face, expressing his pleasure at hearing Zintar's near-desperate plea. Zintar had been manipulated and they both knew it.

Without another word Rom Dasticon nodded, silently moving off until his form was lost in the heavy pervading mist.

Zintar abruptly turned and hurried away, needing to put some distance between himself and Rom Dasticon, and this dark place.

He entered the gargantuan warship's bridge, striding over to an elevated section of the compartment, toward an area encircled on three sides by a waist-high railing. From this higher vantage point, he was able to look down on the deck officers, all busy at work. Zintar saw the empty command chair below. Brakken was up ahead, at the railing. His thick, muscular arms crossed over his chest—a stern presence, overseeing the bridge crew below. As Zintar joined him at the railing, his loyal second waited for him to speak first.

"We have three days."

His second took that in, then slowly shook his head. "Perhaps Jarial should make another attempt himself?"

"No ... he nearly got himself killed. Twice, actually. He'll carry those scars, along with the enduring pain, for the rest of his life. I do not believe he would survive another attempt ... one that will undoubtedly fail, again," Zintar said.

"Of course. You are probably right, my Lord. Better let the girl risk her life," Brakken said.

They both looked over to the forward display where a strangely distorted, oblong planet filled the screen. Brakken chuckled. "The human, along with her three Blues accomplices, has reached the surface."

Zintar watched his second-in-command give a mock shudder. "I hate fucking bugs. As much as I detest humans, and the Blues, I do not envy them—what they are about to endure."

Lord Zintar Shakrim's reaction was far different. Although he smiled, along with Brakken, Zintar relished the suffering the young human would soon be enduring. He said, "This is only the beginning of her suffering. The insects first—later, something far worse."

"Lord Shakrim," came a voice from below.

"Yes, go ahead, Deck Officer Tamma." Brakken had answered for Zintar.

"Commander Jarial is now in position on the surface and has installed the various view pods. Do you wish to observe—"

"Yes ... just do it!" Zintar commanded. He quickly moved to the lower section, joined the bridge crew and assumed the command chair. *This should be quite entertaining*, he thought.

Chapter 35

Boomer counted six or so small hovering pods, placed around the perimeter of the obstacle course. *There are probably more,* she surmised. But looking down from their current vantage point, after viewing three distinct—impossible—stages of the course to come, being observed was probably the least of their problems.

They looked over the obstacle course and prepared to begin.

Earlier, when they first reached Draggim, an odd-shaped world, and settled into a high orbit above it, Captain Brith provided them with a far more detailed accounting of what was on the surface. There were trillions upon trillions of life forms, even excluding things smaller than the average earth-sized cat. Draggim was teeming with life: thousands of insectile species, and, he further clarified, abundant cross-over species, too.

Using the scroll as a reference, along with Brith's excellent ancient Dacci translation skills—not to mention the ship's somewhat limited sensor array—they were able to pinpoint the next won effigy's hiding place in less than three hours. The Sahhrain crewmen again secured into the gunship's hold while the ship's course held steady in a medium-level orbit around Draggim.

The team joined hands and phase-shifted together down to the surface. But the sensor arrays hadn't prepared them for what waited there. They'd phase-shifted atop the carcass of *something* really big and very recently dead. It was slippery and mushy beneath their feet, and covered, head to toe, in creepy-crawly bugs. Within seconds their exposed legs, beneath their Tammy Wrap garments, were tickled by scores of minute legs. Only Boomer, who hadn't disengaged her battle suit yet, was spared.

As the bug-biting started, Rogna was the first to scream bloody murder. Soon, Gain and Drom began screaming too, just as loudly. All three frantically danced about and slapped futilely at their legs.

Boomer needed to get them away from there, and fast. "Grab hands!" she yelled. But no one listened to her, totally preoccupied in their own misery. Boomer grabbed ahold of Gain, the closest one. Spotting a ledge, some thirty or forty feet above them, she phase-shifted him away. She repeated the same action twice, until they were all out of reach of the tiny, biting bugs. They continued to slap themselves silly, until they finally realized that employing teamwork instead might be the best antidote. They began picking the bugs off each other's body, one by one. Hysterical, Rogna pulled her Tammy Wrap over her head and stood naked to let the others rid her body of the parasitic little monsters. Within a moment, Gain and Drom stripped too.

"Don't just stand there gawking! Get them off of me!" Drom pleaded, totally devoid of all self-consciousness about his naked-ness. Boomer's face flushed and she quickly averted her eyes from both Gain's and Drom's now exposed privates. She let them deal with each other's insects and turned toward Rogna, who continued to wail and looked ready to hurl herself off the ledge to escape from the pain. Boomer continued to pluck the tiny beetle-like bugs from legs and arms and back and neck. She stopped and held one of them between thumb and forefinger and inspected it. It was definitely a beetle but also looked centipede-like.

"This isn't working," Boomer said. "There's way too many of them!"

"You got any better ideas?" Drom asked, plucking bugs, one after another, off Rogna's small breasts. She screamed and slapped at his hands. "Get away from me!" Streams of blood trickled down her skin from the many bites, her body quickly becoming a bloody mess. Boomer knew the stricken three were in serious trouble.

"Stand away from each other!" Boomer ordered. "Do it … now!"

They did as she asked, continuing to pluck and slap and swear and scream. Boomer started with Rogna, the loudest, most upset, of the threesome. She raised her enhancement shield and, doing her utmost to produce the absolute minimal emanation of distortion waves, began to direct the rays over Rogna's exposed skin. Immediately, the beetles—hundreds of them—snapped and splattered. To Boomer it sounded like popcorn popping. Rogna's skin began to turn from first blue to a reddish color. Where she'd concentrated the distortion waves for too long, small heat blisters appeared on her flesh. *A small price to pay*, Boomer thought, as she steadily moved the face of her shield up and down Rogna's flesh.

"Okay … okay … they're dead! Get away from me with that thing!" Rogna cried out angrily, suddenly conscious of her nakedness. She looked around for her Tammy Wrap. Finding it at her feet, she snapped it energetically into the air, ridding it of the pesky insects, before covering herself.

Boomer was already repeating the same eradication procedure with Gain, who, standing relatively still, was far easier to assist than Rogna. Lastly came Drom, who stoically looked into the distance, his arms raised over his head. Boomer moved her shield over his body in a now-familiar rhythm. Pop pop pop, the tiny beetles exploded, one by one, off his muscular V-shaped back. It was only when he turned around to face her that she hesitated. Boomer inhaled, recognizing that his penis, hanging thick and long, had four little beasties on it. Their eyes met and Boomer gave him a pained smile. "This might hurt ... a tad."

He looked away and shrugged, not saying anything.

Boomer used her shield and eradicated the tiny creatures from Drom's privates. Four more pops, and he flinched with each one. A minute later, after she'd finished him, she directed the shield over her entire combat suit—up and down her legs and torso.

Only after that could Boomer assess their environment. What she'd first considered to be some form of outcropping, on the rock tower they were on, she realized wasn't what she'd figured at all. They were standing atop a three-story, building-sized hive, though she didn't sense it was an active one. Using the toe of her boot, she dug into the substance beneath her feet and saw it was the color of sand—dried and flaky—dead stuff.

Then she noticed the first of the hovering pods. Lowering now from above, a little reflective lens spun around to face her. She reached out for it but it swooped away, keeping her in its sights from a distance. Over the next few minutes, she spotted five other little flying pods.

"You sure you want to be the one to do this, Drom?" Gain asked, looking from him to Boomer. His meaning was clear: Boomer, wearing a combat suit, might be the wiser choice.

Glancing at the three Blues—each with seeping, bloody, stains on their wraps, looking very speckled—Boomer said, "Gain may be right—"

"No, we've already discussed this. I will be retrieving the statue here."

Boomer stood at the ledge and looked down at the area where the ancients had hidden the won effigy. It was impossible from here to know that this was, in fact, an obstacle course; the gunship's sensors had provided an outline of what lay beneath the overgrowth of foliage.

"Someone's been here ... and fairly recently," Drom said, lowering down to one knee. He pointed off to the distance. "Look at the height of the jungle surrounding us, then look at the plant life below us. It's as if someone mowed this area clear. It's grown back some, but it definitely was cleared."

Boomer had to agree. After their recent experience, at the first obstacle course, she could see some similarities in that construction with this one.

Joining Drom on one knee, she took in the landscape around them. Life was everywhere. It felt prehistoric and dangerous here. She had a bad feeling about this place. They needed to acquire the hidden won and get the hell away.

Chapter 36

Boomer phase-shifted Drom down to the beginning of the new obstacle course, some sixty feet from the hive, then rejoined the others, back on the higher perch above—the best vantage point to oversee Drom's progression.

She gazed out at the green and leafy terrain. What surrounded them were tall trees with thick hickory-colored trunks and the kind of black hanging vines you'd expect to see in a Tarzan movie. From this vantage point she could see numerous hive-like structures. They were probably all deserted ... but there was something different about this place that made her uneasy—uncomfortable. Her eyes scanned the course itself and the ancient Dacci's handiwork. Massive, chiseled stone and more of their ornate ironwork. Obviously, someone had recently cleared the vegetation from the course. She briefly wondered if the hidden *won* prize ... perhaps the Palwon, Nordwon, or Lort-won, had already been scavenged. Risking one's life here was one thing ... but risking it for no reward, well that was another.

They had spent close to an hour discussing the course's various obstacles as they went along. The closer they inspected the various challenges, the more convinced they were that it wasn't similar to the Clorvious Noles course like they'd thought earlier.

Boomer did her best to stay optimistic, supportive of Drom, but it was becoming more and more difficult. Maybe she should insist that it be her, not Drom, to tackle the course. She'd learned years earlier that being the person in charge was not a popularity contest. Tough decisions were part of being a leader. As she watched Drom standing alone in the distance—hands on hips—his concentration focused on the first obstacle, she resolved to let things play out as they were. The truth was, he was an amazing athlete. He also was, as he had pointed out to her, better suited to deal with what might be a big part of these challenges—insects.

Drom shook his head, mentally discounting something, as he calculated his moves.

"What's he waiting for?" Rogna asked. "It's getting hot, and I think I heard something."

"We're going to be here a while. Why don't you sit down ... cool your jets?"

Rogna gave Boomer a confused expression, but she eventually sat down, her back resting against the hive. Gain joined Boomer at the ledge. "Have you ever wondered why they went to all this trouble?"

"They?"

"I don't know ... the ancients. Why not just bury those things, the statues, in a deep hole someplace; put an X on a map and be done with it? Why go to all this trouble?"

"I thought of that too," Boomer said. "All I can come up with is they wanted to ensure that the right person, or type of person, retrieved the effigies. Someone they felt worthy of possessing them, or something like that."

"You mean like you," Gain said flatly.

"No! It could be Drom ... or you," Boomer replied.

Gain didn't seem particularly satisfied with her response, but turned, pointing toward Drom, and said, "Look ... he's starting."

Drom stood up on a rock platform ledge in front of a gap, about six feet in front of a series of individual, three-foot-square, rocks—set up to look like a checkerboard—sixteen cut rocks placed in a four-by-four design.

"How does he know which rock to jump to?"

"I don't know," Boomer said.

Drom leapt and landed on a rock in the row closest to him. Immediately he knelt as the rock began to wobble from side to side. Other rocks within the checkerboard series also began to move. First, a rock in the farthest row from Drom completely flipped over—somehow pivoting on a hidden center rod. Then a rock began to spin in the second row, another in the third row. Soon, all the stones were flipping over, then flipping back. There seemed to be no rhyme, or apparent reason, to when they would flip.

Drom glanced up toward Boomer. "Suggestions?" he asked worriedly.

"Jump atop rocks that just flipped over ... they don't seem to spin more than once."

Drom, watching the rock next to him flip over, sidestepped onto it. But moving then onto the next rock changed everything. With a horrendous crack, two rocks turned sideways and smashed together—held still a moment—then flipped again, perfectly fitting back into the checkerboard's overall design.

"Get between two of those rocks and you'll be flattened!" Rogna said. She'd moved to sit on the hive ledge, letting her feet hang over the side.

Drom jumped to another rock and steadied himself, watching for some place to jump to next. "This isn't making any sense!" he said, sounding frustrated.

Suddenly the rock he stood upon upended, along with the one adjacent to it. Ready for it, Drom used his enhancement shield to propel himself into the air as the two rocks crashed together. Momentarily, he stood on their upended sides before jumping across to a rock in the third row.

"Nice move!" Boomer said. She saw a bemused smile appear on Drom's face.

"I think I've got this one figured out, but I'm not real sure what the point is. Definitely don't want to be hopping rock to rock all day."

Again, the rock he was standing upon upended, along with the one next to it. He propelled himself upward, just high enough to avoid his legs getting smashed together.

"That was close," Rogna said.

"Maybe you need to put full weight down on every square ... every stone," Gain suggested.

Drom jumped onto a new square, then onto another. "How would it know which stones I've jumped onto?"

"Your weight. I can see the rocks settle a bit lower, maybe an inch or two, each time you land on one. Somehow, it's tracking your progress."

"I think the rocks are flipping faster now," Rogna said. "And Drom's getting tired ... look how he's huffing and puffing."

"You okay, Drom?" Boomer asked.

He didn't answer. Between stones flipping over, as well as crashing together, Drom was constantly on the move. One miscalculation and he'd be crushed. Boomer refrained from asking further questions so he wouldn't lose concentration.

The shifting rocks were a constant blur of motion. The clashing of stones as they slammed together was so loud Rogna put her hands over her ears. "When is it going to end?"

Boomer and Gain ignored her. Boomer moved nearer to the edge of the hive, mentally prepared to leap down and do something to help Drom. *But, really, what can I do?* He was moving so fast, a strange flow or rhythm to his jumping now. His breathing rate had settled down too. It almost seemed that he was enjoying the life and death aspect of the obstacle. Boomer contemplated whether or not she could have done as well, or even would have survived. She hoped so, but in all honesty, she wasn't sure.

And then the crashing sounds ceased—the stone checkerboard was still once more. Drom staggered and let himself fall onto his back, across two squares in the middle of the obstacle. He covered his face with an arm.

"Two more to go ..."

"Thank you, Rogna, I don't know what I'd do without your help," Drom said, his words muffled behind his arm. He suddenly sat up, took a deep breath, then stood.

Boomer pointed to a spot just ahead of him. "Over there. I think that's a reset wheel."

Drom nodded and took a step, before suddenly flinching and coming to a standstill. One of the hovering pods had lowered down, hanging inches from his face. His face became contorted. In a flash, he offered up a certain Blues finger gesture that Boomer knew was synonymous with flipping it the bird.

As quickly as the pod had arrived it was gone from their sight. Drom made his way toward the far side of the checkerboard, to once again stand on solid rock. He pushed aside several stalks of leafy green plants and found the metal reset wheel. Before turning it, he looked over to the next obstacle, then up at Boomer.

"Any ideas about the next one?"

"Not a clue. Well, other than there are a lot of little holes bored into that large rock slab."

"Holes?"

"Each about the size of my fist. Must be several hundred of them."

Drom nodded, bringing his attention back to the reset wheel. Using both hands, putting his weight behind it, he spun the wheel clockwise until it no longer turned. Boomer heard an audible *clank*, even from her distance away. Apparently, the first obstacle had just reset, and the next was now engaged.

"Want me to—"

He cut her off, furrowed his brow, and shook his head. "Haven't I proven myself yet?"

"You have. I'm impressed," Boomer said.

"Me too," Rogna said. "I thought for sure you were going to die on the last one."

"Why don't you just shut up, Rogna," Gain said, annoyed.

Drom stood at the jump-off point to the next obstacle. He held up a foot and carefully, gently, stepped onto the surface, before slowly adding his full weight. *Nothing.* He then stepped all the way onto the large flat rock and again waited.

"Maybe it's broken. How old is that thing? I bet it's broken," Rogna said.

Drom began to stroll around the surface of the obstacle. "Maybe I didn't reset the wheel correctly. Or maybe she's right. After a few thousand years, maybe these things need a tune-up."

The words had no sooner left his lips than the first metal spike flew up from the slab of rock he stood upon—out from one of the numerous bored-out holes. The sharp spear, about five feet long, vibrated for several seconds, before it descended, back down into its same hole.

"Uh oh," Rogna said.

Drom stood, holding out his palms while carefully scanning the obstacle course around him.

Boomer didn't like what she was seeing at all. Should one of those spikes shoot up where he was standing, he wouldn't have time to move and get out of the way.

Drom took a leery step backward. The sound of metal engaging metal was so fast he didn't have time to move. Another spear—this one directly beneath his right foot—shot up and cleaved his boot heel—practically slicing it in half. Blood poured down as he screamed and reached down to clutch his damaged foot.

As the one spike descended, another shot up.

Chapter 37

Lord Zintar Shakrim leaned forward and watched the display closely, as the young Blues male screamed out —obviously in agony. In his peripheral vision, Zintar noticed Jarial, standing by his side, had looked away from the display in the same moment.

"This brings back ... not so welcome memories, my son?"

Jarial, suddenly self-conscious, refocused his attention again on the events taking place on the surface of Draggim.

"Those pods were an ingenious idea, Jarial," Zintar said.

The pod's viewing perspective now showed a tight close-up of the Blues male—holding on to his leg and writhing in pain— just as a second spike popped up, mere inches from his head. Zintar knew that even watching it was tough on his son, who'd suffered defeat on the same obstacle course, but he needed to get over it. Although, from the accounting Zintar had received, his son experienced seven separate stab wounds. He lost so much blood he was hospitalized for six weeks and would carry scars on his body the rest of his life—as well as endure a lingering amount of pain. Zintar thought about the never-completed hospital on the StarDome station. Supposedly there were advanced Caldurian medical pods there. Perhaps he'd mention this to his son—but a part of him had not forgiven him for his inability to complete the obstacle course.

The injured Blues player, attempting to stand, rose to his hands and knees. As though attuned—somehow knowing it was the absolute best place to inflict damage—another spike shot up, directly below the young man's abdomen. Even Zintar had to momentarily glance away. Looking back, he saw the shaft protruding from the young Blues' gory back. Then, just as quickly, the spike descended back into the spear's hole.

"As much as it pleases me to see a Blues ... any Blues ... suffer, it is not in our best interest for them to fail here," Zintar said.

"The girl will take over. Perhaps she will be more success-ful," Jarial said.

For the hundredth time, Zintar contemplated how he might take possession of the two remaining won effigies and forgo all this drama. "There has to be a better way ..."

"We already spoke about this, Father. There are two remaining *wons*. I've actually seen the won this team is attempting to retrieve. Remember, each course has its own fail-safe contraption—such as a ten-ton stone mounted above the effigy. Any attempt to circumvent these fail-safes and the player is killed ... not to mention the course destroyed. I assure you; the ancients knew what they were doing. If you still want to gather all four effigies, then our current course of action is still best."

There was a bright flash and a human, hidden in a combat suit, appeared next to the young male. Another flash came and they both disappeared, leaving behind an obscene amount of blood.

Brakken's voice, emanating from the lower bridge deck, said, "Lord Shakrim, Fleet Commander Rolm requests your orders."

Zintar nodded and gestured toward the display. A round-faced Sahhrain officer appeared—his narrow forehead and large protruding ears gave him an almost comical appearance. But Commander Rolm was a proficient fleet officer, with many successful campaigns under his belt. He would be directing the attack, which was to be imminent.

"Commander Rolm."

"Lord Shakrim ... you requested an update, just as soon as the fleet was on the move."

Zintar would have preferred to have all four wons in his possession, thereby completing the bridge to Dasticon, but since their fleet assets had recently been discovered, he could not wait and chance losing any element of surprise. They must attack first, and most decisively. He felt the weight of the moment on his shoulders. From here on in, there would be no turning back. Success or failure—the very existence of his people came down to him uttering the following few words:

"Commence the attack on the Sol System."

"Very good, Lord Shakrim. I will not disappoint you, my Lord. The Alliance has grown fat and complacent. Their defeat will be quick and absolute." The display scene changed, back to a view of the bloodied rock.

"Return to Draggim, then head toward ... The Harpaign moon, Almand-CM5 ... you need to find the last location before the others do so you can observe them as we are now. Jarial, contact me immediately when you find it ... I will personally be the one to take the won from the human. I eagerly count the moments until I can crush her head, like a willow-nut, between my palms." Zintar squeezed the heels of his palms together in a dramatic gesture.

Boomer cursed herself for reacting so slowly. She'd wasted precious moments—first speaking to Gain, telling him to wait for her and not attempt to complete the course on his own. By the time she'd then initiated her combat suit and phase-shifted over to Drom, another spike had already driven through his body.

She phase-shifted them back to the Sahhrain gunship, then hurried him into the small medical bay and onto a gurney. A medical autobot was attending to him now, but Boomer knew Drom's injuries were terrible, most likely terminal. What he needed was a MediPod. *Damn! Why didn't I think of that sooner!* She wasn't accustomed to being connected again with space life. She stepped into the passageway and hailed her father. The connection failed. She tried Orion and was instantly rewarded, hearing her voice come across loud and clear.

"Go for Gunny ... go ahead, Boomer."

"Gunny! I need your help! I have an injured ... person. Where are you ... where's the *Parcical*, Orion?" A brief hesitation followed, and Boomer feared they'd lost their NanoCom connection.

"I've spotted you on sensors. We're relatively close, Boomer. We're here in the Dacci system, but well out of phase-shift range for you to use your combat suit. Also, we have numerous injured people on board already, coming up from the surface of Harpaign."

"Mollie! Is Mollie—"

"No. She's fine. And your father's uninjured as well. Billy's hurt ... had both ears blown off."

It must have been the way Orion spoke that caused Boomer to laugh out loud. Nervous tension getting the best of her. "I'm so sorry ..."

"It's OK, Boomer. He's going to be fine."

"I really need help, Orion. Drom ... my friend; he's dying."

"Let me think." Several moments passed before Gunny spoke again. "Okay, your father's personal yacht has a MediPod on board. I think it's been repaired. Maybe I can get Leon to—"

"Repaired? Yacht? Whatever ... yes ... yes, contact Leon! You have my coordinates?" Boomer asked, exasperated.

"I do but it'll take a few minutes. And it will take multiple phase-shifts."

"Please hurry!"

Boomer stepped back into the medical bay and watched as the medical bot frantically moved back around the gurney, which was now saturated with blood.

"Do you even know what you are doing?" she asked.

Although the bot did not respond, Boomer swore she heard it moan. She saw a myriad of medical stats on the lone display; one was registering Drom's heartbeat. The bot began to make noises, appearing to have ceased taking further action, and was now looking at her.

"What ... what did you say?"

The mechanical voice was tinny and sounded ridiculously old-fashioned: "There are insufficient blood supplies on board for this species."

"Can't you synthesize more?" Boomer asked, looking at the slender-looking bot with apparent disdain.

"This vessel is not equipped for advanced medical procedures."

"Just keep him alive. Do whatever's needed to keep his heart beating. Do you understand?"

"The organism has lost too much blood."

"How about a transfusion? I can bring up another Blues ..." She stopped to accept an incoming hail. "Go for Boomer!"

"Boomer, it's Leon. Hanna and I are here. The *Stellar* is right off your starboard side."

Within thirty seconds, Leon had lifted Drom's body off the gurney and had, just as quickly, phase-shifted him away. Boomer moved over to the closest porthole window and saw the sleek space vessel moored alongside the gunship. Worried sick about Drom, she phase-shifted directly over to the craft, into what appeared to be a luxury cabin, with plush leather seating and sectional couches. Unobstructed observation windows, sited on both sides of the compartment, looked out to space. She disengaged her combat suit and spoke aloud. "Hello, anyone?"

Hanna emerged from a forward compartment, which Boomer guessed was the bridge.

"Boomer!" Hanna yelled. She had the same long blonde hair and a bright sunny smile. She ran up to Boomer and wrapped her in her arms. "We've missed you, girl! Your dad and Mollie will be so happy to see you." Hanna released Boomer from her embrace and held her out at arm's length. "Oh my God ... you're all grown up! And so pretty!"

Boomer nodded, a little embarrassed. She hadn't experienced much in the way of personal contact over the past two years. "Where's Medical?"

"Follow me," Hanna said, heading for a DeckPort. This was quite a little ship ... and it was her father's!

They emerged on a lower deck and Hanna half-ran, half-walked toward the stern. Up ahead, Leon was just stepping out from another compartment. Seeing their fast approach, he raised both palms. "Easy now. He's in pretty bad shape. Medi-Pods can only do so much."

Boomer knew exactly what a MediPod could do, having had her own life saved inside one at the age of eight. She entered the small medical compartment and approached the MediPod. Drom was on his back and looked to be sleeping. She studied the holographic display above and noted his heart rate was slow —perhaps too slow?

"Give it time," Leon said behind her. "I think he'll be fine."

Boomer turned around but caught the concern showing on both his and Hanna's faces. "I need to get back to the surface. I must finish the course."

"We can take you. We're not letting you out of our sight, Boomer."

Chapter 38

The *Stellar* no sooner phase-shifted to the surface of Draggim, to a clearing within visual sight of the obstacle course, than Boomer—impatient to get back to the others—phase-shifted to an area directly beneath the stored coordinates on her HUD of the high up hive perch position. She looked up and saw no one on the ledge.

"Rogna? Gain?" she yelled up toward the empty ledge. *Nothing.*

She double-checked her HUD to ensure no one was standing above her—that she wouldn't be displacing their body mass, knocking them off the hive. She phase-shifted.

In an instant, Boomer knew she was alone. Neither Gain nor Rogna were around. Her irritation with them for leaving was about to boil over. She stopped, closed her eyes, and used her *baskile* meditation technique to bring her nerves back under control. Taking several long, deep breaths—completely and totally clearing her mind of all thoughts and emotions—Boomer felt familiar warmth flow through her veins. With her inner self again centered, she could reason clearly.

Use technology at your disposal, she mentally admonished

herself. She'd forgotten to access technological capabilities readily available to her. Her eyes roved down to the row of life-icons at the bottom of her HUD, recognizing Hanna's, Leon's, and Drom's life forms, emanating from the nearby *Stellar*. She could see her own icon, too—standing on the perch—plus two others, relatively close by. Boomer quickly adjusted her HUD menu to provide a more precise level of meta-info, displayed alongside each life icon. Apparently, her suit's internal AI had accurately assigned proper name designations to each—now floating next to the stationary yellow icons.

Boomer stared straight ahead, studying the flaky husk of the tall, building-like, hive. *But what if it wasn't an abandoned hive?* Boomer tried to recall something Rogna had said earlier—something about *hearing* something. She'd been ignored.

Again, as her eyes took in the row of yellow icons, she realized she'd made a wrong assumption—assumed that the HUD's background, a bright red, was just that—the background. But it wasn't. The use of the suit's HUD was coming back to her and she quickly used the zoom feature to spread out a section of the display. What seemed a solid mass of red only moments before now showed a jittering mass of tiny, individual, bright red life-icons, symbolizing *alien* life. Boomer refocused her sight back onto the hive beyond. Mere feet beyond the flaky husk of a wall were thousands of large insects. According to her readings, the two *friendly* yellow life-icons, hidden twenty feet in front of her, were Rogna and Gain. *Oh my God!*

Feeling an almost overwhelming sense of protectiveness, Boomer didn't hesitate; she phase-shifted into the hive. She could see the insects—*how could she not*—when she was so close and personal with too many to count. The blinding flash must have momentarily stunned them, as they seemed to be unconscious. Just enough light was coming in through the hive husk from the outside for her to see. She expected to find big, bumblebee-type insects and was surprised to see a species totally unfamiliar to her. About the size of the average small dog or cat, they were indeed black and yellow striped, and bee-like. But their bodies were a mix, sort of a cross between a sea crab and a lobster. And they had wings: Black-and-yellow-striped lobsters, winged. Boomer avoided looking too close at their equally oversized claw-pinchers. Again, lobster-like, they looked large enough to encircle a human's neck and snip off the head.

Boomer didn't wait to go on the offensive. But her movements were curtailed by the close proximity of the bugs and a gooey, honey-like, substance, and by the husk walls of the hive itself.

Pinchers opened and closed next to Boomer's helmet. The large creatures were coming out of their funk. Before her brain had a chance to process what was happening, the closest lobster-bee attacked. She felt its oversized pinchers on her neck and was certain, if it weren't for her protective combat suit, she'd have already lost her head. Slowly, she raised both wrists and fired from her suit's integrated plasma cannons. The effect was strange. The honey surrounding her immediately crystalized from the intense heat. The lobster-bee was dead, although its pinchers remained attached—still holding firm around her neck. The crystalized honey broke away in sheets, which then turned to dust.

According to Boomer's HUD, her friends were less than eight feet off to her left. The insects had briefly scurried away from her, after firing the bright plasma bolts, but were now moving back, although hesitantly. Again, she fired—this time selectively choosing her targets—only those blocking her advancement forward, toward Rogna and Gain.

Her progression was slow, and it seemed the insects were getting less and less afraid of the repeated plasma bursts. Up ahead, she saw the outlines of two human forms through the blurry, yellowish honey.

She felt something around her left ankle and saw a pair of claw pinchers doing their best to cleave through her suit. Boomer ignored it for the moment, continuing her slow-motion trek toward her friends. She reached Rogna first. Her eyes were open and her mouth agape—as if caught in the midst of a scream. She could see on her HUD life-icon readout that Rogna was alive but in some kind of suspended state. Perhaps that was best. It would be terrible—being awake through this ordeal—waiting for what? Maybe to be eaten later? Or, perhaps even worse, die slowly from starvation?

Methodically, Boomer used her wrist cannons to clear both the insects and honey away from Rogna's body, leaving several inches of the sappy substance around her. She feared clearing it away any closer, as the plasma fire might burn her flesh.

Boomer heard Leon's voice hailing her.

"Go for Boomer. I'm okay. I'm down in the big hive. I found my friends are ... they're like in a suspended animation. Hey, Leon ... is Drom out of the MediPod yet?"

"No, he has serious injuries. It could be several hours still."

"Maybe I should leave these two in here. Until Drom is out."

"I don't think so, Boomer. As the saying goes, the natives are getting restless out here. I don't know what it was like before, but the bugs ... they're all over the place. I suspected those two were in trouble. Best to get them into the *Stellar*."

"Okay. I'm bringing Rogna out first. Where should I bring her?"

"I've just sent you the coordinates to the *Stellar*'s lower-level hold. Bring them both there. Hanna will attend to them the best she can." Leon cut the connection.

In the few moments spent speaking with Leon, the lobster-bees swarmed back in. Ignoring them for the moment, Boomer took Rogna by the arms and rocked her statue-like form, back and forth, until her feet broke free from the hive. Boomer locked into the coordinates sent to her by Leon and phase-shifted them away.

She flashed into the *Stellar*'s hold and immediately felt Rogna's weight in her arms. The honey formed around her body had turned less viscous—almost water-like—and Rogna began to spasm.

"She's suffocating!" Hanna shouted, joining them. "Turn her over on her side ... clear her mouth of that shit!"

Together, they rolled her over and Rogna began to heave up copious amounts of the yellowish liquid. She gasped for air and began to scream.

Boomer and Hanna exchanged a quick glance. Hanna said, "Go! Get the other one. I've got her."

Boomer flashed away.

Boomer shifted back to the same spot she'd left moments before. The lobster-bees, again stunned back into unconsciousness, seemed to have doubled in number. She turned in the direction she'd last seen Gain and found him gone. She checked her life-icon readout and spotted him, all the way down in the bottom of the hive. How they'd moved him there so fast was beyond her.

She phase-shifted, flashing into the lower part of the hive, and realized the environment down there was very different. No more did a thick honey substance envelop her surroundings. There were countless lobster-bees—temporarily immobile from the last phase-shift flash—and she could see them close up in all their disgusting buggy detail.

Gain, lying nearby on the floor of the hive, seemed to be

coming out of some kind of suspended state. Gagging—barf-like drool flowed from his mouth. Boomer's own gag response nearly caused her to throw up too, into her helmet. Gain's arms were positioned above his head. No fewer than eight lobster-bees had their skinny, insect legs wrapped around his arms, as if they had dragged him—carrying him off to a specific place. How she knew that, she didn't know. Perhaps, after years of home-schooling on board *The Lilly,* or even before that, when life on Earth was *normal?* But one fact she knew for sure—all beehives had one thing in common—a queen.

Chapter 39

E merging from the tree line, and seeing the dramatic structure for the first time, Jason, Rizzo, and Mollie, accompanied by thirty-two Sharks, approached Loma City. Two Sahhrain prisoners, hands bound behind their backs, were with them—periodically shoved along at gunpoint.

Mollie was the first to comment on what the others, undoubtedly, were thinking too. "This is amazing! Beautiful! It's like heaven here. Is this where Boomer's been living?"

"I don't know. Truth is, I don't know a hell of a lot about what Boomer's been doing for the last few years," Jason said.

Rizzo instructed the Sharks to split up into three teams— begin clearing the Glist city. The soldiers double-timed their way up a wide formal stairway that was clearly the entrance into the cliff-side city. Rizzo continued to point his multi-gun at both Sahhrain warriors. One of them spat constantly and sniffed from a bloodied nose.

Jason looked up at the glowing bluish structures built into the side of the cliff. An almost Greek influence was strongly evident in the massive pillars and formal-looking geometric shapes. His eyes wandered across hundreds of protruding balconies, of varying sizes, and scanned for signs of life. He saw none.

Still, Jason was hopeful. "You said you'd only just arrived here?" he asked the uninjured Sahhrain.

The prisoner shrugged and Rizzo flipped his multi-gun over, stock forward, ready to strike the prisoner in the face.

Jason held up a hand and raised his brow—as if questioning the Sahhrain warrior—*is this what's going to be necessary?*

He shook his head. "We arrived less than an hour before you ... hadn't even set up a base camp yet."

"Where is everybody? The inhabitants of the city?" Jason asked.

The Sahhrain slowly answered, showing disgust on his face: "They're up there ... somewhere. Hiding in their little domiciles like scared rodents. Another hour and we would have exterminated the lot of them for you."

Jason saw anger on Mollie's face, then relief, hearing that all the locals were probably still alive. A Shark appeared above them, several stories up, and was leaning over a railing. He waved the all-clear signal—which was necessary, since their comms were still not operational there.

It took some time before the local Blues citizenry began to emerge from their hiding places. Even then, Jason and his crew's presence was regarded with mistrust and a certain level of hostility. Standing now in what he surmised was the city's main hall, or perhaps a governmental chamber, Jason—who could see the Blues in his peripheral vision—was looked at with sideways glances. He heard their low murmuring voices. The first of the Blues to finally speak to them seemed far more interested in Mollie than in the rest of them. Jason listened intently to his reply, when Mollie asked him if she looked familiar to him. He was old, severely hunched over, but there was intelligence in his eyes.

"Were you not here before?" he asked her, then, standing somewhat more erect, he looked more closely at her. "No, it was not you. The hair is different ... you are not the same one."

"You speak of my sister, Boomer. Was she here? When?" Mollie asked, trying to keep the excitement from her voice.

His eyes nervously moved back and forth, going from Mollie to Jason.

"It's okay ... you're safe, I promise," Jason said. "We're not here to harm you. We're here to stop the Sahhrain. Tell us about Boomer?"

"Let him be!"

Jason and Mollie spun around to see an attractive older Blues woman approaching. She wore a long flowing Shadick, and almost seemed to glide across the floor. "I am Elder Pauli. You can speak with me."

The old man bowed to her and quickly ambled away. Both Jason and Mollie instinctively bowed their heads to her.

Rizzo raised his weapon—ushering the two prisoners away.

Elder Pauli stared at Mollie, like the old man had done. A small smile crossed her lips. "You are not sisters?"

Mollie's eyes flashed to Jason then back to Elder Pauli. Almost imperceptibly, Mollie shook her head.

The Blues elder raised a hand and placed it alongside Mollie's face. "Oh my dear, you have no idea how important you are. But there again ... how could you know?" A single tear welled up in the elder's eye, overflowed, and escaped down her lined cheek.

Elder Pauli took her hand away, then placed her attention on Jason. "Much is explained now: The inconsistencies of the ancient writings. The almost contradictory aspects of just who the warrior child would be. They didn't have words back then to explain the miracle that created two children from an anomaly —a once in a lifetime convergence of time and space."

"No, my sister Boomer is the only real warrior ... not me," Mollie said. "If anyone's going to save the universe, or whatever, it's her." Mollie looked uncomfortable—even irritated.

Elder Pauli listened to Mollie with an expression that said *bullshit*. Her eyes went from Mollie's face to the enhancement shield on her forearm. Pauli touched it with an extended fingertip—a bemused smile crossed her lips.

"I don't even know how to use the thing. I should probably take it off." Mollie moved to release the straps but stopped when Elder Pauli placed her hand upon hers, shaking her head no.

Jason silently watched the interaction between the two and knew, at some deep level, Mollie would never be the same from this moment on. Somewhere deep inside, he felt sudden sadness pall his consciousness. Mollie, this child, could no longer be kept safe, ignorant, of those years of madness and violence he and Boomer endured. That kind of existence was never intended for Mollie. She was supposed to live a different kind of life: Protected ... spared. What the older Blues priestess was now implying went against everything he wanted for this daughter. *Is that selfish of me?* Jason wondered. *Probably*. But right then—that very instant—all he wanted was for Pauli to stop talking, to shut the hell up and leave things alone.

Jason was slow to realize that Elder Pauli had indeed stopped talking; that she and Mollie were now looking straight at him.

"You think I don't know what this means to you, Jason Reynolds? I do and I am sorry. I know loss and I know obligation. And we both know only you can make the decision that needs to be made here."

Jason continued staring at the blue-skinned woman, into her

kind, empathetic, eyes. In that moment he became all too aware he was also responsible. He'd allowed Mollie to come along. *Why?* She was a sixteen-year-old college student and, most certainly, out of place here. Why on earth then had he permitted her to become part of this venture? Did he, at some unconscious level, recognize that she and Boomer had some kind of destiny to perform together?

"I need to tell you where young Master Tahhrim Dol ... Boomer ... has set off to." The elder's face became serious. "I did not tell her ... when she stood before me, as you do now, that she cannot defeat the Sahhrain leader ... Lord Zintar Shakrim. That too has been written. She will die attempting to do so. It has been foreseen ... I have seen it myself. Again ... I am so very sorry."

Mollie's eyes went wide as she looked from Elder Pauli to Jason.

"You don't know that! You underestimate the girl." Jason was angry now and only wanted to leave this place. He needed to find Boomer.

Elder Pauli pointed an aged finger at Mollie, her voice low and resolute: "But this one ... she can."

Chapter 40

Upon his return to the *Parcical*, Jason was informed by Orion of Boomer's location and current predicament. That Leon and Hanna had taken the *Stellar* and were with her now. Jason couldn't remember when he'd been more distracted. The words of the old woman, as if on perpetual replay, continued to haunt him: *She will die attempting to do so. It has been foreseen ... I have seen it myself.* He tried to convince himself that the old sage's visions weren't written in stone ... when, in fact, they actually had been.

Jason, stepping out from the shower, toweled off and put on a clean spacer jumpsuit uniform. Looking in the mirror, he barely recognized the man looking back at him. His face was tight with stress and dark circles hung beneath his eyes, like old luggage. He hadn't slept and he hadn't eaten—sick with the burden of making decisions that contradicted everything he wanted. He was well aware he was at a tipping point—all too close to falling over an impending precipice. *I need to get a grip.* He was now being hailed.

"Go for Captain. What is it, Gunny?"

"You have an incoming communiqué. It's Admiral Stark."

"Of course, it is. Well, I don't have time for his bullshit—"

"Cap ... you need to take this. It's evident he's rallying the fleet."

"He's an asshole and an idiot. I'll be on the bridge in a few. Tell him he can either wait or I'll contact him later."

"Copy that, Cap." She cut the connection.

He stood there, continuing to study himself in the mirror. He heard another hail coming in: "What!" he blurted out, before realizing who was calling. "I'm sorry, Dira. It's been quite a morning."

"Sounds like it. You have a second ... you know, to talk?"

Jason knew what those words meant. The words seemed innocuous enough, but everyone knew *can we talk* was synonymous with *I'm splitting up with you.* You just don't wish to come right out and, bluntly, say it. In that moment, Jason's chest tightened, and he was even more conscious of the ever-approaching—inevitable—precipice.

"Don't do this now, Dira. Any other time ... but not now."

The silence was loud in his ears. When she finally spoke, her voice was soft and kind. "What is it you thought I was going to say?"

"Something like *goodbye*, I guess."

"Didn't I tell you I'd never say that? Didn't I tell you that my life means nothing without you in it?"

"People say things, Dira. But the truth is, life isn't stagnant. Things change. People change."

"Have you changed, Jason?"

"Me? Yeah, I've changed. But not about you ... not about us."

"So you don't want to say those words to me? Say goodbye?"

"No, I don't! What I want is for you to be here with me ... now. But I know that's imposs ..."

His words caught in his throat. There was movement

behind him, and he saw her reflection in the mirror. *How did she get here ... when?* Concern showed on her beautiful face. She held her arms out and, with an inward wave of her hands, motioned him toward her.

He melted into her arms and buried his head into her neck. She held him tight for what seemed like an hour but was actually brief minutes. She took his face in her hands and kissed him. She continued kissing him until she broke away and said, her voice husky with passion, "Take me to bed, Jason."

"I should talk to Admiral Stark ... he's waiting for me."

She reached a hand down, and he felt her hand on him—grab him.

"Are you sure that's what you want to do right now?"

With her head on his chest, her fingers gently pulling a few errant hairs on his abdomen, she said, "God ... I've missed this."

"Me too. I didn't expect to see you again, to be honest. At least not here, on the *Parcical.*"

She lifted up from him and faced him. She kissed him gently but didn't look him in the eye. "Jason, I can't do this anymore."

He stayed quiet and watched her long lashes flutter. Deep in thought, her brow slightly furrowed. "My life is here. I'm not saying I won't ever go home, because I will. But this is too hard on both of us. When I'm away from you, my life is incomplete. All I do is wonder what you are doing—if you are in danger—if you have given up on me?" Her eyes finally looked up and gazed deeply into his. "Did you notice what I was wearing? Before you ripped my clothes off?"

He shook his head. "I had other things on my mind." He thought about that, then leaned over the edge of the bed to check for himself. Her spacer uniform lay crumpled on the deck.

"You always looked good in uniform. You're back? Not just visiting?"

"Oh I'm back ... definitely back. If that's okay?"

"Yeah ... that's okay!"

Chapter 41

Jason entered the bridge an hour late. No one turned in their seat to look at him, but he knew they probably wanted to.

"Where are we at, Gunny?"

She turned and gestured toward Gordon, sitting at the comms board. "The admiral signed off a half-hour ago. He wasn't happy."

"He'll get over it," Jason said. "What else? How's Billy?"

Orion smiled. "Well, he has a new set of ears. He seems to be fine and is back in the barracks. Said he wanted to run some new drills with the Sharks."

"Boomer?"

"She's still on Draggim. Two of her team members took turns recuperating from injuries within the *Stellar*'s MediPod. According to Hanna, Boomer's inside some kind of insect hive, rescuing a third. I'm staying in close contact, Cap."

"Damn! I need to be there."

"There's more," Orion said, holding up a restraining hand. "The Sahhrain fleet. It's on the move."

"To where?"

"It's still here, within the Dacci system, but they've broken up, formed into three smaller contingents. Looks like two of them are heading out ... will be leaving the system within the hour. The other one has slowed, moving toward the StarDome."

"Any better idea how many ships are involved?"

"The three contingents have around six thousand ships each ..."

Jason reacted to the figure with a look of astonishment.

"Granted, they're not all Vastma-class warships, or even remotely of that same capability. Though there are several hundred of those. Most are smaller cruisers and gunships. It's the sheer quantity ... military might ... that has me concerned."

Jason thought about the three Sahhrain fleet contingents on the move. "Get me Stark."

"Yes, Captain," Seaman Gordon said.

Jason was surprised how quickly the admiral's ruddy face appeared on the overhead display.

"I've been trying to reach you. It is imperative you bring the *Parcical* back to the Sol System at once." Admiral Stark looked angry.

"That's not going to happen. As we discussed, I do not work for you, Admiral Stark."

"No, you do not. You don't work for anyone. You have been relieved of duty. I've already conveyed appropriate orders to the *Parcical's* crew ... that you are to be taken into custody ... and they are to return to Liberty Station at once, under escort."

Jason could see the satisfaction at uttering those words on the admiral's face.

"The last time we spoke, Stark, I warned you of the Sahhrain's fleet buildup. What have you done to prepare the Sol System? Have you readied the U.S. fleet?"

The admiral hesitated and his thick neck had turned a shade of pink. Jason saw that he'd touched on a sore spot with him. Perhaps it was finally dawning on him what a cluster-fuck move it had been to climb into bed with such a duplicitous partner.

Stark snarled, "The only fleet you need to be concerned with is Star Watch. They will be arriving within the Dacci System within minutes to escort the *Parcical* back to Sol space. You are relieved of duty, Mr. Reynolds. I suggest you not resist. Reasonably, you might be allowed to have confinement within your quarters ... if you follow orders."

Jason looked at the middle-aged man, contemplating what it would be like to put a fist into that smug, pretentious, mouth of his. "Have you not looked at the Sahhrain buildup? The immense fleet they've assembled?"

Stark simply stared back at Jason, looking unconcerned. And suddenly Jason realized what was going on. "You knew about the buildup? Of course! You already knew the Sahhrain have become a military superpower."

"Not only do I, and others, know about it, we fully support it. Good news ... you are no longer under investigation for espionage ... for the transfer of top-secret technology. That wasn't you ... as it turns out."

Jason sat back in the command chair. Things were getting stranger and stranger by the minute. "No, General Reynolds was responsible for that," Jason said.

The admiral shrugged noncommittally. "As of 1400 this afternoon, General Brian Reynolds has unanimously been promoted by the Joint Chiefs to fleet Omni. The president stands behind the decision."

"And the transfer of tech to the Sahhrain? That's all been forgiven?"

"As I've stated ... it was a misunderstanding. At this time, it's a moot point."

Jason contemplated what the admiral was saying. How had

he been so daft as to not see this coming? The truth was, the admiral had warned him. His exploits with Star Watch to the far reaches of the galaxy were a slap in the face to the powers-that-be back home. They wanted a commander who remained on station, minding the store—not gallivanting around space. Jason thought he could have it both ways—be the adventurous warship captain and maintain full command of the fleet. He'd also underestimated his brother. For years, he had relegated to Brian minor tasks, promoting him only enough to keep him happy. What Jason never considered was Brian's deep-seated jealousy and resentment toward him. He wondered how long Brian planned what he had going on with the Sahhrain.

"Tell me, Admiral Stark. How long have you known about the Sahhrain fleet? The buildup?"

"Months ... almost a year."

"And their duplicity, attack on the Blues? Fellow members of the Alliance, mind you?"

"Members of the Alliance come and go, you know that. It was strictly a strategic decision on our part."

"Did you know about the attack on Capital City ahead of time?" Jason knew that the implications, regarding his question, were huge. It was common knowledge Boomer was living there. Not to mention Harpaign was not a military threat to anyone. It was, primarily, an archeological hub for the Blues.

"No ... I would not have condoned such an action. I'm sorry for what has happened there."

"Yet, you still believe ... what? That there can be a pact of alliance with the Sahhrain? Are you fucking nuts?"

"It's not your concern anymore. Your brother is a strategic genius. You, more than anyone else, know about the ever-growing interstellar conflicts Star Watch has had to deal with over the last few years. Sol System ... Earth ... has been in jeopardy far too often. The U.S. and Allied forces were often deployed to too many star systems. No! Thanks to General Reynolds, an opportunity has arisen that will more than double our resources. Hell, it will ensure the safety of all mankind. I'm surprised you didn't take advantage of his skill-sets more often in the past."

"Skill-sets? Now that's an interesting way of putting it. Did you know, when I found him eight years ago, he was working for the Craing? Some kind of negotiator, he said, when in truth he was a traitor to his own kind. Apparently, he is a traitor still."

"I'm tiring of this conversation. You are relieved of duty. I'm surprised to see you still sitting in that chair."

"Where is my brother ... General Reynolds, now?"

"That is not your concern."

"I want you to remember the words I speak, Admiral: I do not relinquish my position as fleet Omni. I am giving you a direct order: Take General Reynolds into custody, until I see fit to deal with him properly. You do not take orders from the Joint Chiefs; not even from the president himself; you take orders only from me."

"We'll see about that," Stark retorted back. The feed went black.

Chapter 42

As the lobster-bees began snapping out of their respective funks all around her—long legs twitching and wings fluttering—Boomer noticed their bulbous heads had conspicuously turned away from her. She figured they'd become leery of her presence. Perhaps they had communicated, however lobster-bees did that, the destructiveness of her plasma weapons, which was fine with her. She wasted no time stepping over three bugs and was ready and poised—her wrists raised up and out—to fire. Gain, still retching, looked up and saw her approach.

"Get me out of here," he croaked.

Boomer knelt down and began to unravel spindly long legs from around his arms and upper torso. Like snakes, they pulled away. One of the insects, apparently irritated at being touched, produced a six-inch stinger from its backside. Not having noticed before that they were vested with an added defense system, Boomer thanked her lucky stars she was wearing a combat suit.

Only one long leg to unravel and Gain would be free. She was tempted to phase-shift the two of them out, but didn't like bringing the large insect along. Tentatively, she lifted the tip end of its leg and began to pull it free, noting far more resistance from this lobster-bee.

Boomer felt a tap on her shoulder and looked up to see Gain above her staring, wide-eyed. His mouth opened to speak but words didn't come out—his eyes flicked to something over her shoulder. Slowly she turned her head—at first not fully comprehending what it was she was seeing.

She shouldn't have been surprised. She'd already figured the queen must be lurking around here somewhere. What she didn't expect to see was how different it looked from its much smaller offspring. The queen stood tall—about Boomer's same size—five-feet-something. But the queen had different features, which kept Boomer staring at it in amazement when she should have been taking action. A noise emanated from the queen's head, which clearly, to Boomer, had a zillion eyes, set on two bulbous protrusions atop its disgusting head. Its arms were thick and hairy and, unlike the smaller versions of the insect, the stinger—easily fifteen inches long—was out and throbbing.

Gain huddled behind Boomer. "Get ... us ... out ... of ... here!"

The queen attacked—bowling Boomer over onto her back—as it repeatedly jammed its stinger at her abdomen with ferocious vigor. In a flash, Boomer phase-shifted out of the hive and back to the nearby ledge, the quickest stored HUD location she managed to call up. In the bright sunlight, the queen, who had shifted along with her—was still momentarily affected by the shift and motionless. But Boomer knew she had only moments. Her mind flashed back to Gain, who was still confined back in the hive—with all those other bugs. Concern and guilt and an obligation to help him pulled at her.

She raised her visor and yelled toward the adjacent honeycombed walls, "Hang on, Gain ... I'm coming back—"

She cut her words short. The creature had twitched. Sure enough, it was snapping out of its funk. With the lobster-bee lying across her chest, their heads mere inches from each other, she glanced down. The queen had positioned not one, but two of her giant pincher claws around her torso. She wondered if her combat suit could withstand the forceful power behind those claws or if she'd be snipped in half like scissors snipping through silly putty.

The queen jerked back to consciousness and became instantly frantic. The thrusting of the stinger resumed. Boomer's arms, now also pinned by her long legs, were steadily being driven down into the dried husk of the hive. About to phase-shift again, she felt increasing pressure on her ribcage as the queen steadily began closing its claws. First came an audible alarm, beeping in her helmet, followed by a text warning flashing on her HUD:

WARNING: Combat Suit Failure Imminent!

Snap! Boomer felt the first rib break on her right side, then *snap!* a second rib broke on her left side. In agony, she screamed into her helmet, certain her life was about to end. Just as her consciousness began fading—a blessing, in light of the immeasurable pain consuming her every thought—bright flashes filled her eyes. Miraculously, the head of the queen lobster-bee flared into a ball of fire; then, an instant later, the enormous insect was reduced to a blackened husk, consumed in burning, red-hot embers. Leon and Hanna, donning combat suits and holding multi-guns, stared down at her.

Hanna was speaking, but Boomer's pain was so intense all she wanted to do was sleep, escape the pain.

Gain!

She suddenly remembered Gain was still in the hive with

all those bugs. "Gain ... he's in there ... in the hive," Boomer said weakly, and then she lost consciousness.

Boomer awoke to bluish light, from the tinted glass on the MediPod's clamshell lid, and mentally replayed events within the hive and that huge queen insect. Reluctantly, she looked down at herself, expecting to see bloody indentations on both sides of her torso, where vicious claws had gripped her, but instead saw only her naked body. She tried moving about some and felt no pain. Suddenly self-conscious, she attempted to cover herself with her arms as a face appeared above her—staring down at her.

"Get out of here!" she yelled, embarrassed Drom had seen her naked. "Wait ... get Hanna and go find me something to wear!"

As soon as she was dressed, Gain was ushered in. *At least he's walking*, Boomer thought. Leon helped him into the MediPod and as the clamshell lid began to close, she heard his voice faintly say, "Thank you, Boomer ... fucking bee-things nearly killed me."

"Can I come in now?"

Leon, at the MediPod's interface controls, looked over to Boomer. "He's been pacing out there for an hour. Guess he's got something important to tell you."

"What's so important, Drom?" she asked, embarrassed still about him seeing her naked.

Drom appeared in the hatchway and smiled. "I've got it!"

Boomer finished tying her Shadick and glanced up at him. "Got what?"

"The course ... I've figured it out. I know how to beat it. At least that one obstacle."

"No ... I'm doing it. You were nearly killed, remember?"

"And you were nearly killed by an insect. None of us are infallible. But that doesn't matter now. I've got it and I can beat it. I promise!"

Boomer looked over to Leon. "Are there extra SuitPacs on this ship?"

"Plenty. But if you're handing them out to others, you'll first need to give them basic instructions on how to use the device ... and the battle suit."

There wasn't time to wait for Gain—who was now in the MediPod. They found Rogna sprawled out on the upper level, asleep on one of the soft leather couches. She awoke with a start and grabbed Boomer—pulling her into a hug. "Oh God ... those things! Disgusting ... that shit got in my mouth." She made a gagging expression that made Drom laugh.

Boomer handed them each a SuitPac device. "We've got to go over a few things. This will take a while, and you need to listen to me. Rogna, this is not a toy. I'm serious, so pay attention."

Over the next sixty minutes, with Hanna and Leon interjecting additional tidbits of information, Boomer went over the basics of both the SuitPac device and the battle suit: How to initialize it—on and off; the basics of using the Heads Up Display, and what some of the icons meant; and how to instantly jump across large areas, using the most basic aspects of line-of-sight, phase-shifting, operations. Rogna looked like a deer caught in the headlights—overwhelmed by the abundance of technical information being thrown at her. While Drom asked a distracting number of questions, Rogna hardly asked any. A bad sign. In the end, Boomer gave them sufficient information to potentially save their lives.

Once she felt they were versed well enough in the conceptual side of things, putting the information into actual practice came next... controlling the suit's functionality. Within the next hour, Drom and Rogna were phase-shifting both in and out of the *Stellar*. One time, Rogna phase-shifted too close to Drom, and he was catapulted across the cabin—up against the opposite bulkhead. It was a lesson well learned, and Boomer was glad Rogna could recognize the importance of remaining aware of her surroundings.

"We know how to use the suits ... at least the basics. So can I get out there now and beat that course?" Drom asked.

The truth was, Boomer had no idea how to beat it. She saw how it had nearly killed Drom. It was incredibly dangerous. There didn't seem to be a rhyme or reason to how it worked. But at least he'd have a SuitPac device on him if he ran into trouble. She gave him a tentative nod.

Chapter 43

"You want me to get rid of those viewing droids?" Leon asked, as they watched three descend from above and disperse over the obstacle course.

"No. I have a good idea who's watching us. Better they view us on camera than actually being here," Boomer said.

Knowing now that the nearby hive was dangerous and inhabited, they found the best vantage point possible to watch Drom compete. Leon and Hanna were standing, while Gain, Rogna and Boomer sat, their legs hanging over one of the *Stellar*'s wings.

Drom, upon returning to the starting point of the second course obstacle, began an exercise routine to stretch his legs and arms. He had removed his Shadick and was wearing some kind of skimpy loincloth. She watched as he lunged—one leg stretching forward—his large thigh muscles tensing. He switched legs, repeating the same movement, then stood, reaching his arms over his head, and bent at the waist. His well-defined six-pack rippled beneath his flawless light-blue skin.

"Should I wipe the drool off your chin for you?" Rogna asked.

Boomer scowled at her, then turned back to watch Drom as he leaned down and picked up his enhancement shield and secured it to his arm. He next attached the small metallic SuitPac device to his loincloth. He looked up and gave those watching a smile. Finally, he stepped out onto the large flat rock. If their earlier discussion had been correct, the obstacle would somehow register his weight. He needed to be ready. On his second step out, a spearheaded shaft rocketed up from the far-left corner of the rock. Startled, Drom froze. Moving slowly, he bent his legs and, with his hands out to the side, surveyed his surroundings—ready for action.

Startled, everyone jumped when the next shaft shot up beside him. But Drom was ready for it. He grabbed the shaft firmly in his tightly clenched fist.

Boomer watched as the spear jerked in his fist—trying to pull back into the hole it had emerged from. But he held fast onto the shaft, keeping it extended out. A second shaft shot up—its point piercing his upper thigh with a glancing strike. He yelped but was still able to use his enhancement shield to raise his body up and out, parallel to the rock. He quickly wrapped his leg around the second spear shaft, holding it steady in the crook of his knee, while keeping his body elevated with his shield.

Boomer made a face and Rogna said, "This is ridiculous, he's going to get himself killed." No one disagreed with her. Another shaft shot up, near Drom's head, and he quickly released his grip on the first shaft and grabbed for it. Surprisingly, the first shaft didn't recede but remained extended.

Almost in unison, those perched on the wing said, "Ahh," comprehending now the young Blues' intentions.

Another spear shot up and Drom tried to grab it before it could recede. But, unable to reach it in time, it disappeared back into its hole. Nearly falling, he kicked in additional distortion waves and his body rose back up, seeming to defy gravity. The next shaft shot up, directly behind him, and he flipped in mid-air to grab it—managing to get a firm hold on it with one hand. Rogna clapped and cheered.

It was slow going. Not every attempt to catch a spear was successful, but in time, most of the spear shafts were locked into extended-out positions. Drom soon became proficient determining where the next shaft would shoot out. Even before one appeared, he'd have a hand out, ready to grab it.

All eyes went to the last open hole, on the opposite side of the obstacle. Drom, looking exhausted, still bleeding from the wound on his thigh, quickly maneuvered around between the extended shafts. He propped himself up—placing his feet on one shaft as his hand firmly gripped another one above his head. He used the same maneuver over and over again.

Boomer puffed her cheeks and blew out in amazement. It looked as if he'd practiced that crazy, sideways-walking movement for months—like it was second nature to him. He arrived too late to catch the last shaft but held steady nevertheless—his hand out ready. When it finally clanged up into position, Drom grabbed for it and held on. Ten seconds later, all the spear shafts shook, then descended in unison—disappearing into their respective holes. Drom gratefully fell atop the spear-free rock, totally spent. He'd beaten the obstacle.

Boomer's respect for Drom's capabilities was already high, but now she was blown away. She wanted to phase-shift down to him—hell, she wanted to wrap her arms around him and kiss him.

He was on his feet now and moving toward the next reset wheel. Boomer phase-shifted onto an open area, between the second and third obstacles, and disengaged her combat suit.

Drom abruptly turned—a broad smile on his face—and lifted Boomer up off her feet. He kissed her squarely on the mouth. With his hands firmly on her waist, he held her out and said, "I told you I could do it!" He kissed her again and put her down. He turned, punching the air and excitedly yelling something unintelligible, and continued toward the reset wheel.

Boomer—frozen where she stood—didn't know how to react. She'd never been kissed before. Perhaps a first kiss was an insignificant moment for some people ... like Mollie ... but it wasn't for her. She tried to wipe the silly grin off her face. No way was she going to turn around and let Rogna see her befuddled delight.

She cleared her throat, and said, "You did pretty good."

Halfway through turning the big metal wheel, he asked her, "The obstacle or the kiss?"

"Ha ha ..."

Hidden workings below them clanged into place as the course reset, poised for the third and final challenge.

Loud sounds came of heavy rocks scraping and Boomer moved into position at the next obstacle as Drom joined her. Together, they watched as two automobile-sized rocks separated, leaving an expanded opening that seemed black and bottomless.

"Smell that?" Drom asked.

She nodded with a questioning expression. "What is it?"

"They make a very distinctive odor. Harpaign has the same ... creatures. Only saw one once, fleetingly."

"What? What kind of creature?"

Drom pursed his lips and nodded. "It makes sense. From what I've heard, they can live a thousand years. Longer, even." He looked away from the black void. "I guess it's an insect ... of sorts. They're simply referred to as *rock burrowers*. Their saliva is really putrid stuff. Like an acid, they spray the shit and can burrow right into rocks. As you can imagine, the things are dangerous, but if left alone, they keep to themselves. Oh—one more thing: You never ... ever ... go near their nests. They protect their young. Become over-the-top vicious."

"Are they like those lobster-bees ... that size?"

"No, they're bigger. Much bigger. Listen, you need to stay away from them. One of those things spits on you and you're instantly a puff of pink vapor."

"So what do I do now? Just jump down in there?" Boomer asked, dropping to one knee and peering into the darkness below.

Drom knelt by her side, and she could feel his bare skin against her arm. Their faces turned toward each other, and this time Boomer kissed him. His lips were salty, and his breath was warm and sweet. She opened her eyes and saw him staring back at her. She put a hand on his chest and gently pushed him away "Oh no ... I need to keep a clear head. You need to get out of here. Practice your phase-shifting and go join the others in the *Stellar*. I'll be right there."

He gave her a quick smile. After fiddling with his SuitPac device, he initiated his combat suit. She heard him say, "See you soon," before phase-shifting away.

Boomer brought her attention back to the awaiting third obstacle. A viewing droid lowered itself to within arm's length, holding steady in front of her. She smiled at it and flipped it the bird. The droid hesitated a moment before, surprisingly, descending down into the open void. Whoever was watching wanted a front-row seat to this next challenge. She leaned in closer, seeing the outline of a roughly chiseled-out staircase. It looked similar to the stairway on the second challenge, back on Clorvious Noles. Down there, somewhere below, Boomer was certain she'd find the next won effigy. And, if she were to hazard a guess, it was also the nesting place for God only knew how many *rock burrowers*.

She stood, initiated her own combat suit, and flashed back to the *Stellar*.

Chapter 44

Geneeral Brian Reynolds moved about the captain's quarters of the *Taurus*, one of eleven Master Class Caldurian technology warships, which—along with the *Parcical*, and several smaller support vessels—comprised Star Watch fleet.

Brian padded down the pitch-black passageway, wiping signs of sleep from his eyes. He raised his hands out in front of him—still not completely familiar with the quarters' layout. He'd temporarily displaced Captain Logenes for this impromptu stay on board the *Taurus*. He shuffled into the equally dark kitchenette and came to an abrupt standstill. Something or someone moved, six or seven feet ahead. He tried to hush his own breathing, knowing whatever it might be was there, lurking in the darkness.

"Good morning, General Reynolds ..."

Hearing the mechanical voice, he nearly jumped out of his skin. "Lights! Put the fucking lights on!" he yelled at the ship's ever-present, listening, AI. Placing a palm over his chest, he felt fairly certain he was near to having a heart attack. The lights came on and Dewdrop continued doing what it was doing. The droid picked up the steaming hot mug of coffee and held it out to Brian.

"Your coffee, sir; a blend of Ethiopian Yirgacheffe ... as specified. Black ... no sugar ... no cream."

Brian continued staring at the hovering droid. He'd forgotten the damn thing was on board—that he'd requisitioned it out from long-term storage. It was Boomer's droid. Put away until she would, *someday*, return from her training and reclaim it.

Brian stared at the sleek, high-tech droid, with its pyramid-shaped torso and small triangular head. It had seemed appropriate to requisition this particular droid—make it his own personal valet—since they'd taken the Hopper from him: A reptilian beast of unquestioning loyalty and a substantial friend of his, of sorts. That foul-smelling rhino-warrior killed the Hopper; but, ultimately, it was Brian's brother, Jason, who was responsible, as he was for many other direct, and indirect, aspersions over the years. But all that was about to change—was changing. Brian was now the U.S. fleet Omni. His brother's constant gallivanting off to the far reaches of the galaxy made it easy for Brian to subtly place doubt on his brother's commitment to a job of such significance. No one ever questioned Jason's earlier contributions. Under his and their father's command, the Craing had been defeated and both the Alliance and Earth saved. But that was then, and this was now. The U.S. fleet was larger now and required constant supervision. It was not a part-time position.

Brian had made it a point to stick up for Jason, convincingly act the part of a loyal brother. But he also placed just enough doubt in the minds of the other officers, namely Admiral Stark, as well as the Joint Chiefs and the newly elected president. It had taken him years, but it was all worth it now. Brian, personally, did not wish to harm his brother. That would come from

Jason's own doing—depending on his actions over the next few days or even hours. As far as that miscreant second daughter, Boomer—that abomination from a distortion in time—she would need to die. That was a condition Lord Zintar Shakrim would not budge from. *So be it.*

Brian took the large mug of coffee from Dewdrop and impatiently waved the droid away. He made his way to the ready room and took a seat at the desk. As he sipped the hot brew, he watched as an icon flashed within the suspended 3D display. Taking another sip, he felt the warm liquid's high caffeine content begin ridding the morning fog from his mind. He knew Zintar was impatiently waiting for him to take his communiqué. *Screw him ... he could wait.*

Eventually, he set down the coffee mug and touched the blinking icon with a fingertip. Lord Zintar Shakrim's face filled the virtual screen.

"Lord Shakrim, how good it is to see you this fine morning."

Zintar looked annoyed and made no attempt to hide it. "So, this is the new normal? Missing scheduled video-com meetings? That does not bode well for our newly formed union."

"I apologize, Zintar. But let's proceed ... shall we? I'm sure you are as busy as I am, having so much to do."

Brian saw Zintar flinch at the casual use of his name, without proper inclusion of Lord, his full title preceding it.

"I see you have entered the Dacci System, General."

"Yes, the last of my Star Watch fleet arrived through an interchange wormhole several hours ago. We are now within the Dacci system," Brian said, taking a long sip of coffee.

"And what of our new fleet of warships, Zintar?" Brian purposely used the term *our*, referring to the new Sahhrain fleet. Few within the Alliance knew about their highly secret joint venture; those trillions of dollars had been diverted from the coffers of the U.S. fleet, Earth's holdings, as well as funds controlled by the Alliance's general council. Brian had also taken it upon himself to sell off certain technologies and warehouse items held within some of the Caldurian ships. That action alone generated close to one trillion dollars. It hadn't been difficult for him to garner support amongst important power brokers—several key admirals, the Joint Chiefs, the President of the United States, and numerous Allied heads of state. Who had easily become convinced that a level of subterfuge was necessary to ensure rapid headway—the construction of thousands of next-generation warships and a military alliance—within the Dacci system. The biggest roadblock would have come from the other Reynoldses: Admiral Perry Reynolds, Jason Reynolds, and Ex-United States President Nan Reynolds. None would support their actions. So, they were not told.

What originally started as a Blues partnership had since migrated into one with the Sahhrain instead, determined to be a far more capable partner. They'd *watch* the Alliance's proverbial 'back' in a quadrant of space that was becoming more and more unruly over the past few years. A win-win for both collaborators. Unfortunately, now that the construction efforts were complete, the need for the Blues' cheap labor force was no longer necessary.

Zintar continued, "The joint fleet is on the move. As discussed, it's been separated into three components to handle various, high-tension hot spots within the quadrant. Namely, the recent military build-up of the Craing within their planetary system; second, the continued disruption of shipping lanes by space pirates within the Corian Nez System. The third fleet component is here ... nearly eight thousand warships."

Brian saw a now familiar cruel smile cross Zintar's lips. He knew the discussion was heading into muddy waters. The Blues would be dealt with, but it had to be with a controlled level of force. There could be no more brazen attacks, such as what had occurred on Harpaign. The loss of civilian life there almost jeopardized everything. He did not want to provide an excuse for others' loyalties to sway. His command would endure only as long as everything went according to plan.

Brian held up a hand: "Hold on, Zintar, one moment; I'm being hailed.

"Go for Omni Reynolds."

"Yes, Omni. You wanted to be notified as soon as we were on our final approach to StarDome."

"Very good, Seaman. Bring the fleet to a full stop."

"Aye, sir."

Brian brought his attention back to Lord Shakrim. "We have reached our designated rendezvous point."

"Yes. I watched the arrival of your small fleet on long-range sensors as we spoke."

"So you are already there ... I mean here?" Brian asked, somewhat nervously

Again, the cruel smile returned.

Another hail was coming in: "Yes ... what is it, Captain Logenes?"

Suddenly a klaxon alarm blared. "It's a distress call coming in. Multiple missile locks, sir ... hundreds of them."

"On us? From where?"

"No sir ... they are targeted on the StarDome. The Sahhrain fleet is targeting the StarDome."

Chapter 45

Jason waited for Seaman Jeffery Gordon to answer his damn question. The comms officer had two fingers up to his ear and was listening intently. Brows bunched together—he shook his head: "Captain ... Star Watch Fleet is now here, in the Dacci system."

"Good!"

"Sir ... Apparently StarDome has broadcasted a distress call. They're saying an attack is imminent. Enemy warships are approaching; they've detected a missile lock."

"Missile lock ... by whom?"

"By the Sahhrain, Captain."

"Exactly who were you speaking to?"

"The *Minian* ... my brother, Michael."

Seaman Jeffery Gordon and Seaman Michael Gordon were indeed brothers. They were also identical twins—down to the same mole on their right cheek. It was impossible for Jason to tell them apart, even after seven years. Jeffery was stationed on the *Parcical*, while his twin Michael was presently comms officer on the *Minian*.

Jason hadn't quite gotten over the fact and found it most

unsettling that Star Watch fleet—his fleet—his command, was now in Dacci system without his prior directive. And an imminent attack was planned on StarDome? "Put Captain Perkins on screen," Jason said, getting to his feet. He signaled, getting Sergeant Major Gail Stone's attention, sitting at the helm panel. "How quickly can you get us over to StarDome?"

"Too far for phase-shifting. We'll need to call up an interchange wormhole, Captain," she said.

Captain Perkins' face appeared in a center feed up on the wrap-around display. Jason gestured for Stone to hold off in implementing any orders.

"What the hell's going on, Perkins?"

"We've been ordered into the Dacci System, Captain. I'm sorry, sir ... we're here to appre—"

Jason cut him off, "Apprehend me ... take me into custody. Yes, Admiral Stark has informed that he would be making that order. But hold on ... hold that thought," Jason said, and glanced back to Seaman Gordon. "Two things ... first ... hail Captain Logenes on the *Taurus* and ensure General Reynolds is not on the bridge. Second, I want all Star Watch captains to join in on this conversation."

It took several minutes, but one by one their faces appeared on new feed segments around the wrap-around display. Added to Perkins' feed, the next to appear was Captain Grimes of the *Gemini*, who looked uncomfortable—even worried. Next to appear was Captain Granger, the Caldurian skipper of the *Aquarius*. Next, was Captain McNeil, skipper of the *Virgo*. One by one, eleven Star Watch captains appeared above, on the open video-comms channel. Finally, after the last captain's face appeared, all feeds were visibly on display, three hundred-and-sixty degrees around the *Parcical*'s bridge. Jason slowly turned his head and made eye contact with each officer. More than one shifted some under Jason's scrutiny.

Captain Grimes broke the silence. "Captain ... I just want to say—"

"Hold on, Captain Grimes," Jason said, and turned back to Captain Perkins. Out of the whole lot of those in command, Perkins was his least favorite. But he had been his XO and he'd worked under his father too, ten years earlier. Other than himself, he was the most senior officer there.

"You've come to take me into custody ... is that correct, Captain Perkins?"

"Those are my ... *our* ... orders, Captain Reynolds."

"That's not what I asked you." Jason noticed Perkins was also scanning the faces around him, in his own three-sixty display.

Ricket and Billy entered the bridge behind Jason. "There's no way I was going to miss this, Cap," Billy said—a full-length unlit stogie in his mouth. He then moved close to Orion and leaned back against her console. Ricket continued over to an open panel at the front of the bridge and sat down.

Bristol entered the bridge and hesitated, noting the officers' faces on display around the perimeter of the compartment. "This isn't creepy ... not at all," he smirked.

Jason wasn't surprised by everyone's need to be a part of this event. It was a pivotal moment in their lives, he knew. He noticed Mollie, at some point, had also entered the bridge and was, with arms crossed over her chest, looking back at him. She too looked worried. Jason waited, knowing one more would soon enter the bridge. Ten seconds later, Dira arrived and moved in close, taking a spot right next to him. She defiantly looked around at the video feeds—at the faces of all those she'd served with for so many years.

Apparently, a new line had been drawn in the sand here in the Dacci System. Jason wondered who among them would dare cross over it? And who would stand firm with Admiral

Stark, and with the new fleet Omni—his brother, Brian? The truth was, Jason was tired. Did he still care enough to deal with all the bullshit anymore? Perhaps it was time to leave it behind. Take Dira far away from here—retreat into a quieter life—somewhere. Perhaps it *was* time for someone else to take the lead.

He thought about it a moment but knew for certain that someone could not be Brian. The recent years dedicated to avoiding another war, like the one with the Craing, would be undone in a matter of days. Brian lived for power: certainly, for the overall power of Earth to prevail, but mostly for personal power. Brian would evolve into a conqueror of worlds—of entire interstellar systems—by partnering with Lord Zintar Shakrim, or even worse, Rom Dasticon. *What was he thinking? How could he be so naïve*—trusting those who'd been their dire enemy a mere five years before? He had to completely accept that there was no greater threat to the Alliance—to humanity— than Rom Dasticon. Hell, wasn't Boomer risking her life at this very moment to ensure Dasticon never ... ever ... entered this realm? Jason felt a wave of guilt for even contemplating quitting.

Now StarDome was under threat by the Sahhrain, whose new fleet of advanced warships was commissioned by none other than his brother and supported by Admiral Stark. Jason needed to know which Star Watch men and women officers would have his back—possibly even go to war with him—right here and right now. Yes, most definitely, a line in the sand had been drawn.

Everyone's attention was back on Captain Perkins. "As I started to say, Captain, my orders were clear. To make haste, enter the Dacci System, and implore you to return to the Sol System ... Liberty Station ... accompanied by Star Watch. If you chose not to comply, I was to take decisive action and take you into custody."

"That's fine, Captain Perkins. I now know what your orders were. So, again, what are your intentions?"

"Personally ... I have no intentions of following those orders. I cannot speak for the other officers here, though."

Jason nodded, studying the faces of the other officers up on their respective feeds. Each Star Watch captain was either smiling or nodding, or both. He should not have doubted the loyalty of these fine officers. The relief he was feeling must have shown on his face.

"You had doubts, Captain?" Captain Grimes asked. "After all we've been through together? After what you've sacrificed for every one of us?"

"I didn't want to presume anything. You all have your own careers to consider."

Captain McNeil said, "We're with you, Captain. That also goes for you being the one true Omni of the fleet, as well."

Excitedly, Orion interrupted, "Captain! StarDome has incoming. No less than five hundred high-yield nukes inbound."

Chapter 46

"Look, I understand you wanting to do this yourself," Leon said, "but all I'm asking is that you let me come down there with you. If what your friend ... Drom ... said is true, that those rock burrower things are going to attack, you'll need someone there to give you cover so you can complete the course. Remember, Boomer, I have your father to answer to. Something happens to you and I'm toast."

Boomer only half-listened to Leon ramble on as she made some last-minute setting adjustments to her HUD. Every so often, she glanced down into the black void, where the third obstacle was situated.

"What he's saying makes sense, Boomer," Hanna said. "Let him watch your back."

"Fine. But you'll have to stay off the course itself. Everything is pressure sensitive down there. You add your weight onto a rock that's supposed to hold only one person—like me—then all we've done could be compromised."

"I'm coming, too," Drom said, emerging from the *Stellar*, looking amazingly handsome and self-confident in Boomer's eyes.

"Let me take a look down there first. Get a lay of the land," Boomer said, as she disengaged her battle suit, and Hanna handed her enhancement shield to her. Once it was in place, she gave the group a curt nod. "Here goes nothing!" Like before, she used her shield to produce low-level distortion waves that illuminated the stone steps leading downward.

"Don't forget ... you have NanoCom, Boomer," Leon said, tapping his ear.

She nodded and descended the steps into darkness.

She sensed more than saw movement in front of her. Then she heard the almost imperceptible sounds of tiny motors, actuators, and servos and could see the hovering viewing droid, illuminated in the soft glow of her shield's violet distortion waves. It too was descending, keeping pace with her. Apparently, whoever was watching wanted a close-up view of her face. *Perhaps scanning for signs of fear?* Well, he wasn't going to see any today. She had to remember to ignore the mechanical annoyance—one misstep, or lapse in concentration, and she could become nothing more than a puff of pink mist, as Drom had put it earlier.

The blackness beyond the steps was so absolute she needed to increase the power output of her shield. Suddenly, the subterranean world began to take on form and shape. She was about midway down a long, narrow stairway when, below her, she saw the third obstacle. It seemed almost identical to the ones she'd contended with up above and on Clorvious Noles. Narrower, it was approximately twenty feet wide by two hundred feet long. Various flat rock platforms, of different sizes and shapes, awaited her.

Boomer continued down steps that appeared to lead directly to the start of the course. Now that she was closer to the bottom, she could see that there indeed was sufficient space around the course for the others to stand on.

She hailed Leon. "You and Drom can come down, but no others. Stay off the course and keep quiet."

"Copy that," he said.

As Boomer reached the bottom of the steps, she heard their footfalls coming down from above. She turned and looked around the underground cavern. One could park a 747 here and still have room to spare. What differentiated the space from other caves she'd been in was the glass-like smoothness of the walls. Several feet deep, the translucent rock surface was beautiful, yet disconcerting at the same time. Non-natural, or external, excavating equipment hadn't created this place. Nope, this unique cave was the work of indigenous life forms—the *rock burrowers*. They'd used their acid-like saliva to disintegrate jagged stone, leaving an amazing, heaven-like cathedral in their wake.

Boomer, contemplating the prospect of sudden danger coming from hidden, nearby *rock burrowers*, next reconsidered —in all likelihood, they were long dead. How else had the ancients built the obstacle down here? Certainly, the acid-spitting bugs had to be long gone. She felt some of the tension ease from her shoulders. Then, breathing in the strong, spicy, sweet smell, she wondered, *If the bugs are gone why does it still smell like this here?*

"Looking at the scroll ... I ..."

"I thought you two were going to stay quiet," Boomer said. She then saw that Gain had made his way down the steps and had joined the group. His usual self-confident demeanor was gone. He glanced away when she looked at him. Perhaps the whole lobster-bee ordeal had stolen some of his cheekiness ... She figured he'd get it back ... in time.

Drom shrugged. "I never promised to stay quiet. That was Leon. Anyway, I think I have good news for you. From what I'm understanding, this particular obstacle should be right up your alley."

"Yeah, why's that?" she asked, watching Leon make his way around the perimeter of the obstacle. He was wearing his combat suit and carrying a multi-gun. Drom now was standing close by, only ten feet behind her.

"You see the walls on both sides?"

Boomer nodded, taking in two parallel six-foot-high walls, running along the sides.

"Also, do you see familiar holes, bored into their surface?"

She nodded again. Although this time the holes appeared larger, not symmetrically placed, and there were far fewer of them than on the previous obstacle.

"Why did you say this was right up my alley?"

"Look down. See the small, raised blocks of stone? You only step on those. Landing on anything else will terminate the obstacle, and probably your life."

"But there's only a few of them. The distance between them …"

Another voice pierced the darkness, "Is really, really far."

Boomer spun around, finding Rogna standing next to Drom. Her head was tilted—emphasizing her disbelief in Boomer's ability to succeed. Tempted to send the lot of them back up the steps, she shook it off—using a *baskile* technique, instead—to calm her mind.

With Drom's information, she could make out the obstacle and what was needed from her: a myriad of gymnastics moves— requiring all the skills she'd learned over the past few years.

Boomer let out a long breath and was about to take her first step when she noticed the hovering droid, two hundred feet away. It was slowly circling something—something metallic.

She answered Leon's NanoCom hail: "Go ahead, Leon."

"I'm standing at the end of the course, and I saw you looking down this way. The viewing droid is preoccupied by a statue ... must be one of your won things. Just thought you'd like to know it's here. Oh ... and another thing."

"What's that?"

"Look directly above it."

Boomer raised her eyes upward into the darkness and didn't see anything. Increasing the power level of her shield, the outline of something substantial came into view—a massive, cube-shaped rock, precariously suspended directly over the last third of the course and over the won effigy. The ancients did not chance it—the wrong challenger, or someone incompetent, attempting to complete the course faced certain death. It also occurred to her, if things go bad, that the hanging rock will, most certainly, flatten her before she would be able to activate her combat suit. This course truly presented her a do-or-die challenge.

"Okay I'm starting No more talking. Everyone just remain still." Boomer traced an imaginary path down the course that lay before her. Drom was right about one thing: This challenge did fit perfectly with her skill-set and what she'd been born to do. The first rock block was twenty feet away, off to the right. She opted to cartwheel into the air, using her enhancement shield to elevate her both up and forward. No sooner had she left the ground, spinning legs-over-head, than two ten-foot-long spiked shafts shot out from opposing walls. One missed her legs by inches, the other her head. The cartwheel maneuver had saved her life. Landing upon the small, six-inch-square rock, she wobbled, but still managed to keep her balance.

For the next section, far more holes were visible on the side walls. *Hmm,* she thought, *a simple cartwheel maneuver here won't cut it.* She mentally tried to come up with a different plan —to reach the next elevated stone—thirty feet away and higher up by ten feet or so. No matter how she tried to envision it, she knew she'd surely be *skewered* along the way.

"I know I told you all to be quiet ... but any ideas?" she asked.

No one said anything. Eventually, Drom said, "Sorry, Boomer. Even the scroll doesn't seem to provide us with any clues."

Boomer continued examining her options. As time ticked by, she was becoming less and less confident of her odds of success. That, and the stupid viewing droid kept hovering in her path—darting around erratically.

"Want me to shoot it down?" Leon asked from the darkness. She considered his option but then began to watch it more closely. "It's like it's trying to tell me something."

"Maybe it wants you to jump on it," Rogna said.

"No ... that's not it," Boomer said, sounding distracted.

A smile crossed Boomer's lips. *Would that work?* she thought.

The little droid kept repeating the same movement, over and over again. Boomer turned and found Drom. "Do you see that?"

He shook his head, looking confused. He watched the viewing droid's repetitive movements for another minute and then, also smiling, said, "It wouldn't be easy ... but ... yeah ... it could work."

The little droid moved up and down and then zigzagged from one side of the course to the other, continuing until it reached the end. Three times, spears shot from the walls and clanged off of the droid's metallic surfaces. As if on an endless loop, it circled back and started over from the same position just beyond where Boomer was situated.

Boomer was well aware the viewing droid was, most likely, the property of Lord Zintar Shakrim. That or perhaps the black clad Sahhrain warrior. Based on the family crest she'd seen, there was clearly a family connection between those two. She was almost positive he was Zintar's blood ... maybe his son. But it all still came down to Zintar. Her mind flashed back, to the immense combat-suit-clad warrior on the battlefield dunes of Harpaign. Zintar ... no, *he* was her one true enemy, yet right now he, or that smaller version of himself, seemed to be helping her complete the course. Helping her retrieve the won effigy. And why shouldn't he? It would serve both of their interests to retrieve it from this place. *Or did it?*

"Why not just let the effigy be destroyed?" Rogna asked as if it was the most obvious question in the world. "Let that big stone fall ... flatten the thing."

"I thought of that, too," Drom said. "Remember ... it's made of Glist, an incredibly hard material, so I'm not entirely sure it even could get flattened. Might be difficult to recover, but not beyond the capabilities of someone with the right resources."

"So, it's back to me finishing up here ... either that or die trying," Boomer said.

Rogna said, "Anyone notice that the smell's getting stronger?"

Chapter 47

"Missiles away, Lord Shakrim," Brakken said, excitement evident in his voice. "Three minutes until impact."

Zintar heard him but his attention was not on the missiles, nor on the impending doom of StarDome. Instead, he watched the grouping, close to a dozen warships, converging hundreds of thousands of miles away from there.

He hefted his large frame from the chair and moved to the railing—his eyes never wavering away from the small cluster of ships.

"Zoom in."

The modest-sized fleet, Star Watch, now filled the split-screen display. Those sleek, distinctive-looking, Caldurian designed vessels would soon be under his complete control. The truth was, he'd gladly trade all the warships in his own, newly amassed, fleet for just one of those highly advanced vessels, with their amazing capability to move around the galaxy. The prospect of commanding all twelve ships—including the *Parcical*, the most advanced ship of them all, but missing from this assemblage—had captivated his imagination for years.

Finally, it now seemed, the time had arrived. The convergence of recent events, and his impeccable planning—manipulating and coercing both friend and foe alike—had brought him to this moment.

His success centered around General Reynolds. Once Zintar had him firmly in his grasp—had appealed to the human's weaknesses—namely his greed, not to mention jealousy, of his younger brother, Jason, the puzzle pieces started to come together.

Zintar's one hesitation was still Rom Dasticon. He too was driven by greed and an ever-growing lust for greater power. He thought himself a god. Perhaps he *was* one. But just like the general, Dasticon's emotions would eventually be his undoing. Zintar realized a long time ago that his own destiny was far more than being conqueror of the Dacci System, or the Sol System, or even the Alliance. Lord Zintar Shakrim was going to take Rom Dasticon's place, as the master of realms, and become the most powerful living being in existence. This wasn't ego ... or need for unbridled power ... it was something else entirely. It was destiny.

Zintar watched the right-hand side of the display as the cluster of bright-blue, glowing orbs—high-yield nuclear missiles —progressed toward their target.

"Two minutes to impact, my Lord," Brakken said.

Zintar stifled a yawn. The destruction of the Blues' space station was already a forgone conclusion. He moved on mentally to other pressing issues. His thoughts turned back to Rom Dasticon's relentless pursuit of the four won effigies—the Goldwon, the Palwon, the Nordwon, and the Lortwon. Zintar knew that attaining the four wons wasn't only a means for Dasticon to simply travel between realms, as he had so often exclaimed. Did Dasticon think him so naïve as to believe such nonsense? Zintar had spent the last five years in an almost scholarly pursuit, studying Dacci history. Of course there were the historical tablets, chiseled by the ancients themselves—which had been hand-written onto scrolls—maps—leading to the hidden won effigies. But additionally, he'd commissioned hundreds of archeological digs within Dacci space, but mostly on Harpaign's Capital City, turning up incredible new finds—finds the Blues Council of One and even the self-serving Tahli ministry were not aware of. Sure, much was open to interpretation ... but he was certain that it was the destiny of his people—the Sahhrain and himself—the true master of the realm—to take their rightful place as the guiding force of the galaxy.

"One minute, Lord Shakrim."

Zintar's eyes momentarily flashed to Brakken. *Does he think I can't track time myself?* He quelled an urge to bark off an admonishment. He looked down into the lower section of the bridge and saw a console display providing a logistical representation of his fleet assets: Nearly eight thousand warships were evenly distributed around StarDome and the Star Watch fleet.

Even the Craing's far-reaching influence across the galaxy did not compare to what was, inevitably, about to happen. He'd studied the Craing, too. Conniving, treacherous little bastards whose mistakes he vowed not to repeat when he pushed into distant systems, within multiple realms. Once the Caldurian warships were firmly under his control he'd have no need for Rom Dasticon's help to move between realms. Their existing technology would take care of that. What possession of the four won effigies, he recently discovered, would provide was actually quite simple: Unification of the four wons allowed for the transcendence of time—the ability to come and go—not only into other multiverse realms, but into other timeframes as well. That is what so consumed Dasticon. As powerful as the demi-god was, others—such as Zintar, himself—would always attempt to snatch his power away. But the one who travelled between the constructs of time itself would be impossible to defeat. He'd have the ability to reset the playing field, whenever necessary.

The forward display changed to a new view. Zintar watched as the *Parcical* now approached from deep space. He hadn't anticipated the vessel arriving prior to the destruction of Star-Dome. It could complicate things.

"Hail General Reynolds on the *Taurus!*" Zintar said, retaking his seat but not taking his eyes from the *Parcical*.

"Yes, Lord Shakrim."

Zintar no sooner heard the general's voice than the *Parcical* moved into an intercept position, coming between the Star-Dome and the inbound missiles. An array of weaponry—plasma cannons and rail guns—emerged from hidden compartments around the black hull and began firing all at once.

One by one, the glowing blue orbs faded from view—their missiles' trajectories cut short.

General Brian Reynolds' face appeared, looking sleepy eyed on the split-screen display. He was wearing what appeared to be nighttime clothes—a bathrobe?

Lord Zintar's voice echoed loudly around the bridge: "Destroy the *Parcical*! Do you hear me, General? I want your Star Watch fleet to engage the *Parcical* and destroy her—now!"

"That was not our agreement. There are Alliance personnel on board. Humans ... innocent Blues ... even Sahhrain—"

Zintar cut him off, "Isn't there a human phrase, *you've made your bed ... now lie in it?* You wanted power, command of the most powerful fleet in history? Well, this is the price you pay. Be wary I don't order a command for the destruction of Earth. Now bring Star Watch fleet into the fight ... destroy the *Parcical* and do so now!"

Brian stared back at Zintar's distorted features. His eyes looked crazed, and his over-sized lips were pulled back into a snarl. Brian nodded and cut the connection. *This was not supposed to happen!* He tapped at the input device and soon was looking at a logistical display. In the center was StarDome—thankfully, still in one piece. There were countless red icons, depicting the Sahhrain fleet's multiple thousands of warships, sited around the periphery. Yellow icons represented Star Watch and his own vessel, the *Taurus*. Lastly, he found the *Parcical*, designated as a red icon *enemy*. Brian's eyes stayed fixed on that singular icon and he froze. *Could he really do it, now that the time had come?* Could he give the order that would end the lives of all those on board the *Parcical*, perhaps hundreds? Could he really give the order that would end his brother's life? Was he that person? That monster?

He hailed the bridge.

"Yes, Omni Reynolds."

"Captain Logenes ... rally the fleet. Destroy the *Parcical*. I repeat, destroy the *Parcical*!"

Brian watched the ship captain's face and was taken aback by his apparent calm demeanor. *Was the man an idiot?* He'd just been given an order to destroy an Allied vessel. Undoubtedly, he had comrades ... friends ... on board the *Parcical*. He should be outraged. Expected to comply with the order, there should be protest or anger.

"About that, General. A meeting was held between Star Watch captains while you slept. Captain ... Omni ... Jason Reynolds also attended the meeting."

"Why wasn't I informed? Rousted from my bed!"

"We're siding with the *Parcical*. And with Omni Reynolds—true captain of Star Watch. You should be hearing someone at your hatch momentarily. You're to be taken into custody and held until the Omni can deal with you, firsthand."

The Star Watch fleet did not move from its current position. Attempts to hail General Reynolds failed and Zintar's heart sank in his chest. He had anticipated the possibility—old loyalties to Captain Reynolds might prevail within the fleet—but still, it was a setback. He only needed one Caldurian vessel to be left intact; maybe there would be several. Eight thousand warships were more than capable of bringing down one tiny fleet.

Lord Zintar Shakrim sat back and, without thought, pounded a heavy fist down onto his armrest, which crushed under the assault and tilted down at an odd angle. The bridge went quiet as all eyes went to him. "It's time ... it's time for war. Commander Brakken, order the fleet to battle stations."

Chapter 48

Mollie awoke to the sound of a wailing klaxon. She knew by its particular alarm cadence that the *Parcical* was now at battle stations. She hurried out of bed and checked the rest of the captain's quarters, finding her father not there. *Of course* ... he'd be on the bridge.

"Mollie ... Mollie ... Mollie—"

She spun, annoyed at hearing the repetitious calling of her name. "Geez! What is it, Teardrop?" Her droid was hurrying toward her from down the corridor.

"I am being hailed."

"Then answer it!"

"It is Dewdrop hailing ... Dewdrop needs assistance."

"What? Boomer's droid? Where is she? Is Dewdrop here?"

"No, Dewdrop is on board the *Taurus*. Dewdrop is currently under attack and needs assistance."

"Attacked by whom? What the hell are you talking about?"

"General Brian Reynolds. He is currently striking Dewdrop with a kitchen appliance."

Mollie stared at Teardrop and wondered if her droid had totally lost it, was in need of some kind of maintenance. Why would Boomer's droid be on the *Taurus* in the first place, and why didn't it defend itself?

As if reading her mind, Teardrop continued, "General Reynolds is using a toaster and smashing it against Dewdrop's head."

"Well, tell it to defend itself! Right now!"

"That is not possible. Droids are programed to ..."

Mollie held up a hand to cut Teardrop off: "I know ... I know. They cannot take action against the one they've been assigned to." She was finding it hard to think straight with the noisy racket overhead. The thought of her uncle harming a droid was ridiculous. He certainly had better things to do than beat up a droid—Boomer's droid. But then again, from the bits and pieces she'd picked up, Uncle Brian had taken over her father's job. *He's the Omni, he'd gotten what he wanted ... so why is he having a ... meltdown?*

"Tell me what's going on with battle stations?"

Mollie listened as Teardrop gave her a rundown of the events that occurred over the past thirty minutes—the missile attack on StarDome; the *Parcical* coming to the space station's defense. And, Teardrop had added, a command by Captain Logenes, ordering the immediate arrest of her uncle. Since the *Taurus* was currently under attack by the Sahhrain fleet, he'd been confined to his quarters instead.

"We're under attack by the Sahhrain fleet? You might have started with that, Teardrop," she said, rushing back into her quarters. Finding her spacer's jumpsuit lying on the deck, she hurriedly put it on. As she passed Teardrop in the corridor, she said, "Stay here!"

Mollie left the captain's quarters, heading toward the nearby entrance to the bridge. Even before she'd reached the open hatchway, she found crewmembers frantically scurrying around. Once inside the bridge she glanced up at the feeds and noted too many enemy warships to count. One of the feeds showed a massive, bulbous-looking nearby warship that seemed to have hundreds of decks. It was like a city in space—many times larger than a fleet dreadnaught, or even a meganaught. Space was ablaze with brightly colored plasma fire. She watched as her father, sitting in the command chair, barked orders at both the helm and Gunny, seated at Tactical.

Orion yelled, "Shields down to seventy-six percent. Incoming barrages from multiple warships!"

Mollie had never seen a space battle like this one—and she'd witnessed plenty. She looked up at the logistical feed—what the *Parcical* was going up against was beyond impossible. So many ships! She found a cluster of yellow *friendly* icons, with the icon-tag Star Watch labeled above it. She squinted her eyes to better read the small print and found the *Taurus* was indeed among them.

She took a step forward, needing but a moment of her father's time, or maybe just a few seconds. She caught Orion's eye—her accompanying serious expression and the quick shaking of her head informed Mollie that *now's the absolute worst time to bother him*.

She backed out from the bridge and returned to the captain's quarters. Teardrop was waiting for her.

"What's the status of Dewdrop?"

"Dewdrop has taken on substantial damage. Several key internal systems have gone off-line. I have instructed Dewdrop to phase-shift away."

"That won't work ... also against its programming." Mollie tried to come up with an alternative when an idea suddenly came to her—sometimes the simplest solution is the best solution. She directly hailed her uncle.

"What! What do *you* want?"

"Uncle Brian? Are you ... okay?"

310

"Don't you dare hail me, you little bitch. Who do you think you are? Have you forgotten I am the Omni of the U.S. Fleet? That I have important duties?" The NanoCom connection went dead.

It was clear Uncle Brian had totally lost it. All she'd done was infuriate him even more. She glanced over to Teardrop, who seemed miserable. Was it possible the droid was actually worried? Feeling an emotion? Yes. Mollie was certain that over the years both droids had somehow evolved. Nobody would probably believe her, but the two droids were far more than servos and memory packs. *So how do I rescue Dewdrop during a horrific space battle?* She had no idea. She also had no idea why it had become so important to her. Since, truth be told, it was only a droid. *But it was Boomer's droid.* With that realization, she had to do something. She hailed Rizzo.

"A bit busy right now, goofball."

"I need your help."

"Uh huh ... well, it'll have to wait. I have a team of Sharks ready to phase-shift onto an enemy ship ..."

"Fine! I'll go by myself."

"What are you talking about?" he asked, barking off orders to someone near him.

"I'm phase-shifting into the *Taurus.* To save Dewdrop. I just thought you might want to know that."

"Where ..."

"It's on the *Taurus,* our own ship, right? Five minutes and we'll be back here."

Mollie waited for a reply and nearly jumped out of her skin when Rizzo, wearing a combat suit, flashed into view, five feet away.

"I'll give you three minutes. This is crazy and your father would f-ing kill me."

"Oh, stop whining. He'll probably be glad you finally grew a pair ... took a little initiative, for once."

His expression told her she'd probably gone too far with that last comment. Their flirty banter had elevated over the past few days. She'd have to watch herself.

"Where are we going?" he asked, in a less than friendly voice.

"Captain's quarters on the *Taurus*. Can we go, already?" She looked at him expectantly. She didn't remember how to set the phase-shift coordinates or she'd have gone by herself. She found her dangling SuitPac device and initiated her combat suit.

Mollie watched as Rizzo spent a moment with his HUD settings. He nodded at her, and together, they phase-shifted away.

In a flash, they found themselves standing in a nearly identical spot within the captain's quarters of the *Taurus*. Mollie flinched, hearing a cacophony of loud metallic bangs and clatters. She ran into the kitchenette and found Dewdrop huddled on the floor. Her Uncle Brian, holding a dented, four-slice toaster over his head, slammed the appliance down onto the droid's exposed back. He screamed something unintelligible and raised the toaster up for another blow.

Mollie leapt, grabbing Brian's extended arm before he could strike the droid again.

His eyes widened in surprise, seeing Mollie's face behind her visor. "Boomer! You bitch! You ... you ... unnatural spawn from hell! I'll kill you ... just as I killed your fucking droid!"

"I'm not Boomer! I'm Mollie!"

Brian, crazed with hatred and venom, struggled and jerked his arm free. He raised the toaster up and smacked it across the side of Mollie's helmet. Although the impact didn't physically hurt, she was hurt emotionally. She loved her uncle; never thought he'd be capable of hitting her. Not ever! For a moment she saw realization of what he'd done in his own eyes. The regret. But Rizzo by then was upon him. One punch to his face was all it took, and Uncle Brian was out cold, falling limply to the deck.

The ship jolted—once, twice, three times—and both Rizzo and Mollie were thrown to the deck. The *Taurus* had taken multiple direct hits. Flashing red lights joined the loud alarm klaxon.

"*Taurus*'s shields are down!" Rizzo said, two fingers up to an ear—a habit all crewmembers, having internal nano-devices, suffered from. "The bridge is gone ... this ship is a goner."

A hail was coming in on her own NanoCom ... *shit* ... "Go for ..."

"What the hell are you doing over there?" her father screamed so loudly in her ear she cringed.

"Uncle Brian ... he was killing Dewdrop." The words even sounded lame to her. She could imagine how stupid they must sound to her father.

"Quiet, Mollie! I'll deal with that later. Now that you're there, you and Casanova can help evacuate the crew. Damn it all!"

Chapter 49

Boomer was aware of the suspended, gargantuan-sized, overhead rock more than ever. She wished it hadn't been brought to her attention.

"You can do this," Drom said.

Boomer didn't reply, focusing her attention fully on the course ahead and the distant, protruding rock pedestal she needed to land on, while dodging multiple spears. The viewing droid had given her the most viable course of action. It had even spun and tilted, mimicking what Boomer's gymnastics needed to look like. It could also be deceiving her—sending her instead to an early death. But she didn't think that was the case. Again, it was in the best interest of all to have the wons retrieved.

"Hey ... don't overthink this. From what I know about you, that's not how you've succeeded in the past."

Drom was right. She was trying to hedge her bets with strategy when she was more a "fly by the seat of her pants" type person.

"It really smells in here."

"Can someone shut her up?" Boomer asked. "I'm trying to concentrate."

"Be quiet, Rogna," Drom said.

The truth was, she'd noticed it too. The heavy smell had become overwhelming. It wasn't that the odor was utterly horrible, for it was not—in fact it was sweet and spicy—like cinnamon.

"Hold on, Boomer," Leon said, emerging from the darkness. "I've got life-form movement now showing on my HUD."

That was all she needed to hear. Boomer leapt, because something inside her told her it was now or never. The growing smell, the hanging stone, and impossible course—if she waited even one more instant, she'd never go. She'd never acquire the next won effigy—hell, she'd probably be dead.

She used her shield to propel herself up high—higher than the two parallel walls—and held there for three seconds, just like the droid had done. She saw a blur of movement beneath her. No less than ten metal spear shafts shot out from the sides of both walls. She didn't need to look at them to know there would be zero room for a body, albeit even her small one, between them.

Boomer flipped forward, letting her body free-fall down to near the rocky bottom of the course. Flattening herself, her hands outstretched before her like superman, she came to an abrupt stop then groaned under the strain. Although distortion waves kept her elevated, the position placed an ungodly strain on her arm and shoulder, keeping the rest of her body parallel above the ground. More spears crossed above her, one nicking her lower right calf. She wobbled and nearly lost her concentration.

"Go now!" Drom yelled, back at the start of the course.

She reached up her free arm, the one not holding her enhancement shield, and found a shaft. Grabbing it, she used it to lift herself up, then used the other shafts, like rungs of a ladder, to climb to the top-most shaft. Even now with both walls, and positioned within the last third of the course, she stood directly beneath the big rock.

Boomer mentally replayed the droid's frenetic movements when it too reached this spot. Here would be the most difficult stretch—no way to avoid getting hit with one or more spears. The best she could do, just like the droid had done, was ensure that it was only a glancing blow. The droid had taken two hits, leaving visible gouges in its metallic plating, but helping to propel it forward.

The spear beneath her wobbled. No ... the very ground around her was shaking.

"We've got company!" Leon yelled. She heard Rogna scream and the *thump thump thump* of plasma fire. Boomer stepped off from the shaft, half-turned, and saw a spear shoot toward her head. She brought her shield up in the nick of time, letting the spear hit the face of the shield at an angle, giving it a mere glancing blow. Immediately, she flipped backwards, and brought her legs in tight, forming her body into a tight ball. Two shafts shot out simultaneously—both razor sharp points meeting together—and, once again, they glanced off the face of her shield. She unfolded her body and, ushering forth distortion waves as powerful as she could muster in the opposite direction, came to a hovering stop.

She was mere feet from the end of the course. She'd made it! There, sitting atop a pedestal made of Glist, softly glowing, was the won effigy. Relief flowed through her entire being.

More screams filled the cavern as plasma fire erupted out from other positions. And distortion waves ... Drom was using his enhancement shield. Then she saw it: Its huge ugly insectile head had risen above the wall to her right and was looking directly at her. But Boomer wasn't looking into the beast's eyes— her attention was drawn to the flailing, frantic young Blues, seen hanging halfway out between large brown teeth.

Gain screamed, "Boomer!" She watched in horror as his body was released—more like flipped up into the air. In the blink of an eye, like a dragon's breath, the beast spat out something. Only a pink cloud—a gooey, disgustingly heavy mist remained. Gain was gone.

Still hovering in the air above the course, Boomer instinctively turned her face away, as an acid-like splatter made contact with the skin on her upper back and neck. She shrieked in agony and fell forward. Her movement triggered the next set of spears to release, and she felt the first one enter her upper chest as a second one split open her upper left thigh. She hung suspended, four feet above the obstacle's stone floor.

Less than a light-year away, also within the Dacci System, Mollie stopped in her tracks and gasped. She brought a hand to her chest and fell to her knees, feeling such terrible pain. Tears flowed freely down her cheeks. "Uhhh!" Then she saw Boomer and cried out, "Oh, God ... Boomer ... what have they done to you?"

Mollie was suddenly aware again of her surroundings—of flashing lights and loud, constantly blaring klaxon alarms—within the main corridor on Deck Five. Dozens of crewmembers were rushing by her on both sides. Several turned back to look at her but kept on running. She knew the *Taurus* was ready to blow. The ship's antimatter containment field, located within Engineering, had been breached. They had mere minutes, if that, to get out.

She felt a hand on her back and saw Rizzo, crouched down next to her, holding Dewdrop's limp form in his other arm. "What's wrong with you? We've got to go ... like right now!"

He juggled the droid, pulling her up to her feet. "The shuttles are filled. We'll have to phase-shift back to the—"

"No!"

"What do you mean no?"

"Boomer ... we have to get to Boomer."

"We don't even know where she is. Absolutely not, I'm getting you back to the *Parcical*."

"She's dying. Right this minute, she's dying, Rizzo."

Rizzo continued to stare at her. Then, as if he'd come to some sort of decision, he phase-shifted them both away.

Mollie was angry, furious when they flashed back into the *Parcical*. Then she recognized the ship's distinctive flight bay. *Flight bay?*

As Rizzo let Dewdrop fall to the deck, Mollie reached out for it.

"Leave the fucking droid!" He pulled her by the arm and together they ran toward a grouping of fighters. "Up!" he yelled, when they reached a dark-red, two-man craft.

"This is my dad's ... *Pacesetter*."

"He's already going to kill me. May as well make it count," Rizzo said, climbing the inset ladder rungs. By the time he was seated in the cockpit section behind Mollie, she had already initiated the fighter's pre-flight operation. The drive roared to life and virtual HUDs popped into view.

Mollie looked through the canopy and saw other fighters, also pilotless fighter drones, blocking both flight bay entrances.

"Screw this!" Rizzo said. With a few settings changes he phase-shifted the *Pacesetter* out into open space.

She knew only enough about piloting a fighter to be dangerous, mostly bits and pieces picked up here and there, that she'd learned as a kid when on flying trips with her father. Still, part of her wanted to have the controls in her hands. It was her connection to Boomer.

Rizzo fired up the drive. "Sit back and enjoy the ride," he said.

Blowing past three enemy gunships, Rizzo dodged left to avoid what looked like a large section of ship wreckage.

"You know where we're supposed to be going?" Rizzo asked, behind her.

"I do. I don't know how I know, but ... I somehow do. A planet called Draggim."

"Hang on then ... this is going to be a wild ride," Rizzo said.

Chapter 50

"Captain, three Vastma-class warships have joined the fight against the *Scorpio*," Orion said.

Jason, standing next to Seaman Gordon at his comms console, was engaged in a yelling match. Gordon and Jason, each holding two fingers to his ear, were participating in individual, heated conversations.

"Listen to me, Stark. If you have any hope of saving your career, or not being locked in the brig for the rest of your pathetic life, I suggest you shut up and do exactly what I say."

Gordon said, "No ... the captain specifically requests fleet groups seven, eight, thirteen and twenty-one. He's speaking to Admiral Stark now. The orders will ... No, the general is no longer fleet Omni ..."

Jason's eyes flashed from the logistical feed above them to the actual visual battle going on around them. The flashes of bright, colorful plasma bolts would appear beautiful to anyone not aware of the horrific death toll currently taking place. The *Parcical* shook violently. Jason stole a glance toward Sergeant Major Gail Stone, stationed at the helm: "Phase-shift us out of here!" he barked.

"That's all we've been doing, Cap. We're all phase-shifted out. Need thirty minutes' time to *regenerate*," she answered unapologetically back.

Jason's eyes turned back to the logistical display, and he zeroed in on the *Scorpio*. Things had changed since Gunny's last update. There were now four Vastma-class warships combatting the *Scorpio*. *Shit!*

A voice kept droning on, over his NanoCom. The words 'Star Watch' brought him back to his still ongoing conversation with Admiral Stark. "Say that again!"

"I said, until I receive confirmation from the general himself ..."

Jason cut him off. "Shut up ... just shut the hell up!" He turned toward Orion. "Where's my brother being held?"

"He's here ... in our brig."

"Find Billy. Have him enter the general's confinement cell. Have him convince Brian to transfer his Omni command back over to me and I don't care what he has to do to get it. Brian needs to be on the horn to Stark within seconds. You understand what I'm saying?"

Orion turned toward her board. Ten seconds later, she nodded back to Jason. "He's on it."

Jason, seeing Bristol enter the bridge, asked him, "What can you do to get the phase-shift synthesizer back online?"

"Other than change the laws of physics ... not much," Bristol said.

Ricket joined Bristol's side. They glanced at each other and Bristol said, "We have a few ideas. One in particular."

"Go on."

The *Parcical* shook. "Shields down to thirty percent," Orion said.

"Our first idea, instead of going toe to toe ... battling ... the

Sahhrain in open space, we start bringing the enemy ships directly into the *Parcical*'s MicroVault."

"That's an excellent idea!"

"No ... it actually isn't. Those Vastma-class warships are immense. We may be able to bring one of those fuckers into the vault, but all our power reserves would be eaten up in the process," Bristol said.

"She's being boarded. Crew on the *Scorpio* are abandoning ship, Cap," Orion said, high stress evident in her voice.

"Tell the skipper he must ensure his vessel doesn't fall into the enemy's hands. At all costs."

Jason felt the weight of those words as he turned back to Bristol and Ricket. "Say what your second idea is then ... do so quickly."

Ricket answered, "Use the *Parcical*'s MicroVault projector to move certain organisms from the vault directly into the enemy ships."

Jason tried to fully concentrate on what Ricket suggested, but his connection with Admiral Stark was still open. He heard the Admiral's voice, as though he were speaking to someone else.

Bristol continued saying, "There's some particularly unpleasant species in the vault, of course miniaturized right now, Captain. But once projected to their full-size ... they're ones that will rampage throughout those Sahhrain ships, killing everything they come into contact with.

Admiral Stark was pleading, with whomever he was speaking to, presumably Brian, to reconsider his orders. "You can't give in to them. Of course, I will ... it's just ... Yes, Omni, I mean, General ... Reynolds. I will speak to Captain Reynolds."

An intense flash filled the bridge and, just as quickly, was gone. "The *Scorpio* exploded," Orion said, her voice just above a whisper. The bridge went quiet.

Jason brought his full attention back to Bristol and Ricket. "We're at war. A war that might last for years, and one we're already losing. So do it ... unleash the scourge of the galaxy into those damn ships. And I don't care which vile beasts you unleash, do you understand?"

"Oh God ... oh no ..."

Jason, instantly uneasy about the dread in her voice, looked over to Orion and saw she was looking up toward the display—an expression of horror on her face.

Her eyes met his. "Cap ... new incoming ... toward StarDome."

Jason followed her previous gaze toward the now center display feed. The space station, StarDome, a gleaming white embodiment of modern engineering along with provocative Dacci design elements that made this station not only functionally beyond anything within the sector, but beautiful as well.

Jason leaned forward on his toes as the faint blur of something blue came into view. The blur soon turned into individual, glimmering, pinpoints of light. Thousands of them.

"Nukes?" he asked.

She nodded, then, snapping out of her momentary paralysis, said, "Over a hundred Vastma-Class vessels unleashed a torrent of warheads ... nothing can stop them. Too many."

Jason watched the scene unfold. He swallowed hard, now resigned to the fact that there was nothing to be done. The bridge went quiet to where only sadness filled the space.

The flash filled the bridge, accompanied by a horrendously loud sound of objects hitting against their outside shields. All eyes were on the feed that had once been StarDome—which was now little more than space debris. Jason felt a tightening around his heart. Tens of thousands of lives had just been snuffed out. This was war, and they most definitely were losing.

Lord Zintar Shakrim went back to pacing the upper deck section of the bridge. He watched the battle raging on his forward display. Already, two thousand of his ships had been destroyed. Their Sahhrain losses, although staggering, were still manageable. He expected no less from that advanced little fleet of ships called Star Watch. A part of him was saddened by the ongoing destruction of such amazing technology. Even watching one Caldurian Master Class vessel destroyed was monumental —but seeing two was catastrophic. It was imperative that they boarded, and held, the rest of those ships. But to do that, they'd need Caldurian combat suits. Unlike his own, a gift from General Reynolds himself, they needed the newer ones, endowed with phase-shift capability. They had secured eight of the small devices—called SuitPacs—or something like that. Now, with fifteen amassed totally, mostly recovered from the dead seen floating about in space, Lord Shakrim gave the order to utilize them—infiltrate directly onto the enemy's bridges. But easier said than done. It had taken hours to figure out the Heads-Up Display, and hours more for their scientists to work out how to phase-shift from one location to another. But, in the end, they did succeed. Zintar reveled at the importance of this moment. The moment when the Sahhrain acquired and used Caldurian phase-shift technology.

"We have taken our first ship!" Brakken said, looking up from below. He was beaming. A cheer went up around the command ship's bridge. Zintar returned his second's triumphant stare and nodded.

The humans had waited too long; had allowed their vessel, the one called the *Sagittarius*, to be boarded. They should have immediately self-destructed her. Her captain, over-confident, hadn't anticipated such overwhelming numbers to flash onto his bridge. It wouldn't be long now before the other ships, including the *Parcical*, would also fall. This was a good day. Indeed, a very good day for the Sahhrain.

Chapter 51

Boomer was well aware her left lung had been pierced. She was continuously coughing and spitting up blood, trying to support herself by holding on to the shaft with one hand. Her eyes squeezed tightly shut and her jaw clenched, she was somewhat aware of the loud voices around her, as well as that in her NanoCom—Leon's.

Her mind flashed to Gain—writhing in pain and then, suddenly, vaporized right before her eyes. She hadn't really gotten a good look at the insect beast ... the *rock burrower*. What an odd creature. In the brief glimpse she did have—it looked to be made of rubber. Like a giant toy, made of something artificial —like silicone. Maybe that could explain why it didn't self-destruct from its own vile secretions.

She moved, and when a hot jolt of pain shot through her chest and shoulder, Boomer screamed out. She tried thinking of things, anything, to take her mind off the pain. The voices around her had morphed into a continuous droning.

"You can't remain in that position forever, you know." Who said that? Had she? Boomer opened her eyes and even that seemed to cause more pain. Mere feet in front of her shone the

glowing blue won effigy. She could almost reach out and touch it—grab it—end this misery.

"Boomer!"

Her eyes moved over to the wall and she saw Drom's legs. *Did he climb the wall from the other side?* No, he'd walked along the top edge, back where the course started from. Apparently, the top of the wall was not pressure sensitive, not considered a part of the course. He crouched down and Boomer could see his face. He looked awful, like he was going to do something stupid.

It came out as a croak. "Don't do ... anything," Boomer uttered.

"I have to do something!"

"... Tell me ... about the bugs?"

"Killed two of them but there are more ... a lot more of them, according to Leon. We need to get you out of there now!"

"Wait." She coughed up more blood, suddenly self-conscious how she must look to him. How disgusting she looked. "I'm so close ... I can almost reach it. But this spike through my ..." she couldn't finish the sentence due to a fresh spasm of pain.

"Leon wants to cut the shaft with his plasma weapon. I'll reach in and grab the—"

"No!"

"It's the only way, Boomer," Hanna said from the darkness beyond, her voice coming from farther away.

"The course knows my ... exact ... weight. The rock will fall. We can't ... chance it."

Boomer felt light-headed. She'd lost a lot of blood. But Drom was right—something had to be done and soon, before she completely bled out.

Something moved before her eyes and she tracked its progression until it became stationary, several inches from her face.

Commander Jarial watched Boomer closely on his small cockpit display. His viewing droid was about a foot from her face and Jarial could just make out the light peppering of freckles across her nose and cheeks. She's really quite beautiful, he thought, though he instinctively knew she wouldn't regard herself that way.

It was strange. Only days earlier, he so badly wanted to kill her, desperately seeking to avenge his uncle's death. To destroy the threat—the one chronicled in the ancient writings— inscribed onto rock tablets two millennia ago.

Now he felt a different kind of desperation. *How had that happened?* Jarial continued to watch as light slowly dimmed from the girl's eyes. She was dying. He tried to think of some- thing, *anything*, to save her. But it always came back to that huge, suspended rock. Any weight change and, within an instant, she would be crushed.

He feared those with her would do something stupid, like trying to cut through the shaft while grabbing for the won. But to do that, someone would need to stand on the rock below her, or balance on one of the other extended shafts. Undoubtedly, any added weight would trigger the booby trap.

Jarial considered his options. His small craft was still in orbit around Draggim. Even if he tried to help, he'd be perceived by them as the enemy he was. Saddened, he maneuvered the viewing drone away from Boomer's face.

Boomer realized the only reason she was still alive was due to the internal nanites coursing through her bloodstream—working overtime, to both stem the bleeding and close the ragged hole in her chest. But that was impossible as long as a metal shaft was sticking into her. Mentally, she thanked the teeny, microscopic wonders just the same.

A commotion could be heard, back toward the start of the course. Lots of yelling—but it wasn't hostile. Boomer felt fresh tears form in her eyes before she even knew why. Felt a lump in her throat before comprehending what was happening. A blinding white flash brought her around from her semi-conscious state. Moving her eyes toward the wall, she saw a new set of legs, clad in a combat suit.

Mollie knelt down, then sat on the top edge of the nearby wall. She retracted her visor and looked over at her.

Boomer said, "It's been so ... long. You look pretty, Mollie."

"Thanks ... you look like shit, Boomer."

Boomer laughed and immediately regretted it, the ensuing pain the most intense yet. She coughed out more blood and swore.

"Why is it you're always getting into trouble?"

Boomer didn't answer her, hoping the look in her eye conveyed the right sentiment. By Mollie's smile, it did.

"We need to get you out of here."

"Get away ... the rock ... above ..."

"You haven't seen me in years, and already you're trying to get rid of me?"

Boomer gave her the same look.

"I have an idea. But for this to work ... I'll need your help," Mollie said.

Boomer stayed quiet.

"I'm going to take your place."

"No!"

"Just listen to me."

"No. Too dangerous."

"Sitting under one hundred tons of rock is dangerous!"

"You have a point there," Boomer croaked.

"I'm going to take your place. We are pretty much the same exact weight, give or take a pound or two. You being the heavier one, I'm guessing."

Boomer winced and smiled.

"Here's the plan. First, you'll initiate your SuitPac device. Leon believes it will compensate around the metal shaft, like it does for other things—like enhancement shields worn on the wrist ... or one's clothes. I suggested you simply phase-shift away, but Drom, here ... says we need to get that statue thing at all costs; that you wouldn't consider leaving without it. Is that right?"

"Yup ... Drom's right."

"So, like I said before, I'll take your place."

"How?"

"We phase-shift at the same instant. You out and me in."

Drom said, "Mollie will need to put herself on an adjacent shaft. Perhaps the one next to you."

"Won't work," Boomer said.

"Why?" Drom and Mollie asked at the same time.

Boomer took several moments to answer, speech taking a huge toll on her waning energy. "When I phase-shift ... I'll probably take the shaft with me."

Boomer heard another voice. It was Rizzo, on the opposite wall. She couldn't see him, from her present angle, but it was nice hearing his voice.

"We'll give Mollie a little extra weight ... to compensate."

Boomer thought about that and said, "She already has a little extra weight ... but ... that could work."

"You don't have to do anything. I can control both phase-shifts from my HUD. You just need to tell Mollie what to do once she's there," Rizzo said.

Boomer thought about it. Had they considered the extra weight of their initialized combat suits? She didn't think it was much ... maybe only an added pound, or two, but she wasn't sure how sensitive the course was. Some kind of mechanical, counterbalance workings were going on below. After ages of time, the mechanics could either be more sensitive or less.

Drom said, "Mollie, you just need to reach out and grab the won. But don't put your weight on anything but the shafts ... the spears. And don't touch the pedestal, either."

Boomer listened to Drom's voice—so soothing and confident. She could listen to him all day. She tried to see his face but winced again at the sudden movement. She noticed then there were more holes, forward of the shaft now spearing her. She tried to raise her arm to point at them—but in the process, everything went black.

Mollie watched Boomer's eyes flutter, then close. She'd lost consciousness.

"Probably for the best," Rizzo said. "She must be in a lot of pain."

"You think?" Drom asked.

Mollie, detecting *something* going on between both males earlier, let it go, and asked, "Are we going to do this?"

From a distance, Leon's voice said, "Better make it fast. More bugs are coming. A lot of them."

Mollie looked at Rizzo, sitting on the opposite wall. Even behind his helmet's visor, she noted a trickle of sweat running down his cheek. He was nervous—probably not as confident of success as he'd portrayed he was to Boomer.

Mollie closed her visor and stood on the wall's narrow top surface. Drom handed her a long piece of metal.

"It's an old spear Hanna found on the ground," he said.

She took it, looking down at the now slack body of her sister, Boomer, and the mostly bloody, dripping, Shadick she wore. *She looks so vulnerable.* Mollie nodded toward Rizzo. "Let's do this."

Chapter 52

The flash came and Mollie suddenly felt off-balance. Her feet landed upon the intended shaft, to the right of where Boomer had been, but there was nothing there to grab on to. She swung the spear in her hand in one direction, then swung her other arm in another—moving them up and down like someone walking a tightrope.

"Use your enhancement shield!" Drom yelled.

"I don't know how!" she barked back, barely able to steady herself. Her eyes took in the open space where Boomer had been only moments earlier. She was gone, along with the shaft and a chunk of the wall. There was a significant weight difference now. Mollie glanced up and saw the massive rock above her sway back and forth.

"Don't look at it!" Drom ordered.

"Were you always this bossy with Boomer?"

He shrugged. "Probably."

"Um ... now what?" Mollie realized she wasn't quite close enough to reach the statue.

"Maybe just jump forward, and grab it," Rizzo said.

"It's not a time to guess. One misjudgment and she—all of us ... die," Drom said.

Mollie contemplated Rizzo's idea. Suppose she did miss grabbing the statue? It looked like the pedestal was within the confines of the course. If she landed on the pressure sensitive rock below, that would be the end. She shook her head, following the course's path back in the opposite direction. There, countless spears jutted up across the obstacle course. How in the world had Boomer made it this far? She was amazing.

"Concentrate!"

She looked at Drom. The guy was really starting to annoy her, but he was right. Mollie looked again at the statue-thing everyone called a won. What a stupid name. Her balance teetered and she used the spear to re-balance herself. *Hey, that's it!*

"I think I can use the spear to lift the won off the pedestal. There's an opening ... like a gap where the wings of the statue are connected."

No one said anything.

She looked at the statue. It was beautiful, like an angel, or something with long wings.

"I don't know if that little gap is big enough," Rizzo said.

"It'll have to be."

Again, no one spoke.

"Everyone get back. Go away from this rock."

"No way, I'm not going anywhere," Rizzo said.

"I'm not leaving," Drom said.

"Everyone! Get back! You're distracting me. I can't do this if I'm worried about hurting someone else. I'm serious! Go now, before I lose my balance."

No one moved for at least a minute. Slowly Drom, then

Rizzo, moved away. Mollie heard their footfalls echoing in the darkness. Only the won effigy's soft-blue glow provided enough light for her to see. Drom had been using his enhancement shield as a light, and now darkness crept in around her. She let out a long slow breath and tried to steady her heart rate. Slowly, she reached the four-foot spear forward, with one hand, while reaching backward with her other arm to counterbalance for the expected weight. She wobbled.

The tip of the spear tapped the top of the won. Somewhat relieved at that small achievement, she tried to maneuver the spear downward and over toward the small gap. Losing balance, she had to abruptly pull back. Overcompensating, Mollie felt herself teetering uncontrollably. It took her several moments to get back into a half-standing, half-crouching, position.

In the distance, a voice said, "You're going to have to use your shield."

Uhhg. It was Drom, again. How had Boomer put up with that annoying Blues ass!

Part of her knew he was right, though. She'd never be able to compensate for the weight of the won and still remain balanced. She studied the enhancement shield and thought back to the last time she'd used it—back at Loma City. She'd gotten somewhat acclimated to the thing. How it felt; how it had ... almost ... become a part of her. She had to try.

"You'll need very little power. Think of it ... like a soft breath, or whisper," Drom said. "Anything more and you'll send yourself right off that spear."

Mollie stared at the curved, triangular face of the shield, obviously made of the same material as the won effigy—*Glist.* She remembered back to Rizzo and his patient instruction on the use of the ancient Dacci weapon. Ever so carefully, she did what she'd done before—what she'd been instructed to do. She connected with the shield as if it were a living thing—part of her very being. Eventually, she felt the gentle stirrings, then the tingle. Violet waves emanated from the face of the shield, and she felt an ever-so-faint pushing-back motion. Mollie increased the energy—the power—and the darkness around her gave way to brighter light.

"That's it, Mollie ... that's how you do it!" Drom shouted.

Encouraged, she slightly increased the power again. "Wow!" she said, bending her knees and teetering. Easing off some in using the distortion waves, she said, "Way too much gusto."

Mollie spent a fair amount of time practicing—increasing and decreasing the shield's power in subtle increments. She knew there'd be no second chances, no retries. While battle was the use of unbridled, destructive power, this task required the utmost tactic in gentleness and finesse. A part of her wondered if she would ever get it right. How long had she been standing there? Thirty minutes? An hour? Her legs were starting to shake and her balance becoming erratic.

Mollie heard footfalls coming closer. "I told you ... all of you ... to stay back."

"Yeah ... that's not going to happen."

Mollie carefully turned and saw Boomer emerge from the darkness, wearing her combat suit. Behind her visor, her face looked drawn and white. She said, "Had them set the timer on the *Stellar*'s MediPod to the minimum healing time." Mollie had never been happier to see anyone. "I'm glad you're here. Any words of wisdom ... how to go about this?"

Boomer sat, letting her legs hang over the wall's side. "In the end, you'll have to go with your gut ... find a way to just go."

"That's the best you've got ... just do it?"

She watched Boomer as she quietly continued to assess her predicament. But just having Boomer there, within reach—was a help. Mollie's legs ceased trembling and her confidence some-what increased. She caught Boomer staring up at the massive rock. "Can't you stop looking at that thing?"

"Oh ... sorry."

They smiled at each other and Mollie raised the spear in front of her. Proportionally, she countered her off-center weight using her shield. This time, she pointed the shield to face down, in the direction of the won. The farther she leaned forward, the more she increased the ray's power. The spear again pointed at the top of the statue. Lowering the spear's point ever so slowly, she let its tip find the small gap where the wings met the base of the effigy. A sound of metal chafing against metal could be heard as the spear slid into the gap. Suddenly, the spear caught, and the statue tilted precariously on its base.

"Raise up the spear, Mollie!"

"I'm trying ... my arm's so tired."

"It's slipping," Boomer barked.

"Shhhh!"

Mollie, ushering forth every ounce of strength she had left, continued to raise both the spear and the won effigy. Now raised high enough, and the angle steep enough, the statue began to slip backwards, down along the shaft. All at once, it slid the rest of the way and Mollie grabbed it.

Both girls screamed in delight, as clapping and cheers erupted from the darkness around them.

Mollie let go of the spear and, holding on to the won in one hand, reached out her other hand. Boomer pulled her up next to her on the wall and they hugged.

"I knew you could do it," Boomer said.

"Really?"

"No ... but I hoped you could."

"You're a brat ... you know that?"

"We're out of time! Need to get out of here ... Now!" Leon yelled.

Mollie triggered her SuitPac device and waited for her combat suit to initialize around her. A moment later, in the bright flash of their joint phase-shift, Mollie saw something horrible, rising above the wall just behind Boomer.

Chapter 53

oomer immediately returned to Medical to finish off her MediPod treatment. An hour later, feeling somewhat back to normal, she and Mollie sat together on one of the plush couches placed within the main cabin of the *Stellar*. Boomer watched Mollie, staring at the won effigy now propped up in her lap.

"It's beautiful," Mollie said. "Perhaps because I helped you rescue it."

Boomer hadn't thought of it in those terms before ... *rescued* it?

Drom flopped down on the other side of Mollie without looking in her direction. She noticed he, at some point, had put his long dreadlocks into some kind of a knot at the top of his head.

He opened Boomer's satchel and pulled out a second, almost identical looking, won effigy. Without saying anything, Mollie and Drom exchanged statues. They also exchanged less than warm glances.

Drom said, "The one you're holding is called the Goldwon.

One thing I just learned ... see that symbol at the front of the base?"

Mollie ran her thumb along the engraved metal.

"That is the symbol for the Goldwon."

Mollie nodded and retrieved the one Drom held in order to hold both herself and looked at the other symbol. She raised her brows toward Drom.

"That's the symbol for the Lortwon."

"They do look like angels to me," Mollie said, looking at Boomer. "To you, too?"

Boomer shrugged. "Hadn't thought about it. Maybe half angels and half some kind of beast."

"So we're guessing Zintar has the Nordwon ... and the last one ... that's the Palwon?" Mollie said.

Rogna, who had been uncharacteristically quiet since the untimely death of Gain, plopped down on the couch directly across from Boomer. She crossed her arms under her small breasts and tilted her head—her face souring into a scowl. "I hope you're satisfied."

"You talking to me?" Boomer asked.

Rogna kept her eyes on the two wons. "How many of us had to die so you could find those stupid things?"

Boomer wanted to say something cutting—something mean back to Rogna, but what could she say? The cost ... the toll ... had been so high.

Mollie ran a finger down the intricately carved Goldwon effigy in her lap. "What happens when you have all four of them ... together?"

"Something we're supposed to ensure will never, ever, be allowed to happen," Drom said.

"It's pretty. They are both pretty. But, come on ... why not just destroy them?"

"It's not supposed to be possible," Boomer said. "But I've been thinking about that very same question too.

"Five years ago, Rom Dasticon came close to entering our ... *this* ... realm. According to ancient Dacci writings, his presence here is inevitable... entering through a habitat on the *Minian,* or a portal created by bringing four won effigies together, or it will be something else. He's apparently immortal... thousands of years old. Maybe more. Yes, we could attempt to destroy the two wons we possess. Throw them out an air lock, or even fire nukes at the damn things, but what about next year? Or five years from now?"

No one had an answer. Rogna continued to fume.

Rizzo entered the cabin from the direction of the bridge. "We'll take off just as soon as we tell Leon and Hanna where we're headed."

Boomer turned back around to see Drom holding the ancient scroll. As he studied it, he said, "I suggest we make a quick stop along the way. We need Captain Brith."

Mollie looked between Drom and Boomer questioningly.

"He's the only one who can read the ancient symbols."

"You should do what your sister suggested and destroy them. Destroy them now," Rogna said again.

All eyes turned to Boomer. It was a full minute before she answered. "No. We're going to play this out. Win or lose ... we're going to play this out."

Their next destination—their final destination—turned out to be in the opposite direction. One of Harpaign's larger moons, Almand-CM5.

En route, they returned to the Sahhrain gunship and retrieved Captain Brith. There was some debate on what to do with the other Sahhrain prisoners on board. In the end, they released them from the hold, disabled the ship's drive, and set the small gunship adrift. Eventually, someone would respond to their distress call ... or not.

At this point, Boomer was under no illusion why Brith was so amiable about helping them. It was no secret his boss—Lord Zintar Shakrim—was after the same thing. By helping them, he would be helping Zintar. Captain Brith probably figured he was sending Boomer and her crewmates to their deaths—and perhaps he was right.

Drom and Captain Brith caught Boomer coming out of the upper level DeckPort.

"It's not another obstacle course," Drom said, looking pleased with himself.

Boomer looked over to Brith: "What's he talking about?"

"I didn't put it together before. The fourth won you're looking for ... it isn't like the other three. It is the actual apparatus ... the portal construct, I imagine, though it may look just like the three smaller versions. That's what threw me. It's a huge, giant-sized, won effigy. The three smaller versions are actually keys to its operation."

"So you're saying we have everything we need to open Dasticon's portal ... his bridge between realms? No more obstacle courses?"

"Hardly!" Captain Brith spat. "Your obstacles are far from behind you. Lord Zintar Shakrim holds one of those three and, I am sorry, but you will not defeat him in battle. My suggestion, give him the two you have and run. Hide, disappear in another sector and hope he never bothers to look for you."

Hanna rushed out from the bridge, looking frazzled. "Your father ... he's asking for you!"

Boomer stared back at Hanna, stunned. Two years had

passed since she'd directly spoken to him. Hanna gestured for her to follow her back into the bridge.

She recognized the *Parcical*'s futuristic bridge, appearing on the hovering display in front of Leon, sitting at the helm. It was evident a battle was raging in space. She didn't see her father on the display but did see other crewmembers scurrying around. Bright flashes, what could be plasma fire reflections, emanated from the bridge's overhead wraparound display. Then her father stepped into view and did a double-take on seeing her. A crooked grin crossed his lips. "Boomer!"

"Hi, Dad."

He stared at her for a long moment—taking her in. "Leon tells me you're close by. You need to turn back. In fact, I want you to leave the Dacci system."

"What's happening, Dad? Who are you fighting?"

"War is what's happening. And it's bad. Even with the recent arrival of the U.S. and Blues' fleets, we've lost many ships. Several Star Watch warships have been destroyed. Two others have been taken by the Sahhrain. It's war, Boomer. Leave here, and don't return to the Sol System, either." There was pain in his eyes as he spoke those last words.

"I can't do that, Dad ... you know that."

She watched as he ordered someone off-screen to ready the projectors—whatever that meant.

"You're with Mollie?"

Boomer nodded.

"I can't lose the two of you. Don't ask me to do that."

"It's been two years, and you have so little faith in me?" This time it was her turn to smile. "Dad, I'm going to bring this Rom Dasticon crap to an end ... once and for all. But first I'm going to end Zintar."

"Oh ... you are, huh? Confident are we about that?" He stared back at her, then shook his head. "Well, the truth is, if anyone can ... maybe besides me ... it would be you. I'd help you if I could, Boomer, but as you can see, I have my hands full right now."

"I know, Dad. I'll let you get back to it."

The feed faded.

Leon turned in his seat. "We're headed headlong into a raging space battle. Your Almand-CM5, it's dab-smack in the middle of crazy—"

Boomer held up a hand, stopping Leon mid-sentence. "I'm being hailed."

"By whom?" Hanna asked.

"I think it's Lord Zintar Shakrim."

Chapter 54

"Captain?"

Jason broke his gaze away from Boomer's now-disconnected feed. "Yes, Ricket. Are you ready?"

"Yes, Captain," Ricket said, standing at his side. "But we'll need to implement the projections directly from the MicroVault terminal."

"Fine. I'll be right down."

Ricket left the bridge.

"Cap," Orion said, "I have the remainder of Star Watch— the *Pisces, Leo, Aries, Virgo, Libra, Aquarius* and the *Parcical*— on a rotating basis, phase-shifting in and out of battle. Currently, the *Leo* and the *Aries* are standing down, two light-years away, regenerating. All of them, including the *Parcical*, have taken on substantial damage."

She didn't need to mention the three Star Watch fleet losses —the *Scorpio,* the *Gemini,* and the *Taurus*. The loss of thousands of men and women weighed heavily on his mind. "What's the status of the captured ships ... the *Minian* and *Sagittarius*?"

"Up until now they have stayed pretty much out of the fight.

I'm assuming the captured crew is not being very accommodating," she said.

"It's only a matter of time before they figure things out enough to bring those highly lethal vessels into the fight. We can't let that happen."

"No, sir."

For the tenth time in that many minutes, Jason studied the logistical display. The Sahhrain fleet had also taken devastating losses. Unfortunately, the Sahhrain came loaded for bear. So many warships—it would be impossible to destroy them all with their current assets. Both the Blues and the U.S. fleets, arriving late to the fight, already were taking devastating losses. The Vastma-class ships were on a whole different level than the old Craing light- and heavy-cruisers. And the Blues' ships were practically useless in actual, real-life battle conditions, so Jason had ordered them back, letting what remained of Star Watch take the brunt of the continuing onslaught. *How did this happen?* And only a third of the Sahhrain fleet's capacity was in use. He inwardly cursed his brother and the entire sneaky admiralty, sitting back safe and sound within Liberty Station. *Fools ... all of them fools.*

The *Parcical* shook and the bridge lights flickered.

"Our turn is coming up. We need to phase-shift out within the next two minutes, Cap."

"You have the bridge, Gunny. I'll be with Ricket and Bristol at the MicroVault terminal.

Jason entered the quasi-circular MicroVault terminal compartment. The virtual wraparound display showed the contents inside just one of many virtual storage vaults. Vast storage placed into high-capacity, almost unlimited, memory tabs. Entire ships were stored in there—plus every conceivable type of technology and living organism imaginable. Scientists at heart, the Caldurians were nothing but thorough when cataloging the galaxy.

Bristol and Ricket turned, seeing Jason enter.

Jason spoke first: "Whatever you send onto those ships, make it lethal—the most lethal kind of sons-of-bitches in the universe."

"How about the second most lethal kind of sons-of-bitches in the universe?"

Ricket clarified. "At some point, we'll need to take those ships back, especially those captured Star Watch vessels."

Jason saw their point. "Show me what you have."

Bristol did something at the pedestal and the display zoomed into the vast, warehouse-like vault. The background, almost blindingly white compared to the row after row of miniaturized objects, began to take form as Bristol went first from faster-scanning to slower-scanning, then to a complete stop. Jason didn't quite know what it was he was seeing. He tilted his head and then grimaced.

"Is that a ..."

"Mosquito?" Bristol said. "No ... it's actually only partially organic. It's a bio-droid ... an insectile cyborg ... of sorts. Highly complex for its small size." He held up a clenched fist. "About this size. One small prick from its labium—its snout—and it's all over. Lights out! Organics bitten, like us or the Sahhrain, pretty much turn to slime in a matter of seconds. Very nasty fucker."

"And those are the second most lethal kind of sons-of-bitches in the universe?"

Bristol zoomed out, then zoomed over to another section of the vault.

"That doesn't look so bad. It's kinda cute, actually," Jason said. Pinkish in color, to him it looked like a friendly-faced, floppy-eared bat, which seemed appropriate ... it's chasing after mosquitos.

"No, Captain, this is another bio droid. Once programmed, it seeks out targets, its prey. It has a 99.97% success rate. It never gives up," Ricket said.

"And you have enough ... of both?"

"No. Not even close to infiltrate all of the enemy warships. But the good news is, I have already started to replicate both droids within the onboard phase synthesizer."

Bristol said, "Even with the ability to replicate them, which takes quite a bit of time, we'll have enough for twenty of those Vastma-class ships as well as our own captured vessels. We're hoping it will scare the rest of them off ... until we can deal with them later."

Jason thought about that and saw good logic. Plus, there were very few other options. Again, the display changed. Three large Vastma-class ships filled the display, each firing off plasma fire from multiple guns. A U.S., once Craing, dreadnaught began to tear apart—then violently exploded.

Jason gasped. "What do you say we start with those three Sahhrain vessels," Jason said.

Jason heard the familiar sound of the MicroVault terminal projector spinning up. Crosshairs locked on to the first of the three ships, followed by a quick flashing and clicking sound. The crosshairs then moved to the next ship, and then the next, with resonating clicks for both following after.

Ricket turned to Jason. "Captain, at this time, there are over one thousand swarm-droids on board each of those vessels. I imagine they are already attacking the crew ... anything alive is running for its life."

Jason nodded. "What about combat suits?"

Bristol said, "Someone would be safe in a suit, though I don't think too many Sahhrain warriors are running around in combat suits."

Jason thought about that and hoped he was right. He watched the three Vastma-class warships. One ceased firing its plasma guns. A good sign.

Chapter 55

Boomer sat quietly within the confines of one of the *Stellar's* guest suites on Deck Two. The overhead lighting had been sufficiently dimmed, and she, deep within a *baskile* meditative state, was unconcerned with the small vessel's rocking and the commotion on the upper deck. What lay before her now was what the last two years of training were all about. Perhaps she was born for the upcoming challenges ahead. If she took the ancient writings at their face value, then that was exactly why she'd been born. Not as a savior—her role wasn't depicted that way—but more like a causal effect—an act of nature. Like a storm or a tornado, an unpredictable occurrence, which could be seen coming, although the actual extent of the effects—the damage—was indeterminate.

She brought herself out of her deeply relaxed state and opened her eyes. She was ready. She thought back to her brief conversation with Lord Shakrim. His deep, heavily accented voice was not what she'd expected to hear. He sounded so ... *what?* Normal. He'd asked her if she'd sustained any long-lasting injuries from her experiences with the obstacle courses, actually sounding concerned.

"I commend you for following the dictums of the Dacci writings: That you personally chose to physically challenge those obstacles. It says much about you as a person. The gateway to distant realms must be opened, young human. It has been foreseen."

"I agree," Boomer said.

There was a hesitation. Zintar must not have anticipated her reply. "Then we no longer are warrior enemies?"

Boomer continued, "Rom Dasticon ... he cannot be allowed to enter this realm."

"No ... that too we agree on ... We will defeat him together."

This time it was Boomer who was taken aback. "Do not take me for a fool, Lord Shakrim. You and I will never be on the same side."

"In the end ... no, we will not. You must answer for the great injustices you and your kind have perpetrated against the Sahhrain ... against me."

"Look, your brother, Vikor ... he started this war. No one went looking for him," Boomer said.

"He did what was expected of him; what had been chronicled thousands of years ago to occur. I too am bound by my Dacci heritage. My brother was indeed a crude ... insensitive individual, but he was my brother. I am bound by law and personal pride to avenge his killing. I am honored that my opponent, as small and insignificant as you are, is a master Tahli warrior, in the ancient Dacci martial arts of Kahill Callan. That honors me ... it honors the Sahhrain."

"I'm not here to honor you, nor your murderous people, after what you've done to the Blues. And for what you are now doing in space to my people. I will end you ... and the Sahhrain will be stopped ... for good."

"No, young Tahli warrior ... the war that rages will continue on. With or without me, the war will continue so the Sahhrain can take their rightful place within the galaxy ... within the universe. The outcome of the battle between you and me ... that is separate. That is personal."

"And Rom Dasticon?" Boomer asked.

"My hope is for us to put our inevitable conflict aside; that you will join me in defeating that one true scourge. Understand, Dasticon has one intent only ... to bring darkness and to smother the light ... to bring misery and suffering to all reaches of the universe, to all realms of existence."

"I suspect your own aspirations are not so different," Boomer said.

"Do not mistake a rightful and just ruler with what Rom Dasticon offers."

"I'm not under any illusions where Dasticon's got to go. But, in the end, you're going with him."

Her words made the Sahhrain leader laugh uproariously. Eventually, he coughed and cleared his throat, saying, "I do admire your spirit, little human. Now, let me tell you where the final won is located. Massive amounts of Glist make finding it with sensors impossible."

The *Stellar* dropped out of low orbit around Almand-CM5. Considered a moon of Harpaign, it was only somewhat smaller than its mother planet. Boomer had heard stories that Almand was always storming—that thunder and lightning struck non-stop, and the sun's rays almost never penetrated through the moon's thick dark cloud layer. Where Harpaign's landscape was devoid of plant life—due to brutal, unrelenting sunshine—Almand-CM5 exhibited an equally lifeless landscape, but for just the opposite reason—minimal sunshine if any.

Leon was at the Helm and Hanna at her Tactical panel

position. Boomer, Mollie, Drom, Rizzo, and even Rogna stood shoulder to shoulder, staring out the forward observation window, inside the cramped luxury space yacht's bridge. The ship descended downward, toward jagged black mountain ranges, and maneuvered between angry-looking peaks into an ominous-looking valley.

"There!" Rogna said, pointing off to the left.

Boomer followed the direction of her finger and saw something metallic, reflecting in the near non-existent daylight. The *Stellar* banked, maneuvered around two tall peaks, before straightening out and heading for what could be seen as a structure of some kind.

"Ouch!" Rogna shouted—pushing Rizzo backward with both hands. "That's my toe, *Calhoom*."

"Oh ... sorry," Rizzo said.

Now, closer to the structure, it became evident what they were seeing. They had to be nearly upon it to differentiate it from the surrounding craggy peaks—but, sure enough, it was unmistakable. Supported on a round, metallic base—stood a won effigy, hundreds of feet tall. If it weren't for a rare beam of sunlight, emanating from a break in the clouds, the effigy would have appeared just like the other rocky spires surrounding it.

Similar to the two small versions, even though this won effigy was immense, it too had a half angel, half beast appearance. The chiseled face showed its Dacci heritage, and long dreadlocks billowed over slim, feminine shoulders and down the tall effigy's back. Like the two others, the wings weren't extended, but nestled in close to the body, though still high enough to see the wing tips above the figure's head. Boomer wondered if the effigy was a heavenly symbol, like biblical angels on earth, or if there really were, once upon a time, beings that resembled this statue living within Dacci space.

"It has the same type of symbol," Rogna said, pointing.

Sure enough, etched along the forward face of the base was a unique, although similar, geometric symbol. Boomer was certain it would correspond to the name Palwon.

Leon piloted the craft around the far side of the statue and found, hidden between two tall rocky ridges, a valley wide enough to land into. "Looks like we're not the first ones to arrive," Leon said.

A Vastma-class warship hovered far off in the distant mist. Leon landed the *Stellar* gently on the rocky valley surface and powered down the drive. "Someone should stay with the ship."

"I will," Rogna said. Her offer didn't seem to surprise anyone.

Boomer said, "You can stay if you want, Rogna ... but you can't fly this thing come some emergency. Hanna ... do you mind staying?"

"Fine with me," she said, looking over to Leon, who nodded back in agreement.

Chapter 56

One by one, they exited the *Stellar* and headed down the extended forward, lower deck, gangway. All five were wearing combat suits. Leon and Rizzo had multi-guns slung over their shoulders.

Boomer felt strong winds buffeting her back and more than once nearly lost her balance. Rogna was already complaining over the open channel and Boomer tuned her out.

"Steps ... over here," Rizzo said, gesturing, and all heads turned toward the base of the great statue. Boomer hesitated when she saw movement, more than fifty feet above them at the top of the effigy's base.

"I wondered what happened to them," Drom said.

Boomer watched as a procession of hooded, long black-robed Blues moved out along the perimeter of the curved base, coming to a halt and looking down at them. They were the Tahli ministry members—all ten of them. Boomer looked up at them with contempt as her mind flashed back to the massacre in the arena and the conspicuous departure of the ministry members, just prior to all hell breaking loose.

One by one, the ministry members pulled back their

draping long robe sleeves to reveal enhancement shields. Reflexively, Boomer and Drom raised their own shields and assumed defensive Kahill Callan stances.

But the ten, bright-violet distortion waves were sent over their heads. Boomer and the others turned to see the ten waves merge into a singular spotlight that shone on a large figure, a half-mile back within the valley's darkness.

"Stay here," Boomer said. "The plan is for me to simply talk to him at this point. We need each other to open the bridge. With that said ... if he kills me ... or incapacitates me ..."

"We'll kill him," Mollie interjected. "You can count on that."

They had already discussed the upcoming encounter. Boomer had argued, and eventually everyone conceded, that she had to face him alone, at least at first.

Boomer took her first steps away from the others and felt something land on her shoulder. She turned to see Mollie, standing behind her. Tears were in her eyes.

Mollie said, "Wait ... I didn't realize how big he'd be. He's ... a fucking monster!"

They both laughed and Boomer said, "The bigger they are ..."

Abruptly Drom was there too, beside Mollie. He raised his visor and immediately wind and rain blew into his helmet. He gestured towards Boomer's helmet.

Embarrassed, she glanced at Mollie then raised her visor. He wasted no time, moving in and kissing her on the lips. She felt his arm around her waist as her body was pulled close to his. Eventually they separated.

Mollie's eyes were wide, and she was smiling. "Well, well ... I'll need more details about this later ... many more details."

Drom said, "You need to reconsider speaking to him alone."

"Don't worry. And keep an eye on the ministry members ... I've already learned turning my back on them is a mistake."

Drom looked back over his shoulder and nodded. He did not look convinced about her going near Zintar alone but offered no further argument.

Boomer closed her visor and turned away from the team. Lord Zintar Shakrim was still standing in the same position he'd been in minutes earlier. She slowly approached the Sahhrain leader. At fifty yards away, she marveled at his ... grandeur. There was no better way to express it. He was wearing a combat suit, of sorts, although he had rigged it so his billowing crimson cape, and his gold breastplate, were worn on the outside. She had to give it to the giant warrior ... he had style.

When she was close enough to see his eyes, enclosed behind a helmet, he said, "Master against master. You honor me, Master Tahhrim Dol."

Her expression changed at hearing his words.

"Yes ... I know much about you," he said. "That you have been a master of the Blues' Kahill Callan since what? The age of twelve?"

"Eleven."

"Yes, eleven. And here you are, soon to die at the age of seventeen. Prepare yourself for battle, human."

She was about to correct him on that number, as well, then realized—it was true. As of today, she was seventeen. She put her hands on her hips and looked up at him defiantly. "What are you talking about ... battle? What about all that ... us working together stuff ... stopping Dasticon, combining forces ... at least temporarily?"

She heard a snicker emanating from the large, elongated helmet. "I could tell you that circumstances have changed. The truth is, I do not need your help, human. You have what I need right there in that satchel. You are far too trusting ... naïve, in

357

fact. In time, if you had lived, you would have learned to be more cunning. Obviously your training was far from complete. If only you had been trained by true Sahhrain Kahill Callan masters ... you would have been more prepared for today."

She slowly nodded, "Fine then." Her mind reeled. She wasn't mentally prepared for this ... not now. She noticed movement—first off to her right then behind Zintar. Viewing droids were back.

"Then let's get this over with. I have a few other things to do today," Boomer said, sounding bored. She suspected he was smiling beneath his mask-like helmet. He bowed to her and took up the traditional Kahill Callan opening stance. She mirrored his form and both released bright distortion waves from their shields simultaneously. His quickly turned a bright red and Boomer's instantly followed suit.

"Perhaps your training was better than I suspected ... young human."

Instead of answering, she opted to attack—bringing the face of her shield quickly down while elevating her body upward and sideways. Her distortion waves missed the mark, which she hadn't anticipated, when he turned his body sideways, using little movement and energy. Smart for a combatant hefting that much weight around. He returned fire, making an upward S swiping movement with his shield that created an impossible-to-dodge span of energy. Clipped on her upper right shoulder, Boomer, on her way down from above, was catapulted backward twice while in the air before crashing down to the rocks below—both stunned and hurt.

Zintar was upon her without hesitation. He leveled his shield at her and fired. She rolled away as far as she could, before hitting something big and hard that stopped her progression. She took a new distortion wave directly in the chest and felt the most searing white-hot pain of her life. Warnings flashed on her HUD along with shrill audio alarms. Instinctively, she disengaged her combat suit, as it was now nearly useless in protecting her. The sudden act of removing her suit must have surprised Zintar, because he momentarily relented in his attack. Boomer dove and tumbled then cartwheeled away. The telltale sounds of massive energy waves following only inches in her wake were all she needed to keep moving—dodging one way then the other. She needed to get back on the offense. How quickly he'd taken control of the battle, and she became his prey.

"Dodge right and go high!" Rizzo said in Boomer's Nano-Com. He knew just enough about Kahill Callan—its various *jarta* moves—to be dangerous, but she followed his guidance anyway. She used the edge of her shield to elevate herself up and sideways, adding a vertical spin to the mix that caught Zintar by surprise. She leveled her shield at his oversized head and fired off bright-crimson energy waves, using all the power she could muster—reaching inward and giving it her all—from the very deepest level, where she felt her very soul resided. Bright waves of energy struck him with enough force to melt his helmet and upper battle suit. A fleeting glimpse of simmering, blackened like charcoal skin now replaced his once pale exposed flesh. *Why didn't he cry out in pain?* He dodged both left and right, as Boomer continued to track his movements, firing relentlessly. He was incredibly fast—even agile. Knowing he'd suffered what must be immeasurable pain, she had to give him his due. In a blur he was up in the air, completing a complex move that Boomer was not nearly as adept at. She dodged a barrage of incoming distortion waves and, once again, found herself on the ground and on the defense. Bringing her shield up she fired. He spun away, momentarily hidden behind his wide—billowing—red cape.

Zintar spun away, a captivating spectacle in itself. Bright

light flooded around him—silhouetting his gargantuan stature—
and Boomer chided herself for momentarily hesitating. He must
have fired powerful distortion waves while turned away from
her—right through his cape.

Boomer moved, figuring out what was happening, but was a
moment too slow, as waves hit her stomach area. She doubled
over and grabbed herself, expecting to feel and see something
akin to what had happened to Zintar's face and shoulders. But
then she remembered: The distortion waves were no longer red,
nor even violet in color, but more bluish. He'd made a grave
mistake. His stupid cape—probably made from some kind of
protective material—had dissipated the strength of those energy
waves. She was fine.

Boomer watched as he stumbled and fell forward. Trying to
get to his feet, he was breathing hard. A rasping sound could be
heard coming from his ruined face. He momentarily turned to
face her, and she got a full view of the damage crimson distortion waves could cause. She felt the taste of bile in her throat
and had the urge to throw up. It was far worse than she'd imagined. He was missing his lower jaw.

He stood up tall—surprisingly, considering his injuries—and
raised an arm. Not his shield arm but his other arm. Confused,
Boomer glanced backward, over her shoulder. He had signaled
the Tahli ministry members, standing above them on the upper
base of the won structure, who then began firing. Bright distortion waves rained down through the misty air toward her friends
and Mollie. Although they scrambled away, two had already
fallen. Rizzo was returning their fire with his multi-gun as Leon
leaned over one of those fallen. *Oh, God ... please don't let it be
Mollie!*

She was sure it was her. Boomer ran, using her shield to
propel herself even faster, practically flying across the rocky
surface toward the others. She reached Leon, positioned over

the prone body, and fell to her knees next to him. Leon stood and joined the fight. Distortion waves continued to streak by overhead and around them. *Thump thump thump* erupted from Rizzo's, and now Leon's, multi-guns. But none of that mattered —all that mattered was the figure lying so still before her. The surface of her visor was a melted mess.

"Mollie! Oh, God ... Mollie!" Boomer pulled the lifeless body into her arms and screamed and wailed. She knew she was dead. She'd been around enough dead to know. She knew there would be no bringing her back in the MediPod. She was gone ... her sister—a living part of herself—was gone forever.

At some level she sensed the team around her had moved toward the base of the statue. They were attacking the ministry members. *Kill them ... kill them all!* Boomer thought. She buried her face into Mollie's chest.

At some level she heard it. A distant—wet—slurping sound coming from behind her. Boomer knew it was Zintar, but at that moment she didn't care. He could kill her too. It didn't matter now. *Let him.* Without Mollie ...

"Boomer?"

Boomer froze, her back to the approaching Sahhrain leader. It wasn't his voice, added to the fact he didn't have a mouth to speak from. She knew it was Mollie's voice. Boomer spun around, seeing Lord Zintar Shakrim's two hands stretched out in front, with Mollie dangling four feet in the air. His hands were tightly clasped around her neck. Boomer could see the desperation on her face, even behind her visor. Boomer stole a quick glance down at the inert body on the rocks. It must be Rogna. Rogna had been killed—not Mollie. *When had she joined them?*

Boomer stood and faced them. Zintar released one hand's hold but still continued to hold Mollie into the air with the other. She kicked and flailed but his arm didn't waver. He pointed to Boomer's shield and shook his mangled head—his meaning clear: *Remove your enhancement shield or I'll snap her neck.*

Boomer briefly wondered if the Sahhrain still had the strength for such a feat, but did she want to chance it? She removed her shield and threw it to the ground. "Now what, asshole?"

He raised his free arm, the one holding a shield, and pointed its face at Boomer. Mollie screamed for Boomer to run—get away—but Boomer simply stared back at Zintar. He was going to kill her, she was sure of that. At this range ... he couldn't miss.

Lord Zintar Shakrim fired.

Chapter 57

Jason left Ricket and Bristol at the MicroVault terminal and headed for the bridge. As much as his mind was on the ensuing space battle—Boomer and Mollie truly consumed most of his thoughts. Gunny had just informed him of the presence of a lone, Vastma-class warship down on the surface of Almand-CM5—one of Harpaign's moons. The same desolate moon Leon had navigated the *Stellar* and his daughters to in search of the last won effigy. His thoughts raced, and his heart rate doubled within his chest. Were his daughters alive? Had they arrived there only to discover a trap waiting? Was Zintar finally getting his revenge on him at this very moment?

Jason strode onto the bridge, grabbing a quick glimpse at the above logistical display.

"Cap ... I believe whatever Ricket and Bristol devised may be working. It's a bit early to tell but—"

"Gunny! Dammit ... the girls!"

Orion, shocked by his anger, pointed at another, separate, logistical feed on the wrap-around display. Jason stared at it but wasn't mollified in the least. "What the hell am I looking at?"

"I've zeroed in on the surface of the moon ... of Almand-CM5. There's a large structure there that's not in our database. I've locked on to the team's combat suits."

Jason now spotted the yellow icons—several stationary, others moving. Above each one was their respective callout. When he saw Mollie's, some of his tension eased. He then saw Leon's and Hanna's, then Rizzo's, and several names he didn't recognize. He also noticed several red icons that were immobile. He looked over at Orion, his eyes pleading.

"I'm sorry, Captain. I ... I ... haven't been able to locate Boomer yet. We're too far a distance for precise organic scans. And ... it's reading similar to Loma City ... there may be high amounts of Glist in the area. I wouldn't take it to mean anything."

"I need to get down there."

"Now?" Orion asked, staring up at the wrap-around display and at the multiple battle-feeds showing.

Jason looked up at the war now raging in progress and eventually nodded. A ship's captain does not leave his post in the midst of battle ... not ever ... no matter what the circumstances. He sat down in the command chair. "Give me an update on the swarm droids ... tell me they're working out."

Orion gave him a sympathetic nod. "I think they are, Cap ... I think they are."

Boomer, upon seeing the flash of bright light emitted, waited. She was still waiting and still standing. Her chest hurt like blazes, but that was from before. Why was she still upright? Still alive? Boomer's eyes had never left Mollie's.

Only then did it register on her: The huge flashes weren't from distortion waves but from multiple plasma bolts.

Mollie fell to the ground—released from Zintar's now-wavering grasp. She clutched her throat but otherwise seemed okay. Zintar, on the other hand, was not. Boomer saw two blackened scorch marks on his abdomen. The Sahhrain leader teetered about on his feet, and then, like a toppling sequoia, fell backward—dead even before hitting the ground.

"It took me a while."

Boomer watched as Mollie rose to her feet. "It took me a while to remember that these new suits have integrated wrist-plasma guns. Then I had to figure out how to shoot the damn things."

Boomer rushed forward, throwing her arms around Mollie. "I thought he was going to kill you for certain."

"I wasn't going to let that happen," Mollie said, hugging her back.

They separated and stared down at the motionless Sahhrain. Mollie said, looking at what remained of Zintar's face, "That has to be one of the most disgusting sights I'll ever see."

Boomer had to agree—it was pretty nasty. She looked up, hearing running feet, as the rest of the team approached them. She did a quick headcount and thanked the stars above that no one else had been killed.

Drom, the first to reach them, said, "We've captured three of them ... Tahli ministry members. They're tied up and not going anywhere."

Rizzo, somewhat out of breath, slowed to a halt. "Found an entrance into the statue. There are three open slots that look to be the size and shape of those two smaller won effigies we have."

"We need the third one. Zintar's," Drom said.

As if on cue, their heads turned toward the distant warship.

Rizzo said, "There must be thousands of warriors on board. There's no way ..."

Boomer cut him off with a sudden, abrupt movement,

lowering herself down to Zintar's side. She'd noticed the pouch, hanging from his side during their battle, and thought it seemed relatively small in comparison to his huge, eight-foot-something, stature. But now, as she untied it from his belt, she realized the pouch was large enough. She stood, holding the satchel-like pouch in her hands, and handed it across to Drom. "I'll let you do the honors."

Drom hesitated, then took the satchel and quickly opened its top clasp. He reached in and pulled out the third won effigy. After a quick look, he handed it back to Boomer, then unslung the satchel and draped it over his shoulder. "Now we have all three won effigies."

Boomer smiled and looked at the others. "C'mon, let's go see if they fit inside those keyholes!"

Chapter 58

Boomer was the last of the team to crest the narrow rock stairway leading up to the top plateau surface of the Palwon effigy. She craned her neck to look up toward the looming statue's face. It ... she ... didn't look particularly happy.

Leon and Rizzo were busy hefting the lifeless corpses of fallen Tahli ministry members to the far side of the area. Rizzo unshouldered a body right onto another one—the way one would add one more log to a stacked wood pile. She had no affection for the cunning ministry members, but did feel they deserved some level of deference—if not respect—for their years of training ... or maybe even their advanced age.

She heard excited voices and walked around the curved base and the effigy's almost human-looking, automobile-sized two feet—each with ten toes instead of five. The three surviving Tahli ministry members were on their knees with their bound hands behind their heads. Boomer was about to protest but remembered what had recently happened to Rogna—whose body was now growing cold down on the rocks fifty feet below them.

Hanna had a multi-gun pointed at their heads. "What are we doing with them?"

"Hopefully getting some answers," Boomer said. "They're highly trained ... not to mention devious ... I wouldn't take my eye off them for a second."

"Over here!"

Boomer recognized Drom's voice. She continued on around the base and found Drom and Mollie standing together in front of a protruding arch that was about five feet across and rose up about three feet in the air. It was nestled in between the backs of the effigy's two big heels. As she approached, she saw the arch was flat on top, like a table or console.

"It's made of Glist ... like the rest of her," Drom said, using a flat rock to scrape at a small section on the surface. A bluish glow emanated through the scrape marks. "Volcanic sediment makes everything look black here."

Boomer stood before the surface and took in a myriad of intricate symbols. There were also three cut-out openings. "These are where the wons go?" she asked.

"Definitely," Drom said.

Boomer lowered a shoulder and grabbed the strap of Lord Zintar's satchel. She opened it and pulled out the small seventeen-inch-tall statue and looked at it. She glanced back and forth between the base of the statue and the three odd-shaped openings. "These match," she said, gesturing between the middle positioned opening and the effigy in her hand.

"The Nordwon," Drom said.

He brought up the two statues from the satchel lying at his feet.

"You've got the Goldwon and the Lortwon," Mollie said. "They go here and here," she said, pointing to the other two openings.

Lightning flashed across the dark sky, quickly followed by

three nearly eardrum-shattering thunder cracks. The wind came up and driving rain began to splatter the arch top surface.

"Any idea the order they need to be inserted ... which one goes first?" Boomer said with her statue already poised over the center opening.

"Not that one!"

The voice had come from the darkness between the statue's massive feet. Hidden behind a section of long, draping Shadick, the warrior in black stepped into view. He was holding a multi-gun. Not the most recent model, but a multi-gun just the same.

Rain bulleted his face—while his thick matted hair seemed to repel the moisture. His eyes were on Boomer. "I am Commander Jarial Shakrim ... and I watched as you killed my father."

Boomer hesitated, then said, "I'm sorry. Sorry you had to see that. I didn't want to ..."

"Shut up ... just shut up ... *Calhoom*." The hatred in his voice was audible.

She stopped talking. Boomer felt Drom tense and wondered if he was thinking of making some kind of move. That would be a mistake. He was fast—certainly a great warrior. But he wouldn't be quick enough to beat plasma bolts. She looked at Drom and, almost imperceptibly, shook her head. She hoped he'd gotten the message.

Using the muzzle of his weapon, Jarial gestured toward Mollie. "That one ... it goes there. Insert that one first."

Mollie glanced at Boomer. She shrugged. Mollie took one of the statues from Drom and moved to position the Goldwon above the right-hand side opening.

"No ... ignorant human ... the other way ... head in first."

Mollie hesitated before flipping the statue around—she squinted her eyes at the Sahhrain warrior. Eventually, she slowly lowered the Goldwon into the hole and quickly found that it needed to be turned until the head and shoulders and wing tips were aligned with the identically shaped cutout. With that done, the statue dropped all the way into the opening until there was a clang—its downward progression stopped by its wider base.

"Now that one ... it goes there!" Jarial said, indicating for Boomer to go next with the Nordwon.

Boomer flipped it around as Mollie had done and, while looking at its shape, matched it to the opening and then lowered it into the middle hole. She dropped it and it too made the same clang sound. It had come to rest with only the base visible.

Drom held the last remaining won effigy statue and leaned forward. Boomer watched as he positioned it over the left-side hole and stopped. He looked over his shoulder at Boomer. "If these are indeed keys ... like to a gateway to a distant realm ... are you sure we want to do this?"

"You there ... Blues mongrel ... don't look at her ... look at me. Do it ... do it now!" Jarial ordered.

Drom ignored him. "You know ... this probably can't be undone."

Boomer had been thinking the same thing. This could be one of those epic moments in time. Perhaps it was a moment that had already been scribed onto stone tablets two thousand years ago. Her indecision was paralyzing. But what had really changed? Wasn't the original plan to temporarily work with Lord Zintar Shakrim to open the gateway? Her intent had been to defeat Rom Dasticon ... somehow ... once and for all. Make it so he could never threaten this realm ... not ever, while Zintar's plan had been to defeat Dasticon also, but then to take his place as some kind of master of the multiverse. That in itself was ridiculous. But either way, both of them had planned to kill Dasticon.

Boomer said, "I know what your father wanted. He told me. Why don't you tell me what your intentions are?"

Jarial furrowed his brow. "I don't have to tell any of you anything! Least of all you. You murdered the only person that meant anything to me." His eyes leveled on Drom. "You ... drop in the statue or I'll kill you where you stand."

Drom held fast and continued to look back at Boomer.

"Perhaps you are less of a warrior than your father was," Boomer said. "Perhaps you intend to do Dasticon's bidding. To be Dasticon's ..." Boomer searched for an appropriate word.

Mollie said, "Bitch."

"Yeah ... Dasticon's bitch," Boomer said.

"No. I will not be Rom Dasticon's bitch. And I will honor my father ... take his rightful place as the leader of the Sahhrain people. Soon the U.S. fleet ... the Alliance will fall to our superior forces in space. And Sahhrain supremacy will not stop there."

"One way or another, Dasticon is coming. And he needs to be defeated. Your father knew that, and I know that. He wasn't smart enough to comprehend one simple fact."

"And what is that?"

"Only together can that happen. He is far too powerful to be defeated by any one of us alone." Boomer took a step forward and placed a hand on top of Drom's. She held it there and turned to Mollie. Mollie smiled and placed one hand on the others. All eyes turned to Jarial.

He looked from Boomer to the others, and then back to Boomer.

"You and me ... we're not done."

"Agreed."

Jarial lowered his multi-gun and let it fall to the ground. He stepped forward and placed his right hand on top of Mollie's—

completing the four-hand mound. Drom looked into Boomer's eyes and waited. She nodded.

He released his hold on the last won effigy. Gravity pulled it down and, like the previous two, it clanged into place.

The arched flat top surface began to rise up while increasing in size. The four of them stood back as the archway continued to rise up.

For the first time, Boomer noticed that Leon and Rizzo had been standing several paces behind them. Hanna, presumably, was still keeping watch over the three Tahli ministry prisoners.

Made of Glist and glowing bright blue, the archway continued to rise up high in the air—not unlike what that monument ... the St. Louis Arch looked like back on Earth. She'd never seen it in person, but she had seen pictures. Obviously, what they had been standing at was just the top—the pinnacle— of something much ... much larger. By the time the arch slowed and came to a full stop, it had widened beyond the sides of the base and loomed as tall as the effigy itself, well above the effigy's head—as if she, angelic with her high tipped wings and defiant far-reaching look off to a distant horizon, was standing within a doorway of sorts.

They were all looking up—shoulder to shoulder. Boomer felt Drom to her right and Jarial, now to her left.

He looked at Boomer, his expression intense. "Are you ready for this ... for what is about to happen?"

"I don't know. Are you?"

Both Boomer and Jarial hadn't noticed what the others— those still looking up at the archway—had.

"Oh ... my ... God!" Mollie said.

Rizzo said, "Did that just happen?"

Leon said, "Yup ... think it did."

Boomer looked up and then forward. It didn't register at

first. Register that the huge Palwon effigy was gone. The archway had remained, but the statue was no longer there. In its place was a tunnel—carved out of roughly chiseled Glist blocks —a tunnel that looked as ancient as the ruins back on Harpaign. Somewhat larger than a subway tunnel, it was perfectly straight and looked to span many miles—the walls converging down to a distant tiny point of light that twinkled every so often. She stepped away to the side and, just as she figured, the tunnel was only visible while looking directly into the arch. The arch ... or the tunnel ... or both were a portal. How long it would stay open she had no idea. But something told her waiting much longer was not a good idea.

Boomer looked over her shoulder and found Leon. "Think the *Stellar* would fit ... could fly through that opening ... into the tunnel?"

He shrugged. "Probably."

Thank you for reading ***Boomer, Book 3 in the Star Watch series***. Want more?

GOOD NEWS—The entire ***Star Watch series*** is available now on Amazon.com

If you enjoyed this book, please leave a review on Amazon.com – it really helps!

And to find out about future books, please join my mailing list -

I hate spam and will never share your information. Jump to this link to join: **http://eepurl.com/iCGBXk**

Thank you, again, for joining me on these SciFi romps into space.

Acknowledgments

I am grateful for the ongoing fan support I receive for all of my books. This book—number eleven, Star Watch, Ricket—came about through the combined contributions of numerous others. First, I'd like to thank my wife, Kim, for her never-ending love and support. She helps make this journey rich and so very worthwhile. I'd like to thank my mother, Lura Genz, for her tireless work as my first-phase creative editor and a staunch cheerleader of my writing. I'd like to thank Mia Manns for her phenomenal line and developmental editing ... she is an incredible resource. And Eren Arik produced another magnificent cover design—maybe his best yet! Thank you, Lazar, for the incredible website warship floor plans ... it adds a whole new dimension to reading these books. Thank you, Taryn Ikenouye, for and amazing website experience ... you've outdone yourself. A special thanks goes out to L.J. Ganser, who produces the audiobook versions of my books. Anyone looking for a truly immersive, not to mention 'fun' reading experience—with all his wonderful character voices ... you have to try the audiobook version. I'd also like to thank those in my Tuesday writer's MeetUp group, the Writer's Idea Factory, who have brought fresh ideas and perspectives to my creativity and elevating my writing as a whole. Others who provided fantastic support include Lura and James Fischer, Sue Parr, Stuart Church, and Chris DeRrick.

About the Author

Mark grew up on both coasts, first in Westchester County, New York, and then in Westlake Village, California. Mark and his wife, Kim, now live in Castle Rock, Colorado, with their two dogs, Sammi and Lilly.

Mark started as a corporate marketing manager and then fell into indie-filmmaking—Producing/Directing the popular Gaia docudrama, Openings — The Search For Harry.

For the last fifteen years, he's been writing full-time, and with over 45 top-selling novels under his belt, he has no plans on slowing down. Thanks for being part of his community!

Also by Mark Wayne McGinnis

Scrapyard Ship Series

Scrapyard Ship (Book 1)

HAB 12 (Book 2)

Space Vengeance (Book 3)

Realms of Time (Book 4)

Craing Dominion (Book 5

The Great Space (Book 6)

Call To Battle (Book 7)

Scrapyard Ship – Uprising

Mad Powers Series

Mad Powers (Book 1)

Deadly Powers (Book 2)

Lone Star Renegades

Star Watch Series

Star Watch (Book 1)

Ricket (Book 2)

Boomer (Book 3)

Glory for Sea and Space (Book 4)

Space Chase (Book 5)

Scrapyard LEGACY (Book 6)

The Simpleton Series

The Simpleton (Book 1)

The Simpleton Quest (Book 2)

Galaxy Man

Ship Wrecked Series

Ship Wrecked (Book 1)

Ship Wrecked II (Book 2)

Ship Wrecked III (Book 3)

Boy Gone

The Expanded Anniversary Edition

Cloudwalkers

The Hidden Ship

Guardian Ship

Gun Ship

HOVER

Heroes and Zombies

The Test Pilot's Wife

The Fallen Ship

The Fallen Ship: Rise of the Gia Rebellion (Book 1)

The Fallen Ship II (Book 2)

USS Hamilton Series

USS Hamilton: Ironhold Station (Book 1)